TAFF LOVESEY

# THE SHIMMERING GATE
## BOOK TWO OF THE PORTAL CHRONICLES

2007

# The Shimmering Gate

First Edition

www.lovesey.net

# The Shimmering Gate

THE PORTAL CHRONICLES SERIES:
Book 1: The Spider Gem
Book 2: The Shimmering Gate

# CONTENTS

# AUTHOR'S NOTE

At the start of this book you will find a detailed synopsis of Book One of the Portal Chronicles, The Spider Gem. I have produced this for those of you who may, like myself, dislike having to read stacks of repeated text, as authors recap previous events in their subsequent work.

Therefore, within the story of The Shimmering Gate, with the exception of the prologue, there is only passing reference to much of the detail of the story laid out in book one and generally just a small reminder of who is who and who did what. If you would like a more detailed reminder, or indeed, if you are reading book two without having read book one, then the detailed synopsis is what you will need. Beware though, if you do plan to read The Spider Gem in full, then the synopsis will be a 'spoiler' for you as it is quite detailed.

On request of readers, I have also added a glossary for The Portal Chronicles at the back of this book.

When I read fantasy novels I rarely reference any provided maps, but I know they are popular with many, so I have sent a fire eagle to Rhys to ask that he draw a map for us. This map will appear on my web page, along with other Portalia snippets.

My web site is www.lovesey.net and I am happy to receive emails from readers so click away! I also link to my blog from here which I try to update regularly, so drop on by.

I hope you enjoy The Shimmering Gate and the Portal Chronicles as a whole. I look forward to sharing more stories with you in the near future.

Keep adventuring
Taff Lovesey
May 2007

*For My Family And Friends Who Have To Put Up With My Constant Mumblings About The Portal Chronicles...*

*...for My Wonderful Team Of Volunteer Proof Readers: Martin Daniels, Margaret Gill, Leonie James, Bridget Lovesey, Ceri Lovesey, Danni Marrison, Mike Shepherd, Leigh Simmonds & Rob Turner...*

*...with Thanks To Jnb Graphics For The Cover Image...*

*...but Most Of All, For All The Readers Of The Spider Gem Who Encouraged And Inspired Me To Write On.*

# DETAILED SYNOPSIS OF THE SPIDER GEM

I f you intend to read The Spider Gem, Book One of The Portal Chronicles, in full, I would not advise that you read this synopsis as the following provides a comprehensive summary of events that led up to the story of The Shimmering Gate.

However, for those who would like to go straight into book two, or who may require a refresh of the story so far, read on...

<u>CH1</u>: Opens in the world of Portalia. Shangorth the warlock and his minion Zarn the dwarf use their army of lava made creatures, the Graav, to secure the Spider Gem. This gem gives the bearer the power to command a great army of spiders. The Graav are successful in their attempt, but during the acquisition a blast of magic turns Zarn into an albino and he is branded with a new name, the White Dwarf.

<u>CH2</u>: Rhys, a 13 year old Welsh boy is staying with his Aunt on the coast of West Wales. He wants to explore a local cave with his friend Michael and so his aunt directs him to her loft to locate some items that he will need for the exploration. While there he finds a pendant that is emblazoned with a Celtic knot.

<u>CH3</u>: Ashley Rees-Jenkins is a 14 year old, soccer mad girl living in Oregon USA. Ashey tries to persuade her parents to take their vacation in Wales where her ancestors originated. They refuse and she goes to bed disgruntled as she dons her

nightwear she removes a Celtic knot pendant given to her by her grandmother.

CH4: Back in Portalia, Gorlan, Warlord of Pinn, is leading a band of fire eagle riders to assist the outpost of Fortown. The town had sent out messengers to the various races of Portalia, as they had seen evidence of a return of the evil Black Eagles which had been prevalent during the Warlock Wars, many generations before. Molt, a young man, was sent to Pinnhome, the capital city of Pinn, and he was now accompanying the Pinn warriors back to his home town. During the journey Molt befriends twin brothers, Stern and Carl, both Pinn fire eagle riders. The brothers describe the nature of their magical mounts to Molt and explain that the eagles were formed by the magical bonding of a phoenix with an eagle. They also tell him that the Warlord possesses the Horn of Summoning which, in dire need, can call forth a red dragon. Meanwhile, as the Pinns make camp next to the Yew River for the night, two forest half-men, camouflaged in the undergrowth by their black skin, spy on the band.

CH5: Back in Wales, Rhys and Michael explore the cave and surprise Zarn gathering spiders for the warlock's army. The albino dwarf makes his escape through a blue pulsing portal. The boys then stumble across a gold ring on the cavern floor which matches Rhys' pendant. They touch the ring to the pendant and both boys, Ashley and a curious insane, old and bedraggled man are transported to a sealed chamber in Portalia.

CH6: Gorlan and his men travel deeper into the Halfman Forest. Meanwhile, Zarn visits the Halfmen via another portal gateway and orders the Halfmen clan to attack and kill the Pinns.

**CH7**: There is battle in the woods between halfmen and the Pinn warriors. The canopy of the trees prevents the fire eagles from assisting their riders and the Pinns are eventually forced to flee. As they escape the woods only Gorlan, Molt and ten riders remain.

**CH8**: The teenagers are still trapped in the runestone chamber but they learn that the octagonal platform is some form of transport device. They meet Lan, the old man, who is very scared of them and clearly quite mad. Unable to escape the chamber the trio are relieved when they discover and befriend a young female centaur, Kyrie, who visits the runestone chamber to practice pipe music. Kyrie informs them that they are in a sealed chamber in the centaur city of Eumor but does not let them out.

**CH9**: Meanwhile, Gorlan and his men are continuing towards Fortown. They stumble upon a small farm and discover the houses empty other than for web wrapped corpses picked clean of any flesh. They continue to Fortown where they find a similar fate has befallen the town. Bodies lay all around and they discover mounds of hot rock which they later learn are the remains of slain Graav. There is no sign of Molt's family or his friend Briana. In desperation Molt leads them to escape tunnels beneath the city but there no survivors there either.

**CH10**: The teenagers are still shut in the runestone chamber and have strange dreams of warlocks. Kyrie returns as promised but with her mother and father, Karia and Fyros. Fyros decides that the teenagers must be taken to the Eumor Centaur council elders for a decision to be made on what to do with them. While talking to the centaurs, Rhys touches the control pedestal of the runestone and is immediately overwhelmed with images of different gateways and worlds. He collapses and is brought around by Karia. Fyros takes them to the council.

At the council they meet Meld, Molt's brother and the messenger dispatched by Fortown to the Eumor centaurs. The council hear the story of the teenagers and Meld's request for help and decide that they will send forth a band of centaurs to assist and that the teenagers will accompany them. Before they depart, Cambor tasks Michael and Kyrie to visit the Dramkaan, an ancient guardian that lives in the nearby hills. The Dramkaan holds the Cormion Crystals that allow communication over long distance but it will only release the crystals to the bearer of the Celtic knot ring. Michael argues with the Dramkaan but recovers the crystals.

CH11: The centaurs set out for Fortown but first the teenagers have to select mounts for their journey. Lan surprises all by being chosen by a Cloud Horse called DiamondCrest. During the journey Rhys touches the Cormion Crystal which triggers a violent psychic reaction in which Rhys actually creates a random portal gateway.

CH12: In Fortown the Pinn riders begin the cleanup of the town, burying the skeletons in mass graves. Meanwhile the centaurs continue their journey and have a precarious time when crossing a deep canyon in high winds as they enter the town of Raleigh. They make camp outside the town and Griff, the leader of the centaur expedition, enters the town to pick up supplies. While here he is watched by a strange shape shifting creature called Ohrhim. The creature changes into a crow and spies on the camp. After gathering information it changes again, this time to a large black dragon and flies to Shangorth to report its findings.

Griff arrives back at camp to find that Ashley has taught his centaurs the game of soccer.

CH13: Gorlan and his remaining riders spot movement in the hills. Closer investigation reveals an army of dwarves, led by Swiftaxe the Dwarven King, escorting the survivors of Fortown back to their homes. Molt learns that the enemy army have taken Brianna alive and that his parents were not amongst the survivors.

CH14: Shangorth speaks with Ohrhim at his tower fortress in the Dargoth mountains. He orders Zarn to deliver the latest women captives to the half men horde for breeding. Opening a secret portal gateway he returns to the island of the Graav where he has built his own runestone and where he trains a coven to follow his commands.

CH15: Ohrhim returns to the centaur camp to watch over the teenagers during the journey. Here he learns about Rhys, who has another dream episode that creates a portal gateway in his tent. Mistaking Michael for Rhys, the shape changer slithers into their tent and abducts Michael, taking his comatose body back to the warlock Shangorth. As a result the warlock captures the Celtic knot ring and a Cormion Crystal before stealing Michael's mind and spirit with a device called the Soul Orb.

CH16: Shangorth learns of Ohrhim's mistake through the use of the Cormion Crystal when he overhears a communication from the centaur party. He decides not to punish the ShapeChanger and sends him back to spy on the centaurs. He learns of a mind bending spell and uses it on Michael. Not only has the boy now lost his soul but he is a willing guardian to the Warlock ready to lay down his life for his new master. He possesses no free will of his own.

CH17: The centaurs camp a short distance from Fortown where Ashley organises a soccer tournament. Reinforcements begin to arrive at Fortown as they prepare for battle.

CH18: Nexus, human minion of Shangorth is in the hills near Fortown. Formerly he was an advisor to Toran, OverLord of Pinnhome, but he was banished after being found dabbling in dark magic. He has returned and under the cover of a cloak of invisibility he attempts to assassinate the OverLord, but as he is about to strike a deathblow, he is thwarted when Shangorth uses his mountain runestone artefacts to recall him to Dargoth. Meanwhile the centaurs and the teenagers arrive in Fortown, where Rhys demonstrates his growing ability to create, but not control, a portal. This time he is assisted by Lan and this helps to solidify a portal. Kyrie attempts to use the portal and finds herself in a strange world populated by centaurs and horses. She returns unharmed.

CH19: Shangorth returns to his island via a portal to speak with his coven and to ask his lead apprentice, Stack, to prepare additional Graav for war. In Fortown, Stern and Carl are flying on a scouting mission when they stumble upon a band of women who have escaped from the enemy. The group is led by Brianna and they return her for a reunion with Molt.

CH20: Shangorth sends Nexus south east to intercept the approaching Pinn reinforcements. Stack is sent west to intercept reinforcements sent from the town of The Gates. Both are provided with a large force of Graav. Nexus' army meets the Pinns head on but he is a poor leader and the Pinns overwhelm the Graav. Nexus escapes by using the cloak of invisibility but his Graav are destroyed.

CH21: The defenders of Fortown build a huge fire pit to protect the city. Shangorth sends his army through the portal but the Graav and spiders are held back by the defenders. Slowly however, the Graav make progress and the tide of battle turns to the evil forces until elven reinforcements arrive to aid the defenders. As sunset fades Shangorth withdraws his army back to the hills to regroup. Meanwhile in the West the Graav army led by Stack slaughter the human reinforcements from the Gates.

<u>CH22</u>: In the Pinnacle Mountain far away Fangtor the last of the dragons lays partially embedded in rock as he uses the fading power of the Peak to will his flesh to stone.

<u>CH23</u>: The next morning the Allied force awakens to find that the warlock has created a huge storm that extinguishes the fire pits. Gorlan aware of the danger sounds the Horn of Summoning. As the battle turns towards the evil forces the horn is answered by Fangtor. With Gorlan riding him, and followed by the teenagers riding with the fire eagles, the Warlord leads them to a confrontation on the hillside with Shangorth.

Gorlan and Fangtor are intercepted by Ohrhim now in the shape of a huge black dragon. A dragon battle rages and eventually Fangtor tricks the shape-changer and destroys it.

On landing the Pinn riders are swiftly dispatched by the warlock and as Swiftaxe and Meld attack, he binds them in a field of force preventing any movement. Furious at the warlock Ashley rushes forward. Zarn the White Dwarf faces her but as he is about to strike Rhys conjures up a portal gateway. The dwarf's momentum takes him through the portal to another world and Rhys closes the portal to trap him there. Distracted by this Rhys had not noticed that Shangorth had ordered Michael to kill him. As his friend steps forward to murder him, a horse leaps into the fray. It is Lan on his Cloud Horse. He knocks the Warlock to the ground and tears the Soul Orb from around his neck.

His concentration broken, Shangorth loses his hold on Swiftaxe and Meld. Swiftaxe responds quickly to protect Rhys and buries his axe into Michael's chest, slaying him. Lan destroys the Soul Orb with two rocks and his soul is freed and returns to his body. Lan is actually Farspell, a great and ancient wizard. He reveals that the warlock is not Shangorth, but a lesser wizard called Weldrock, corrupted by dark magic. The warlock and wizard give battle and the Spider Gem is knocked from the warlock's hands. Meld recovers it and the attack on the town is ceased as the spiders run off in all directions, now free of any control. Seeing his plans falling apart Weldrock creates a portal and returns to Dargoth. Swiftaxe chases after him and enters the portal. As Weldrock exits he notices Swiftaxe following and closes the portal to trap the dwarf king in limbo. Before departing for his island stronghold, Weldrock destroys the mountain runestone, removing the chance for the teenagers to use it to return home.

CH25: At the end of the battle Fangtor lays dying from his wounds. Gorlan speaks to the dragon who tells the Warlord to remove his heart. Gorlan removes it and pushes a slice into Michael's chest. The heart bonds with the boy's own and Michael is resurrected, at the same time gaining dragon knowledge and memories.

CH26: Farspell and the teenagers travel to Shangorth Towers in Dargoth and find the runestone destroyed. They search the buildings and find a map that shows a chain of islands in the Sea of Mist. Farspell suggests they return to Pinnhome to translate the map and to try to find a way for teenagers to return home.

Book one ends with the teenagers heading back to Pinnhome and with Nexus following in their wake.

# PROLOGUE
## The Corruption of Sagot

Nexus pulled his cloak over his head and disappeared from view.

Someone, or something, was approaching his wooden shack. He slipped out of the partially open door and moved quietly into the trees.

A lone human hunter was approaching his hideout, cautious in his approach. There were a number of hunting shacks in the woods, generally shared by all, but not this one. The hunter knew that this lodge was marked for private use and had been the property of the OverLord's advisor before he had been banished from the lands.

Hidden from view Nexus, the Dark Assassin of Weldrock the Warlock, followed the man as he approached the open door. The hunter used his left arm to slowly push it fully open. As it swung inwards he paused before stepping inside.

The man noticed immediately someone was living in the supposedly empty shack. Turning to look out of the door for signs of the owner he satisfied himself that he was alone and walked to the bedside cabinet. He pulled open a drawer searching for valuables.

He saw objects within and reached inside. Before his fingers found their target the hunter's eyes suddenly opened wide in surprise. Pain tore through his midriff as Nexus slipped a knife between his ribs. The hunter let out a quiet grunt and fell to the floor, dead.

Nexus removed his cloak of invisibility and cleaned his blade on the hunter's clothing. Dragging the dead man into the woods he left him a few hundred metres away. The carrion eaters would take care of the rest.

Returning to his shack he closed the door and sat on his bed. He looked at the open drawer of his bedside table. Reaching inside he pulled out a torn and faded photograph. It showed a small church and a happy couple, bride and groom arm in arm. A wedding. One from a past life that he had all but forgotten.

Liam Sagot was French by birth. He had moved to Wales with his parents when he was five years old. He had hated it almost immediately. Leaving his friends behind he had been forced to learn English and attend an English speaking school. As a French boy he was not popular with the other kids and was constantly teased and bullied. They gave him the nicknames "Froggy", a cruel jibe at his nationality and "Sagot the Faggot", pronouncing his family name in an English way, rhyming it with a curious British meatball, often created by using the poorer cuts of meat mixed with offal.

When playing sport, he found himself on the end of some very rough treatment from the other pupils as, where he was concerned, the teachers turned a blind eye to any foul play.

As a result he grew to hate Wales and the Welsh and became a loner, choosing to distance himself from others. The only sport that he had enjoyed was football. He had inherited some of his father's skills for the game and it was one of the few things he could do where he was almost accepted by the others.

The practice of bullying continued all through his school years and he earned a reputation for being moody and distant although everyone acknowledged the fact that he was a brilliant scholar. He never moved on to university, but stayed living with his mother and father on the Welsh Coast. It was here that he heard about the young woman who, after tragically losing her family in an accident, now lived alone in a large and secluded house on the cliff tops, overlooking the sea. Taking an opportunity to move away from his parents and into a grand house he decided to woo this young girl.

Her name was Glenys and it appeared that they had attended the same school at the same time. They had been a grade apart in the school year, and he had no recollection of her. She also had an older sister who had moved away years before to build a life of her own, but he could not recall her either. Sagot decided to use their common schooling as a way to gain an introduction and so set about his plan of making her his bride.

The lonely young lady, attracted to his brilliant mind and intrigued by his foreign background fell for his false charms and a few months later they were married and he moved into her cliff top home.

He tolerated married life for over a year before he became restless. Although she was still tender towards him his wife was clearly getting frustrated with his reclusive ways. She was content to live in the seclusion of their home, detached from the village, but she loved the company of others and so volunteered her services in the community. As a result she spent most of her time away from their home, which suited Sagot.

He stayed at home and earned money from writing short stories and producing various documents for educational bodies. It was while developing a paper for Cambridge University that he first came into contact with the world of magic. It involved investigating the work of a group of druids based out of the town of St Davids in South West Wales. Although the modern day druids proved to be frauds, Sagot was intrigued by the stories of the use of alchemy, necromancy and enchantments by the previous generations of druids. In particular his interest was piqued by some of the old parchments that he had found in the vaults of St Davids Cathedral. It was this that had later caused him to dabble with the dark arts and become tainted by its perversion to become what he now was, a minion of a dark warlock.

Over the months he became increasingly bored with his life and found the presence of his wife intrusive. He had started to delve deeper into the study of magic and had learned a great deal about its use in ancient Britain. However, he found that his exposure to current magic use was very limited in South Wales so he decided to travel further a-field and visit other countries and cultures in an effort to gain more knowledge. One dank and miserable rainy day, when his wife was out of the house, he took a rare journey to town and emptied their bank account. Returning home he packed his bags and scribbled a brief note informing her, rather impersonally, that Wales offered nothing for him anymore and that he was going to sign up with a merchant vessel bound for South America.

He spent the next three years travelling the world, living from day to day, jumping from port to port. At each new stop-over he gradually frittered away their savings in the pursuit of further knowledge of magic and myth. Occasionally he would send back souvenirs of his travels to his wife in Wales, but this practice soon dried up as money became scarce.

It was in Peru that his life changed. He had been studying the history of the Incas and their habits of sun worship and the related stories of stones which possessed magical properties. This led him and his hired interpreter to the ancient town of

Cuzco where he met an elder who spoke to them of a gateway high in the mountains. A gateway that legend said linked to another world.

The old man claimed that the mountain retreat of Machu Picchu had been built to honour those who travelled through the gateway and that this magical portal had been used to transport the stone to the high mountain top where Machu Picchu was built. Sagot knew that experts had been puzzling for years over how the Incas had transported the heavy stone to the mountain top. He felt that there may be more to the man's stories than just the exaggeration of tribal beliefs.

After a heated negotiation involving money and cigarettes, the elder provided Sagot with a map. It showed a trail that ran from Cuzco to the old Inca site of Quenko, a few miles to the northeast. From here it headed in a North West direction toward Lake Pieray.

Approximately three miles up this trail the map showed a small building. He explained that it was once the entrance to a large underground chamber, similar to one found at Quenko. This was the Chamber of the Shimmering Gate, a holy place that allowed travel between worlds. When Sagot had asked why this entrance had not been previously discovered, the old man explained the entrance no longer existed and that the chamber had been buried many generations before.

Sagot was suitably intrigued to investigate further. He conned some locals from Cuzco into accompanying him on a short expedition to find the buried chamber.

Days rolled by, but eventually their efforts were rewarded and the site was located, the old man had been wrong. The entrance had indeed been blocked and hidden, but on clearing the doorway, the chamber beyond proved to be intact. After some heavy graft, an entrance was cleared, large enough to allow human entry to the chamber.

Sagot had demanded to be the first to clamber through and the Peruvians did not need persuading. They had become increasingly uneasy as the doorway was cleared and none were keen to go further into the chamber.

Armed with a bright torch, Sagot had descended into the dark. Going down the steep stone stairway he noticed ornate stone carvings on either side. Various animals and acts of sun worship were depicted, but nothing unusual for Peru until he got to the lower part of the staircase. On the wall here were depictions of centaurs. He had examined them closely; often the Incas drew the invading Spanish Conquistadors in a centaur-like manner, a two headed horse-man beast. Having no indigenous horses in Peru they had, at first sighting, believed the rider and horse to be a single beast. The artwork here though definitely depicted a centaur, a four legged horse-like body and tail with a single human head.

Excitedly he stepped off the last step into the chamber to find…nothing!

The chamber was completely empty. No magical gateway, no Inca treasures, just more carved walls with stone seats around the outside. He had been so sure that this was leading to something. Even then, confronted with the evidence of the empty room, he could not throw off the gut feeling that there was something more to be found.

Behind Sagot, at the top of the stairs, the Peruvians had recovered their bravery and followed him into the chamber. When they saw it was bare and derelict a few offered words of consolation to the Frenchman which irritated him immensely and he snapped back at them rudely.

The group had scoured the chamber and eventually, disappointed at finding nothing of value, began to filter away to make their way back to home. Sagot however was sure that there was more to be discovered and he had steadfastly refused to leave. They tried hard to persuade him to return, but he was not going to budge and eventually he was left alone to wallow in his misery.

He had set up his tent at the top of the staircase just outside the chamber and, as night drew in, he built a fire. Taking a bottle of scotch from his pack he decided to drown his sorrows and fell asleep in an alcohol induced haze.

He awoke in the middle of the night. At first he thought that the campfire provided the illumination in the dark but then, his mind gradually waking, he realised that the hue of the light was wrong. There was a deep dark blue tinge to it. Sitting up he saw that it emanated from within the chamber. Standing, he hurried down the stairs and, as he had entered, he had his first sight of The Shimmering Gate, a portal that linked worlds. He did not hesitate. Breathing deeply and closing his eyes he had walked through the gateway.

There had been a momentary feeling of weightlessness, but then he felt solid ground beneath his feet again. The transition was almost immediate, a few steps and he was through.

This was how he had first arrived in Portalia. The Shimmering Gateway had transported him to a ruined city, not unlike Machu Picchu, which was located high up in the Pinnacle Mountains. Here he had discovered a ancient buildings and, from the carvings and artwork still remaining, he had correctly deduced that it had been the home to a race of men who regularly traded and communicated with centaurs.

Shortly after arriving he had felt a moment of panic as the Shimmering Gate had closed to reveal no sign of its existence. He examined the walls and in the dim light he found a large slab that had a depiction of the Gate etched on it. Feeling all around he was frustrated when he could not find a way to trigger the gateway. Tired, irritated and somewhat concerned that he would not be able to return to Earth, he had decided to camp at the ruins and wait in the hope that it would re-open at some point.

Over the next few days, as he waited, he explored the rest of the buildings. Other than the wall carvings depicting the use of the gateway and drawings of more centaurs, dwarves and humans, he had found nothing else of particular interest and nothing that suggested any solution to his dilemma.

Occasionally he caught sight of birds unknown to him and once witnessed the flight of a huge eagle, its plumage a golden colour with head and tail adorned with red, yellow and orange feathers. He had later learned that this was a fire eagle from Pinnhome. At night he heard larger animals moving through the undergrowth, but it appeared that they were more scared of him than vice versa as they never left the cover of the vegetation.

On the fifth day he was finally rewarded and the Gate shimmered into life once again. He had swiftly passed through and with extreme relief he had found himself back in Peru. There was no-one to be seen at the ruins and he noted that his tent and belongings had been removed. He laughed to himself when he speculated on what the locals must have thought. Returning to the Peruvian town, he had acquired enough provisions to last him a number of months in the wild, making sure that he kept away from areas where he was known and that his brief visit had not aroused any suspicions. He returned to the chamber and waited for the Shimmering Gate to re-open.

After four frustrating days and restless nights in a light sleeping bag, once again the night was illuminated by the dark blue glow.

With another sigh of relief, Sagot stepped through once more and returned to the ruined town.

Setting up camp he had decided that he would make this his base and explore the local area in more detail. A new life demanded a new name and it was here, high in the Pinnacle Mountains, that he chose the name Nexus. Not only because the name suggested the centre of things, a connection between events and places, but also because of an ancient story referenced in his copy of the Agrippa's Three Books of Occult Philosophy, a story that involved a centaur called Nessus.

Legend stated that Nessus was ultimately responsible for the death of Hercules. During their travels, Hercules and his wife Deianeira were helped across a swollen river by the centaur Nessus. The centaur is attracted to Deianeira and tried to force himself upon her but Hercules intervened and shot him with an arrow tipped with the poison of the Hydra, a seven-headed monster. As Nessus lay dying he told Deianeira to gather drops of his blood to act as a love potion that would bind Hercules to her forever. Years later, when Hercules was away from his wife he fell for Viola. In an effort to restore the love bond that they shared, Deianeira soaked a cloak in the blood of the centaur and gave it to Hercules. On wearing the cloak the great warrior was immediately poisoned and suffered a slow and painful death, finally bringing Nessus his revenge.

Sagot had always admired the cunning and guile of the centaur and so Nexus was born.

He had spent the next few weeks exploring the wilderness and was thrilled by the sight of both familiar and alien flora and fauna. It was while returning from one of these trips that he had made his most exciting find.

One of the buildings of the town was octagonal in shape and still partly roofed. With the sun low in the sky rays shone into this building illuminating areas within that were normally shrouded in shadow. In the far corner Nexus noticed an abnormality on one of the walls. On closer inspection he realised that this was a compartment of some kind, hexagonal in shape and with a hidden hinge to the right. He worked at the edges of the compartment for almost an hour and was eventually rewarded when he cleared a slot which allowed him to prise open the door.

Inside he had found a small, dark wooden box, decorated with a bleak painting of a coastal cave. He stared at it, the cave seemed strangely familiar. Next to the box was another small, pale wooden box. He picked up the larger one first and opened it to find inside an octagonal object, a dark and smooth stone, emblazoned with a Celtic knot. Next he opened the light wooden box and inside he found a dark metal pendant and a gold coloured ring, both of which had also been etched with the figure of the Celtic knot. Under these two items sat a scrap of paper on which had been written a short verse;

*Portalia south, north, east and west,*
*To ease the travel on any quest,*
*The knot, the peaks and the old oak tree,*
*Servant chains amount to three.*
*A ring to trigger a call to home,*
*Returns all three to their Runestone.*
*A stone-made key makes up the set,*
*Unlocking the paths of the portal net.*

Using his logic he assumed that the verse related to the items and that he held in his hand three magical artefacts, a pendant, a ring and a stone-made key and that they held some form of property similar to that of the Shimmering Gate. Storing the items back in their boxes he placed them in his backpack and returned to his makeshift camp. Later he was to learn that these items were artefacts of the Celtic knot, the Runestone of Eumor. Centaurs had hidden away the artefacts generations ago to prevent the use of the runestone at their capital city. This had been carried out in secret and not even the Eumor Council were aware that the items had not been lost or destroyed.

A few more weeks had passed and during this time Nexus had closely monitored the Shimmering Gateway as it opened and closed. It re-appeared at very sporadic intervals. On one occasion it had opened twice in a single night while another time it had remained closed for almost ten days. The length of time that it remained open was also random. The longest was over five minutes while some nights it flashed for only a few seconds. However, now confident that the Gateway would provide a way back to Earth, Nexus had decided to leave his mountain ruins to explore this strange new world.

Eager to find some signs of intelligent life, he had decided to break camp and had struck out towards the south as it was from this direction that he most often saw birds approaching.

After picking his way through the mountains he finally had finally discovered a lush open valley and the city of the Pinns, Pinnhome. He found the people friendly and accommodating. Through tact and cunning and using his keen mind and off world skills and knowledge, he had advanced his station to become a trusted advisor to Toran, OverLord of Pinnhome. Initially he had genuinely enjoyed his new role and revelled in the access it gave to the magical tomes hidden away in the Pinnhome vaults, but driven by an intense desire for more knowledge and power, he began to delve into the dark magic secrets that had been locked away within Pinnhome. Eventually, his use of the dark arts was uncovered and with great sadness Toran had banished him from Pinnhome.

After this exile, and fully aware of the significance of the runestone artefacts that he possessed, he had made his way to

Eumor City with the intent to test the devices and to ascertain whether they were genuine. While in Pinnhome he had learned of the superstition and lack of trust that the centaurs felt towards the runestone so he was careful not to let others know why he was there.

While there he had found precisely what he needed in a centaur called Hesh. This high ranking centaur official was as ambitious as Nexus and so the pair teamed up. They met secretly and the Frenchman had shared with the centaur the knowledge that he believed that he had possession of the runestone key. Not fully trusting Hesh he did not mention the ring and the pendant. A few days later and with the assistance of the traitorous centaur, the pair gained entry to the sealed runestone chamber. Once inside they inserted the runestone key into the control pedestal. The runestone hummed into life and, as they watched, a portal gateway grew at the centre.

In Pinnhome Nexus has studied the use of the runestone portals and, although most linked to portals here in Portalia, he was positive that five of the pedestal settings led to locations on Earth.

Even more remarkable than this was the realisation that one of these portals was located inside Salty's Cave which lay on the coast, within walking distance of his home in Wales. It had taken him a while but eventually he had recognised the cave on the box that he had found. He had seen that cave many times before, less sea battered on the box but unmistakably Salty's. It seemed that the magic of the portals was even greater than any knew. Had it been the magic that had lured his father to Wales so many years before? Had it led himself to Peru? For him this confirmed that his chosen path had been his destiny and that he should continue to follow it to greater things.

Aware that Hesh held a keen interest in the ancient history of the centaur race, Nexus had told him of the story of Nessus and persuaded him to guard the runestone chamber while he, Nexus, used the portal to return to Wales. In exchange he promised Hesh that he would recover the copy of the Three Books of Occult Philosophy and that he would bring it back for the centaur. Hesh, eager for more knowledge and keen to build his personal wealth, readily agreed.

Turning the portal key to the required setting, a gateway shimmered into life and Nexus stepped through. He smiled broadly as he exited. He had been correct; the setting did lead to a cave and, within a few minutes, he had followed the length of it to exit onto a familiar beach.

Removing the runestone key box from his belongings he had compared the painting on the lid to Salty's Cave itself. He had hoped to get some indication of the age of the box, but other than confirming that much erosion had taken place since the painting was created, he could not determine anything useful. Carefully he had placed the box back in his pocket alongside the smaller box containing the Eumor pendant and ring.

He ran along the beach and made straight for his home. Wishing to avoid contact with his wife he had remained on watch from a distance until he saw her leave for the village. He sighed when she stepped out of the front door. She had passed close by his hidden position in the undergrowth. He had forgotten how beautiful she was and despite himself he could not help but feel small pangs of regret at leaving her.

He had watched her disappear into the distance before entering the house. Cautiously listening for any sound of occupancy, he made for the loft where he recovered the occult volume and a number of other valuable books for himself, placing them in an old kit bag.

As he had opened the front door to leave, he had seen a wedding photograph of Glenys and himself. He scooped up the photograph, still in its frame, and threw it into his kit bag.

Reaching into his pocket he had then made a decision that he would later regret. He removed the Celtic knot pendant from the box, grabbed a pen and paper and scribbled a brief note, ensuring that he disguised his hand writing.

It read;

*Dear Mrs Sagot,*

*I apologise for informing you in writing and not in person but you were not at home when I visited and I am required to rejoin my ship, which sails at midday today.*

*During a recent trip to Peru where I worked on board the Castrolis, a small cargo ship based out of Florida, we took on board your husband, Liam Sagot as a deck hand.*

*While sailing from Peru to California we hit a storm and I regret to say that Liam, who was on deck at the time, appears to have been washed overboard. A search was carried out but no trace of him was found.*

*I later went to his cabin to pack his things, but sea life being what it is, it had already been gutted. However, I was lucky enough to find the enclosed pendant. I am sure he would have wanted you to have this as a memento.*

*I realise that this is impersonal and I apologise for this but I am sure you will understand my haste.*

*My sincere sympathy for your loss.*

He had left the letter unsigned in the fear that Glenys may try to track down this mysterious visitor and discover that he did not exist. He placed the note and pendant inside an envelope and posted it back through the letter box as he had departed.

With kit bag in hand he made his way back down the cliff and along the beach to the cave. The bag was heavy and before stepping back through the open portal to Portalia he placed it on the floor to stretch his back which ached from the weight. As he lengthened his spine stretching it for relief, Hesh suddenly leapt from the portal and grabbed him roughly. "Quick, we must hide. Fyros is coming! He is the keeper of the runestone chamber. He must not discover our intrusion"

He had pulled Nexus back towards the portal and the momentum caused them to stumble to the floor. Hesh quickly recovered all fours and continued to pull Nexus towards the portal. Fortunately, just as Hesh yanked him violently through the portal gateway he was able to reach out his hand and firmly grasped a bag handle. Kit bag and man disappeared.

Hesh had quickly removed the runestone key and the portal closed. In the nick of time he extinguished their lantern and the pair shrank back into the shadows.

Fyros had opened the chamber door and looked inside. Satisfied that all was well he did not step into the chamber itself and so did not discover the hidden pair. They had listened to the chamber guardian's hooves as they faded away and then Hesh relit the lantern and turned to Nexus. "I should never have listened to you!" he said angrily. "If I had been caught I would have lost all that I have built up over the years. I would be an outcast."

Nexus scowled in response. Reaching into his bag he removed the volume of the Three Books of Occult Philosophy and threw it at the centaur. "Don't give me that! You knew what you were doing. Here is the book as promised."

Hesh picked up the volume and once again glared at Nexus. "Human, consider our little 'partnership' terminated!"

"Fine!" replied Nexus, "Give me the runestone key. I will find someone else to help me."

Hesh shook his head, "I don't think so. This key shall remain in my safe keeping. The key belongs to the centaurs so a centaur shall own it. You will leave Eumor immediately or be killed."

Nexus then swore at the centaur profusely but the creature just laughed back.

With little choice the Frenchman had left that same day. He made camp to the south of the city and it was here that he discovered to his horror that he had not only lost the runestone key, but that the box with the ring was missing too. Casting his mind back he realised that it must have fallen out of his pocket as Hesh had dragged him to the floor in the cave.

Cursing he regretted his rash action of leaving the gift of the pendant for Glenys and chastised himself for trusting the centaur Hesh. He vowed to return to Eumor and one day seize back the runestone key. Neither would he be so sentimental on his next journey to Wales. He would recover the pendant and ring, even if it meant he had to kill to do so.

Nexus shook himself from his reminiscing. Taking one last look at his wedding photo he placed it back in the drawer. He no longer had time for sentimentality. For now he would do the bidding of the warlock until his own knowledge of the dark arts exceeded those of Weldrock. Then he would be the one to rule over all of Portalia.

# CHAPTER ONE
## A Body in the Sand

Gatherer looked across the desert towards a long line of sand dunes.

A scorching yellow sun blazed down. No breeze blew to disrupt the fine white sands and as usual, a cloudless sky offered no respite for the creatures below.

He closed his inner filter eyelid, restricting the bright light to allow his yellow eyes greater definition of his surroundings. Bending his three metre tall, stick-like, bronzed and hairless frame, he placed his hands on the ground and stretched his long bony fingers so they lay flat on the sand, five short claws penetrating the top surface.

He looked towards the dunes and shut down the rays of the sun by closing individually his remaining two pairs of open eyelids. Breathing deeply and slowly he directed his thoughts to the sand and opened his mind to sense his surroundings.

He could feel the energy of living creatures close at hand. He sensed numerous insects and sand parasites and noted that the energy level was much stronger than earlier sensings. Increased activity like this usually meant that there was food to be gathered and as tribe gatherer it was his responsibility to ensure that this resource was found and brought home for the others.

Gatherer became very excited. The sensing was extremely powerful and this often meant that there was meat to be found.

Usually his gathering activities brought home pulp fruit, the hardened yellow bulbous seed pods of the desert cactus. Occasionally the death of one of the few living creatures that roamed this inhospitable land would bring meat to the smaller creatures of the desert and, if he was fortunate, to his tribe of desert striders.

Opening his eyes once more, Gatherer raised his frame and stretching his long legs he began to jog. His sensing had told him that whatever had caused the disturbance should lie close to the dunes ahead. He had not detected any other large hunter presence in the area so there was no need for a more cautious approach. This was not always the case though as Gatherer had discovered far too often for his liking. Even so, as he jogged effortlessly up the first dune, he momentarily focused his attention on his outer skin to ensure that its pigment changed, chameleon-like, to the sandy white of the surrounding dunes.

As he crossed the peak of the second dune he slowed his jog. There at the foot of the dune, some fifty feet below, lay a body of some kind in the sand. Gatherer smiled, his pleasure growing even greater as he moved closer and saw that the creature was only recently dead and hence remained largely intact with only small areas devoured by the insects and parasites that crawled over it.

Gatherer used his foot to roll the body onto its back. The small creatures, their feast interrupted, scurried quickly away, tunnelling deep into the sand seeking the protection of concealment. Gatherer looked at his find and frowned. At his feet lay a short, two-legged creature of a type that he had never seen before. The white and lifeless eyes of a being that had once held intelligence stared up at him. Gatherer slowly bent his frame to get a closer look.

Placing his hands on the pale, cold flesh he estimated that the corpse had been dead for less than a day. By desert standards this was fresh meat and the tribe would be very pleased when he returned home with his haul. Not only had he found this meat to nourish them but also he had already discovered a large amount of pulp fruit on this gathering. He stared at the strange lifeless face; white hair framed the pallid skin that would not have held any colour even in life.

Gatherer frisked the corpse and found a number of interesting items. Apart from some gold coins there was a small crystal that shone brilliantly in the desert sun, a metal pendant decorated with the symbol of a mountain and an ornate gold ring. He placed all of these into a large pocket sewn into his leather jerkin.

He then reached towards his leather waist belt on which hung three weapons and a small bag. The first was a sling shot made from bone and fine cartilage. Small heavy stones weighted with metal ore compounds provided ammunition and filled the small bag. The pellets were round at one end but tapered at the other and terminated in a sharp point at the rear to streamline their flight through the air.

The second weapon was a double-edged scimitar, useful for hand-to-hand fighting but it was for the third weapon that Gatherer reached. This was a stubby knife with a serrated edge on one side and a keen-edged blade on the other. He dropped the backpack that he carried and from within removed some fine skins. Carefully unfolding them he spread them flat on the fine sand.

Holding his knife in his right hand he grabbed the white hair of the creature with his left and began the job of removing the clothes and skin, paring away the meat from the bone. Working meticulously Gatherer placed the flesh in one of the fine skins and the bones in another. Taking two large sections of skin he folded these into a small cloth pouch and placed them with the bones. He left smaller sections of skin and bone where they lay, adding to these two long strips of flesh from his gathering of meat. This would help feed other creatures of the desert and help to maintain the very delicate ecosystem that survived in this inhospitable land.

Folding the skins to protect his gathering, he refilled his backpack, storing not only the flesh and bones but also the clothes of the corpse. Finally, he reached into another pocket and drew out six small seeds. Digging beneath the mound of remaining skin, meat and bone Gatherer planted the seeds deep in the sand. Before refilling the hole, he used his tongue to squeeze a gland in his mouth which immediately secreted a small amount of water. He spat it onto the seeds and buried them.

All desert striders possessed the water gland. This small biological factory could produce its own water from the oxygen and hydrogen that existed in the air. Although the amount of water that was produced was very small it was enough to help maintain the life force of the desert striders and allowed them to travel across large tracts of desert for days at a time without the need for additional water. The fine balance of the desert also relied on this small gland for the continued survival of the desert cactus which, through years of cultivation by the desert striders, relied heavily on the water provided by the tribesmen.

Gatherer steadied himself. It was less than a half day journey to Dry Dune, his home village. This gathering had been a short but fruitful event. Often he would be out gathering for weeks at a time, but on this occasion, it had taken only three days to fill his pack. Surveying the area once more and taking one final sensing for any signs of danger or resources, Gatherer threw the heavy backpack over his shoulders with an ease that belied his stalk-like frame. As he strode out for home, behind him on the desert sand the insects returned to lay waste to what remained of the body of Zarn, the White Dwarf.

He had been walking for only an hour or so when his earth senses began to tingle. Dropping the pack he bent to the ground to take another sensing. Something was approaching from the east. He stood and drew his scimitar, adopting a combat position with knees slightly bent and the sword held raised and ready for battle.

As a result, when this hunter came sprinting towards him over the dunes, Gatherer was poised and ready for combat. He saw that his attacker was a razorback, a fierce desert carnivore. Similar in shape to a kangaroo, it had strong lower legs and long upper arms which terminated in vicious clawed paws, three finger-like digits on each. Its head was also kangaroo shaped, but this creature was hairless and possessed tough leathery skin. Down its long back it had a large boned spine that formed a thin sharp ridge, hence providing its name. When it sat up on its back feet it stood as tall as Gatherer.

Without pausing the razorback attacked. The desert strider moved swiftly to the right and, as the creature passed him, in one smooth movement he swung his scimitar in a wide arc directly towards the creature. The sword slid across the hard skin at the midriff of the razorback, drawing blood.

The creature screeched as it felt the pain of the gash. Furious, it stopped and turned, pausing to survey its prey. Gatherer gave his weapon a sharp flick in the air and the blood flew from the blade and onto the ground, leaving the blade almost clear. Still screeching, the razorback crouched and using its strong lower legs it made an enormous leap into the air clearing the ground by some twenty feet. It pointed all four sets of claws at Gatherer and angled its descent towards him. As the creature bore down on him Gatherer rolled to the ground to avoid being impaled by the sharp claws. However, the razorback responded instinctively and swung out a leg raking the cheek of the desert strider. As the claws came free of his cheek, Gatherer twisted with the direction of the blow and athletically carried out a cartwheel to avoid further injury from the flailing legs of the creature. Recovering his balance he raised his sword as the razorback approached once more. It charged again and Gatherer easily avoided it, once more swinging his scimitar in an arc to bite even deeper into the flesh of the creature's side.

Once again the razorback shaped to make a giant leap at its prey but Gatherer had learned the pattern of the attack from the earlier blow and, as the creature leapt into the air, he rolled to the floor and lay flat, sword upright facing directly towards the descending claws. As the creature made contact, Gatherer thrust his arms upward, plunging the sword deep into its chest. He pushed his body to the side to avoid the descending beast, releasing his weapon. With the blade buried deep inside the animal, Gatherer rolled as the full weight of the creature fell onto the spot where he had lain only moments earlier. He swiftly jumped back onto his feet, drawing his knife at the same time. Turning to face the beast, the small weapon held out in defiance, he saw that he could relax. The razorback lay impaled on the scimitar, twitching in its final death throes.

Breathing heavily from the exertion, he waited for the creature to become still before turning the razorback onto its side to remove his sword. He cleaned the blade on the creature's skin and wiped it dry before re-sheathing it. He then withdrew his skinning knife and once more set about the task of removing the flesh of his kill, wrapping the meat in the skins as he had done earlier with the body of the dwarf. He could not believe his luck.

Carrying out the same ritual as he had earlier, he once again left some remains for other creatures and planted cactus seed before turning for home once more, his pack now bulging with one of the most successful gatherings that he had ever had.

A few hours later he came to an area of desert which sat surrounded by dunes dotted with projections of bare light-grey rock that jutted up beyond the sand. He moved to one of these projections, a small square of rock that possessed a flat top. Deep into this rock someone had etched a depiction of a sand dune. Gatherer stepped up onto the rock and raised his hands out in front of him where they came into contact with a cold surface, invisible to the naked eye but solid to the touch. Closing all three sets of eyelids, Gatherer allowed his senses to flow down his arms and through his hands onto the cold surface. There was a flicker of light and, in silence, a large dome appeared, translucently reflecting the image of the sand and sky around it. Where Gatherer had laid his hands an opening appeared in the dome and he immediately stepped inside.

On entering the protective dome, the gatherer paused to breathe deeply and allow a sense of calm to wash over him. He was home. In an almost schizophrenic change of character, his fearsome hunting persona slipped away and, as he relaxed and his mood mellowed, he looked at the home of his tribe and his loved ones.

Ahead of him was the small village of the Dry Dune tribe. Gatherer and around fifty other desert striders lived here, mostly adults but with a few elders and a handful of children.

The houses of the village were formed from blocks of rectangular stone, mined and moulded from the grey bedrock on which the village was built. They each had solid rock walls with small windows and doors but with no roofs. No wind or rain could breach the energy force of the dome so the owners could leave their homes open to the sky.

Unlike the view from the exterior, from within, the energy dome could be seen easily and, while it allowed the sunlight to filter through, it was very much diffused giving the whole village a pastel glow, while ensuring that the temperature inside remained much cooler than the hot desert beyond.

The base of the dome was approximately five hundred metres in diameter. Around the base, at the edges of the village, sat sixteen stone pyramids spaced symmetrically around the circumference, thirty metres apart. Each pyramid was around a metre and a half high. Beneath the pyramids the sand had been swept away to allow their bases to make solid contact with bedrock below. The pyramids were the energy source for the dome, the shape and structure of the devices allowing earth energy to flow up to the peak and spread in an arc around the device. Each energy projection met the forces emanating from the next pyramid, bending and stressing the flow to mould the shape of the dome.

The houses of the village were dotted around in a circle. A thin layer of soft sand covered the ground, deep enough to provide a soft base on which to walk. Similar to the scene outside, grey rock occasionally projected through the sand but here it had either been etched or painted with depictions of desert animals and plants.

In the centre of the village, at the very heart of the community, the sand had been cleared to expose bare rock which had been decorated with an intricate symbol of the sun, vibrant with reds, deep ambers and yellows. Gatherer walked to this clearing and the villagers, gradually acknowledging his return began to congregate, all eager to see what their gatherer had brought home.

A female desert strider approached Gatherer and hugged him. They touched noses lovingly.

"Welcome home Gatherer. It is good to have you back" she said running her hand along his cheek as she spoke. Where her fingers touched his skin the pigment of his flesh changed to a soft pink in pleasure.

She looked at him and smiled, "I take it from your swift return that it was a fruitful gathering?"

Gatherer looked into the eyes of Sandmover, his mate. Unlike most desert striders, who possessed yellow eyes, hers were a light shade of amber, which Gatherer felt supplemented her beauty. She was by far the thinnest of the females in the tribe and almost the tallest.

Gatherer nodded in response to her question, "A VERY fruitful gathering," and so saying he emptied his pack to display the pulp fruit and the remains of the dwarf and the razorback.

The tribe murmured in excitement. Four of the adults and one older child stepped forward to collect the meat. To them would fall the responsibility for curing the joints and for preparing meals. Next, an elder, with the assistance of two young apprentices, gathered up the bones and cartilage. They would work both into implements to provide a medium for artwork and decoration. Two females collected the cloth and skins. These they would rework into clothing and material for the tribe.

By law, the other items that Gatherer had brought back would remain his property to dispose of as he wished, but as custom demanded, he displayed the items to the rest of the tribe.

Taking the pendant with the adorned mountain symbol, Gatherer pulled Sandmover to him and placed the pendant around her neck. The pendant sat comfortably on her chest and she looked at it in admiration before rubbing her nose against Gatherer's cheek in affection and gratitude.

He then took the ring and lifting her hand he attempted to place it over her finger. "No you don't," she smiled and taking the ring from him she slipped it over his own finger, "For Gatherer, our glorious tribe provider and my most loved one." The tribe called out loudly in appreciation and Gatherer could not hide his embarrassment.

When the noise had subsided he withdrew the final item, the crystal that he had taken from the body of the dwarf.

Turning to a robed elder who stood authoritatively at the centre of the crowd he said, "Tribemaker, I also found this item but I do not know what it is."

Tribemaker took the proffered crystal and turned it over in his fingers. Holding it up to the sun, the crystal's chain hung down, and he smiled when he saw the myriad reflections and refractions that occurred. Tribemaker was the eldest of the Dry Dune tribe and although not an official leader, he was the person that all went to for advice. Over the years he had seen and learned much.

"I once came across stone similar to this many years ago but much, much smaller. It was found lying within a piece of grey rock that we were working. I think I still have it somewhere. It was not as intricate as this though." He held it up to the sun once again and turned it so that the refracted rays moved around. Looking thoughtful he said, "Let me ponder this for a while. I am sure we can find a use for it," and so saying he placed the crystal in his pocket.

Now addressing everyone, Tribemaker announced, "We have truly been blessed with a great gathering. Let us have a feast this night to give thanks and to show our appreciation to Gatherer for his efforts."

An excited cheer went up from the crowd. Tribal feasts were extremely rare but always resulted in a fun time for all. So, with celebratory thoughts , the tribe dissipated to prepare as Gatherer walked arm in arm to his house with Sandmover.

This had been one of his best gatherings yet and he felt very content as he pulled his mate closer to him in satisfaction and pride.

# CHAPTER TWO
## Pinnhome

Rhys looked out through his bedroom window across a sun swept green and luscious valley. Farm animals grazed in the meadows and, to the north, snow capped mountains provided a stunning backdrop to the scene. He breathed in the air that was cool and crystal clear and was reminded of when he had travelled to Switzerland with his school three years ago. This was not Switzerland though. You didn't get to see centaurs and elves roaming the mountainsides in Europe. This was Pinnhome, the capital city of the Pinns.

Rhys sighed, now missing his home, his parents and his aunt. He wondered what they were doing. They must have been so upset when they found that he had gone missing. A small tear trickled down his cheek as he thought of his mother and aunt grieving for him. They would have thought that both he and Michael had been swept out to sea by the turning tide, although they must have wondered why the boys had not radioed for help. After all they had taken the walkie-talkies with them.

That had been months ago. Rhys was not sure precisely how many but he believed that it was probably a year since they had entered Salty's Cave at the start of this adventure. So much had happened since then but ultimately they were stuck here with no way home. If only the ancient wizard Farspell could find a way for Rhys to control the new powers that he possessed. he could then create a portal back to Wales, but so far, the efforts of the wizard had been in vain.

Since leaving the shattered Runestone at Dargoth, Farspell and Rhys had discussed his power at length and while Rhys had created numerous portals and could view what was on the far side of the portal, he had no way to conjure up a specific location on demand. Now, with the runestones at Dargoth and the Forest of Old destroyed, and the runestone key for Eumor lost, there was no way back to Earth for his friends, Michael and Ashley, or himself. He was their only hope. If he could not learn to control the portals then they would be stuck here forever.

Rhys jumped as he was suddenly hit across the back of his head by a cushion. "C'mon gloomy, cheer up! It can't be all that bad, remember that Carl and Stern have promised to take us fishing this morning". Wiping the tears from his face Rhys turned. "Oh. Hi Mike. Sorry I'd completely forgotten," he replied.

Michael smiled at him, "No problem. C'mon then. Get your kit on. It's still fairly chilly out there even though it looks warm from inside."

Michael did not ask Rhys why he looked so upset or why there were tears in his eyes. He already knew.

They had learned not to discuss things when they felt homesick. Better that they help each other by trying to take the thoughts away from home. They had found that this worked well for all of them as they were rarely gloomy at the same time.

Rhys got washed and dressed while Michael waited for him; soon the boys were heading to the kitchens to grab some breakfast. They gobbled down bacon and bread washed down with sweetgrass tea before setting off to meet Stern and Carl in the main courtyard.

There was already a hustle and bustle about the town as the citizens of Pinnhome went about their daily business and when they arrived at the courtyard they found the twin warriors waiting for them.

"OK you two, let's go," said Stern and so saying he picked up a handful of fishing poles and tackle. His brother, Carl, carried two wooden boxes. He saw the boys look at the boxes questioningly. "One box for bait and the other for lunch," Stern replied, his blue eyes glinting at the very mention of food.

Rhys laughed and turned to Stern, "You don't mean you actually trust Carl with the food box?"

Stern paused and harrumphed, "A very astute observation young Rhys." He turned to his brother and handed him the fishing poles, "Carl, you take these and I'll take those. That way we can be sure that there is not one fat belly and three empty ones by the end of the day."

Carl feigned a crestfallen look while handing the boxes over and the quartet left the city, laughing as they strode out across the open meadows.

"How far is it to the stream Stern?" asked Michael who was a keen fisherman.

"Not too far, it's just a short walk. The stream is a tributary of the Snake River. It's one of the many snowmelt streams that run down from the Pinnacle Mountains to form the Snake. This one is a major route for salmonfish. There's not another run like this within half a days travel. You'll see, we'll be heading home loaded up with fish by the end of the day."

"Awesome!" replied Michael, "I'm really looking forward to this. It's been ages since I've been fishing."

The four continued to make their way to the stream occasionally disturbing wildlife. Along the way they met a few other people, all human. Most were farmers out tending their animals but there were also a few fishermen. Some of these were returning after a night fishing session and they reported that the stream had provided a good catch.

By and by they arrived at the stream and found a spot to set up their tackle. Carl gave his assistance to Rhys while Stern offered help to Michael. As they prepared the rods, Stern watched Michael inquisitively. Pausing after tying Michael's hook he gently put his hand on the boy's chest. "So how is that old dragon heart of yours? Has anything unusual happened yet?"

Michael shook his head, "No, not really. I occasionally get glimpses of memories that obviously belong to Fangtor, but these are usually mixed up images. Farspell says that these images will make more sense as the heart adjusts itself to my mind and body, and vice versa, but I guess we'll have to wait and see." Michael pulled his jerkin open at his chest to reveal scaly skin beneath, "Of course I still have this, the mark of the Dragon Heart. Apparently this will stay as it is. I don't mind though. It doesn't look very nice but given that it saved my life I can't grumble and I can always cover it up with some make up if it bothers me."

"It doesn't look that bad anyway," replied Stern, "A little scaly but nothing that would upset anyone."

Michael smiled, "Thanks, but I think you're just being nice." And with that he covered the patch of skin again.

"No really," insisted Stern, "I think you'll find more young ladies wanting to check out your unique feature rather than being turned off by it. Could be quite a lady puller that dragon skin of yours."

Michael blushed, "Shut up will you," but inside he felt cheered by the words of his friend as Stern had hit upon the very thing that Michael feared. He was convinced that any girl who saw his chest would find it repugnant and would run a mile.

To hide his embarrassment Michael grabbed the rod from Stern and said, "Are you going to talk or fish?"

Stern laughed out loud, "Well said young earthling. Fishing it is!"

\*\*\*

Ophra, daughter of Toran and Melis, OverLord and OverLady of Pinnhome, walked through the palace gardens arm in arm with her new found friend, Ashley. The coming of spring had brought out some early bulbs and, after a winter of sleep, the garden was beginning to come back to life, revitalising itself and those who walked its paths.

The two teenage girls had met shortly after Ashley's arrival in Pinnhome and being around the same age, had hit it off almost immediately. Ashley had been surprised at herself befriending Ophra as, given that she was the daughter of the OverLord, she had received a rather different upbringing to her usual group of friends. Ashley's tom boy past and love of soccer had always resulted in her teaming up with other girls who were similarly branded. Ophra however had been brought up in palatial luxury and the pomp and ceremony that surrounded it. She was very feminine, interested in jewellery, clothes, perfumes and anything that would attract the interest of the handsome young men that lived in and around Pinnhome.

Ashley unlinked arms and walked to a striking red bloom that filled one of the circular beds. It was similar in size to a large tulip but two enormous petals opened out fully to reveal intense splashes of crimson red at the top of every stem.

"Whoa! This is stunning. What is it?" she asked.

"It is called Lady Kiss. See the way the petals overlap each other to form a shape like a pair of lips. They are very popular and often given to their sweethearts by the men of Pinnhome."

She winked as she bent and picked one of the flowers and attached it to Ashley's white shirt, where the contrast of the red against the bleached white was stunning.

"Let's have some fun. We'll both wear one of these and have everyone wondering which of the boys had sent them to us," said Ophra picking another bloom and attaching it to her own blouse. "I know there are a few who hope to catch your eye and this will drive them crazy!" The two girls laughed.

"This garden must be wonderful in the summer," suggested Ashley.

Ophra looked around, "It is. The colour starts now, with these early bulbs, but you'll see how quickly the garden blossoms over the next few weeks. There'll be colour right through until deep into the winter." She paused, "That is my favourite area of the garden." Ophra pointed to a wooden bench a hundred metres away at the end of a long pergola corridor. Thorny bushes had already started to wind their way up the pergola's columns.

"The climbing plants are Pinn Roses. They'll climb their way all over the pergola and will flower from now right the way through to mid autumn. It's beautiful when they are in full bloom. They are a mix of different shades of red, yellow and purple and they possess a strong scent that is wonderful."

Ashley looked closer at the plants. "They look very much like the roses back home, although the colours seem far brighter and more vibrant."

Beyond the roses there was a large bed filled with a waist high plant that was overloaded with flowers of the purest white. The blooms literally glowed in the spring sun as their fist sized heads opened in a sphere formed by petals.

"Oh my god!" said Ashley, "What are these? They are absolutely superb. So white!"

Ophra smiled, "They are snowbloom. They only blossom at this time of year and as well as being beautiful they have a unique property. Touch one and you'll see."

Ashley hesitated before touching the flower. "It's not gonna sting me is it?" she asked.

Ophra laughed, "No, it won't hurt. Go on, touch it."

Ashley reached out and as the tip of her finger made contact with the petal she shivered.

"Oh my god!" she exclaimed, "It's so cold. I can feel the chill spreading up my whole arm."

Ashley looked at her finger and a thin veil of frost had formed where she had touched the flower.

"That's amazing! How's that possible?" she asked.

Ophra shrugged. "I don't know. It just is. Legend says that the flowers came into the world when a princess of Pinnhome was abducted for ransom. Her attackers hid in the Pinnacle Mountains and were killed by bears, but the animals did not know that the princess lay within an ice cave nearby and she died of starvation and cold. Months later, a hunting party found her remains and where she had fallen the snowbloom had grown amongst her bones."

Ophra indicated large beds of the same plant that were growing in the area near the kitchens. "The blooms are only just starting to form. The flowers are only in blossom for a few weeks but the kitchens like to collect the petals so they grow loads of them. They actually have fields of them just beyond the city wall to the north. They don't have any taste but they do chill things rather well and you can make some wonderful dishes with them. They'll probably start to serve some in a week or so. You'll see, I bet you'll love them."

Ashley grinned. "Now that is one of the neatest things I've ever seen." She shook her head in disbelief.

Ophra grasped Ashley's hand and led her to the wooden seat.

"Come, we shall sit and chat a while!" she said enthusiastically.

Ashley obliged. She was eager to hear the latest gossip.

"Has your father heard any news from Fortown?" she asked.

Ophra smiled, "A little. Do you want to know about anything or *anyone* in particular?"

Ashley's cheeks went red, "Perhaps!" she replied.

Ophra laughed, "Meld is doing fine. He is working with the town officials to repair the damage done by the conflicts. The town is more or less back to normal now. They have left the fire-pits in place as a precaution but have built a number of bridges to allow people to cross to the town. The hills have been quiet though, no Black Eagle sightings or anything unusual. It looks like the warlock has returned to wherever he came from although my father is convinced that he will return.

The Fortownians have also erected a large memorial to honour all of those who fought in the battle against Weldrock and in remembrance of those who lost their lives during those awful weeks. We are all invited and my father and mother are working out details of who should attend."

Ashley beamed in excitement, "Hey that's great! When is it? Do you think they'll allow me to go?"

Ophra smiled, "It's not for a few months yet and I'm sure they will if they think it's safe." She paused before continuing.

"You really should write to Meld you know. I'm sure he would be thrilled to hear from you."

Ashley shook her head, "No, I don't think so. I think we only got close because we were both so frightened. He's three years older than me. I would think he's more interested in girls his own age. Anyway, if he wanted to get in touch then he would've written to me, don't you think?"

"Perhaps, but maybe he is in Fortown thinking exactly the same as you! Anyway, what does the fact that he is three years older than you have to do with anything?" exclaimed Ophra. "My father is six years older than my mother and she was only seventeen when they married. Even I have my eye on one of the new guard recruits and he is almost nineteen. He's really handsome and I'm sure he finds me attractive. Every time I meet him in the grounds he seems lost for words and finds it difficult to talk to me. I think he may be in love with me!"

Ashley shook her head, "Sorry Ophra, I don't mean to disappoint you but don't you think that this may be to do with the fact you are the OverLord's daughter?"

Ophra shrugged, "Probably, but that's boring. Much better to think that he is dumb struck with adoration!"

A short silence followed. Both girls lost in their own thoughts and fantasies.

Ashley spoke first, "Seeing as you are the OverLord's daughter won't this mean that you have to marry some Lord or Lady's son? I know that in my world royalty nearly always marries royalty."

Ophra shook her head, "No, we don't have any restrictions like that. I am free to court with anyone who I choose. The OverLord position isn't really royalty and the position does not follow the family line. It is an elected position chosen by the Pinnhome people."

Ashley nodded, "I see, so a democracy, very much like we have in the USA."

"I suppose. I wouldn't know though," Ophra looked pensive for a moment, "It would be nice to visit your world. From what you have told me it sounds so different and so exciting."

It was Ashleys turn to shrug. "Not really, it doesn't have the adventure and excitement of Portalia, most days are just school work, homework and then bed."

"Maybe not, but it does sound like there are other exciting things to do and at least it is a relatively safe place to live," Ophra responded.

Ashley had to agree with this comment.

"Also from what you tell me your world is so much bigger than Portalia. There must be so much to see and new places to visit."

Again Ashley nodded before replying, "All true, I guess that it's difficult to compare as things are so different. I must admit, I do miss my family and friends and the things that we used to do, even though some seemed boring at the time. If I went back today though I'm sure that I'd probably miss Portalia as much."

"What? Even the part where an evil mad warlock tries to bash your brains out?"

Ashley laughed, "Yeah, especially that bit!"

The girls fell silent again.

This time Ophra broke the silence, "I can't imagine what that must have felt like Ash. You must have been terrified, especially when you had to face Weldrock and you were attacked by the White Dwarf."

Ashley looked down at her feet. She shivered as she recalled that moment.

"Yeah, it was scary but the worst part was when Swiftaxe killed Michael to save Rhys. I can still see the axe biting into his flesh. I know, he's OK now, but the shock of watching him die won't go away."

Ashley looked up at Ophra, "Has your father heard anything of Weldrock since he fled Fortown?"

Ophra shook her head. "No, not a thing. We have joined up with the dwarves, elves, centaurs and other human settlements to search for any sign of him but there has been no word. He seems to have disappeared as suddenly as he appeared. Some think that he has moved to the home islands of the Graav which are said to exist beyond the Sea of Mist, but no-one knows for sure. Others say that the stone creatures are not the Graav of the story-song, but creatures that Weldrock created."

Ashley frowned, "But what does you father think?"

"He is a supporter of the idea that the warlock has retreated to the Graav homeland. He has to be careful though. Our justice demands that he also hears the thoughts of those who would call for more immediate action, those who wish to scour the world to find the warlock and destroy him once and for all, regardless of what it may cost in lives. Some of the town officials are ambitious and a few have started to whisper that the warlock should not have been allowed to escape, even suggesting that Gorlan was incompetent to allow this to happen."

Ashley raised her voice in protest but Ophra raised a hand to calm her, "Oh don't worry, it is just a small handful of individuals who think themselves clever. They will ultimately destroy themselves. Everyone knows the heroics that were performed defending Fortown."

Ashley calmed herself before responding, "Ophra, if Weldrock has returned to the Graav homeland why can't Portalia send a force to finish him? I guess that you have boats that can sail beyond the Sea of Mist?"

Ophra nodded, "Yes we do but the journey is a perilous one. Usually boats that sail deep into the Mists are never seen again. Even so, my father is planning to travel to the twin towns of the Gates to commission a ship and to send out a scout team to determine if there is any truth in the old legends about the islands beyond the Mists. I believe that Gorlan is putting together that scouting team and may lead it himself."

"That doesn't surprise me," replied Ashley, "Gorlan is such a great leader and he is incredibly brave. I bet your father didn't even have to ask him, I bet he volunteered."

Ophra nodded. Ashley continued, "So when will the expedition depart?"

"Not for a few days yet. I'm not sure if you have heard but two of our Pinn fire eagle riders are retiring so there will be a Ceremony of Choosing in two days. Everyone will be there as it has been some time since this has happened."

"Oh excellent!" replied Ashley, "I'd love to see that. Meld told me about the ceremony. I can't believe that I'll actually get to see one."

"Yes, you are lucky. It is a great celebration. While it is sad to see the warrior retire and lose his life bonding, it means renewal for the fire eagle so everyone celebrates. Of course, after the fight at Fortown it has even greater significance. Only fifty-one fire eagles remain from the battle against Weldrock. My father has asked Farspell if he can help create new fire eagles, but unfortunately the wizard does not possess the knowledge."

A shrill chirping from the rooftop of a nearby outer building interrupted the girls. "Oh wonderful!" exclaimed Ophra, "Fledglings. Another sign that spring is in the air."

The girls watched as an adult bird flew to the rooftop and disappeared under some tiles, mouth stuffed with worms.

"How are you progressing in your studies with Farspell?" asked Ophra.

"Pretty good," responded Ashley, "He doesn't work us too hard and the subjects that he teaches are really interesting as everything is so new and fresh. He can be a bit nerdy at times though and I think his brain is a bit screwed up as he forgets things." Ophra knew what she meant.

Farspell had volunteered his services to act as mentor and tutor to the three Earth teenagers almost as soon as they had arrived in Pinnhome. Although Ashley was a year older than the two boys, it did not matter, as the subjects that they were being taught were far from the normal lessons they would have received back on Earth.

Language did not seem to be a problem here in Portalia as everyone seemed to understand everyone else. The teenagers had not noticed this at first, but later marvelled at the fact. They quizzed Farspell on why this was the case, but could hardly make sense of his mumbled answer quoting magical energy flows and life forces. Secretly they felt that Farspell did not really know himself.

Similarly, the geography that Ashley had worked so hard at back in her Oregon school was useless here as they all had to learn about the new world of Portalia.

All three of the teenagers were strong on mathematics, which delighted Farspell and he was able to advance their knowledge in this subject, a skill that would be useful in any world. Similarly Ashley's aptitude for music helped her too.

Farspell had insisted that they have four hours study every day and he split this into two equal sessions. He put lots of emphasis in teaching them the geography, history and customs of Portalia and gave them more insights into the various species that existed in this world. Although Farspell was obviously ancient and had been alive at the time of the original Warlock Wars, it was clear that the years spent as Lan, with his soul and life essence entombed in the Soul Orb, had severely damaged his memories. In fact he often had to turn to library books to remind him of some of the basic facts. Usually though, after such prompting, his own memories would be triggered and he was able to elaborate on the information provided in any of the standard textbooks.

Rhys and Michael both had extra sessions with Farspell. Rhys to explore his ability to open portals and Michael to explore any dragon memories that arose. Ashley had to admit that she felt a little envious of the boys and was disappointed that she did not possess any 'special' abilities herself. That said, it did allow her more time to spend with Ophra and for doing other things that she enjoyed.

"I hope Farspell can find a way to help the fire eagles," said Ophra. "It would be so sad if they became extinct and with only fifty-one left that could easily happen if our Pinn riders have to fight again."

Ashley nodded. "Let's go and see if the warriors are training with their eagles today. I love watching them fly together. I can't understand how they do it. I'd be terrified. It was bad enough just riding on the eagle at Fortown and that was a fairly gentle flight."

The pair stood up, and arm in arm once again, made their way out of the garden and through the main gates of the town to the fire eagle training area to the north where they sat on the grass to watch.

There were over a dozen eagles and riders training. This involved feats of amazing aerobatics and intricate weapon exercises carried out at high speed and in mid flight. Ashley recognised a handful of the riders, some from the battle at Fortown and others whom she had met since arriving at Pinnhome. She noticed that Kraven, the bard-warrior of the riders and now promoted to sergeant, was busy training some of the more junior riders. The current lesson involved the art of undertaking a steep dive attack, a tactic used to help support ground based warriors. Kraven waved cheerily to the girls when he saw them watching.

"It must've been a brilliant sight when there were hundreds of fire eagles," commented Ashley.

Ophra nodded. "Yes, I should think it was. I've dreamt about it a few times. I remember as a small child waking and rushing to my bedroom window to see the fire eagles. In my dream the sky over the valley was filled with them. There were hundred and hundreds of them and they were even more majestic in my dream than they are in real life. I felt so disappointed and let down when I realised they were just a figment of my imagination."

Their conversation was suddenly interrupted by another voice, "So young ladies, what brings you out here to the training fields?"

It was Gorlan, Warlord of Pinnhome and one of the heroes of the Fortown conflict.

Ashley and Ophra smiled and nodded a greeting. "We just wanted to watch the eagles and riders for a while," replied Ashley.

"And I cannot think of a better way to idle away a few hours," replied Gorlan and he plonked himself on the ground between the two girls, pushing them both over as he did so. They laughed and pushed him back.

"Haven't you got anything better to do than pester young girls!" joked Ashley.

"Of course I have, but it's nowhere near as fun as annoying you Ash," he teased back.

They both smiled. After a slight pause Ashley said, "I hear that you may be going on a journey soon. Perhaps you'll be doing a little warlock hunting while you are away?"

Gorlan looked at Ophra and scowled, "I think that some teenage ladies should learn to keep their counsel. Sometimes knowledge should not be so openly shared."

Ophra went bright red and suddenly found intense interest in her shoes, looking down to avoid eye contact with the Warlord.

"Ah! I suppose no harm is done. I would have told you myself soon anyway" continued Gorlan softening a little when he saw he had upset Ophra. "We should be departing to the Gates in a few days. There we will choose a ship and hire an experienced crew. I have chosen a selection of soldiers from the barracks and I will take a handful of my riders as part of that crew."

Ashley interrupted, "I know why you have to go but please be careful Gorlan. I want you to promise me that you will return safe and sound!"

Gorlan looked serious, "I cannot deny that the mission is a dangerous one. There are few who have sailed into the Mists and returned to tell the tale. As such I can only promise that I will do my best to return safely and to protect all those that travel with me. My hope is that the stories have been exaggerated over the years and that the journey will not prove as treacherous as we fear."

They paused in their conversation as they pondered the dangers that may lie ahead.

Overhead a firebird swooped low, the rider waving at them as he sped by.

"So who will go with you Gorlan?" asked Ashley.

The Warlord looked apologetic, "I'm sorry, I cannot tell you yet. I need to agree my team with the OverLord and Farspell. In fact that is precisely where I'm going now. I bid you good day young ladies. I dare say we shall discuss this further a little later." Gorlan stood and slowly walked away.

When he was out of earshot, Ashley whispered her apologies to Ophra for mentioning the mission. Her friend dismissed the incident assuring her that it had been her own fault, not Ashley's and that no harm was done. With it forgotten they returned their attention to the fire eagle training. Both laid back on the lush fresh grass, bathing in the warmth of the spring sun as they watched the giant war birds and their riders, weaving their intricate patterns in the skies above.

*** 

Farspell looked thoughtful as he contemplated Gorlan's plan.

"My biggest worry is that we do not have any sea charts for the waters of the Sea of Mist. When you add to this the atrocious visibility caused by the thick fogs the risks of being grounded or sunk are very high," he said.

"I agree," added the OverLord, "You will be sailing almost blind on an unknown ocean."

Gorlan nodded his understanding, "And that is precisely why I want to take a few fire eagles and riders. They can help by scouting our way ahead from the air."

Farspell shook his head, "I fear that will not be sufficient either. The fogs of the Sea of Mist are incredibly thick as I have seen with my own eyes. Your firebirds may be able to rise above it but they will not be able to see through it to help steer the ship safely." He pushed back his long grey hair with the fingers of his right hand before continuing, "However, I do believe that the fire eagles will be an asset. If your journey does lead you to Weldrock then the fire eagles will be needed for any battle that may ensue. Secondly, if you do break beyond the fog then the eagles can be used for guidance as you suggest."

Gorlan looked encouraged by this, "So our eagles may be able to help us locate the islands from the air!" he exclaimed.

"Possibly," replied Farspell, "Although I believe that the retelling of the legend may be inaccurate and the islands actually lie within the Mists."

"Why do you think this Farspell?" asked Toran.

"Simply because we have no record of the islands. I believe the Graav to be ancient creatures and their island to be an early formation of Portalia. If that is so, and the islands are visible from the air, I am surprised that there are no previous records of any sightings by riders. Remember that Pinn riders once flew the length and breadth of Portalia during the Warlock Wars."

Toran nodded, "A point well made."

"It is for that reason that I suggest one further modification to the plan." Gorlan and Toran looked questioningly at the wizard. "On leaving The Gates I would suggest a slight south-westerly detour to dock at Seahome on the isle of Llan and to request assistance from the sea-elves."

Toran raised his eyebrows, "Do you think they will help us? It has been over a year since Fortown sent out their messengers to ask for help against Weldrock. In that time nothing has been heard from the sea-elves. It would seem that they have no desire to get involved."

"Possibly," responded Farspell, "But Meld has informed me that his cousin, the messenger sent to Seahome has never returned. It could be that he never made it to Llan."

"Or it could be that the sea-elves took exception to his visit and killed him," responded Toran.

Farspell shook his head, "No, that is not the way of the sea-elves. It is true they like to keep themselves isolated from others but they are not as paranoid about strangers as the dark-elves of Rusinor. I believe that if they had received the plea for help from Fortown then they would have responded."

"I think that this is a good suggestion OverLord," offered Gorlan, "We do not know much of the sea-elves but living so close to the Sea of Mist they may well have information that could benefit our search for the island of the Graav."

Toran thought on the suggestion for a few seconds before replying.

"Very well, I approve the plan as stated." He turned to his Warlord, "Gorlan, you will leave for the Gates in three days time, the day following the Ceremony of Choosing. You will take more than the requested six eagles though. Ten fire eagles and riders will accompany you. The journey to the Gates will be much faster using the fire eagles as transportation and I have a feeling in my gut that time could be of the essence. However, as Farspell suggests, you will make the detour to Llan to request the assistance of the sea-elves. You may leave us to prepare."

Gorlan saluted in acknowledgement and left the room.

The OverLord turned to Farspell, "I fear for those undertaking this journey Farspell. Is there no other way of searching out Weldrock?"

Farspell shook his head, "Not that I know. I have tried various spells and incantations in an effort to discover his location but all to no avail. It may be that his whereabouts are being shrouded by the Sea of Mist. If so then this journey may be the only chance we have of finding him. However, I will continue to search for alternative solutions."

The OverLord rubbed his face in frustration. "And what of your search for the precise location of the Pinnhome portal gateway? Have you made any progress?"

Farspell nodded, "Indeed. I have better news regarding this issue Toran. As you know only too well, there are over a dozen sites around Pinnhome and the Pinn valley that claim to be the location of the ancient portal."

Toran cursed under his breath, "Incredible isn't it," he replied, "For years no-one really cared about the true location and we were all happy to visit the various sites that claimed authenticity. Now here we are with egg on our faces! Vulnerable due to our own ignorance and stupidity."

Farspell looked at the OverLord sympathetically, "You should not be so hard on your ancestors. No-one could foresee the threat which the portal once again presents!"

"Maybe not," responded the Pinn leader, "But this is a lesson that we had learned long ago during the Warlock Wars. We should not have forgotten it! We should have vowed never to let it happen again."

"Be that as it may," countered the wizard. "We are where we are and I have narrowed the site down to one of three locations. Over the next few days, with further reference to the volumes and diaries held in the vaults, I believe that I will finally know the true location." Farspell's expression turned to one of frustration. "If only my full memories would return. Each day something else returns to me but my time as Lan has numbed my brain and so much is lost within, unreachable until a memory or thought is triggered by a sight or event."

The OverLord's face relaxed a little and looked sympathetic, "Do not blame yourself my old friend. Over time your full powers and memories will return. At least the progress that you have made so far will allow me to offer some immediate relief to our forces. They have been guarding all locations around the clock since the battle for Fortown. It is obviously taking a toll on the troops and impacting morale. May I ask that when you leave today that you notify Tosh of the three locations and have him adjust the guard shifts accordingly."

Farspell nodded his acceptance and turned to leave, but the OverLord interrupted his departure once again.

"One last thing. I know I ask a lot of you, but please continue to research a solution regarding the fire eagles. I fear that our mission to seek out Weldrock may see the loss of yet more of the poor creatures. We need a way to protect them."

Farspell gloomily acknowledged the instruction and departed. Toran, feeling exhaustion sweep over him, slumped in his favourite chair, left alone to contemplate the dangers his men would face and to ponder the possible repercussions of his orders.

# CHAPTER THREE
## The Ceremony of Choosing

For Ashley, the days leading up to the Ceremony of Choosing had passed extremely slowly. She was so restless and eager to view the spectacle of the ceremony that she could not concentrate.

Finally, the day of the Choosing arrived. The previous twenty-four hours had been very wet with very heavy rain showers and moderate winds, but today the town awoke to blue skies dotted with white puffy clouds. Not a grey rain-laden cloud in sight.

After spending the morning tidying her room and working through some centaur history research that Farspell had set, she ate a light lunch and was now on her way to meet with the wizard for daily lessons with Rhys and Michael.

When she reached Farspell's quarters she knocked and entered. The two boys were there already and were chatting to the old wizard.

"Hi guys!" said Ashley as she took her seat.

"Good day Ashley," replied Farspell, "You seem much brighter and alert today. I wonder why that is?" He turned and winked at the boys.

Ashley didn't rise to the bait, but merely smiled and concocted a witty response. "Sir, I'm sure you know that I am bright and breezy every day. The only variable is the intensity of my brightness! However, no matter what the level of that brightness, whether it is low, like a night-light, or as blinding as a super-nova, I always shine light and happiness around me!"

The boys stared at her in amazement. Rhys looked at Michael and put two fingers in his mouth to mimic a vomiting action. Farspell chuckled, "Well said my dear, and who could argue with that!"

The wizard turned away from his pupils and reached for a large chart that was propped against his desk. Lifting it onto a pedestal he re-addressed the trio. "I thought I'd talk a little about Portalia's Western region today, the sea that lies beyond the mainland."

Pointing to the chart Farspell indicated the western coastline of Portalia and the outline of a large island which lay some way off-shore, towards the Sea of Mist.

"Previously we have discussed the coastal towns of Norgate and Sougate. Also, from your time in Fortown you are familiar with the city of Dargoth Sands, a place teeming with cut-throats and villains of many sorts. However, beyond these, further to the west lies Llan, the Isle of the Sea-elves." Farspell paused in his monologue, "Have you heard much about Llan and Seahome?"

All three shook their heads.

"Well, as I said, Llan is the home of the sea-elves and Seahome is their capital city. Much like their cousins, the elves of Lorewood and the dark-elves of the Forest of Old, the sea-elves prefer to keep their own counsel. They rarely involve themselves in the issues of Portalia and, unlike the elves of Lorewood; they do not welcome visitors, a trait that they share with the dark-elves. That said, unlike the dark-elves, who can have a tendency for violence towards strangers, the sea-elves are not aggressive and merely treat strangers with certain coldness and with a tendency to be somewhat brusque and impolite."

The wizard paused, deep in thought as he searched for a lost memory, finally continuing as he brought it to the fore.

"They are a very proud race and one of the oldest in Portalia. Once they were part of one large elf nation but, as the world changed, the elves were forced to divide. The majority moved deeper into the eastern forests to form the realms of Lorewood and the Forest of Old. The elves of Llan however, turned to the west and settled on the forested island of Llan, creating a sea locked refuge. Here they built a new capital city, Seahome. Whether through the work of magic or through the nature of evolution, the elves, who became reliant on the sea for food and protection, became part shape changers. When on dry land they resemble the Lorewood elves but possess a pale green tone to their skin. However, once in the water they are able to transform their two legs into a single tail and flipper, whale-like in appearance." Farspell picked up the chart and turned it around to display the picture of a sea elf family, mother, father and two children. The parents were standing on the dry land while the children played in blue waters.

Rhys, Michael and Ashley looked at each other and said as one, "Mermaids!"

Farspell raised his eyebrows in surprise, "Now that is a term that I have not heard used in a very long time. Where did you hear it?"

Ashley responded for the teenagers, "Back on Earth. There are loads of legends about merfolk. Most people do not believe that they are real and think that they were mythical beings created by the ramblings of lonely sailors, imagining human form as whales and dolphins played and swam in the waves."

"Fascinating!" exclaimed the wizard, "Well, I can assure you that they do exist, although they are sea-elves, not merfolk. The term merfolk was used by sailors of the coastal towns and villages of Portalia when the elves first settled on the island, before they became aware that they were relocated elves. I suppose that those tales spread to your world during the time when the portal gateways were in more frequent use."

Farspell indicated the tails of the elven children which could be seen beneath the water level. "When they are in salt water, the legs join and form this solid mass of blubber-like flesh. The feet turn sideways, swell and flatten into a flipper. This gives the sea-elves incredible speed in the water, as fast as some of the whales that frequent the oceans." Moving his finger up he pointed to the mid riff of the elves, "They also possess magnificent lungs with a large capacity that allow them to remain below water for hours at a time. They do not possess any gills, so, like other sea mammals, they eventually have to come to the surface for oxygen or they will drown."

Rhys looked thoughtful, "I wonder if the sea-elves ever visited Earth. Maybe it was not the story that travelled through the portals but the sea-elves themselves."

Farspell nodded, "I suppose that is possible but I doubt it. The sea-elves were never portal travellers and they generally seek out the companionship of their own race. It is extremely rare for any to leave Seahome although I did witness it during the Warlock Wars."

The wizard opened a large cupboard to his left. He lifted out a long, light grey-green bow and a quiver full of arrows.

"This is the preferred weapon of the sea elf. The bow is made from whale cartilage which provides the elasticity needed to launch the arrows." Farspell removed the arrows. "There are three main types of arrow. The first is made of bone, whale or seal." He removed the arrows and passed them out to the three pupils. "The second is made of the wood from the Llan forests, tipped with hard stone or bone worked to a sharp point."

The teenagers noted the difference between the two types of arrow as they passed the shafts around.

Farspell rummaged in his cupboard again and drew out a long, thin, wooden box with a hinged lid. He opened the lid. "The third is extremely rare. These are made of a scarce substance called seametal that is only found beneath the water level off the southern coast of Llan. The elves discovered the sea-metal seams accidentally and found that by working this metal they could make arrow shafts that rivalled the arrows of the Lorewood elves in power. Not only are these arrows capable of penetrating heavy armour but also they are immune to any enchantment, possessing their own magical ability. The sea-elves jealously guard the secret of the location of the seametal ore deposits and also their knowledge of how to forge these arrows from the ore."

Farspell removed the seametal arrow and passed it to Rhys.

"Gosh, it is very light!" commented Rhys.

"Remarkably so," replied Farspell, "But even given its lightweight shaft, the distance that this arrow can be fired is substantial. Note though that it is not just the lightness of the seametal that provides this ability. The weight is reduced still further by the use of elven magic. A complex elevation spell helps the arrow stay in the air as it travels to its intended target. Of all the elven races the sea-elves have the greatest involvement and knowledge of the magical arts." The old wizard frowned and looked serious. "Unfortunately that knowledge has not always been used for good. Although it is true that the sea-elves are rarely aggressors, they have dabbled in both light and dark magic."

"So sea-grey magic," interrupted Rhys smiling.

"Quite!" he replied looking at Rhys with the contempt that the weak pun deserved. "As an example of how their magical knowledge has been, at times, misdirected; The Soul Gem, that cursed device that Weldrock used to trap my soul, was created by a sea-elf. I believe that is why I chose the name Lan when Weldrock used the power against me. I knew the nature of what held me and, in my poor state, I used the name of the island of Llan possibly as a reminder of what had happened to me."

"I guess that makes sense," responded Rhys, "You were pretty messed up."

Rhys placed the arrow in front of Michael who picked it up.

Almost immediately Michael let out a cry of pain as his head began to throb and he was overwhelmed with visions flooding from his subconscious. He began to writhe and groan and he gripped the arrow so tightly that his knuckles went white. As Farspell stepped towards him, Michael jumped to his feet and lifted his hands to his head. The arrow, forgotten in his panic, scratched against his cheek and the sudden pain made him drop it in shock. The visions stopped immediately and he realised that Farspell was at his side steadying him.

"Are you alright?" asked the wizard.

Michael nodded, "Yeah, I'm fine. I think. My mind just seemed to explode with images; dragon memories and visions."

Blood welled up in the scratch on his face and a trickle ran down his cheek. Farspell took a cloth and wiped the blood away and, whispering a quiet spell, helped the wound seal itself over.

"It is only a small scratch. Nothing to worry about," observed the wizard. "Can you remember what happened? What did you see?"

"I can remember some of it, but the thoughts were coming so fast that I couldn't concentrate on anything," replied Michael.

"Sounds a bit like when I first started to experience the power I have to create portals," commented Rhys. "The thoughts and images fly by so quickly that your head hurts."

"Exactly," replied Michael. "I do remember certain things though."

"Excellent, tell us what happened and I'll brew up some feyberry tea. That will clear that headache of yours," urged Farspell.

Michael began. "The memories and visions were all jumbled but I remember that I was flying above a large island and someone was shooting arrows at me. I think the arrows were made of seametal as they looked just like the one I was holding."

"Continue," said Farspell, now frowning.

"Well, like I said, it was all jumbled up. The next thing I remember is being on a boat. There were sea-elves all around and they were talking to me but I could not understand what was being said as there were too many voices. There were other boats too. All were sailed by a mix of sea-elves although I remember seeing a handful of humans. Sometimes the boats were sailing in the sun and at other times in the mist. "

Farspell handed the feyberry tea to Michael, who drank down the warm brew thankfully.

"Next thing I remember was that I was flying again. I was up high, looking down on heavy cloud and suddenly I dived into that cloud. Everything was grey and dark, but then the mist thinned and I saw I was flying over another island, smaller this time. It passed beneath me and I was engulfed by mist once again. Then the mist thinned and I saw another small island. Something was moving around on this one although I could not make out what. The last thing I remember is the face of a sea-elf; at least I guess that's what it was as it had the same colour skin as the pictures you showed us. This elf wore a silver crown and he was talking to me. He seemed to be pleading for me to help with something but I have no idea what that was."

Michael took another slug from the tea cup, "Then I put my hands to my face and cut myself with the arrow. As soon as I dropped it the images stopped."

Farspell nodded. "Thank you Michael. I'd suggest that you do not touch the arrow again right now. However, I do think that later we should explore this a little more. The seametal seems to have tuned into your dragon aspect and pulled forward images that were locked within, memories of the sea-elves and of the island of Llan."

Michael needed no encouragement with regards to staying clear of the seametal arrow. Although he knew he was safe and these were only dragon memories coming to the fore, he did not like the experience of being so out of control.

Farspell smiled, "I think at this point it may be a good idea to bring a close to studying today. I'm sure that you have things to do before the Ceremony of Choosing later this afternoon."

***

The rest of the afternoon had proven uneventful and time seemed to drag, but finally, the time for the Ceremony arrived. Ashley had picked out a white blouse and a sky blue jerkin with a pair of light brown leather trousers. She arrived at Michael's room ahead of Rhys and in her eagerness found it difficult not to snap at him when he arrived later than they had arranged.

The three walked swiftly to the arena where the crowds had already formed and filled the stands on all four sides.

"Gosh, everyone is here," said Rhys, "We may have to split up to get a seat."

Ashley was livid, "Well if you had been on time then we wouldn't have had this problem," she snapped.

Rhys reddened and in an unsuccessful attempt to respond he merely opened and closed his mouth a number of times. Finally he decided on a tactful reply, "Yeah, you're right. Sorry Ash. I just hadn't expected so many people to be here."

Ashley was just about to have another nag at him when they were interrupted by Gorlan. "Ah, there you are. Come on you three. You can come and stand with me on the arena floor. You'll be close up to the Choosing there."

Rhys grinned at Ashley; "See!" he said, "No problem, I knew that we'd be OK."

Ashley scowled at him and let out a harrumph of disdain.

They followed Gorlan. When the crowd saw the Warlord enter the arena they let out a loud cheer. The spectators launched handfuls of coloured paper cuttings into the air and confetti fell all around, dancing on the light breeze.

Gorlan stepped up onto a small platform at the centre of the arena. OverLord Toran and OverLady Melis were already there with their daughter Ophra.

Gorlan bowed his head to the OverLord who stepped forward to greet them. Toran indicated to Rhys, Ashley and Michael that they should stand to his left, while his family were standing to his right. He then turned to the crowd and shouted, "Let the Choosing begin!"

A fanfare of horns trumpeted and the crowd cheered in jubilation as over two thousand Pinn warriors marched into the arena in straight columns. They were dressed in bright red shirts with thin, golden-mesh armoured vests laid on top.

Their legs were covered to the knee by pairs of long green leather shorts. Whilst impractical for battle, their attire was magnificent for show as the metal glinted in the amber sunlight of late afternoon. The sound of their feet made a resounding thump as they marched in time and streamed around either side of the arena. They curved their march to form a large circle surrounding the central platform and, with their ranks spread three metres apart, came to a halt.

Once all were in position another fanfare rang out and two hundred cavalry men, led by Kul, their captain, cantered into the arena on their great mounts. They were dressed in similar fashion to the infantry except that the shorts were replaced by long trousers and they wore black leather boots decorated with gold paint. The horses were clad in show armour too. Their black saddles were decorated in the same gold paints as their rider's boots and their heads were adorned with bright red and gold cloth that reflected the descending sun. The cavalry took up position behind the warriors and, as Gorlan stepped forward to address his troops, the crowd hushed to a dull murmur before falling silent.

"My warriors, you have trained long and hard to earn the right of presentation at the Choosing. To be selected as a soul partner by the fire eagles is the ultimate honour for a Pinn warrior and falls only to the minority. For those who are successful today you will be enriched in your bonding. For those that are unsuccessful do not despair. There will be other Choosings and there are other ways in which you can serve Pinn at the highest level."

Gorlan turned his attention to the crowd, rotating to address all as he spoke.

"People of Pinn and honoured guests, I am delighted that you could be with us today to honour our warriors and bear witness to the Ceremony of Choosing. May I bid you all stand

and raise your voices in welcome for our fire eagles and their flyers!"

The crowd went crazy as fifty-one fire eagles blazed a path above the arena in full flight. Farspell added to the effect by creating a fantastic magical pyrotechnic display that filled the skies around the eagles with fantastical colours and loud explosions.

The riders flew their eagles for three laps above the arena before carrying out a sharp dive. Dividing into three lines as they plummeted towards the arena, they skimmed across the heads of the crowd, the air pressure ruffling the hair of the spectators. The cheering and excitement reached a crescendo as the crowd savoured this experience and the eagles turned to make another pass across their heads in the opposite direction.

Finally, they climbed sharply and spiralled down to land in front of the OverLord.

Tosh, the newly appointed captain of the riders dismounted and stepped forward to salute the OverLord and OverLady, trying hard to hide a smile but failing hopelessly.

Tosh took a deep breath to regain his composure and uttered the traditional summons.

"Toran, OverLord of Pinn, your riders salute you and charge you to carry out a new Choosing. We have warriors who require removal of the bonding. Will you release them?"

Toran responded, "Captain Tosh, I honour all of the riders and pay homage to those who will lose their bonding. I thank them for their service and so agree to the breaking."

"Thank you, My Lord. Will you also permit a new Choosing for the fire eagles that have lost their soul mates?"

Toran looked across the lines of warriors, "There is no greater honour for a Pinn than to bond with the fire eagles. I do agree. Let the Ceremony of Choosing continue."

Another great cheer was raised and Toran bowed his head as he turned to his riders.

"Those who wish to undertake the ritual of breaking dismount and step forward."

Two warriors dismounted and stepped forward to face Tosh.

Tosh saluted both, "Creel and Korgan, you have served Pinn well. You fought gallantly and rode skilfully. You have kept your promise to the fire eagles and cherished your bonding. We honour and thank you for calling to break the bonding and to allow renewed life for your fire eagle soul mate." As these words were uttered, Tosh, the Warlord, the OverLord and the OverLady all bowed their heads and knelt onto one knee in respect."

Creel and Korgan spoke together, "We thank you for allowing us the honour of the bonding. We now agree to release our eagles for the Choosing." Both then turned and returned to their eagles. They stood in front of their mounts in anguish and touched heads with the eagles. Turning they said a sad goodbye and rejoined the ranks of the foot warriors.

Gorlan unsheathed a small dagger and approached the two solitary warbirds. Glancing at the sun, which was now setting in the west, he addressed them directly.

"Trusted friends. We ask that you continue to serve Pinn and request that you select a new soul for the bonding."

The birds stared back at the Warlord before they too glanced towards the setting sun. Utter silence spread across the arena as all waited with bated breath.

Ashley looked on from her central position in anticipation; she glanced briefly at Michael and Rhys and noticed that they were equally transfixed by the scene.

Then, as the sun started to sink behind the horizon and the daylight began to wane, the excitement grew and while the last rays of sunlight flickered and died the two rider-less eagles leapt into the air. Climbing. they burst into flames, the intensity of the fire burning white hot and adding a new level of illumination around the arena, which was now as bright as the midday sun.

The eagles continued to climb, higher than Ashley had ever seen them fly before until they almost seemed to be brushing the very heavens with their wings. Suddenly the light of the burning eagles extinguished, their body mass fully consumed.

The excited buzz that had built around the arena once again quietened as all awaited for the ash to fall.

In their excitement and eagerness the Pinn warriors had lost a small amount of their discipline and most were searching the skies, moving from left to right in an effort to see the falling ash and all hoping that the ash would land at their feet, indicating that they would be the one selected by the fire eagle. The atmosphere was so tense that Ashley felt it could be cut with a knife.

Toran leaned towards the teenagers and whispered, "This can sometimes take a little while. At the last Ceremony of Choosing it was almost fifteen minutes before the ash returned. As you can tell it is a very trying time for our troops, but it does add to the spectacle of the event." He smiled and returned his attention to watching the skies with the others.

The minutes ticked by as everyone waited and finally there was a shout from someone standing behind the teenagers. They turned as one and saw white ash floating downwards like snow. The ash fell on the boots of a tall and sturdy built warrior in the second rank of the ring and standing a long way from the central platform. Ashley cursed under her breath as this warrior was a long way from the platform, back in the third row, so it would be difficult for her to witness the transformation from where she was standing. She tried to change position but failed to get any real improvement in her view.

The warrior beamed with pride and great cheering went up as the ashes continued to fall at his feet. Gorlan too was smiling. He did not need an introduction to this warrior. This was Foile, born of Pinnacle mountain stock and cousin to Carl and Stern. He was a fine warrior and had waited patiently for this moment; this was his fourth Ceremony of Choosing. The ash built up at his feet into a neat pile. Gorlan stepped forward and handed the dagger to Foile who immediately cut his palm and allowed his blood to dribble and drip into the pile of ash.

Almost immediately the ash began to sizzle and white smoke began to rise. Then, slowly, it began to move, growing and moulding itself as it was metamorphosed into the approximate shape of a fully grown fire eagle. Still grey and ashen the form began to quiver, and, as it did, red, orange and yellow flames began to dance from within. The flames burned brightly for a few seconds then began to turn to a deep blue and started to recede. Beneath the flames the fire eagle had reformed and exhibited a blaze of red and yellow feathers. With a loud, eardrum shattering cry, it spread its seven metre wingspan and stretched its body. Foile approached the warbird and placed his forehead against the eagle's head. The bonding was complete. Foile and the fire eagle were now joined.

The cheering crowd and warriors began to quieten once more waiting for the second set of ashes. Another fifteen minutes went by. Toran frowned and turned to Gorlan, "I have never known it take this long. Has something gone wrong?"

Before Gorlan could answer Ophra interrupted, "There, here it comes!"

Everyone looked to where she was pointing and, sure enough, they could see the snow-like ash drifting downwards.

Ashley whispered to Michael and Rhys, "Cool! It's going to be much closer this time so we'll get a better view." The boys nodded and continued to follow the ash as it floated down and down, getting ever nearer to them until finally it came to rest...at Ashley's feet!

There was a stunned silence and then murmuring in the crowd. Ashley stared at the ash in disbelief. Rhys and Michael were standing open mouthed too as realisation dawned. Sensing Ashley's discomfort and fear Rhys felt he had to say something to reassure her but all he could imagine was, "Look Ash, ash!"

Ashley was completely oblivious to this; she was staring in horror as the ash continued to pile up in front of her. Gorlan and Toran looked at each other both frowning, unsure of what to do. From the ranks of warriors, Farspell pushed forward and spoke. "Gorlan, the eagle has chosen, complete the ceremony."

Gorlan looked from Toran to Farspell and back to the OverLord again. Toran nodded his consent, and Gorlan, who had recovered the dagger from Foile, stepped up to Ashley and handed her the blade.

Ashley looked up at him as he touched her arm. He held out the dagger for her.

"But, it can't be me! Why has it chosen me? I'm not a warrior and I don't know how to fly an eagle." Tears began to well up in her eyes.

Gorlan looked at her sympathetically, "Be brave Ashley. There must be a reason for this. Take the dagger and join with the eagle."

Ashley accepted the dagger from the Warlord almost robotically. She placed the sharp edge against her palm but her fear stopped her from cutting.

"Go on Ash, do it,"

"Yeah, come on Ash. The fire eagle must have a reason for this." The two boys encouraged her to complete the bonding.

Ashley looked at them both and took comfort in their support. With a quick slash she cut a small line in her palm, wincing with the sudden pain and then she let the blood flow onto the ash pile.

As before, the ash began to bubble and smoke and formed itself into the grey eagle shape. Once again the shape burst into flames. Rhys and Michael felt the heat of it against their skin, Ashley however did not. She was aware the flames emanated heat, she could see the skin of the people around her redden in the warmth and yet she felt no change in the temperature whatsoever.

Then the flames were gone and she was looking into the regal face of a fire eagle.

Gorlan instructed her to step forward and to place her forehead against the bird as Foile had done.

Nervously and yet strangely elated, Ashley did as she was told and placed her forehead where Gorlan had indicated.

It was nothing like she had expected. She had anticipated that there would be a complete joining of minds and that the great eagle would communicate with her and talk to her through her thoughts, almost like a conversation. It just wasn't that simple. Ashley sensed and instinctively knew how the eagle was feeling as if those feelings were her own. On bonding she knew immediately that the eagle was full of trepidation mixed with elation, in exactly the same way as she was. Once joined though, both the young human and the eagle knew instinctively that all would be well. They loved each other in a unique way. Both felt a part of the very life essence of the other. There was no 'conversation' to convey this, it simply was not needed. Their minds were as one, their feelings and basic thoughts interlocked. For a brief moment Ashley wondered if the bird had a name, but realised it did not need one. The eagle simply 'was', it did not need to be branded with a title anymore than she did herself when thinking her own private thoughts. Ashley's link with the creature made her understand this without question.

As she relaxed, she felt the will of the eagle and understood why the great creatures served the Pinns. Without the magic of the wizards that weaved their spells, the fire eagles themselves would never have come to be and indeed, without the Ceremony of Choosing and the sacrifice made by the old human warriors, they would not continue to be. She felt a deep and unquestioning loyalty within the bird and understood why the bond with the creature was so tight. She marvelled at the very nature of it and shed a tear as she thought of how the retiring warriors must feel to lose this bonding.

She sensed how the eagles felt when they soared and hovered in the clouds and how free they felt when unfettered by human riders. She knew too that the birds understood their duty and that they would gladly carry human Pinn riders for the rest of their lives. Ashley smiled as she recognised pure goodness. The very soul of the eagles overflowed with pure thoughts and good intentions. There was not an ounce of evil flowing through the veins of these majestic birds.

The eagle too was exploring the thoughts of Ashley. It marvelled at the intricate nuances and feelings that she possessed. It understood the emotions that existed within her. Love, hate, anger, happiness and then it sensed her deep fears and discovered her acrophobia, her intense fear of heights. The eagle became agitated, unable to grasp a concept so alien to its very core. It shook its head as if to clear its thoughts and then nuzzled its beak against Ashley pushing her around to its side.

Ashley felt and understood this consternation and also knew what the eagle intended. She paused, "I don't think I can," she said out loud, reverting to normal conversation as if to reassure herself that this was not a dream.

The great bird stopped and looked at her with its huge eyes. Ashley felt its determination as it nuzzled her again towards its back. She knew that it was hopeless. The bird wanted her to mount, but her fear held her back, not just due to her acrophobia but also because of the added fear of never having ridden an eagle on her own.

"Please eagle!" she cried, "I can't! I don't know how."

The great warbird did not even pause on this occasion but continued to nuzzle Ashley towards its back. Slowly and reluctantly she gradually eased forward until she was standing against the eagle's midriff.

During this exchange the crowd had fallen silent as Ashley stood at the bird's side, neither mounting nor acknowledging the presence of others in any way. Gorlan, possessing knowledge of Ashley's fear of heights, realised the conflict within her. He stepped forward; "Here!" he whispered softly. "Let me help you".

He offered his hand to Ashley and she looked at it with a slight frown. Slowly she held the Warlords hand and allowed him to help her onto the back of the fire eagle, *her* fire eagle!

As soon as she was sitting firmly the eagle let out a great cry and leapt into the air. Ashley was almost overwhelmed by the elation that swept through the eagle and into her own thoughts. She grasped the bird tightly, wrapping her fingers in it's feathers she shut her eyes as they climbed higher and higher. Finally, some level of confidence returning, she opened her eyes and glanced to the side. Immediately wishing she had not. The ground was far below, the arena now just a small dot and she was overcome by terror as her fear of heights rose back to the surface. Feeling nauseous she started to panic and was physically sick. Sensing Ashley's thoughts, the power of her fear washed away the eagle's elation and the great bird was itself suddenly over-powered by the terror that Ashley felt. Suddenly the great bird, confused by the rising panic that swelled in its mind, glanced down and saw the great height, once an everyday image but now a threat. Its mind began to lose focus and it stopped beating its great wings as its vision blurred. With no control over its flight the eagle began to spiral downwards and Ashley had to hold tightly to the feathers to prevent herself falling to her death.

There were screams and cries of terror as the crowd watched the giant bird falling back to earth. Michael and Rhys looked on helplessly. Their happiness at seeing Ashley mount the great bird now swept away by terror as they saw their friend clinging on tightly, seemingly falling to her death. They tried to call to her to hold on but their voices were lost in the noise of the arena. Tosh and a dozen of his riders had mounted their birds and were racing towards the stricken eagle; they were now close enough to hear Ashley screaming as the eagle continued its free fall. Tosh felt a wave of hopelessness sweep across him as he realised that the bird had now ceased flying completely and was dropping like a stone to the jagged rocks below. They would not be in time, the pair would be smashed to pieces.

On the eagle's back, Ashley dug her fingers so deeply into its feathers that she could feel its flesh below. Aware that it was her fear that was the cause of the eagle's distress she fought to regain mental control and started to breathe deeply in an effort to calm herself.

The pair continued to plummet as the confidence of the eagle battled with the fears of Ashley's acrophobia.

As bare rock flashed towards them the eagle regained some of its composure and with a violent shiver it began to beat its wings again. They fell between two rock outcrops and were lost from sight to those in the arena. Everyone held their breath waiting for the thump of bodies hitting the ground, but within a fraction of a second, they saw the eagle re-emerge from behind the arena walls, slowly climbing once again in a stuttered flight, with Ashley still clinging tightly.

The eagle steadied its flight and descended back to solid ground gliding down to the arena entrance. Tosh landed next to it and Gorlan had already begun to sprint to where they had alighted.

Tosh grasped Ashley's arm, "Are you alright Ashley? Here let me help you."

"No let go!" snapped Ashley, "I'm OK." She softened a little as he released her in surprise. "I'm sorry Tosh," she said in a softer voice, "But we have to get back in the air. The eagle remembers my fear of heights and I don't know what that will do. It may harm him."

Tosh stepped back understanding her concern.

In an instant Ashley directed her thoughts back to flight. As Gorlan reached her he uttered a surprised grunt, as the great bird once again took to the air with Ashley looking uncomfortable on its back.

This time Ashley was more prepared for the flight and she kept her gaze ahead as the eagle climbed high into the sky. Some of the crowd cheered, but others, including Michael and Rhys, looked on with frowns of concern.

When Ashley felt the bird level its flight, she summoned up her courage and, with a deep breath, she turned to look down.

After an initial moment of dizziness her head began to clear. Her mind was full of the wonders of the sights below. The beautiful city of Pinnhome nestled between the red hills to the south and the snowy Pinnacle Mountains now below her and to the north of the town.

She felt the power of the bird and a great sense of freedom as they glided high above the crowded arena. Other than the rushing wind there was no other sound here in the skies and Ashley began to feel an overwhelming sense of calm.

The eagle, sensing her growing confidence, ensured that its flight was balanced and level. No sudden jerks or violent movement to trigger any concern in its new soul partner. Ashley was now entirely at ease and looked around, enjoying the experience.

She looked below her and saw that the other riders had joined her. They flew at her left and right in case she needed assistance, but it was no longer necessary. She knew that she had a lot more training to do, but with her fear of heights almost forgotten, she felt confident that she would master the art.

Swinging back around and spiralling down towards the arena, the pair made a smooth landing as the crowd cheered and clapped their approval.

Ashley dismounted and had a huge smile on her face. Rhys, Michael and Ophra rushed towards her to hug her. "I thought you were a gonna there Ash!" exclaimed Rhys.

"Me too!" added Michael, "What happened?"

Ashley explained and the others looked on in amazement.

"So you're cured of your fear then?" asked Rhys

Ashley thought on this before answering. "Well not really. I think it is more that I get help from the eagle which allows me to overcome the fear."

Michael turned to look at Ashley's eagle, "What's he called?" he asked.

Ashley looked at him and started to laugh.

"What?" said Michael looking quizzically at her, "What did I say?"

"Come on," she replied, "Let's go and find somewhere quiet and I'll try to explain".

As they made their way back to the town, Ashley's eagle spread its wings and took to the air.

*** 

"I will not hear of it!" exclaimed the OverLord. "The mission is far too dangerous and Michael is still a child."

Farspell frowned; he had not expected such a reaction. "Toran, Michael may be young but he is far from a child and he possesses the knowledge of an ancient dragon locked away in his mind. His reaction when he touched the sea-elf arrow was intense. I believe that his presence may prove of benefit not only in locating the home of the Graav but also in our dealings with the sea-elves."

Gorlan interjected, "Do you think that Michael would agree to go? I do not think he would want to leave Rhys and Ashley behind. They are from the same world, and although they are adjusting to our culture, their desire is still to find a way back to their homes."

Farspell nodded, "Yes, I have thought of that too. I would suggest that Rhys and Ashley accompany him on this journey."

"You are joking!" exclaimed Toran. "Now you are suggesting that we take three youngsters into danger. It just doesn't seem right. We can't ask this of them."

Farspell sighed and his shoulders sank. "It is a very hard thing to ask but my instincts tell me that the teenagers should undertake the quest with Gorlan." The wizard walked to the window and looked out to the west, down the valley and beyond the horizon where, far out of sight, the Sea of Mist ebbed and flowed.

"Ashley is now a fire eagle rider, so she enjoys the protection that the war birds bring. Rhys has his own unique power that we have only just started to explore. His skills, in mind generating portals, have greatly increased so I would put it to you that none of these 'youngsters' are as helpless as we are suggesting. All could look to their own abilities to protect themselves as well as Gorlan and his men."

Toran frowned and pondered on the wizard's words. Gorlan, rubbing his face in resignation offered his comments. "My Lord. Perhaps Farspell is right on this. It does seem a lot to ask of the young Earthlings but it is true that they possess skills that will offer them unique protection. They also share a bond that makes them stronger when they are together.

Toran looked into the eyes of his Warlord and saw the truth within, "Very well. We shall ask them, but, if they choose not to undertake the journey, then I shall not order them to do so."

Gorlan and Farspell accepted this, both sharing the confidence that Rhys, Michael and Ashley would not refuse.

Toran sent a messenger to collect the teenagers and, within a few minutes, all three were standing before him. Toran explained the mission and Farspell's belief that Michael might possess knowledge of the Sea of Mist that would benefit the mission.

"So what do you think Mike?" asked Rhys when they had heard Toran out. "Weldrock may possess knowledge that could lead us home again. Whadja reckon?"

Mike agreed, but thought for a few seconds before he spoke. "If it is my ability that you need then I'll come, but there's no need for Ash and Rhys to come too. They should stay here where it's safe."

"No way!" shouted Ashley and Rhys in unison.

"Mike, if one of us goes then we all go," added Ashley. "I can't explain it, but I know we need to stay together."

Michael looked at his two friends and smiled. "Are you sure?" he asked.

"Positive!" said Rhys.

"You betcha!" confirmed Ashley.

Gorlan looked humbled, "My thanks to you all. This is a dangerous mission and we do not know what we will find and whether we will return. You honour us with your presence. Leave now and get some sleep. My men will prepare for the journey and I will ensure that they pack provisions and clothing for all three of you."

As the trio turned to leave Gorlan called to Ashley. "Ashley, your eagle will fly with you. The flight to The Gates should be uneventful so it will be good practice for you to become more familiar with your bonding. I will ride with you when we fly west tomorrow and I will ask Kraven to personally carry out your training during our journey. By the time we return you will be the equal of the other riders."

Ashley gave a small nod, "Thank you Gorlan. I think I'm gonna need a lotta help. I just hope that I don't let you down."

"I am sure you won't Ashley. You have already faced your fear and won and you have gained the hearts of the people of Pinn." The Warlord wore a serious expression as he continued, "I will not lie to you. There may be some warriors in my ranks that are not happy about the choice of the fire eagle at today's ceremony but I am positive that the eagle had a reason for choosing you that goes beyond our understanding. No, I am sure that you won't let me down young warrior," replied the Warlord.

Ashley could not suppress a smile at being addressed as a warrior. She didn't really feel like one yet, but she realised with surprise that she liked the thought of being part of Pinnhome's finest, and relished the chance to fly with the other riders.

"Young Warrior." she repeated. "I like that."

They all laughed as Ashley followed Rhys and Michael through the door.

When they had left, Farspell offered up another suggestion.

"Gorlan, Ashley still possesses one of the Cormion Crystals. We should send a flyer to Eumor to recover one of the two that are in Cambor's possession. Cambor will support us in this and as Head of the Centaur Council in Eumor, he will not be challenged. Cambor should retain one for himself and the other should sit with me as I possess the Eumor runestone pendant. This will allow us to communicate during your mission."

"An excellent idea," replied Toran. "We will send Tosh. The fact that he is Captain of the Fire Eagle Riders will demonstrate to the centaur council the importance of this request."

Gorlan acknowledged the order, "I will send him immediately OverLord."

Thirty minutes later, Tosh was mounted and heading to Eumor. The flight would take almost two days and his brief was to make the utmost haste. He did not plan to stop so he carried dry rations in his pack which he could eat en route.

Gorlan watched his captain disappear into the distance and silently wished him well before he too retired for the night to rest before the morrow's journey to seek out Weldrock and his Graav.

***

From the shadows beneath the arena grandstand, a lone figure watched the events unfold while hidden beneath his cloak of invisibility. Nexus, formerly a counsellor to Toran but now an agent for Weldrock, looked with interest at the teenagers. So these were the children from Earth. He had crept close enough to hear them clearly. The boys were clearly Welsh, the girl an American. He was not confident with regional accents, but he placed her as being from the US West Coast.

*Amazing,* he thought, *an Earth-child now rides a fire eagle.*

He allowed his memories to come to the fore, visions of his life on Earth and how he had used the Shimmering Gate to travel between worlds.

He had not revisited the mountain location since arriving in Portalia and he wondered if the gateway was still functioning. He pondered too whether the teenagers had entered Portalia via the same route, but given the isolated location of the Peruvian portal he thought it highly unlikely. He therefore presumed, correctly, that the two Welsh boys had found the artefacts, which he had lost on his last visit to Earth, and that they had invoked the magic of the Eumor runestone, transporting them to Portalia. As for the American, he puzzled on how she had travelled with them and finally decided that she too must be in possession of a Celtic knot pendant. So he now supposed that Hesh still possessed the runestone key of the Celtic knot and that these kids held two of the pendants. He also knew that Farspell wore the third pendant and that the ring had been lost with Zarn, the White Dwarf. He stored this knowledge away, confident that it would later be of use.

Nexus knew that there was more to the magic of this world than just the portals. Too many coincidences were in evidence to be through chance alone.

Turning away from the arena he started to make his way back to the hunting lodge where he slept. Here he would ponder events and decide on his next course of action. Since his banishment from Pinnhome, and his unsuccessful attempt to assassinate Toran, the security around the OverLord had been increased, making it far more difficult to get anywhere near him. Nexus also feared the presence of Farspell, who had more than once looked in his direction curiously, even though he was blanketed beneath his cloak of invisibility. He sighed realising that his desire to kill the OverLord would have to wait. One day though, the time would come and the opportunity for assassination would present itself. Until then he would bide his time and work with Weldrock to further his skills and knowledge, then Pinnhome, and the Pinns, would bow to him.

# CHAPTER FOUR
## Premonition

Sandmover and Gatherer lay together in their bed, she stroked his head. "I love you," she whispered. "Don't go on a gathering today, I have a bad feeling about this one."

Gatherer looked into the eyes of his mate. "Lover, you know that I must go. The tribe rely on me for survival. If I failed to go on a gathering every time one of us had a bad feeling then the tribe would fall apart or starve."

Sandmover turned away fighting to keep tears back. She knew that Gatherer was right but she could not shake off this feeling of impending doom. It was stronger than she had ever felt in the past. Her fear made her irritated and she suddenly turned back to him with anger in her eyes.

"Gatherer! I am not asking for you to miss many gatherings, just this one. Something is not right."

Gatherer looked at her sympathetically and sighed. "Sandmover, you know I cannot. The tribe…."

"The tribe this! The tribe that!" she interrupted, "Well what about you? What about us? I tell you that this trip should not go ahead. I sense danger."

Gatherer bowed his head, "Sandmover! Nothing means more to me than our bonding and happiness. I would lay my life down for you but this is serious, you ask that I risk the safety of the tribe. If the sand storms come early and we do not have enough food gathered then what will become of us?"

Sandmover looked crestfallen, "I know but the feeling I have is so strong otherwise I would not ask this of you," she replied, the tears now running down her cheeks.

Gatherer softened his voice and tried to smile to reassure her, "Very well. We will talk to the Tribemaker about your fear. He will know what we should do."

Sandmover frowned but nodded her agreement.

"Then that is settled. Let's rise and go and talk to him now," he said, speaking as he swung his tall frame out of bed and rose to dress.

Sandmover watched him, the daylight reflecting off his lean and tanned body. She felt so lucky that she had such a kind and handsome mate. She did not want to lose him.

Rising herself she washed and dressed and soon the pair were winding their way to the home of the Tribemaker.

The ancient desert strider listened to Sandmover's concerns and paused a while, deep in thought. The couple waited patiently and silently for a response, after a short while the elder stood. He picked up his long staff that he used to help him walk and limped his way to face Gatherer. Suddenly and with a lightning movement that belied his age and frame, Tribemaker swung the staff at Gatherer's head. The agile desert strider dived to the ground but the staff caught him a passing blow against his shoulder. He rolled to recover his balance and stood to face the old man. Tribemaker immediately stopped his assault and spoke, "Sandmover. Did you sense danger before I struck out at Gatherer?"

Sandmover, still shocked at the sudden attack, stuttered a response, "Uh, I, well, I, uh, no."

"But the attack was real and if Gatherer had not moved swiftly my blow may well have done serious damage. Do you not agree?"

Sandmover nodded while Gatherer stood in silence.

"So in this instance, danger existed and yet you had no sense of it. Could it not be likewise that you sense a future danger that does not actually exist? You are not a shaman Sandmover. You do not possess the sight. I think what you feel is the normal apprehension that one feels when a loved one undertakes a dangerous task."

Sandmover shook her head, "No, it is not the same!" she exclaimed, "The situation is different. I *know* that there is danger ahead on this gathering. True I did not sense danger when you attacked Gatherer but then neither did you actually harm him with your strike. With respect Elder, I would ask that you give Gatherer leave to cancel the next gathering."

"Enough child! You know this cannot be. It is vital that we provide for the tribe before the arrival of the storms. Gatherer must fulfil his duty." He placed his arm around Sandmover and whispered to her, "Sandmover, your love for Gatherer is strong. You need to rise above this feeling as there will be many times in the future that you feel this way. It is essential that you learn to control your worries and allow Gatherer to depart on his gatherings without undue concern for his well being. There are always dangers out there in the desert and Gatherer cannot afford to have any distractions when gathering."

Sandmover looked ashamed. She had not considered that her concerns might play on her mate's mind as he undertook his gathering duties. She looked into the eyes of the elder who was now smiling at her kindly. "I am sorry Tribemaker. I have been selfish and stupid. I will do as you ask."

"Thank you. In return for your understanding I will grant your wish in part," he replied. "Gatherer, you may remain at Dry Dune for an additional day. Tomorrow will be early enough to start the gathering."

Gatherer smiled and Sandmover positively beamed, "Thank you Tribemaker," they said simultaneously. Sandmover turned to Gatherer and hand in hand they returned to their home.

# CHAPTER FIVE
## The Collection

On his island Weldrock was sitting at a large wooden desk in his runestone chamber. In his hands he held the ring of the island runestone. He slid open a desk drawer. It was divided into four compartments, which in turn, were identified by a small symbol at the base, a Celtic knot, a tree, a mountain and an island.

Weldrock examined the contents of these compartments. Looking thoughtful he called out to Stack. His loyal apprentice, leader of Weldrock's coven, responded swiftly. "Yes, my lord, how can I serve you?" He noted that the warlock was examining the contents of the drawer.

"Stack, I want you to travel through the portal to the Fortownians hills."

"Is that wise my Lord?" questioned Stack. "Our enemies are sure to be guarding the portal site."

Weldrock snapped back at him, "Of course it is not wise but I have a task for you that is of such importance that I cannot entrust it to others."

The warlock pointed to the items in the drawer. He indicated the first compartment. "The Runestone of the Celtic Knot, a functional runestone that sits in Eumor, the city of the centaurs. As you can see, this compartment is looking rather bare. Two of the Earth teenagers wear pendants of the Celtic knot. Farspell bears the third. That fool of a dwarf, Zarn, left our world when he fell through the portal carrying the Celtic knot ring and one of the Dargoth pendants with him. The runestone key is long lost and I have had no luck in locating any information of its whereabouts."

Moving his attention to the second compartment he continued, "The tree, runestone symbol of the Forest of Old. The dark-elves destroyed their runestone long ago to ensure that they were cut off from outsiders. The three tree pendants and the ring are all lost, presumably destroyed by the fools at the same time. However, I wonder if that legend is true? As you can see, I have been able to acquire the Runestone Key of the Tree." He pointed to a grey stone that filled a pocket in the compartment. "If the runestone key still exists, then perhaps the other artefacts of the Forest of Old remain intact."

Skipping the third compartment he pointed to the fourth. "The Island Runestone. My very own creation. Of course, I possess the runestone key and the ring, and unlike the other runestones, there are four pendants. The first my own, the second you wear yourself, the third is in the hands of Nexus, my human minion and the last we will present to the most promising of my coven when ready."

He returned his attention to the third compartment.

"The Runestone of the Mountain, the Dargoth runestone was located at Shangorth Towers. As you are aware, the runestone itself was destroyed after the unfortunate turn of events at Fortown. Notice that I not only possess two of the pendants, but also the runestone key and ring. As I mentioned, the third was lost by Zarn when he departed this planet. However, when I crafted the island runestone I was left with enough runestone ore to forge a fourth pendant for Dargoth. This fourth pendant was in the possession of Ohrhim the Shapechanger when he was destroyed at Fortown. That pendant now lies in the hills above Fortown. The task I want you to complete is to find the pendant and return with it."

Stack thought on this and frowned, "Sire, with the Dargoth runestone destroyed why the importance to find the pendant? Surely the power is spent and it cannot be used. Why undertake such a dangerous mission to recover a useless item?"

Weldrock looked furious, "You disappoint me Stack. Are you not my star pupil? Have you learned nothing of the unique powers of the runestone? Even with the Dargoth runestone destroyed there is still power locked within the pendant. Now that Farspell has escaped the Soul Orb I cannot afford to leave such power lying around. Like me he is highly skilled in the magics, although thankfully it will take him some time to recover his full powers after being so long entombed by the Soul Orb."

Stack looked suitably chastised, "I understand my lord. When do you wish me to undertake the task?"

"You will leave at first light, taking with you a dozen of the Graav. I will leave the portal open for your return and I will place additional Graav to guard it while you search for the pendant. We will carry out the mission in daylight rather than at night to prevent the town watch from observing the glow of the portal gateway when it is opened. You should move quickly, the element of surprise will be vital to overwhelm any guard placed at the portal entrance."

The warlock opened the top drawer in his desk and pulled out a long, thin amber crystal shard that was glowing brightly. "When Ohrhim was destroyed his body was spread over quite a distance. I have tuned this crystal to the power of the runestone. While it does not possess any great power in itself, it is sensitive to the runestone magic and will glow in its presence, as it is now." He lifted the crystal which was literally throbbing as it pulsed due to the close proximity of the island runestone and other artefacts.

"You will take this and it will lead you to the pendant. Use the intensity of the glow to track down the artefact and then return to the portal with the utmost haste. The Graav will alert me to any danger at the portal entrance so wear your island pendant and I will recall you using the island runestone if necessary. Understood?"

Stack nodded confirmation as he struggled to keep his apprehension hidden.

***

The next morning Stack arrived in the runestone chamber as ordered. He wore his island pendant and carried a short sword strapped to his waist. He had replaced his usual cloth robes with a tough covering of hardened leather armour.

Weldrock was standing at the Runestone control mechanism. Two dozen Graav guards surrounded him protectively. Nodding a welcome to his apprentice he inserted the key into its slot in the pedestal. He turned his head and looked approvingly at his apprentice, "Excellent Stack, all is prepared. I have merely to turn the key to the correct portal slot and the gateway will be opened." He reached into his robes, "Here, take this. Without it you will not be able to locate the pendant." He handed the amber crystal to Stack.

"Ready?" asked the warlock.

Stack nodded and Weldrock turned the key stone. There was a slight tingling in the air as the portal glowed into life. Weldrock immediately ordered a dozen Graav through. Addressing Stack he waved for his apprentice to follow, "Be quick, speed is of the essence. If Fortown is alerted to our presence I will have to close the portal immediately."

Without hesitation Stack stepped through. Behind him the remaining twelve Graav took up position to surround the open portal.

Stack felt the familiar light-headed sensation as he floated through the blue aura of the portal gateway. He had experienced portal travel a number of times in the past, and after at first seeming strange, it now felt comforting and natural. He let himself float towards the portal exit.

Stepping out onto the hills of Fortown, he was suddenly struck by how dark it was. At first his brain could not comprehend what was happening but slowly his senses came to him as he saw the Graav in front of him standing stock still against a solid rock wall. The only illumination came from the blue glow of the portal. He stepped forward to examine the wall.

It had been built of solid mountain rock. It formed a large circular chamber surrounding the portal that provided only just enough space to accommodate Stack and the Graav. He followed the wall around the entire chamber confirming his suspicion that there was no door installed. Looking upwards, as far as his eyes could see in the gloom, he saw that the solid walls climbed over ten metres in the air before they started to taper inwards. As he could not see the roof of the chamber due to the lack of light, he correctly presumed that the walls sloped in to a conical apex directly above the centre of the chamber. There was not a window or door visible at any point in the entire chamber.

Cursing to himself he turned and stepped back through the portal.

The twelve Graav guarding the open portal raised their weapons but before they could strike Weldrock had called them off.

"What is it Stack?" he asked.

"The Fortownians have built a chamber around the portal exit. There are no doors or windows and the walls appear very thick and solid. Not even the Graav will be able to force their way through," mumbled Stack.

"Hmmm, a sensible precaution but sadly futile," Weldrock stood as he spoke and stepped towards the portal, "I shall resolve this. A solid wall will not hold back Weldrock."

The warlock stepped through the portal closely followed by Stack.

Weldrock walked the circumference of the guard tower and smiled. Gathering himself he began to mutter words of power and a glow formed around his feet. After a few seconds he began to levitate.

As he rose towards the tower roof, the tone of his incantation changed and Stack watched as the warlock began to glow as he had when he had unleashed the intense shock of power to destroy the runestone at Dargoth. However, on this occasion, rather than a powerful blast of power, while still suspended in mid air, Weldrock used his body and mind to focus a narrow beam of white hot energy which he focused on the rock wall at the junction with the roof.

High above the heads of Stack and the Graav a small hole began to appear in the wall as the rock turned to molten lava and flowed down the inside wall. After a few minutes of concentrated heat the warlock had succeeded in burning a hole all the way through to the outside. A metre long tunnel had now been created and formed a make shift peephole. From where Stack stood he could see a beam of light shining through the hole as daylight streamed in.

Weldrock completed the energy spell and, muttering quietly once more, he floated towards the hole. Through it he could see a seventy degree view to the North West, looking away from Fortown which lay to the east. Weldrock noted the surroundings and let himself float gently back to the ground.

He addressed Stack, "There is only one guard to the west and he patrols between the north and west points of the tower.

I would guess that there are four guards in total, one for each quadrant. I can melt a doorway through to the outside here but it will call the attention of the guards. We will need to move quickly. All four guards must be slain before they raise any alarm."

"My lord, we could easily handle any that choose to attack us but what if any choose to flee. The Graav are fearsome fighters but they are not swift of foot," said Stack.

"Do not panic! I will handle any that try to flee," snapped Weldrock.

As the warlock prepared himself to create a doorway, Stack watched the immobile Graav. He looked into their cold staring eyes and a shiver went up his back as goose-pimples formed on the surface of his skin. At his side Weldrock began to summon more energy force and soon a larger beam was being projected from the warlock to the tower wall. Where the beam hit the stone below, it began to melt rapidly and silently.

Stack stepped back as the liquified rock began to flow onto the floor. The Graav seemed oblivious to it and bathed their feet in its warmth. This time the warlock did not burn all the way through the wall. Instead he removed the stone until only a thin layer of rock remained. Stack watched as the stone of the wall cooled and solidified at an unnatural rate.

Warlock pointed to the thin layer of remaining rock.

"The Graav can break through the final layer of rock. It will be much quicker than melting a doorway and should allow us to retain the element of surprise." Weldrock gasped for breath as he spoke, clearly drained by his prolonged spell casting.

Stack examined the alcove that the warlock had created, "My Lord, if you produce four such openings then we can use the Graav to attack all four areas at the same time," he suggested.

Weldrock shook his head, "A good thought but that will take too long and the magic will weaken as I tire, but I will cut a second doorway on the opposite side of the tower. This will allow the Graav to attack on two fronts."

Secretly the warlock doubted that he would have been able to channel the power for the length of time it would take to cut four alcoves but he did not voice this to his apprentice.

Stepping to the opposite side of the tower the warlock repeated his incantation and manufactured a similar alcove.

When completed he turned to his apprentice. Even in the dim light of the tower Stack noticed how pale and drawn the warlock had become after his spell casting. "Are you ready?" he asked.

Stack nodded and with a wave of his hand Weldrock willed the Graav to advance.

The stone creatures obeyed the command immediately and swiftly smashed their way through the thin layer of remaining rock. Weldrock had assumed correctly, four guards were posted at the tower. All of them turned in surprise but recovered their focus quickly. Stack thought that these men were well trained not to panic and run. Three of the guards raised their swords to meet the Graav while the fourth, to the north east, turned to run towards a large bronze bell that had been placed at the tower as an alarm.

Stack began to sprint to intercept the warrior but, as he did, he felt a blast of incredible heat sweep past him and saw a large ball of fire flying through the air. The fireball hit the guard in the back and he exploded in a ball of flame. The guard did not even have time to scream as his charred remains fell to the ground.

Weldrock noted that the three remaining guards all carried enchanted weapons, their sharp magic-tainted blades slicing through the protective metal collars of the Graav, removing the heads of the stone creatures with ease. Four Graav met their end this way before the warriors had been overwhelmed and killed. The whole incident was over in seconds and the raiders had achieved their mission of striking quickly and relatively silently. No alarm had been raised. For the moment there would be no reinforcements from the town.

Weldrock gave his orders to Stack and the Graav. "I will return through the portal. You use the crystal to find the pendant. The guards will be on a rotation basis and we do not know when the next change of shift will take place. I will hide the Graav in the trees to the east in an effort to cut off any approaching guard. The two doorways in the tower are visible from quite a distance so move quickly before they are noticed by the town. Take only a few Graav as it will be easier to hide if you stumble on any of our enemies. If you have not returned within three hours I will close the portal. I will not wait!"

Stack nodded and taking the crystal in his hand he began the search. Weldrock positioned the Graav in the trees and around the portal entrance. Before returning he called upon his magic one more time and carried out a make shift repair of the crude doorway that faced the town. It was not perfect but all would look well from a distance. Happy with the situation he stepped back through the portal to the safety of his island stronghold and collapsed in a chair, exhausted from his spell casting.

*** 

Stack had been searching for over two hours. On a number of occasions the crystal had flashed brightly for a few seconds and he picked up a trail only to lose it again after a short distance. The Graav that accompanied him followed close on his heels, eyes staring in front but ready to protect the human should the need arise. Looking around and keeping track of the direction and time it would take to return to the tower, Stack decided it was time to retrace his steps. He realised that it was unlikely now that he would locate the pendant and he was not looking forward to facing Weldrock with his failure.

Turning a full three hundred and sixty degrees on the spot, he held the crystal in front of him and studied it hard for any sign of increased activity in the amber pulse. With nothing conclusive he shrugged and began to retrace his path towards the open portal. Suddenly the Graav guard rushed past him to form a barrier in his path, their backs turned to him and their stone blades aloft.

After a few seconds Stack heard the sound of movement in the trees ahead. Something or someone was moving through the cover towards where he stood. He did not want to face a foe out here alone, even protected by six Graav and so he began to sprint to the north, away from the movement and towards some thick bushes. The Graav followed him and encircled Stack as they ran. Diving into the cover he laid flat and urged the Graav to do the same. The stone creatures obeyed, the only noise was the slight grinding of stone on stone as they bent their knees to hide in the undergrowth. It was not their way to hide and their bodies were not designed for it. Fortunately their stone grey colour meant that they were well camouflaged amongst the vegetation.

Stack waited patiently as the sounds came ever nearer. Eventually a group of soldiers appeared from the trees ahead. There were over twenty and all were heavily armed with both sword and bow. Stack felt relieved that he had chosen to hide and held his breath as the unit came to halt just a few metres from his hiding place.

The leader turned to talk to his soldiers. Stack could hear the odd word but the leader's back was to him and the breeze carried away most of the monologue. Suddenly, to the left, there was a loud rustling in the bushes. The soldiers reacted quickly and ten drew swords while the remainder notched an arrow to their bow. Taking up a defensive posture the soldiers watched the bushes and awaited the command of their leader.

Stack, now terrified of being found began to recall spells that his master had shown him as he sunk further back into the shadows of the undergrowth. His concentration was suddenly broken however as the amber crystal began to pulse brighter than ever. Moving swiftly he pushed the crystal into his robes to hide the light. One of the soldiers must have seen the glint and pointed in his direction. The Graav squatted ready for action.

The bushes close to Stack's position suddenly parted and a black, hairy spider, the size of a large dog crawled, its way out of the undergrowth. The soldiers immediately fired their arrows. The shafts sped through the air to bury their heads deep into the body of the huge arachnid. There was a loud clicking noise and a hiss as air and blood oozed out of the wounds and the spider rolled over, legs in the air, as it went through its death throes.

With the spider dead the human leader held his hand up and called for his soldiers to hold their position. They continued to watch the bushes, vigilant for further danger or movement. After a few minutes they relaxed and Stack noticed that the Graav also lowered their defensive posture.

The leader walked over to the spider and kicked it with his foot. "Damn ugly things," he said.

One of his colleagues advanced to his side. "That's the fifth one today. I wonder how many more survived the battle at Fortown and roam these hills? A relative of mine says that the creatures have actually taken young lambs from his farm. They found the bones wrapped in spider silk, completely fleshless."

"I can believe it," replied the first. "I know men that have been bitten by these things. It's not fatal but the venom stings like hell when it takes hold and it burns like acid. The sooner we can hunt all these down the better."

The leader turned back to his men. "OK, let's get going again. We can sweep to the south and head back to Fortown and make it back before sunset. Drinks on me this evening!"

A loud cheer went up from the group.

Stack sighed in relief and was finally able to uncover the crystal. It was pulsing strongly. Watching the amber glow, Stack followed the path indicated by the increased activity. Moving deeper into the undergrowth he came to a point where he had to crawl through heavy thorn bushes which scratched his arms and back as he snaked his way through. Suddenly the crystal gave one bright flash and throbbed with the strength of the pulsation, much as it had done in the runestone chamber.

Running his hands through the loose leaves, Stack's fingers came into contact with a metal chain and grabbing hold he withdrew the lost pendant of the mountain. He grinned in relief as he eased his body back through the thorns. Returning to the clearing and with a glance at the sun, he realised that his three hours were very nearly up. There was only one way that he could make it back to the portal in time and that would mean sacrificing the Graav that had accompanied him.

Calling on his newly acquired sorcery skills Stack began to call forth the power of nature. Not dark magic but natural magic, used by both wizards and warlocks alike. A green aura started to flow from the ground at his feet. Stack began to mould the glow so that it totally immersed his feet up to his shins and then, with a loud hoot of satisfaction he began to run. The nature magic weaved its spell and his feet moved in a blur. He raced through the forest and across the hills back towards the safety of the portal. His Graav were soon left far behind, deserted without a second thought.

Arriving back at the tower he was relieved to see that the guard had not been renewed. He approached the tower cautiously, creeping towards the forced opening that the warlock had created.

Skirting quietly along the wall, Stack peeped inside and let out a deep sigh of relief. Inside two Graav stood sentry at the entrance to the portal gateway, still pulsating brightly in the dim interior.

Moving swiftly Stack stepped into the portal followed closely by the Graav and, after a few moments of the familiar floating sensation, he stepped back out into Weldrock's runestone chamber.

The raised Graav weapons were swiftly dropped when Weldrock recognised his apprentice. Stepping purposefully up to his minion, Weldrock snatched the crystal without a word of thanks and a manic grin spread across his face.

# CHAPTER SIX
## Journeys

Gatherer rose very early. By desert standards the morning was relatively cool and a few small clouds splashed blobs of white on the blue canvas above.

He grinned as he thought about the previous day. He had enjoyed the extra hours spent with Sandmover. During the morning they had worked together in the conservatory, sowing seed and tending the small shoots that thrust their heads from previously planted trays, taking care with each delicate stem to ensure that they did not damage them as they transplanted them to provide for improved growth. Following this they had spent a peaceful afternoon together sharing stories and drinking cactus wine.

Sandmover seemed a lot happier now but he knew that she was still uneasy about this gathering. He had promised to be especially careful and hugged her long and hard as he kissed her farewell, gently rubbing her cheek with his own as they broke contact.

He had decided to head south to Wildrock Oasis. Now an area of dried mud and sand, this had once been a vast but shallow lake. Although creatures no longer enjoyed the once cooling waters, it was still a good spot for a gathering. There were four other Desert Strider tribes that gathered in this area and all were careful not to over-farm there. Protection of the plants and animals was critical. Survival of the flora and fauna was as important as gathering food. As a result each tribe only visited the areas once in each season.

Checking his equipment and readjusting his scimitar so it sat comfortably in its scabbard, Gatherer set out.

It would take him most of the day to get to the oasis. He would not carry out any sensing until he was there which would conserve his energy and allow him to move quickly.

This would mean travelling a long distance with no warning of any lurking danger. He thought about his promise to Sandmover but decided that the route was so well used that it would be safe and this way he could carry out a swift gathering and return to her with the utmost haste. Satisfied that this plan was not breaking his word he continued swiftly towards the oasis using his eyes and ears to monitor his surroundings for any sign of danger or indeed, any chance of gathering resource while en route. Striding out, his long legs eating up the ground, he was positively flying across the hot sands. Smiling to himself he allowed a lively tune to play in his head though he dare not sing it out loud for fear of drowning out any telltale noise that would warn of predators. All seemed well with the world today and he soon forgot about Sandmover's trepidation as he relaxed into his task.

*** 

Rhys hammered on Michael's door. "Come on lazy git. We've got to meet the others. Wake up!"

Michael pulled open the door. He was still in his nightgown and rubbed his eyes sleepily.

"Huh, what's up?" he said stifling a yawn.

"What's up? Whadja mean what's up?" replied Rhys, "We've gotta be in the courtyard in about ten minutes. Get moving or Gorlan will go berserk!"

A look of panic crossed Michaels' face. "Oh hell! Sorry Rhys. I didn't sleep well at all last night. I kept having these dreams. They were really weird. One minute I…"

"Tell me later Mike. You need to move," interrupted Rhys.

Michael quickly splashed some water over his face and brushed his teeth and then he dressed swiftly. Gathering up a few belongings he nodded to Rhys that he was ready to go and soon the boys were hurrying down to the courtyard.

Rhys took the opportunity to ask Michael about his dreams.

"They were really mixed up," replied Michael. "I think that there were dragon memories mixed up with my own imagination. One minute I'd be flying through the air above the ocean and the next I'd be deep in the sea chasing sea-elves and watching them mine the sea-ore. At one point I was fighting a huge sea snake and as I was about to win I changed from a fearsome dragon back to myself. I woke up just as the snake was going to make me his fast food lunch!"

"Make mine a Big *Mike* and make it large!" Rhys joked.

Michael laughed. "I managed to get back to sleep after laying there for a bit but then the dreams came back. This time I was the dragon again and I was in a city surrounded by sea-elves. They were cheering and waving, but as I walked forward, the ground turned into a huge swamp and everyone disappeared. Then the swamp turned to lava and I was being torn to pieces by the Graav." Michael shivered.

"Sounds like you had too much cheese for supper. My Nan always said cheese gives you nightmares."

Mike looked thoughtful, "Don't think I've had any cheese in days," he mumbled thoughtfully. "What about sweetgrass tea? I drank gallons yesterday. Does that make you dream?"

"I don't think so but I reckon that you'll be peeing for a week!" replied Rhys with a smirk. Michael pushed him playfully and they broke into a run.

Not surprisingly they were the last to arrive. "Ah, here at last." said Gorlan.

"And about time too!" added Kraven who followed this with a mumbled word that the boys did not quite catch but which they knew was not particularly complimentary.

Carl handed the boys a large backpack that had been stuffed with food and extra provisions for their journey. They put their smaller bags of belongings into these packs and slung them over their backs.

Michael, looking about, suddenly gave a wolf whistle. Rhys turned to look and was bowled over by what he saw. Ashley, who was stood with her fire eagle, had been decked out in full rider leather uniform and the lightweight wrought ore armour breastplate. She also wore a gleaming scabbard in which held a sharp but plain metal sword, typical of the weapons carried by the Pinn riders.

"Whoa Ash! You look fantastic," whistled Michael in admiration.

"Yeah Ash," added Rhys, "Absolutely incredible."

Ashley beamed. "Thanks guys. Feels kinda cool too and it's not like the armour from the old days back on Earth. This stuff is really light. Feels like I'm wearing a heavy shirt."

They were prevented from chatting further as Gorlan gave out the orders.

"I will ride with Ashley. Rhys and Michael you will partner up with Stern and Carl. Kraven, I want you to fly up front with Ashley and myself. As we travel you can help train Ashley and give her the benefit of your experience. Pinnel and Lloyd, you will take the left flank. Flare and Tor will hold the right flank. Green and Herd, you will bring up the rear."

There was a mumble of acknowledgement. "Any questions?" asked the Warlord.

There were not. "Fine, then let's go."

The ten eagles, their riders and passengers took to the air. They circled the city once, waved to those on the streets below then adjusted their course towards the west.

\*\*\*

Gatherer's gamble had paid off. He had moved swiftly across the desert sands without incident and was now in sight of Wildrock Oasis. He knew that now was the time for caution so he slowed his pace and progressed with stealth to the peak of a tall dune that overlooked the large oasis area.

Wildrock Oasis was a large oval shaped dust bowl that resembled a shallow volcanic crater. Now bone dry the lakebed displayed signs that it was once a rich treasure for desert creatures. Thorn cactus still clung to the lake floor and pulp fruit grew in large quantities, the plants fed by some remnant of water that still existed far below the blazing hot surface. The pulp fruit was in abundance and it looked like Gatherer's luck was in as it appeared that no other tribe had undertaken a gathering at the oasis recently. This meant he could fill his bags with ease.

The dark green thorn cactus, named for its quarter metre long needle like prongs, was also growing well. Gatherer would be able to harvest this too for its fleshy, watery main stem. He would have to be wary of the sharp thorns though. One prick could inject a poison that, while not fatal, would cause severe swelling and temporary paralysis.

The third plant that usually grew well here was not faring as well as in the past. This was the dry lake creeper, unique to Wildrock Oasis. This had once been a spongy and mossy creeper that grew in the waters of the old lake. Now, with shorter roots than its botanical competitors, it was starved of all but the bare minimum of moisture. As a result, the plant had adapted and now continued to grow with a crisp, dry skeletal frame that nurtured thousands of small seed pods each year. The plant was not much use for gathering other than for collecting the dried seed pods for use in cooking. When added to any dish they produced a pleasant, hot and spicy flavour. Even though the tribes were careful not to over harvest the seed, Gatherer had noticed that this plant was struggling to survive. On a number of occasions he had taken seed back to Dry Dune but the creeper refused to grow anywhere other than in the sands and dry mud of the old lake bottom. Gatherer felt saddened as he thought about the decline of this plant. If this continued then within another ten years or so the plant would be gone.

The desert strider searched the area around the oasis for signs of wildlife but all was quiet. To be sure he decided to carry out a sensing. Blocking out the sun by closing all of his eyelids he began to focus on his breathing to relax and to allow his mind to join with his environment. The familiar feeling of oneness began to build and he became more aware of his surroundings, feeling the life force of the plants and creatures for miles around.

As he increased his focus on the energy flow, he became aware of something new. A sensation that was unknown to him, something that felt foreign and threatening. The shock of it broke his concentration and the sensing was lost. Gatherer frowned and snapped open his eyes to look around him anxiously. What was that?

Satisfied that there appeared to be no danger he returned to his sensing, once again building the bond that connected him to the desert to feel as one with his surroundings.

There it was again, a strange unfamiliar energy flow. This time it came more suddenly and with greater power and Gatherer focussed intensely so that he did not break the sensing. However, this alien force demanded his attention and he turned his mind towards it, immediately losing contact with his desert. As Gatherer realised his mistake his consciousness was overpowered by the draw of this intrusive energy flow.

Above him the skies darkened, lightning flashed, thunder cracked and a strong wind blew as a torrent of rain fell on the oasis for the first time in a millennia. Gatherer was only partially aware of the violence of the storm as water soaked his skin. He struggled hard to regain control of his thoughts but it was too late. Once he had focussed his sensing on that strange energy form it expanded rapidly, overwhelming his thoughts with a sea of shimmering blue energy. On his finger the ring that he had recovered from the dead dwarf felt hot and he forced open his outer eyelid to see that it too was glowing, emanating a bright blue aura.

Suddenly, Gatherer felt himself being pulled upwards. Fear ate at his soul as he felt his feet leave the familiarity of his desert world. Recovering his composure a little he found himself floating through a strange sea of blue energy. He knew instinctively that he was no longer in the desert. He started to panic and tried to turn back towards where he had come from, but not only did he find it difficult to control his movement, but he realised in horror that he did not know which way was back. Around him all he could see and feel was this strange blue ooze that held him. His thoughts turned to Sandmover and her predictions of doom and realising that he may never see her again he felt a peak of fear and panic that he had never experienced before.

The panic made him start to thrash around furiously but this did not seem to help in any way. He did not know how long it was before he stopped struggling and shouting, but eventually overcome by tiredness he slowed his wild movement and allowed himself to float along the energy flow, resigned in the thought that he was hopelessly trapped.

***

Tosh, Captain of the Pinn riders and his fire eagle were making excellent time. They had climbed high and found a current of wind that carried them in the direction of Eumor. He estimated that if the wind prevailed they would reach Eumor around midnight, well ahead of expectation.

Tosh had remained awake through the night and was beginning to feel weary. He lay forwards on his eagle. The bird sensed his need and adjusted its body position to flatten the area around its neck and upper back. Tosh snuggled into the downy feathers and began to doze.

It seemed like only a few minutes had passed when the violent movement of his fire eagle suddenly roused him. The wind had increased dramatically and despite the strength that the eagle possessed it was getting thrown about by the turbulence.

Tosh grabbed onto his bird even tighter and willed it to descend to a safer altitude, but every time the eagle tried it was hit by a severe updraft that pushed it higher. Tosh realised that they were in trouble. He had never experienced turbulence like this.

Focusing his mind to calm himself, he willed his support to the eagle and once again requested that it descend. Six more times they tried and each time they were pushed ever higher by the uplift. The bird was no longer flying but was merely gliding along out of control as hurricane force winds pushed it along.

Tosh tried to focus once more, not an easy task as the sound of the howling of the wind had reached epic proportions. He glanced back over his shoulder but the sky had become as dark as night and he could make out very little in the gloom. Suddenly, without warning the pair were hit by an incredible force of wind from behind and beneath. The strength of it pushed the giant eagle tail over head as it floundered hopelessly, rolling over and over as it was blown through the skies.

Even with his vast experience he was unable to stay mounted on his bird and he became separated from his eagle. Initially he was blown along with the bird but, without wings to help him catch the breeze, he soon began to fall, slicing through the updrafts like an arrow through the air.

Now in freefall, he felt a violent pressure change as his body fell below the jet stream and his ears popped loudly, causing his head to hurt. He spread his arms and legs and steadied himself to slow his fall, looking all around but failing to see his eagle anywhere. Glancing at the ground he realised that he only had seconds to live as the Eumor Plains rushed towards him.

High above his eagle had seen his fall and knew what it must do. Folding its wings flat, it angled its body so that its beak pointed downwards towards the ground with its tail in the air. This was a most unnatural position for the bird.

The change in body shape worked and the eagle was now diving swiftly through the updraft racing towards the falling warrior. The ground was getting precariously close as the eagle finally reached its bond partner. Tosh saw the bird arrive and felt the eagle clutch his foot in its beak. His moment of relief was brief as it quickly turned to horror when he realised that the velocity which they had reached would not allow the eagle to unfurl its wings to decelerate before they hit the ground.

The eagle, also clearly aware, tried nonetheless, but finally, as the ground unavoidably sped towards them it unfurled its great wingspan and turned its back to the ground, chest up to the stormy skies.

"No!" screamed Tosh suddenly aware of what his bond partner intended as it pulled him into its chest.

They hit the ground with a sickening thump and Tosh heard bones cracking in the eagle's chest and back. At the moment of impact the great bird folded its wings around the warrior and rolled with the impact. Its momentum caused it to spin, tail over head several times and Tosh heard more bones breaking on each rotation until finally they came to a halt.

Tosh lay still, all the air knocked from his body but otherwise unharmed. His bird was wrapped around his body like a protective cocoon. It was not moving and Tosh felt isolated as the awareness of the eagle's consciousness deserted him. He felt lost and alone. He had forgotten what it was like not to share the bonding.

Catching his breath in great gasps he eased the bird's great wings from him and crawled out of the mass of feathers. His eagle was a mess. It was covered in blood and bones were protruding from its body in a number of places. There was no sign of life.

Tosh was speechless. He had thought the fire eagles immortal if their bond partner remained alive. He did not know that they could die this way. He began to shake as he was swept by a feeling of desolation, his bonding with the great bird now lost to him. He hugged the eagle around the neck, he felt as though he was in a dream. No, not a dream, a nightmare.

He was so lost in his grief that he failed to notice the centaurs as they raced towards him. They had witnessed the fall and were now making haste to his assistance at full gallop. He heard them before he saw them but did not look around; he did not want to leave his eagle. As helping hands reached his shoulders he resisted for a moment but then, exhausted, he felt his head start to spin. The last thing he saw before he blacked out was the worried expression on the face of a young female centaur as she lifted him onto her back.

***

Gorlan had changed mounts and now rode with Tor. This allowed Ashley to ride alone while Kraven gave her some training on riding her new partner.

When she first mounted her eagle she had expected her old fears to return but there was not even a hint of it. It seemed that the battle that she and the fire eagle had experienced at the Ceremony of Choosing, had won over her acrophobia and cured her completely. When this realisation had dawned on her she could not help but laugh out loud in relief.

Kraven had started her training explaining that all of the skill came from the mind bonding with the fire eagle. Rather than directing the eagle through body movement the secret of success was through clear and concise thinking. The key was to focus the mind on precisely what you wanted to do but to remain open to suggestion for the eagle as it used its own experience to suggest how to achieve the goal.

Ashley realised that her soccer training would help her in this. When in early grade-school back home she had a coach who had played professional football for Spurs in England. He had taught her that apart from ball skills, the secret to a great player was to know the layout of the field around you even when you did not have the ball. This would allow you to know where your opponents were and where your team mates would be, hence providing the opportunity for a quick pass if needed. This required focus and quick thinking as players changed places quickly in this fast sport. As a result she was used to high levels of concentration and fast modification of her thoughts and ideas.

Her belief proved accurate. After only an hour training with Kraven her mentor expressed how delighted he was with her. "Incredible Ashley!" he stated. "You have picked up some complex skills faster than any Pinn warrior that I have known. It seems that you were born to fly with the eagles."

Ashley smiled in response and, with mind focused, carried out a tight mid-air loop in celebration.

Kraven laughed, "OK, stop the theatrics. Now for some combat moves. Follow me and do what I do."

The Pinn removed his sword from its scabbard and bird and man carried out an agile direction change to angle sharply towards the ground. Ashley mimicked her tutor and swiftly followed.

Kraven shouted to Ashley, "See the bushes on the hill ahead?" She nodded her affirmation. Kraven continued, "Imagine that they are Graav. The topmost leaves are their heads. Time to fight!" Kraven let out a loud battle roar as they sped towards the bushes. Swinging his blade skilfully he chopped in a downward arc that sliced off the top of the bush in one clean cut. Immediately the eagle went into a steep climb to gain height once more.

"Easy!" mumbled Ashley but as her great bird swept above the bushes she got the timing all wrong and slashed at empty air, missing the bushes by half a metre.

The pair joined up again high above the valley. "No need to worry. This is a hard skill. The war bird is fast and the timing is difficult at first. Let's keep practising. It will come."

Further attempts were made and each time Ashley mis-timed the strike, sometimes too early but usually too late. On the seventh attempt she did manage to brush the leaves of the bushes but her sword was not angled correctly and she merely pushed them aside with the flat of the blade. She cursed under her breath in utter frustration. She could fly like the best of the Pinn's but she was having great difficulty in using a sword during flight. After another dozen failed attempts Kraven called for a rest and they returned to the others, Ashley's early euphoria now dampened.

*** 

Tosh groaned as he regained consciousness. He opened his eyes slowly raising his hands to shield them from the torch light. His head hurt and his body ached. Slowly his senses returned and he remembered what had happened. Tears welled again as he remembered the torn and crumpled body of his fire eagle. He sat up and took in his surroundings.

He was lying on a pile of blankets on a soft mattress in the corner of a bedroom. He knew immediately that this was the home of a centaur and correctly made the assumption that he must be in Eumor City.

An arched window revealed that although it was daylight outside, the skies were still dark and the rain was teeming down as the storm continued its relentless beating of the land. As he looked out, he saw a couple of centaurs trotting along the largely empty streets, heads bent down to shield their eyes from the wind and rain.

The bedroom itself was brightened with burning torches attached to the walls, which removed shadows that otherwise would have clung in the corners. The paintwork was bleached white; but this bedroom had also been decorated by simple, yet colourful drawings of centaur life. The entrance to the room was a large stone arch, door-less and wide enough to allow centaurs to pass through with ease.

Safe in the comforting thought that he was amongst friends, Tosh relaxed and allowed his aching body to sink into the soft mattress. He closed his eyes and began to drift back to sleep.

Almost immediately he sat back up., Startled, the comfort of the room suddenly gone, Tosh felt a presence in his mind, probing and nudging. It was as though someone was spying on him, watching his every move. No, even more than that, something or someone was trying to invade his mind, to share his thoughts.

Tosh breathed hard and deep to calm the panic. Slowly his alertness returned and realisation dawned. Leaping into the air he let out a yell of joy and surprise. Sprinting out of the bedroom and into the main living area he startled a number of centaurs who were eating. Without hesitation or apology, he continued his charge through their home to exit into a small covered courtyard at the back of the house. There sat on a pile of straw and looking content was his fire eagle.

Tears now flooding down his face, Tosh did not pause as he threw his arms around the neck of his warbird and he fully opened his mind so that man and beast were one again.

"You beauty!" he said as he rubbed the bird's great neck. In response the bird pushed its head against the warrior and made a low purring noise in its throat.

Tosh, still hugging the eagle gradually became aware of another presence. Turning around he saw that he was being watched by a female centaur. He looked up at her and bowed his head by way of greeting.

"It is good to see you are well," said the centaur. "My name is Kyrie and this is the home of my father, Fyros."

Tosh raised his eyebrows, "Fyros?" he replied. "I know your father. We fought together at Fortown. My name is Tosh, Captain of the Pinn Riders."

Kyrie did not look surprised, "I know your name Tosh. My father recognised you and has told me of your valour and your actions at Fortown. It is good to meet you. You are most welcome here."

The warrior looked at his eagle once again, almost as if he felt that the huge bird would wash away in the rain if he turned away. "I thought my friend here was dead. Did you heal him?"

Kyrie shook her head. "No, his recovery was nothing to do with us. We too thought the bird dead but we carried it back here so that you could be near it when you recovered. We thought you could give it a fitting burial. We were amazed when we found that it had started to heal itself. The bones started to slowly re-knit and the flesh reformed. We kept checking on it and after a few hours the bird had returned to normal. We had heard that the eagles cannot die if their bond partner lived but none of us had ever witnessed this. It was magical and very moving."

Tosh paused and hugged his warbird again. "I've seen eagles get injured and recover before but I have never seen one so lifeless. He was completely dead to me, both in mind and body. That is something that I have never witnessed in all my years as a rider. I was sure I had lost him."

Kyrie nodded. "There are so few left now. I am glad that you have both recovered and are rejoined."

She offered her hand to Tosh to help him stand, "If you are feeling better my father is with Cambor, Head of the Eumor Council. They would like to speak with you."

Tosh nodded, "That would be good. I have a message for Cambor from Toran that is of the utmost importance," and so saying he followed her out of the courtyard.

"The storm is still blowing strong, but we are only a short way from the chambers," she passed Tosh a cloak. "Here, put this on it will help keep the rain off."

Wrapping the cloak around his shoulders he followed Kyrie out into the rain lashed streets. After only a few blocks they came to the council chambers but, even so, Tosh was glad of the cloak as the downpour was torrential. Fortunately the centaurs had excellent drainage and, although water sodden, the rain was continuing to drain away from the paths.

As they entered the chamber Tosh removed his cloak and shook off the excess water. Inside he saw two centaurs deep in conversation. They paused as he approached and warmly greeted the Pinn captain. He recognised the first as Fyros and he correctly surmised that the other was Cambor.

"Tosh! It is good to see you again and even better that you are back on your own two feet," said Fyros as he put his arm around the Pinn's shoulders in welcome.

"It is indeed good to see you have recovered," added Cambor smiling a welcome.

"Thank you," responded Tosh "although the manner of my arrival is somewhat embarrassing."

"Embarrassing?" questioned Cambor, "Why do you say that?"

"Well, it is hardly normal for the captain of the Pinn riders to be blown from his mount!" replied Tosh.

Cambor looked at him curiously. "There is no shame there Tosh. I must admit it is an unusual occurrence but so is the strength of the wind that caused your fall. It is common for the Plains of Eumor to suffer storms and sometimes even powerful tornados, but this storm is very unusual, not only in strength but in its form. Although strong here at ground level it appears to increase at higher altitudes. Also the storm does not appear to be moving away, it is spiralling but with the focal point centred on our city. This is no normal storm."

Tosh nodded, "The wind was strong indeed and seemed to come from nowhere. It was like nothing that we had experienced. It picked up my eagle as though it were a feather and blew us around as it pleased. Have you witnessed this before?"

Both Cambor and Fyros shook their heads. The latter spoke, "Never. I have discussed this with Horos, one of our wiser council members. At first I feared Weldrock's hand, but it would appear that it may have been caused by another event, that being the appearance of a curious creature in the Eumor runestone chamber. Indeed, the storm does appear to be centred on the runestone chamber."

Tosh raised his eyebrows. "What is this creature? It is not the White Dwarf is it?" he asked, aware that Weldrock's minion had been in possession of the Eumor ring when he had been spirited out of Portalia by Rhys.

Again the centaurs shook their heads. "No, thankfully not that disgusting creature," answered Cambor. "We'll introduce you to our new arrival shortly but first tell us about your mission. Were you heading to Eumor, or elsewhere?"

Tosh confirmed his mission and explained to Cambor the request for him to loan one of the Cormion Crystals to Farspell for communication with the expedition to the islands. When he finished speaking Cambor responded, "It is not usual for the crystals to leave the possession of the centaurs but a precedent has already been set with the children from Earth. Given the dire need of the times I am sure that the council will agree to this. Obviously the remaining stone will have to remain here in Eumor."

"Of course," replied Tosh bowing as he thanked the centaur.

Cambor reached for a rope that hung from a large bell mounted on the wall, "Now, if that concludes our business let me introduce you to our new friend." He pulled the rope and in response to the bell a young male centaur entered. Cambor addressed him, "Kurl, please ask our guest to join us. I would like him to meet Tosh."

A few minutes later the doors to the council chamber swung open and Tosh gasped as a giant of a creature came into view. He was taller than the centaurs themselves and had to bow his head slightly as he entered.

"Tosh," said Cambor, "I'd like you to meet Gatherer. Apparently he is one of a race known as desert striders. Needless to say he is not of our world."

Tosh was still gaping but managed to mumble a greeting, "Uh, um good to meet you Gatherer. Welcome to our world."

Gatherer bowed in acknowledgement, his great frame bending nimbly at the waist as he showed his respect.

"Thank you, although I am afraid I am not here through choice," replied the desert strider.

Gatherer explained how he had come to enter the portal web after invoking a sensing and found himself floating in the blue aura. After an indeterminable time the current of the web had brought him to the Eumor runestone, presumably drawn there by the power of the Celtic knot ring which he wore.

Gatherer displayed the ring to Tosh. As was the custom of Portalia the centaurs had made no attempt to take the ring from his possession. It was a law honoured by all races of Portalia that a ring or pendant bearer should not have their device removed from them unless so offered by the bearer.

"It was at the point of Gatherer's arrival that the storm intensified," interrupted Fyros, "We believe that the nature magic that brought Gatherer here fed the storm in some way. Gatherer also mentioned that a rain burst was created on his world at the point of creation of the portal. The desert striders live in a desert region where rain has not fallen for generations. The two are obviously linked in some way. It cannot be a coincidence."

Tosh glanced at the giant's finger, "How did you come to wear the ring Gatherer?" he asked.

The desert strider explained how he had found Zarn's body and recovered the items from it. He told of the whereabouts of the pendant and the crystal.

Cambor spoke, "Curious indeed would you not say Tosh? The very day you arrive to request one of the Cormion Crystals we learn of the whereabouts of the fourth." The centaur explained to Gatherer the purpose of the crystals and the giant became excited. He looked at his runestone ring.

"So if I use this to trigger one of the Cormion Crystals then I can speak with my tribe?" he asked.

Fyros replied, "Possibly. The crystal must be in the possession of a bearer, either worn or held in the hand. If it is not then the link will not be made. There must be a life-force of some kind in contact with it."

Gatherer nodded, "I understand. It is born of nature magic and needs life essence as the trigger. Can we try to make contact with my people? Tribemaker, our elder, possesses the crystal and may be carrying it."

Cambor nodded, summoning Kurl. Once again he asked his assistant to collect the Cormion Crystals. A short while later the young centaur returned bearing both.

He handed the first to Tosh, "Take this and give it to Farspell with my blessing. I will inform the council of my decision. I am sure Hesh will object, but I would worry if he agreed with anything I did these days." The old centaur winked at Fyros who laughed. The relationship between the ambitious centaur Hesh and Cambor had deteriorated over the months and Hesh took every opportunity to try to undermine the council leader.

Cambor placed the chain of the last crystal over Gatherer's head.

He spoke softly to the desert strider, "Place your runestone ring against the crystal and do not be alarmed. It will not harm you."

Gatherer did as he was bid and as soon as the devices made contact they started to glow brightly. Within seconds images appeared in mid air.

The first two were as seen through the eyes of Tosh and Gatherer. A third showed Gorlan on the back of a fire eagle riding high above the ground, clearly the view through the eyes of Ashley. To Gatherer's disappointment there was no fourth image. No-one was wearing the crystal that he had given to the elder. He cursed quietly under his breath.

Gorlan a little startled by the sudden appearance of two images of Cambor, one as viewed by Tosh and the other as viewed by Gatherer, recovered his composure and spoke.

"Cambor! It is good to see you. I presume that Tosh made it to Eumor. Is all well with you and your people?"

"Thank you, yes!" replied the centaur, "Tosh has briefed me on your mission and I am happy to offer our assistance. We will send one of the Cormion Crystals to Farspell with Tosh. Is there anything else you require of us?"

Gorlan shook his head, "No, but thank you. We will keep in contact with the crystals and will let you know should anything arise. We are making good progress at the moment."

"How is your training progressing Ashley?" enquired Tosh.

The voice of Ashley came across loud and clear, "Fine thanks Tosh although I am having problems with my battle training. Flying seems like second nature to me but I think Kraven is tearing his hair out trying to teach me some of the battle moves."

"Don't worry Ashley," replied Tosh, "It will come, just be patient and listen to Kraven. You could not want for a better teacher."

"Gorlan, you should know that Tosh and his eagle had some problems getting here but there is no cause for alarm, both are well and unharmed. It is a story that can wait until you return," said Cambor.

Gorlan looked concerned nevertheless. "Tosh, what happened? Are you sure you are not injured in any way?"

Tosh reassured his leader, "No, I am fine Warlord. As Cambor says there was a slight incident but all is well and I will return to Pinnhome tomorrow."

Having heard it from the lips of Tosh himself Gorlan relaxed, "Very well, but take care my old friend."

"Gorlan, there is something else I wish to share. The centaurs have a visitor." Tosh turned his gaze to Gatherer who was standing next to Fyros to give Gorlan a perspective of his height.

The Warlord whistled, "Who and what is that?" he exclaimed.

Gatherer looked annoyed, "The who is Gatherer. As to the what, I am a desert strider, a gatherer of Dry Dune."

Gorlan looked embarrassed, "Please accept my sincere apologies Gatherer, I meant no offence. Sometimes it is difficult communicating with these crystals. I should have addressed you directly."

Cambor interjected, "We believe that Gatherer was pulled here from his desert world by the power of the portal web," offered Cambor, "He bears the Celtic Knot ring which he took from the dead body of Zarn."

"But how?" replied Gorlan, "He does not have a pendant does he?"

"No, but Gatherer does possess the ability to sense the natural forces of his world. We believe that this is achieved through a similar magic to that which controls the portal web. Our supposition is that the combination of the runestone ring and his sensing opened a unique portal that brought him here. Something is amiss though as since his arrival we have been beset by a huge storm centred on the chamber. It is as if the magic of Gatherer's world clashes with the portal web."

Gorlan frowned, "Can Gatherer not re-open a portal to return to his own world? Maybe this would calm the storm?"

Gatherer rubbed his bald head and looked uncomfortable, "I have tried to reopen a portal by carrying out a sensing but I do not possess the sense ability here in Portalia. It is difficult without it as it makes me feel...." He struggled to describe his feelings, "...uh...alone. Cut off from my life and isolated from all I know."

Ashley's voice came to the fore, "Gatherer, my name is Ashley and I am here with two of my friends Rhys and Michael. Like you we aren't from Portalia. We are from a world called Earth and we're also searching for a way home." Ashley then whispered something to Gorlan.

"Ashley has made a good suggestion," said the Warlord. "Gatherer, in Pinnhome there is a wizard called Farspell. He is searching for a way to return Ashley and her friends back to Earth. If anyone can help you he can. I would suggest that you accompany Tosh when he leaves so you can request the assistance of Farspell."

Cambor nodded and placed his hand on the shoulder of the giant, "If anyone can get you back home then it is Farspell. We do not possess deep enough understanding of the portal web here in Eumor and the runestone is useless without the runestone key. I think Ashley's suggestion is a good one. You should travel with Tosh to see Farspell."

Cambor waited for a response. When none came he looked more closely at the desert strider.

Gatherer had gone a deathly white and his stare had become vacant. The giant creature began to shake and convulse. Moving swiftly Cambor reached forward and pulled the ring away from the crystal. Gatherer's convulsions stopped immediately and he quickly regained his senses.

His head was throbbing with pain and he squinted at Cambor.

"What happened?" he asked.

Cambor frowned, before responding he issued a request for feyberry tea to be prepared.

"I am not sure Gatherer but I would hazard a guess that you were once more affected by an incompatibility with the energies of your world and our own. I believe you had some form of fit in response to invoking the magic of the crystals."

Cambor, with permission, removed the crystal from around the neck of the giant and placed it around his own.

"I think it best that you avoid contact with the magic of our world. I fear that it may do you harm. Perhaps it would be better if you passed the runestone ring to another."

"No!" snapped Gatherer and as if in objection an enormous lightning strike lit up the sky immediately followed by a deafening thunder-clap. "I may need the magic of the ring to return to my home. I will not give it up."

Cambor raised his hands to calm the giant. "Do not fret my friend. My words are in concern for your welfare, nothing else was intended. If you choose to carry the risk then no-one will dispute your decision."

Gatherer toyed with the ring as he apologised for his outburst. At his side Tosh looked through the open door as the rain intensified once more.

Cambor followed his gaze and a worried look crossed his face, "I hope this storm lets up soon. A few days of this and the city will start to flood. I do not relish the prospect of evacuating my people."

Gatherer sighed aware that this storm was of his making. He vowed to himself that he would put this right before he returned to his world.

# CHAPTER SEVEN
## Transformation of a Minion

Weldrock stood in his island runestone chamber. He wore both the island ring and pendant. Eager to receive a report from Nexus on events in Pinnhome he had decided to recall his minion.

The warlock brought his ring finger up to the pendant and inserted the small notch in the pendant slot.

There was a momentary shimmer and after a few seconds he was joined on the runestone by Stack and, a few moments after that by Nexus.

His apprentice was not fazed by this recall as the warlock had warned him of it earlier. Nexus had clearly been caught off guard though and appeared wearing only a pair of baggy trousers. His chest was bare and his jaw-line covered in white foam. He had been shaving when Weldrock had summoned him.

When he saw Nexus' face Weldrock began to laugh, and Stack soon joined in the merriment.

Nexus frowned. "Impeccable timing as usual."

Weldrock stepped towards Nexus, "Looks like you've missed a bit," he said with a grin and as he ran his finger along the human's cheek bone, a soft glow emanated from its tip and hair began to sprout, pushing its way through the soft foam until Nexus sported a full grown beard.

Stack double up with laughter while Weldrock smirked.

"Very funny," responded Nexus, "Now what can I do for you Weldrock."

The warlock stopped smiling and scowled, "Watch your tongue Nexus or it will be more than a simple beard that bursts forth from your skin!"

Nexus cowered away from the warlock, "I apologise your greatness, I did not mean..." His words were cut short as an electric charge burst from the hand of the warlock. Pain racked his body as it struck his chest.

Nexus fell to his knees and Weldrock lowered his arm, ending the spell.

"Stand up Nexus and report to me. What news do you bring of the Pinns? Do they still plot my downfall?"

Humbled by the show of power. Nexus staggered back to his feet. He looked down as he delivered his report, unable to meet the eyes of the warlock. Inside his hatred for his current master rose to another level. "They do indeed. A party has left the capital to search you out bent on your destruction."

Weldrock looked excited and extremely interested, "The fools! So they have left Pinnhome poorly protected?" he asked.

Nexus shook his head. "No my lord. They have sent only a small party on the expedition. Ten fire eagles led by Gorlan. The Earth teenagers are with them too."

"And I suppose my nemesis Farspell accompanies them?"

Again his minion shook his head. "No. The wizard remains at Pinnhome."

The warlock looked thoughtful and then let out a loud guffaw. "Gorlan with ten riders and a handful of children. Is that the best effort they could muster?"

"No sire, nine riders. The Earth girl now rides a fire eagle. She was chosen at the recent Ceremony of Choosing."

Weldrock looked surprised, "An Earth child bonded with a fire eagle? You jest with me!"

Nexus shook his head once more, "No Weldrock, it is true. The eagle chose her as its bond partner despite her alien roots."

The warlock stopped laughing and considered this information. After a few seconds he shrugged, "Curious, but hardly a cause for concern. What do they plan Nexus? Surely they cannot hope to overthrow me with such a small handful of riders. There must be something else?"

"I have not been able to gain details of their plan but there are rumours that they travel to the Gates to hire a ship that will carry them on their expedition. Some also say that they will seek the assistance of the sea-elves."

Weldrock looked thoughtful once more. This time it was a few minutes before he responded.

"The sea-elves are too wrapped up in their own concerns to offer any assistance. However, Gorlan can be persuasive and the Earth children bring an unknown factor to this situation. The boy Michael possesses the dragon heart and Rhys the power of the portal web. The sea-elves will recognise these powers and may well be influenced by them."

The warlock walked to his desk and removed the island runestone key. "Nexus, I need to think on these events for a while. I will open a portal gateway to return you back to Pinnhome."

Nexus waved his arms to indicate his lack of clothing, "Umm, I may be somewhat conspicuous dressed as I am. Or should I say 'undressed' as I am."

Weldrock looked him up and down. "A good point." He turned to his apprentice. "Stack, please remove your robe and give it to our friend here."

"No need!" replied Nexus. Reaching into his pocket he pulled out his cloak of invisibility and smiled, "I carry this everywhere, even into the shower. You just never know when a covert escape may be necessary!"

Weldrock inserted the key into the runestone control pedestal and turned it to the slot that would open a gateway to Pinnhome. "Nexus, I wish to ponder the information that you bring and to formulate a plan. I will recall you soon, either by a runestone summoning or via messenger. Be prepared next time. I have no desire to see your half nude, pallid body again."

"I will get as close to the wizard as I can my lord. He worries me though as sometimes I am sure he detects my presence even when I am shielded by my cloak."

Weldrock nodded, "It may be that he is partially aware of you on a subconscious level but if he had even a small suspicion of your presence then he would have uncovered you by now. His powers and sharpness of mind have not yet returned to him fully but he will gain power day by day. You will do well to be cautious. For now though I think you are safe. Now go!"

Nexus turned his back on the warlock, something that he never liked to do. He threw the cloak over his head and stepped through the portal. Back in Pinnhome his network of misinformation was working well; the Pinns had still not discovered the true location of the portal so no city guard rushed to meet him.

On his island Weldrock sighed. Events were moving faster than he had expected. He was not unduly concerned however. The small party sent to search him out were a mere annoyance and, even given the unknown factor that the Earth children brought to the situation, he could easily overcome such a small band. However, up to this point he had all but discounted any interference by the sea-elves. He laughed as the seed of an idea came to him. Rising from his chair he headed for his library to consult his growing collection of magical arts and tomes.

A few hours later, while scanning the pages of a volume entitled "Transfigurations and Deformities" he found reference to a spell that added water to that seed and his plans began to grow.

***

It was morning of the next day when Nexus was once again summoned to Weldrock's island.

On this occasion he was ready for the summoning, having risen early from bed he had dressed and was preparing to walk into Pinnhome to spy on Farspell. The summoning saved him this task and he stepped through the blue ooze to face Weldrock and Stack once more.

"Nexus, I have a task for you. I want you to gain service on board the vessel that Gorlan hires for their expedition. I need you to spy on the Earth children to determine the limit of their powers and also to report to me on any contact with the sea-elves. The elves were friendly towards the dragons and Fangtor was well known in Seahome. I am not sure how they will react to the boy with the dragon heart."

"But sire," responded Nexus, "I am well known by Gorlan and his men. They would recognise me immediately!"

"Do you think me a fool?" he snapped in reply raising his hand beckoning silence. "You will not be recognised. I have the power to prevent this. Physically you will remain unchanged but to all that look upon you your outward appearance will be disguised. Your real self will remain hidden to them. It is an ideal spell for spies and assassins as not only does it hide your true appearance but others will find that while they learn to recognise you, they will find it hard to describe your looks and will be unable to picture your image in their minds."

Nexus nodded his approval but inwardly wondered why the warlock had not used this spell in the past.

From a bench top that held a mass of alchemic equipment, Weldrock withdrew a small vial of cloudy liquid. He passed the vial to Nexus and gestured that he should drink the contents.

"The solution is tasteless and will do no harm. Please, drink."

Nexus frowned but reassured by Weldrock's words he pulled the stopper and drank the fluid in one gulp. As Weldrock had indicated the liquid was without taste but it did possess an unpleasant gritty texture similar to stomach salts. As Nexus drank, Weldrock waved his arms and gesticulated in the direction of the human, muttering words of magic as he circled him.

There was a faint blurring of Nexus' visage and then this cleared to show his new appearance.

Weldrock smiled, "Excellent and very effective. What do you think Stack? Close your eyes and describe to Nexus how he looks to you."

Stack did as he was ordered, "Well, you blurred for a few seconds but then reappeared and looked entirely different. Your hair had gone grey. No wait, it was brown." Stack frowned. "You looked older and seemed shorter, but that can't be right because I was looking up at you so you must have grown."

Stack opened his eyes. "Now that is curious. I cannot recall your features. Now I am looking at you I can see that you are taller than you were with long dark brown hair to your shoulders. You are muscular and have steel blue eyes. You have the looks that will melt the hearts of the ladies but which will still allow you to gain the trust of the hardiest of men. Your skin is tanned which will give the impression of being of outdoor stock and should fit well with your mission. You will need new clothes though as the spell has not changed your clothing and you look rather curious in that cloak. It doesn't suit your new look at all."

Nexus grinned, "I sound really hunky." He walked to the far side of the chamber and looked into the mirror that was hanging there.

"Hang on! I look exactly as I usually do! Is this a trick of some kind?"

Weldrock laughed, "No trick Nexus. As I said, your true self has not changed. To the two of us you continue to look as you always have. It is only others who see you in your new form."

Weldrock turned to Stack once more. "Now that you have seen and described him in your own words, turn away and describe him to me again."

Stack span away from the pair. He stammered out some conflicting descriptive features and then gave up.

Nexus found this incredibly amusing, which irritated the apprentice even more.

Weldrock gave his orders, "Stack, get a couple of the coven members to gather some clothes for Nexus and have Kraan conjure up some work documents. Nexus will need these to gain employment on board. On this mission he will be called Grant Landman, son of a farmer who left his home on the Meadows for a life on the waves."

He turned to Nexus, "Not far from the truth which should mean that even you can pull this off."

Nexus feigned a hurt look, wiping away an imaginary tear, "Now that is cruel Weldrock. I'll have you know that I was renowned for my acting back on Earth. Richard Attenborough would have been proud to have me."

"Richard who?" questioned Stack, "Wasn't he a fisherman out of Sougate?" and with a confused expression he left the chamber to carry out the warlock's instructions.

"Nexus, I have something else for you." Once again Weldrock rummaged amongst the alchemic equipment. This time he pulled out a small black leather case that had been secured shut with three buckles. He opened it and handed it over. Inside were two small vials containing clear liquid, two small white pills, three dried leaves similar in size and shape to a miniature rose leaf and a tube filled with a dark green fluid that seemed to move under its own volition.

"The two vials contain quick acting poison that will kill the drinker in seconds. They should be poured into a larger vessel and mixed with a drink. They possess no taste so will not be detected. The tube contains a disease. Once its contents are consumed the disease will become active and will begin to eat away at the victim, rotting him from the inside. Death will not come for many weeks and the victim will experience incredible pain. The flesh will slowly blacken and rot and will give off a smell of such putridity that even those of the strongest disposition will find it difficult to stomach. As far as I know there are no cures."

Nexus pointed to one of the dried leaves, "Another poison?"

Weldrock shook his head, "No, not a poison." The warlock took all three of the leaves from the case and broke each in half. He ate three of them, one half of each leaf. Nexus looked puzzled.

"These are a little creation of my own," said the warlock, "They are dried leaves of a Pinn rose that have been covered with runestone dust and dried in the sun."

Nexus picked up a leaf and looked at it. It looked like any old dried leaf. "What does it do?" he asked.

Weldrock swallowed the leaves on which he had been chewing and smiled.

"These will allow us to communicate while you are on your little spying mission. When you want to speak with me, eat one of the leaf halves. Our minds will then be connected, but only for a few minutes so use them wisely.

Nexus nodded an understanding; he correctly surmised that the runestone dust allowed the consumer of the leaves to tap into the portal energy to communicate. He had no idea how Weldrock had created the link between the two leaf halves but there would be time to find that out in due course. He carefully placed the three leaf halves back into the leather case.

"And the pills?" asked Nexus.

"Ah yes. They are the means by which you will gain suitable employment. Place one of these pills into a target's drink and they will be susceptible to suggestion for ten minutes or so. When you reach the Gates find out which ship will carry the Pinns and where the captain or first mate lodge when in town. One of these dropped in their ale will allow you to suggest a suitable role on board their vessel. Be cautious though as you should choose a task that will allow you to roam freely and without suspicion. Perhaps a deck hand? Don't request anything lofty as it will draw attention to you."

Nexus nodded, "I have been to sea on many occasions, both on Earth and here in Portalia. I think a cook would be a good role. It is a skill I possess and it will allow me to spy freely on others."

"Good," replied Weldrock. "I will open a portal to The Gates for you. Move swiftly in case you are seen, the portal opens into the outer fringes of Norgate and although not a busy area, it is populated. We do not want to give the position of the portal away at this point. The fools are still floundering in their search for its location which is to our advantage."

Weldrock turned to the runestone and made the required adjustment. As the portal solidified Nexus once again donned the cloak of invisibility and stepped through to the twin towns of The Gates.

# CHAPTER EIGHT
## The Gates

Rhys, Ashley and Michael were sitting on wooden crates on the dockside. They had arrived in Norgate earlier that morning and it was precisely how Rhys had imagined it. A busy port with a hive of activity and a dock packed with a dozen large sail ships. It was just like old Victorian paintings that he had seen hanging in the museums back home in Wales. Well, other than the fact that not all the seamen and passengers were human. Here different races went about their business, dwarves, elves, humans and even a few centaurs.

The teenagers watched as one of the ships, now fully laden, hoisted sail and slowly left the dock. It was a spectacular sight, the brilliant white sails sharp against the blue sky and the azure seawater. They continued to follow its path in silence, each lost in their own thoughts as the vessel veered left and disappeared from view

"Look at him," said Michael in a hushed voice and clearly suppressing a laugh.

Rhys and Ashley looked to where Michael indicated and saw a large chubby dwarf arguing with a man who was clearly trying to gain access to one of the ships. The man was almost two metres tall and dressed in a silk white blouse and dark green knee length breeches. On his feet he wore a pair of long black boots which possessed a platform sole that added six or seven inches to the man's height. In truth he was only a little taller than the dwarf. His face was contorted in rage but, as he was too far away to be heard, the teenagers had no idea why he was arguing, although they could pick out his rather squeaky voice in the distance and the odd word or two.

After a few minutes of heated discussion the man clearly lost his patience and, clenching his fist, he struck out at the dwarf. His target stepped backwards and the man, his weight thrown forwards, stumbled as he lost balance on the platform boots. As he fell to the floor the dwarf shouted for assistance and five burly deck hands sprinted from the ship. Before the fallen man could recover he was roughly hoisted into the air and, with consummate ease, the deck hands tossed him off the dock and into the sea.

A great cheer went up from all around as onlookers laughed openly. Clearly the subject of the dunking was not popular. The teenagers joined in with the laughter, but showed a little concern as the man thrashed about in the water, clearly not a strong swimmer. To their relief, the same set of deckhands threw him a rope and dragged him out before sending him on his way.

Michael smacked his lips, "I'm hungry," he said, "Fancy some nibbles?"

The trio stood and walked along the wooden decking towards the town. The dockside end of town was packed with small shacks selling all sorts of hot and cold food and drink. Most catered for the working men and offered cheap snacks but a few were more upmarket, aiming their goods at the higher class customers of the passenger ships that sailed in and out of port.

As they had eaten soldier rations for a great part of their time in Portalia, the teenagers were content with the cheaper offerings and they suspected that they were not much worse than the dressed up offerings of the more expensive establishments.

"Have you tasted the Hyrax patties?" questioned Michael, "They are superb."

Ashley frowned, "Is that one of those big pig thingies?" Rhys and Michael both nodded, "What does it taste like?" she asked.

"Roast pork and crackling," replied Rhys, his mouth watering as he thought of the succulent juicy meat.

"Go on then and can I have mine with fries. Oh and make it large!" said Ashley with a smile.

Michael approached the vendor, "Three Big Hyraxes please and hold the mayo!" he said laughing.

The vendor, a rugged looking old man with deep creases in a sea worn face stared at Michael without humour.

Michael stopped laughing and his face went bright red. The vendor continued to stare at him, "Well! Are ye going t'order something or not?" he snarled.

Michael replied sheepishly, "Um, uh, yes please. Three Hyrax patties please."

"In't cornbread or plain?" the old man seemed to mellow a bit.

"All three in cornbread please."

The vendor cut three huge chunks of cornbread and divided them up the middle. He then filled these with equally large slices of Hyrax meat. Picking up a large ladle he removed the lid of a large vat of red boiling liquid.

"Blood Sauce?"

The three Earth teenagers looked at each other, "No thank you!" they replied as one.

Taking the patties Michael paid the man and they returned to the dockside where they found Kraven waiting for them.

"They look good," commented the Pinn sergeant, "Where did you get them?" Rhys gave him directions.

"I think I'll head over and buy one too. Gorlan has asked me to send you to the Unfurled Sail. It's an inn further up the dockside. We're going to make it our base while we search out a vessel that will take us into the Mists. Keep following the dockside until it turns to the right and head northwards. Just after the wooden decking finishes you'll come to a stone track and the inn is a few hundred metres up the track on the right, facing the open sea. It's about fifteen minutes walk."

The teenagers followed his instructions and soon arrived at the inn.

"Awesome. What a neat place," said Ashley, "Looking out to sea and with a great beach just across the track." The inn itself looked similar to an old English country pub. It was thatched but to prevent the loss of the roof to high coastal winds, the thatch was covered in thick wooden slats that held the dried grasses below firmly in place. " I hope I get a room looking out to the sea!" added Ashley as they entered the inn.

Inside it was equally welcoming, possessing open stone floors with a large fire in the centre of the bar area. Unlike the wooden benches and stools that most bars contained, this one boasted large brown leather chairs with comfortable arms arranged around low tables. The furniture was not what they expected and added to the warmth of the place.

Rhys looked around, "Cor, this is the sort of place my Dad would like. I could just see him sitting at that window over there on a Sunday afternoon eating roast beef and drinking a pint of bitter."

The other two did not comment. They knew better than to dwell on life back home.

There was an awkward silence for a few seconds but fortunately this was broken as Gorlan descended the open staircase and entered the bar.

"Aha, you've arrived, excellent. Come with me and I will show you your rooms."

They followed Gorlan back up the stairs and down a long corridor that ran the length of the inn. Gorlan paused at the second door on the right, "Ashley, this is your room. It is small but as the only female in our expedition we thought you'd like a place of your own. I am hoping it will only be for one night so make the most of the comfort. The sooner we can find passage to the Mists the better."

Ashley walked into the bedroom. As Gorlan indicated it was small but it was soft, clean and had a comfortable looking bed. In one corner stood a stoneware sink. The room also looked out westwards across the sea, granting Ashley her earlier wish.

"You boys are next door."

All three followed the Warlord to the next room.

He continued, "It's a larger room but three of you will be sharing."

Rhys and Michael made disgruntled noises at the thought of sharing, "Oh, I don't think you'll mind too much. You already know your room mate."

Gorlan knocked the door and a voice bid him enter. He opened the door.

"Hello my friends!" Meld was sat on one of the three beds in the room. He stood and hugged Rhys and Michael; it had been some time since he had seen them and they greeted each other warmly.

He paused when he approached Ashley.

"Hello Ash! Quite a surprise huh?" he said.

Ashley stared at him in disbelief, "Uh, um, how did, I mean, why are..." She gave up trying to speak and threw her arms around him hugging him tightly.

He squeezed her back, equally tightly and her eyes filled with tears. Behind their backs Michael looked at Rhys and raised his eyebrows. Rhys smiled and winked at him.

Ashley held the hug a little longer than is normal for 'just good friends' and it gave her time to regain her composure. Wiping away a tear she said, "What are you doing here Meld?" Then, not wanting to be misunderstood she quickly added, "Not that I'm complaining it is *so* good to see you."

Meld smiled and kissed her lightly on the cheek, "and you too Ash." He scanned the faces of his friends. "As to how I came here? It is mere chance. I am here on official Fortown business delivering invites to those who may wish to attend the memorial festivities later this year. I did not expect to meet you here so I can assure you that the pleasure is all mine!" He beamed at them before addressing Ashley again, "You look terrific Ash, I love the uniform! Gorlan told me all about your new found role. It's amazing, I thought he was joking with me at first and I think it is only now that I see you dressed in a rider's uniform that it has really sunk in. My little Ashley a fire eagle rider! Incredible!"

Ashley forced a smile; she had not liked the 'little' reference. She swallowed her anger and replied. "I know, couldn't believe it myself. Cool huh? Betcha thought I'd fall off!"

"Well um, not really, but I was worried about your fear of heights. Are you OK now?"

Ashley realised that she was still holding Meld's hands tightly and letting go she said, "I think so but there was a moment at the ceremony when disaster nearly struck."

She explained what had happened and Meld whistled in awe when she described how the bird had momentarily been overcome by her fear of heights. When she had finished, Rhys and Michael started to talk quickly about their journey to

Pinnhome and all the things they had seen and done. After a few minutes to give them time to get re-acquainted Gorlan interrupted with a polite cough.

"I am sorry to break up the reunion, but Meld has promised to accompany me to the docks to help secure a ship. I want to get this done as soon as possible so we can be underway. There will be time to catch up with events this evening. Come Meld, we should be on our way."

Addressing the teenagers he continued, "There is no need for you to come with us but I would ask that you do not wander around alone. Stick together if you go into town although I would prefer that you stay here in the vicinity of the inn. The innkeeper is running a tab for us so order what you need."

Gorlan and Meld wished them a good day and left the three alone in the boy's room.

"Now is that a coincidence or what!" exclaimed Michael. "What are the chances that he would be visiting here at the same time we turn up? If I was at home I'd get Dad to buy us a lottery ticket, it must be our lucky week!"

Ashley looked pensive, "Sure thing Mike. Let's go back down to the bar. That patty has left me thirsty."

As she left the room Michael mouthed a question at Rhys, "What's up with her?"

Rhys shrugged his ignorance, "Who knows, she's always like this when Meld is around. One minute happy, the next minute gloomy. It drives me mad!"

Michael nodded, "Yeah, me too. Come on let's catch up with her. Maybe a walk on the beach will cheer her up."

They followed Ashley down to the bar where they found her chatting with the barman. As they approached Ashley introduced them. "Oh here they are. Rhys, Michael, this is Clave, he owns the inn."

Clave greeted them warmly. "It is good to meet you. Gorlan has told me a lot about you. I wish you luck on your journey and hope you can find a way to get back to your homes."

The boys thanked him.

"Now what can I get for you? Some ale or perhaps a lighter drink?" continued Clave.

Tempting as the offer of beer was, all three decided that now was not the time to be drinking alcohol so they ordered kelp wine, a refreshing drink, which, as the name suggested, was fermented using kelp gathered locally. Despite its green colour it produced a tasty, fruity beverage and had an almost negligible alcohol content.

Clave poured the wine and handed it to them.

"So tell me. How are things back in my home land? It has been a while since I last went home."

Rhys and Michael looked confused.

"Oh sorry," added Ashley, "Clave is a Pinn. He moved here ten years ago to open and run this inn. That's why we are staying here. He is an old friend of Gorlan."

Michael responded first, "Oh, I see! Pretty good really. Although we want to get home to our families Pinnhome wouldn't be a bad place to live. Everyone is really friendly and lots of people have helped us settle."

"That's true," added Rhys, "It's amazing how everyone teamed up to help us and provide what we needed to feel at home. I guess the people are still worried about Weldrock but even so everyone seems happy."

"Well that's one thing Pinn's are good at. We remain calm and cheerful even during troubled times. It has brought us through many a conflict and crisis over the generations," replied Clave.

"I know another thing you're good at...fishing!" offered Michael enthusiastically.

Clave laughed. "Well I'm not sure about that when you see some of the catches that the men of the Gates bring home. There are some huge fish out there in the Sea of Mist."

Rhys asked Clave if they could take their drinks out to the beach and he readily agreed. "Just remember to bring the glasses back again though. I lose plenty each year through my customers leaving them on the sands."

"OK! We won't forget," they replied as they left the inn.

At a corner table in the inn a man was sitting watching the teenagers. As they left he downed the remnants of his glass and paid his bar tab.

Clave watched him closely and noted that he had taken the same path as the teenagers, towards the beach. With a frown he decided that he would make Gorlan aware of the stranger and his apparent interest in Rhys, Michael and Ashley. Curiously, as he thought about this he struggled to grasp a physical impression of the man and after a few minutes the incident had faded from his memory.

Outside the inn Grant Landman followed the teenagers down the beach and towards the open sea.

# CHAPTER NINE
## A Tear in the Fabric

Ashley paused as they neared the shoreline. She glanced at Rhys and Michael and an unspoken thought flashed through their minds almost simultaneously. Grinning from ear to ear she said, "Last one in the water is a dork!" Immediately, all three stripped down to their underwear and sprinted into the sea, water splashing high as they met the oncoming waves together. Kicking high to maintain speed against the pull of the water they continued to run until finally diving under the cooling waters.

"Ooooo it's blooming freezing!" exclaimed Rhys jumping up and now standing waist deep.

"It's lovely," replied Ashley, "Stay under and you'll stay warmer. Your body gets used to it."

Michael, a strong swimmer, was in his element and he had already started to do underwater handstands. Rhys relaxed and joined in the fun and was soon diving about and playing water tag with his two friends.

Thirty minutes later they emerged from the sea to fall on the sands, their bodies drying in the sun.

Ashley soon tired of this and went for a walk along the beach. She had only gone a short distance when she noticed something that had been washed ashore.

Unsure of what it was she approached it slowly. The object itself was almost perfectly round, about the size of a soccer ball and greenish colour, *similar to the colour of snot*, she thought to herself.

She poked at it gently with her toe and it rolled away from her. It appeared to be some form of seed pod.

She kicked it a little harder and it soared into the air. It was relatively light for its size and was obviously full of air. Pretty soon she was juggling the seed pod like a football and excitedly she returned to show the boys.

"Look what I found!" she shouted.

Rhys and Michael joined her.

"It's like one of those indoor five a side footballs, "observed Michael, "What is it?"

Ashley shrugged, "I'm not sure, seaweed seed I think! Come on, let's play some one on one!"

Rhys made a goal out of their discarded clothing and took up position in goal with Ashley and Michael fighting for the ball.

"We'll do three and in," said Rhys.

"OK", replied Michael, "First to three chooses whether to go in goal or stay out," and he kicked the seed pod to Rhys.

"Ready?" asked the keeper, "One, two, three, GO!!!" Rhys punted the pod over the heads of his two friends and they raced to get to it.

It was no surprise to either boy when Ashley reached the pod first. It was more of a surprise when she flicked it up with her left foot completely over Michael's head, rushed around him and hit a half volleyed shot that absolutely flew past Rhys.

Rhys laughed, "OK, maybe it's a little heavier than those five-a-side footballs, there's no way you could kick one of those that hard!"

Ashley smiled back, "Wanna bet?" she said and winked at him.

***

Nexus, also known as Grant Landman, was lying stretched out on a small sand dune a few hundred metres along the beach from the teenagers. He watched them playing with a glazed look on his face.

It had been so long since he had played football and his thoughts drifted back to his childhood and some of the few happy memories of those times.

"What could it hurt?" he said to himself. "I could introduce myself to them and ask about their game. I'm sure they'd be willing to teach me and play some two-a-side."

He knew that Weldrock would be furious if he knew the chance he was taking, but the draw of playing a game of football again was just too big.

Rising, he took a deep breath and waved a friendly greeting.

Within a few minutes he was chatting to the trio and Ashley's competitive nature meant she was only too quick to offer to teach him the rules and suggest a two against two game, Ashley and Grant versus Rhys and Michael.

They played for over an hour and Nexus was enjoying himself so much he almost forgot who he was as he laughed and played around with the earth born teenagers. All too soon for his liking Rhys suggested it was time to return to the inn and so, reluctantly, he agreed to a 'next goal is the winner' suggestion from Michael, even though Ashley and himself must have been a good six goals ahead.

As they walked back to the inn Nexus chatted idly to them.

"Thanks for teaching me the game," he said.

"You're welcome," responded Ashley, "Seems to me you're a natural, you picked it up real quick!"

"Yeah, too quick for my liking," responded Rhys, causing Nexus to flinch, concerned that he may have given away the fact that he too was earth-born. Rhys continued, "You walloped us! Two experienced soccer players against a girl and a newbie. You should have been hammered!" Ashley scowled and Rhys winked at her. She took a deep breath which stopped her rising to the bait that Rhys was dangling.

Turning her attention to Nexus she asked, "Do you live here Grant?

Nexus shook his head, "No, I come from The Meadows. I lived with my father and mother on their farm but I lost them both to Weldrock's spider army." Nexus feigned sadness and the teenagers offered their condolences.

Nexus continued, "Home didn't feel the same after that so I decided to travel."

He told them that he had just arrived in town and was looking for employment and that he too was staying at the inn.

"So what brings you to The Gates?" he asked.

Rhys flashed a look of warning to the others but he need not have worried.

Michael responded quickly, "As you can tell we are not from Portalia."

Nexus nodded, "Yes, I know, I realised who you were when I saw you on the beach. You are unmistakable, especially with Ashley's eagle hovering above."

Rhys and Michael looked up. They had not even realised that the bird was there. Ashley did not need to look, she was fully aware of the presence of the warbird.

Rhys smiled, "Yeah, I guess we have become a bit famous since Fortown!"

Michael interjected, "It's weird. Back home I always wanted to be famous but now I think I'd be happy with being plain old me again. That's why we are here; Gorlan is helping us to search for a way back to our world." Wisely, none of them mentioned their mission to search out Weldrock's island.

They arrived at the inn and said their goodbyes. As Nexus watched the teenagers head for their rooms his thoughts turned to The Shimmering Gate, a possible route for the teenagers to return to Earth and he wondered whether he should share this knowledge with them. He felt a warm glow of friendship, a feeling that had been long lost. There was also something about the boy Rhys that bothered him, something familiar that he could not quite place. The feeling was only momentary though. Pulling himself back together he shook off this sudden spark of humanity and reminded himself that it was Grant Landman these kids liked, not Nexus or indeed, Liam Sagot. He could not afford sentimentality, particularly as before his task was done he may well be forced to kill all three of his new 'friends'.

*** 

Standing two metres tall with a long thin frame, the Dramkaan glowed with pleasure. Throwing back his head he let out a roar of laughter, his large goat like horns shining in the blue aura of the portal web. Unlike when Michael had visited the Dramkaan to collect the Cormion Crystals, the creature displayed no ethereal tail and was in full solid form, his lower torso possessing long muscular legs.

Surfing the portal web was no fun in his energy form, there was simply no sense of danger or challenge. In this form, when he fell from his surfboard, he could actually feel pain. This gave him the incentive to stay aloft.

Watching the ebb and flow of the portal energies the Dramkaan picked his moment. As a surge of force rushed towards him he threw his surfboard onto it and rode the wave as it screeched through the cosmos. His body was thrown from side to side and up and down as he rode the oscillations, but, by concentrating hard on his centre of balance, he was able to stay upright until finally the wave that he had been riding dissipated.

The Dramkaan screamed out in elation and threw his arms in the air, "Yes! What a ride!"

This had been one of the big ones and for him to surf the entire length of such a large surge was rare. He flicked up his board and readied himself for the next wave.

Turning his attention to the portal web he noted with disappointment that the energy had calmed, in fact unusually so. Something was not right. There was a disturbance in the flow.

Returning to his pure energy form, he followed the disruption to its origin and stared in horror.

There was a tear in the portal web!

The Dramkaan watched as the familiar blue flow met a green tinged energy that was seeping in through the tear. Where they met they flashed briefly and were replaced with an utter blackness. A growing nothingness that threatened to wipe out everything in its path as it expanded.

Instinctively he knew what he must do. The tear must be repaired.

Left unchecked the forces would spill between dimensions and the very fabric of existence would be threatened.

This was not a gentle folding of the flow, as generated by the runestone portals, or the intricate twisting of the flow, as produced by the oscillating gateways of the ancients, this was a brutal and unskilled tear in the very fabric of the flow.

For thousands of years he had been guarding against this. The ancients citing him with this task. Never had such a tear appeared. Not even the warlocks at the height of their powers could damage the flow. But now someone or something had. Something had wrenched open a link between dimensions. A link that was against all the laws of nature. A link that would destroy all before it and allow nothingness to become the fundamental force of the cosmos.

The Dramkaan frowned. It was one thing knowing that he needed to close the tear but it was another to know exactly how to administer the repair.

Analysing possible solutions he decided that there was only one real option. Significant energy and life force would be needed to seal the lesion. It was time to call upon all his knowledge and strength. He would need conjure and control levels of energy the likes of which he had never before attempted.

Settling his fear, the Dramkaan focussed his efforts on his inner self as his consciousness searched for the power he required. Pulling increasing amounts of portal energy to him, he moulded them with his own life force and his form began to glow with power. Continuing to build his energy store he began to spin. As his form rotated it drew in ever increasing levels of portal energy that, in turn, accelerated the spinning, amplifying the level of transfer.

Finally, when the Dramkaan felt he could take no more, he released the built up energy in one sudden emanation and thrust it towards the tear in the form of a pulsating blue energy ball.

The ball hit the fissure and the Dramkaan held his breath as he watched it fall into the growing blackness. It disappeared, engulfed by the darkness.

For a few seconds nothing happened but then, just as the Dramkaan felt pangs of disappointment, there was a violent explosion and the concentrated power of his energy ball burst back out from the nothing to form a large sphere encircling the boiling mass of colliding energies and nothingness.

The Dramkaan probed the sphere with his mind. It was opposing the rift but was not strong enough to close the fissure. He could feel the force of his energy ball trying to push back the boiling mass of the conflicting energies, but he realised that it simply was not strong enough to force the closure of the tear and that it merely slowed the reaction.

Once again he focussed his effort on creating energy and began to spin until he released a second energy ball.

This time the ball hit his original sphere and the energy dissipated increasing the overall strength of his shield.

It was still not enough; the protective sphere was merely slowing the growth of the blackness but it was not healing the tear.

The Dramkaan tried again and again, recharging the sphere, but the forces involved were too strong. In utter despair he realised that he would need to seek help. His significant powers alone would not be enough to close the fissure. Feeling utterly drained and exhausted he allowed himself to manifest in his solid form. He would need to make a journey but first he needed to rest and recharge. Exhausted, the Dramkaan fell asleep for the first time in his long existence.

# CHAPTER TEN
## The Shii

Weldrock's coven stood before him. Earlier he had unexpectedly asked Stack to call them to an assembly in his runestone chamber. Walking around the gathering he spoke to them as a group. The coven members could not help but notice that Weldrock literally glowed with power.

"My students! You have worked hard in your studies and showed that you are worthy to follow my path. It is now time to recognise your effort and reward your achievements."

Their faces lit up in expectation. Twelve pairs of eyes watched him expectantly.

Thirteen key members in total. Always thirteen, a number denoting power to those that followed the path of the warlocks.

"Kraan!" There was a murmur of surprise when Kraan was the first to be called. He had been one of the less ambitious students, talented but with little drive to seek real power.

Weldrock faced him, almost nose to nose. Kraan trembled as he looked into the warlock's eyes.

"You have studied hard and have mastered the basic skills of manipulation. Your control of the elements of wood and paper are admirable. However, you lack the strength to become a leader of others. Here is your reward."

Weldrock placed his hand on the head of his student and before Kraan could object his body was consumed in a raging fire that within a few seconds had reduced him to ash.

Weldrock paused to enjoy the moment. He watched as the excited expectation of his students changed to one of fear. Earlier he had prepared himself for this ceremony, drawing on the power of fire and stars to charge himself. He knew that the display of power would enthral his students, and indeed, that it would be necessary to kill Kraan in order to make room for a new coven member.

Weldrock smirked as he continued, "I see fear in your eyes." He looked each full in the face as he walked past them. Only two of his coven continued to display any level of self confidence, Stack and a solidly built warrior-like human, Tiborous, another of his star students.

"You are right to fear me but you need not be concerned. The reward for the remainder of you is not death."

There was an audible sigh in the chamber as his students relaxed at his words. Only Tiborous remained impassive to the events. The fighter had seen many strange things in his time as a mercenary and battle hardened, he knew the benefits of hiding emotion and staying focussed.

Weldrock turned his back on his coven without fear and from the corner of the chamber he collected three staffs. Each was approximately a metre and a half in height and topped by a fist sized jewel. The first displayed a rich red ruby that shone with a crimson aura. The second emitted a green hue as the light reflected off and through a magnificent emerald. Finally, a dark blue sapphire displayed its charms as it glimmered.

"These are the Staffs of Light, one for each of the primary colours of light; ruby red, emerald green and sapphire blue."

Turning back to his students he held them out, "Zephyr. Fenwaer and Ryne, step forward. The staffs are your prize. You are deemed fit to bear the name of warlock."

The three students beamed as they stepped forward to take up their reward.

"Your staffs are linked. When used individually they can emit a beam of energy that itself possesses power. However, if you combine the forces of all three staffs they form a brilliant white light that can burn flesh to a cinder within seconds."

The three newly appointed warlocks thanked Weldrock and stepped back into their place amongst the others.

The warlock paused and allowed a moment of silence to increase the tension before approaching Tiborous.

The giant northlander looked straight into Weldrock's eyes; no fear was evident on his face.

"Tiborous, not only do you possess the strength of three, but you have proven to be particularly adept in your manipulation of the forces of nature. Whilst not as advanced as my own skills, your efforts in the generation and control of weather patterns and storm creation have been most encouraging. Further your loyalty would demand a more fitting reward. To you I give the pendant of my Island runestone. You will become one of my most trusted followers and I will teach you all I know of the magics of weather control."

Weldrock held out the pendant and the big man bowed his head to allow him to slip the chain over it. He gave the smallest of nods in recognition of his gift.

Weldrock turned his attention to the remaining six students.

"The rest of you shall be honoured by completing my coven." Signalling to Stack, his lead apprentice removed six jet black rings from a small leather pouch. He handed the rings to each of the remaining students.

"Place these on the index finger of your left hand," ordered Weldrock. All obeyed without hesitation.

We must now join together, hand in hand to form a circle of power. To return our numbers to thirteen I must call forth our final member. For this I will need your combined energy and focussed efforts.

All in the chamber formed a ring, hands joined except for Weldrock and Stack. The warlock whispered a sharp command to Stack who immediately approached the three warlocks of the Staff of Light and Tiborous.

"The four of you must join with me to form a second circle. You do not possess rings so you cannot be part of the circle of jet." So saying he led them to form a second circle immediately to the side of the first.

Weldrock now addressed the six who wore the jet rings. "Together we will perform a conjuration. What you see may alarm you but there is no need for fear."

He held out his hand. Sat on his palm was a small round object, similar to a glass marble and also made of jet. It seemed as black as the deepest of caves. Taking the sphere Weldrock ducked under the joined arms to sit at the centre of the larger human circle.

"This object will allow me to control the creature that we will raise. While I possess the sphere it will be powerless to cause harm, unless I command it to do so. So fear not. You must keep the circle complete until I have the beast under control. If you break the circle then the binding will also be broken and, at best we will lose the creature from the summoning, or at worst, we will summon it without any control." Weldrock turned his head as he spoke to meet the eyes of all six of the bonded humans. "Believe me, if that happens, then you truly will know fear."

Satisfied that he had invoked sufficient terror in his minions to prevent them breaking the circle of summoning, Weldrock began to chant.

"Restorum aliarius Shii. Amorial conjector Shii. Helender ha luciva aliarius! Restorum aliarius Shii. Amorial conjector Shii. Helender ha luciva aliarius!"

There was an ominous silence in the chamber. As the warlock continued his chant the temperature in the room began to drop and the students held onto their colleagues just a little tighter, faces now full of uncertainty.

The black sphere held in Weldrock's open palm began to hum. It rose into the air, hovering a few inches above his hand and began to spin. As its momentum increased the humming noise grew in intensity.

Weldrock was now shouting the spell, *"Restorum aliarius Shii. Amorial conjector Shii. Helender ha luciva aliarius!"* and the black ball was spinning ever faster, the sound filling the runestone chamber.

At a point where some of the coven felt unable to continue the humming suddenly stopped and the sphere fell back into the warlock's hand.

As it hit his skin, black ooze seeped out of it and soon filled his palm overflowing onto the stone surface at the his feet.

The warlock continued the spell in a whisper as even he was feeling some of the trepidation that had filled the room.

When the sphere had stopped emitting the ooze the students noticed that the warlock's hand was now clean but that the pool on the floor had started to bubble and boil.

Weldrock closed his hands, holding on tightly to the orb.

The dark black slime was beginning to expand. From the centre of the bubbling mass a figure was starting to form, pushing its way upwards until a mound of boiling gunk bubbled and frothed, two metres tall. Then, with the warlock still mumbling the spell, the column began to take shape. Two legs formed first, short but strong and muscular. Next came two powerful looking arms, the hands terminated in five long finger like talons. A torso formed, clearly female, still solid looking and displaying full breasts.

As the coven watched, the sound of tearing flesh rang out and two slits formed in the back of the creature. The black ooze spilled out like blood but did not drip to the floor; instead it began to dance in the air until two dragon like wings positioned themselves on the creature's back.

As these wings grew, a heart shaped head moulded itself on top of broad shoulders.. Two sockets formed above high cheekbones and a few in the chamber gasped as these opened to reveal eyes that screamed of evil, two blood red irises surrounded thin, insubstantial pupils. The sclera, normally the white of the eye, was instead as black as night, matching the slit like pupils.

Dark full lips formed as grey teeth grew, the top row protruding out of the lips ending in sharp points overlapping the bottom lip, all except for two lower jaw fangs that grew to almost four inches in length as they jutted upwards. If the creature had possessed a nose then it would have been pierced by these large fangs, but instead, nature had blessed it with two nostrils that were merely slits in the face, lending almost reptilian qualities to its features.

Likewise, the ears too were small slits in the side of the head, no auricle or lobes formed to channel sound. The head remained smooth and hairless.

As the creature stabilised its form, the black ooze turning to a more solid dark blue flesh like substance, Weldrock stopped his chanting and held the black sphere between his fingers.

"Welcome Helender. I have summoned you to serve me. I am the possessor of the sphere and I claim the right to command you."

The creature glared back at him. It hissed a response, the sound of its voice raising the hairs on the back of the necks of those that surrounded it.

"Who are you that daresss to sssummon the Shii? Can you not let me ressst!"

Weldrock stared back defiantly, "I am Weldrock the Warlock and I claim the right to command you as Shangorth did before me. You must summon your sisters. It is time to fly the skies of Portalia once more.

The Shii glared at him angrily. "No, my sssisssters have sssuffered enough. Leave them be! I will not sssummon them." Helender leapt forward and raked her claws at the warlock. Stack jumped to protect his master but stopped as he saw the Shii's talons meet an invisible obstacle.

Weldrock smiled and made a tutting sound as he replied, "Now, now Helender! You know that you cannot touch the bearer of the sphere," and without pausing he squeezed the black orb between his fingers. The sphere was now pliable and soft, malleable to the touch.

Helender the Shii screamed in agony as her body started to contort in synchronisation with the black orb. Her newly formed shape began to twist and the flesh started to seep black ooze once more.

"Enough!" she screamed, "I will obey. Are the hossstsss prepared?"

Weldrock looked at his students nervously, initially seeing only confused expressions and then raw fear as realisation dawned.

"Yes, "he replied, "In a manner of speaking they are. Proceed!"

Not even Tiborous remained impassive during the chain of events that followed.

Helender suddenly vomited and six more small black orbs burst from her mouth. These never hit the floor.

As she spewed them out, the room filled once more with the loud humming, this time six times as loud.

Almost instantly the students broke the ring, raising their hands to their ears to protect themselves from the noise.

The six that ringed the Shii had no time to react as the spheres flew at them. Aiming straight at their heads they entered the men, choosing the closest path to the host brain, through nose, mouth, ear or eye.

The six students fell to the ground, tearing at their faces and hair as the spheres began to spread their black ooze inside their heads. Within seconds the gunk had destroyed their brains and their screams subsided. Then it was flowing back out of every orifice, engulfing its prey as Helender's sisters re-entered the world in solid form.

The other members of Weldrock's coven had made a tactical retreat and had backed themselves towards the main entrance, their faces contorted in horror and disgust.

They watched as Weldrock spoke with the Shii. Eventually, confidence returning as they realised that the beasts were under the control of the warlock, they inched their way back to his side.

Weldrock laughed as they approached, "So now my coven is complete. Kneel before me my faithful flock, show me homage and I will lead you to great things."

Without a thought the five warlocks dropped to their knees. The Shii hesitated and watched Helender. She glared at Weldrock but as he toyed with the black sphere between his fingers she succumbed. As she fell to her knees, her sisters followed suit. Weldrock sighed with relief and pleasure, content that the Shii were his and that his coven was now complete.

# CHAPTER ELEVEN
## The Red Serpent

White foam splashed as the ship skimmed its way across the water. On board the crew were comparatively relaxed as they watched the rigging and kept an eye on the ocean for there was little to maintain on board a Flowrider vessel.

In the galley Grant Landman busied himself preparing food for those on board. It had not been difficult for him to secure the position of cook on The Red Serpent. He had listened intently at the inn and easily discovered the poor wretch who currently fulfilled the role. Befriending the man he treated him to a copious amount of alcohol. Later, as the man slept in a drunken stupor, Nexus crept into his bedroom and poured the contents of the disease potion into him as he snored loudly. By morning the virus had already started to do its work and Nexus smiled when, at breakfast, he witnessed a doctor being escorted upstairs to the lodgings.

Later that day, as Captain Fishnose left the bar to relieve himself, a surreptitious placing of a persuasion pill into the captain's ale had resulted in Grant merely having to suggest that he was searching for employment and he was quickly drafted onto the crew.

Captain Jack Fishnose had skippered The Red Serpent for over twenty years. He had heard of Gorlan's need for a vessel and so had searched out the Warlord at The Unfurled Sail to offer his services.

Gorlan and Meld were surprised when approached by Fishnose, or JF as he liked to be known, as he had understandably taking a dislike to his own rather comical family name. The Red Serpent was well known throughout Portalia and was one of only four remaining flowrider vessels. Gorlan quickly accepted the offer and was delighted when the rugged seaman had agreed terms, even after he had explained their mission to the captain. His day was made even brighter when Meld, lured by the presence of Ashley, readily agreed to join them on their quest

Flowriders were skippered by captains who possessed a unique skill, the ability to channel small amounts of energy from the portal web to 'blow' into the mesh sales of their ships, allowing them to travel even during what would be becalmed days for other vessels. This allowed for travel at full speed in any direction, regardless of the wind strength. While a flowrider could not outrun a standard sailing ship steering its course with a full wind behind, it more than made up for this shortcoming by being highly manoeuvrable and due to its ability to be totally independent of the wind direction.

As Nexus chopped vegetables, high above him JF sense-checked the flow against the heavy mesh sails. The sails of a flowrider had to be made strong to withstand the forces pushing against them, especially when the web forces fought against the blowing winds. If made from standard canvas they would have been torn to pieces so they were crafted from a fine metal weave.

Gorlan approached JF and noticed that he was in an almost dream like trance.

"Is all well captain?" he asked.

JF shook himself back to full consciousness and smiled, "Aye it is," he replied. "You will get used to my little trances. Once I have set the energy flow it rarely falters, but there is a need to check the force occasionally to prevent us veering off our course."

JF was stood on a traditional ship's bridge next to a rather normal looking steering wheel made from a honey coloured wood.

"This is my first sailing on a flowrider," commented Gorlan, "I am surprised to see that you have a wheel for steering."

JF nodded and laughed heartily, his round sea-worn face smiling. He was a handsome forty year old with darkened colouration, his skin tanned by the sea, salt and sun. He looked fit and moved with a litheness that belied his age, clearly the years had been kind to him.

"A wheel is not necessary in truth although it does help when turning the vessel. The steering is done almost entirely by directing the energy flow. Of course, it also makes our crew a little more at home by having a large ship's wheel that they can steer."

Jack kneeled to ruffle the coat of a large friendly looking creature that sat beside him, "Mind you, when Howler here was a pup, we had to teach him not to cock his leg on the wheel shaft or the mast. Thankfully he picked up that discipline very quickly." JF laughed again and the dog looked up him, its large tongue lopping out of its mouth as it nuzzled his hand and face.

Rhys, who had accompanied Gorlan to the bridge, looked at Howler. The dog was very similar in shape and size to the large Irish wolf hounds of Earth but its coat was very short and almost whippet-like in appearance. "What sort of dog is he?" he asked.

JF patted the dog's head as he replied, "He's an Urthound. They originated in the northern part of the Blistering Desert. There are few left in the wild these days, most were domesticated generations ago. A few packs still run the borders of The Meadows and the Desert though. They were originally a pack animal and built to hunt so when domesticated they make great guard dogs and their pack instinct makes them very loyal."

Rhys kneeled too and Howler cautiously scuttled over to him. A word of encouragement from JF made him relax and he was soon licking Rhys's face much as he had done with JF. Rhys laughed as the huge wet tongue coated his face affectionately.

"Yeuch! Get off you big lummox!" he joked pushing the dogs face away from his own playfully.

"How long before we reach Seahome?" asked Gorlan.

JF looked southwest, "At this speed just a couple of days. The energy flow is strong at the moment and I don't sense it weakening at all."

Rhys wondered if the captain's skills were in any way similar to his own. Perhaps he could learn something that would help him to better control the portal gateways.

"How do you direct the energy?" he asked

JF shrugged, "It's hard to explain really, I just concentrate and I can feel the flow, by focusing on it I can bend it to the sails. I've been able to do it since I was a small lad. I used to lie in bed at night and as I dropped off to sleep I'd see these dim patterns swimming around the room. I found that if I concentrated hard enough I could move the patterns, changing the direction of the flow a little.

Pretty soon I was able to do it while awake, but it wasn't until much later, when I reached my teens, that I realised it was the portal web that I was interacting with."

Rhys thought about his own experience, "So when you direct the energy what do you do to control it."

JF shook his head, "I'm not sure I'd say I control it. All I do is bend it a little so that it flows in the direction that I need to steer the ship. As for how I focus; I guess I don't really do much. I just close my eyes and I let myself become aware of its existence. The patterns then form in my mind, they are invisible to the eye."

Rhys sighed in disappointment. It seemed there was nothing to be learned here about how he may control his own abilities for manipulating the portal web forces.

"Hey Rhys, you hungry?" Michael and Ashley were calling up from the deck.

Rhys shouted a reply, "Yeah—a bit peckish!"

"We're going down to the galley. Wanna come?" responded Michael.

"Yep, will be there in a mo'," he turned to Gorlan and JF excusing himself.


Down below decks the galley was quiet.

Grant was busy serving up some soup and bread to the ship's first mate, Ves, and there were three sailors, plates now clean, quietly chatting in the far corner their faces lit by the glow of a ship's lantern that hung above their table. The galley was not large but it did provide an adequate cooking area and four moderate sized oak picnic style tables that allowed for four men to sit in comfort.

The Red Serpent was carrying twenty-seven souls, twenty-eight if you included Howler. Jack had two regular crewmen. His first mate Ves, who was responsible for directing and overseeing the work of the deck crew and his second mate, Trall, a dwarf who maintained navigation charts, publications, and instruments.

Ves, a surly looking human with a bald head and a long deep scar on his right cheek, was an experienced sailor and was tasked with pulling together the deck hands for each trip. His crew of nine split into three shifts, were well managed and his men treated him with great respect, for while he was hard and demanded discipline, he was also fair and treated them well.

This crew, together with the teenagers, the Pinns, Nexus and Howler made up the full ship's complement. Of course that excluded the occasional sea bird that perched itself on the masts as the ship flowed across the ocean.

Ves took his full bowl and tore a large chunk of bread but did not offer any thanks to Landman as he sat on his own at a table next to the other crew members.

Ashley noted that, although it was his usual way with people to be stand offish, Ves seemed to have taken a particular dislike to Grant and avoided any direct conversation with him. Unbeknown to Ashley, the first mate was very unhappy that JF had appointed the new ship's cook without consultation with him, this was an appointment normally made by the first mate. JF had apologised profusely when he realised that he had cold shouldered his first mate and truly did not understand why he acted on impulse. Ves had forgiven his captain but did not yet trust this new member that had so suddenly appeared as part of his crew.

"Hello friends, what can I do for you?" asked Grant turning to the teenagers. "I can recommend the fish soup."

"That'll do me then," replied Michael.

"Me too," added Rhys.

"And me" answered Ashley.

Grant served up three bowls for them and they made towards an empty table. He watched as they sat and noticed that his earlier supposition about Ashley had been correct, she did possess a pendant. What he could not understand was how she had come into possession of it. He had only taken one pendant to Wales so this must mean that someone else had once travelled between worlds and taken a pendant to Earth. He decided he would quiz her on this when the situation presented itself.

Busying himself around the galley, he manoeuvred to a position where he could work but also overhear their discussion.

Between spoonfuls of the creamy fish soup Rhys made conversation.

"This is nowhere near as bad as I expected it to be," he said. "I thought we'd be working our butts off but we seem to have loads of spare time"

Michael agreed, "Yeah, pity there's not more land about though. It does get a bit boring looking at the sea and I've hardly seen any fish or sea creatures since we left the Gates."

Swallowing a lump of white fish Ashley joined in, "That may be a good thing Mike. Have you noticed that the eagles have not left us since we arrived on board? As you know they normally only stay with their riders if there is some kinda danger. All the riders are a little jumpy as a result."

The two boys raised their eyebrows. Neither had noticed the night presence of the eagles.

Ashley continued, "Ves says that he has only sailed with a fire eagle rider once before and the bird never left it's rider that time either. He says it was just as well too!"

"Why?" asked Michael. "What happened?"

"Dunno the full story as he wouldn't explain. Said he didn't want to spook the crew but later Jack told me that they had been attacked by a sea serpent. If it hadn't been for the fire eagle then Jack reckons they would have lost the ship."

Rhys and Michael stopped eating.

"How big was this thing?" asked Rhys.

"Dunno!" she replied. "Clearly big enough to sink the ship though."

The boys continued to stare at her in disbelief until a lump of fish fell from Michael's spoon and splashed in his soup.

Rhys decided a change of subject was in order.

"Had any sea-sickness Ash?" he asked.

"Nope. How about you?" she replied.

Rhys shook his head.

Michael, now knocking back his soup again spoke, "I've felt a little queasy a few times but I've not spewed up! The sea seems really calm and the ship seems to just skim along," he added.

"Yeah, I noticed that too," said Rhys, "I reckon it's 'cos it's a flowrider ship. I've been sailing with my Auntie Glenys and a friend a few times back home. The boat was much smaller though and the trip was much rougher even though the sea looked no choppier than today. Both times we went out I threw up after just a few minutes."

"I didn't know your Auntie had a boat," commented Michael.

Rhys shrugged, "She doesn't have it anymore. She sold it a few years back. Apparently it belonged to my Uncle Liam and..."

Rhys was suddenly interrupted by a loud crash. Grant Landman had dropped the pan that he was wiping. The teenagers turned to the cook and noticed that he had gone white and seemed to be staring at them.

Ashley stood and walked over to him, "Are you OK Grant, you look terrible?"

Ashley's voice brought him back to awareness, "Oh, um, yes!" he stammered. "Sorry, I just feel a little sick. I turned around quickly and got giddy. I think I'll lie down for a while."

As Grant made for his bunk Michael kicked Rhys under the table and whispered behind his hand, "That's your fault talking about throwin' up. I reckon our new ship's cook gets sea sick. How weird is that?"

Rhys shrugged with little interest as he finished his soup.

\*\*\*

Farspell swore, as a rather large and dusty book fell from a shelf above him and struck him solidly on the head.

He was on his hands and knees, crawling on the floor of one of the Pinnhome vaults. A few minutes before, while leafing through some hand written journals, he had found reference to a hidden store room. This room was only accessible through a crawl-way located behind a stone panel at the rear of the fifth vault.

"I'm too old for this!" he said out loud to no one in particular.

Dragging aside a number of boxes and items that blocked access to the rear of the chamber he finally felt the hard wall beneath his fingers.

Mumbling a spell, he waved his hand to create a small orb of light that illuminated the darkness beneath the shelving.

Sure enough, there at the back he could make out a rectangle in the stone work. At the centre of this rectangle there was a circle indentation about the size of an orange.

Farspell pushed the circle and with a scraping of stone on stone the crawl way covering slid aside.

The cubby-hole revealed was almost a perfect square metre at the entrance and only two metres long. The wizard was easily able to scuttle his way through to enter the room beyond. His light orb followed him.

The stone chamber in which he now stood was almost identical to the vault which he had just left. Increasing the illumination of his light orb he saw that the walls were lined with volume after volume of books. He sighed, although it was good to have found the room he had hoped that it would hide a single and powerful secret that would aid him in his studies and help restore some of his dormant memories. Of course, there may well be some critical secrets locked away in these books but it would take months to pick through this new material.

Farspell squinted as he looked along the lines of books. He estimated that there were around five thousand in this section of the vaults. As he scanned the volumes on the shelves above the entrance crawl way he noticed a dark cube that sat nestled among the bindings. Dragging over a stool that also served as a small steps, he climbed up to the shelf and picked up the cube.

The object was made from a dark storm grey stone. On one side the word PORTALUS had been etched. He noticed that a small line stretched across the horizontal plane of the cube that divided it into two identical halves. Raising the object closer to his light orb Farspell ran his finger along the line, then, with his right hand grasping the top half and his left the bottom, he twisted the cube halves in opposite directions.

The faces twisted with hardly a sound. As they did they divided down a fine hinged edge and locked into place. They were now one hundred and eighty degrees apart, forming a small oblong block. From the centre of each cube, two telescopic projections extended downwards towards the floor.

The wizard immediately realised he was holding the device upside down and, turning it over so the projections pointed upwards, he placed the open cube onto the floor.

Once still the block emitted two beams of light, one from each telescopic antenna. The projections overlapped and an image was projected that stretched for some four metres in diameter. Farspell stood next to the block at the centre of this projection.

At first it looked like random patterns of blurred colour but then, as the antenna adjusted height, the beams became focussed and Farspell realised that he was looking at a three dimensional map of Portalia.

At first he marvelled at the workmanship of the device but then his wonder changed to excitement as he realised that various features were indicated on the map. Could it be that this included the location of the runestone chambers and the portal gateways?

He glanced towards Pinnhome on the projection but, to his disappointment, he realised that the scale was too small to offer much help of the location of the portal. However, in order to gather as much from this map as possible, he walked towards where Pinnhome was highlighted to take a closer look, the light splashed around him as he advanced. He reached the spot and stopped. Almost immediately the projection grew, leaping from the floor to surround him. Startled he made to step away but then stopped as he realised that he was now stood inside the city, or at least a projection of the city.

In the image he was at the centre courtyard of Pinnhome, still recognisable even though the projection was clearly very old. Farspell turned his head to look around and the deserted town felt strangely eerie and alien, despite the familiar features.

He stepped towards the main tower but immediately the picture dropped away until he was once again looking at the flat map.

Instinctively he realised that to travel in this projection he would need to use his mind, not his feet.

Entering once more he concentrated on where he wanted to go and pretty soon was able to easily control his direction and speed.

He now had only one objective. Speeding up as fast as the map would allow he hurried towards the locations rumoured to be the co-ordinates of the original portal gateway. Within a few minutes he had found it. There, just a few hundred metres from a current guard site, sat a glowing portal.

Stepping out of the projection Farspell wasted no time. He crawled back through the entrance and made straight for Toran's chambers, not only to tell him the good news but also to get the guard posts changed to the correct, currently unguarded location.

*** 

An added benefit of being the ship's cook was that Grant Landman, also known as Nexus to some and Liam Sagot to others, did not have to share a cabin. Instead, he was given a small area behind the kitchen which provided a secluded compartment for him to live and sleep. It was here, in his bunk, that Grant laid back with troubled thoughts triggered by the overheard conversation of the teenagers.

*How could this be?* He asked himself.

*But then, was it so strange? After all, fates had worked to bring him to Portalia so was it so amazing that Rhys, his very own nephew, had also found his way here?*

Nexus frowned, his mixed emotions causing confusion. He simply could not think clearly.

He raised his hands to his forehead which was now pounding as a headache bit deep.

*I need to think! I cannot let this boy change my plans! He is nothing to me! Until today I did not even know that I had a nephew!*

Nexus was pushing himself hard, trying to overcome the softer feelings that were rising to the surface. First he had befriended the teenagers and found that he enjoyed their company and now this.

He snarled! *Pull yourself together Nexus. Think! Refocus your thoughts!*

He turned on his side but knew that he would enjoy little sleep this night.

*** 

Toran had wasted no time. As soon as Farspell had confirmed the accurate location of the portal gateway he had reassigned the guards and work had begun on the defences.

He stood on a makeshift wooden platform, overlooking the location. Below him, illuminated in the light of a hundred torches, men shifted copious amounts of earth.

As the men dug deeper into the ground, ropes and pulleys were set up to extract the dirt from the expanding pit. This earth was then dumped around the rim to form even higher walls. A gap had been left on the south side to allow access for the digging and excavation equipment but this would be filled later.

On top of the mounds that formed the makeshift walls, large wooden platforms were being constructed. These would provide walkways and battlements for archers should the need arise to protect the town and prevent anyone, or anything, climbing from the pit.

Kul approached his OverLord and addressed him.

"Sire, work is progressing well. A few more hours and we will be at the seventy metre level that was requested."

"Excellent!" replied Toran. "Once the level has been reached arrange a change of shift and focus on strengthening the battlements."

"Yes sire!" responded Kul. The cavalry captain looked a little awkward as he shifted from foot to foot and lowered his voice a little as he continued, "Sire, may I ask a question?"

Toran frowned uncertain as to why his captain showed concern.

"Of course Kul, what is it?"

"Well, this may seem a stupid question but the men have been arguing about what would happen if someone tried to use the portal? Would they appear in mid air and fall to the bottom of the pit or does the portal sink to ground level?"

Toran laughed, "That is not such a stupid question Kul, I asked Farspell the very same! Our wizard is certain that the portal will fall to ground level."

Kul nodded, "I see. And what happens as the pit fills with bodies? Will the portal become blocked or will it rise with the level of the dead and wounded?"

It was now Toran's turn to frown.

"A point well made. Unfortunately we do not know. Farspell suspects that the portal will adjust so that it does not become blocked. If bodies do obstruct the exit then the portal will rise as the pit fills. That is why we want the pit so deep. With the Graav turning to rubble and ash when they die they will have to take heavy casualties to fill it."

Kul nodded understanding and offered a salute as he left to carry out the orders of the OverLord.

***

Farspell felt the tingling of magical energy seconds before the Dramkaan appeared.

The guardian appeared in solid form. He bowed as he addressed the wizard.

"Wizard. I seek your assistance!"

Farspell raised an eyebrow in surprise.

"Now what could the Dramkaan possibly want from me?" he asked. "Have you become bored in your ethereal world?"

The Dramkaan ignored the sarcasm in the wizard's tone. He wasted no time in coming straight to the point.

"Something has ripped a tear between dimensions! I have slowed its expansion but I am unable to close it. I need your help."

Farspell stared in disbelief.

"In all that is holy! I felt something was amiss but I could not place the uneasy feeling that I was experiencing. Hurry, we must go immediately."

Without further comment the Dramkaan grasped the arm of the wizard and both disappeared in a flash as they left the world of Portalia.

# CHAPTER TWELVE
## Desert Encounter

Gatherer was sitting perched on the back of the giant war bird close behind Tosh. He admired the strength of the bird and understood the bond relationship between eagle and rider. As the sun rose in the east, he marvelled at the lush vegetation of the green lands that stretched out below, so different from his dry and barren home world.

Tosh leaned back and shouted above the wind.

"We'll be within sight of Pinnhome soon." He pointed to the east.

"Follow the line of the valley and you will see the buildings rise in the distance."

Gatherer nodded and watched for first signs of the town. A few minutes passed before he was rewarded by the sight of a handful of roof turrets that popped their tops above the horizon.

As if inspired by the sight itself, the eagle beat its wings even faster and they accelerated towards their destination.

Circling the town as they approached a handful of eagles, some carrying riders, flew to meet them. Tosh waved a greeting and looked quizzically at a huge pit that had been constructed on the town outskirts. He directed his bird to land in the central courtyard.

They dismounted. Gatherer became embarrassed, suddenly aware that he was the centre of attention as the eyes of humans, elves and dwarves all stared at him in disbelief.

As he caught the stare of those around him, the crowd, conscious of their rudeness slowly turned away and after shouting a greeting to Tosh went about their daily business.

Tosh offered reassurance, "My apologies Gatherer. It is just that they will not have seen the likes of your kind before and they are naturally curious. Do not be alarmed. No-one will wish you harm."

Gatherer nodded, "No need to apologise. I too am somewhat overwhelmed by your world."

Tosh led Gatherer across the courtyard where they met Toran who, having been informed of their arrival, had hurried out to greet them. Tosh admired the control of the OverLord as after welcoming Tosh he introduced himself to Gatherer without a hint of surprise or bewilderment in his expression.

Gatherer felt immediately at ease and as he relaxed he provided a brief explanation of how he came to be here and his intent to ask the assistance of Farspell in helping him find a way back home.

The OverLord looked saddened, "Gatherer, you are most welcome in our town and I will make arrangements to ensure you are comfortable. Unfortunately I fear that you will be unable to ask Farspell for his help at present. The wizard disappeared last night. We have no idea what has become of him although it seems he left his rooms peacefully as there are no signs of conflict or abduction. We can only hope that he is well and that he is undertaking some important task. I am sure he will return soon but I cannot help but be slightly concerned as it is not like Farspell to disappear like this."

"I am sure that you are right sire," added Tosh, "The wizard is more than capable of looking after himself and I am sure he will return soon. He cannot have gone far if he left no word of his departure."

Gatherer shrugged, "I hope that you are both right. It seems that Farspell may be the only one who can help me return to my world." He bowed his head to Toran, "I thank you for the invitation and for your hospitality. I will await his return as you suggest."

Toran shouted for one of his staff to escort Gatherer to a guest room and to ensure that he had everything he needed to make him comfortable. As Gatherer left their presence the OverLord readdressed Tosh, "And what of the Cormion Crystals Tosh? Were you able to persuade the council to part with one?"

Tosh smiled, "No persuasion was necessary. Cambor gave me one almost without question." He reached into his cloak, withdrawing the crystal he handed it to Toran.

"Excellent," said the OverLord. "Now we need to find Farspell as without his runestone artefact we will not be able to invoke the magic of the crystal."

"That would be desirable sire," countered Tosh, "But if he cannot be found our new friend Gatherer possesses the runestone ring of the Celtic Knot. He will aid us if necessary."

"How in hell's thunder does Gatherer come to be in possession of a runestone ring?" asked Toran in surprise.

They told the OverLord of Gatherer's find in the desert and he nodded his understanding.

"It is good that we have an option, however, I would still rather we find Farspell. His sudden disappearance greatly troubles me. I fear that he is in great danger."

***

Farspell stared at the tear in the energy flow. The gaping centre of nothingness had now expanded to the very edges of the shield formed by the Dramkaan and it was about to break through.

He frowned, "You have done well Dramkaan but we need to move quickly. The tear is likely to accelerate as it grows and if it breaks out of your shield then I fear it may be too large for us to control."

The Dramkaan grunted in response, fully aware of the dangers.

"Then let us begin wizard," he replied and once again he began to spin, gathering in energy.

At his side Farspell went down on one knee and focussed his mind on the singular objective of channelling forces from both the portal web and the alien force into an energy ball of his own.

They did not speak but both knew that they would need to combine the forces that they were gathering and simultaneously thrust them towards the fissure. Both also knew that the magnitude of the forces on which they were calling could easily destroy them in a fraction of a second.

Sweat formed on Farspell's brow and he dropped onto two knees as he felt himself tiring, all of his energy being pushed into his spell. His energy ball was now pulsing with a blazing blue-white aura as it grew in intensity.

The Dramkaan, now spinning at a rate the likes of which he had never experienced before was drawing ever increasing levels of force towards him, storing the energies up like a giant capacitor.

He watched as Farspell, now almost falling forward in stress and strain, directed his energy ball towards him. It floated closer and closer until suddenly the outer edge touched the boundary of his force.

The Dramkaan was racked with pain, a sensation which he had never experienced. He screamed in agony as, fed by the power ball, his rotation began to accelerate faster and faster, he was completely out of control.

"Ddddddo it nnnnnnnow!" yelled Farspell.

Fighting for control as the wizard's energy ball enveloped him completely; the Dramkaan gave a scream and released their combined spells into the fissure.

As the conflicting forces of tear and spell met there was an enormous but silent explosion of light. The back-draft of the collision hit them and threw them into the air.

The Dramkaan, still in his solid form swiftly changed to ethereal as he felt his body being ripped apart, even so, his cloud-like form was thrown over and over until finally, the force dissipated and calm returned.

The Dramkaan immediately turned his attention to the fissure. Elated he saw that the tear had been repaired. The undulating currents of the portal energies now flowing normally once more, the nothingness dispatched back to where it belonged….nowhere.

He turned triumphantly to the wizard.

"Wizard, we did…." He stopped short.

Farspell was nowhere to be seen.

\*\*\*

Nexus checked that the galley was empty and took a position where he could see clearly if anyone entered. Taking one of the rune leaves from his box he popped it in his mouth. The bitter taste was a shock to his taste buds so he swiftly chewed and swallowed the leaf.

After a few seconds he began to feel light headed and he fell into almost a trance like state, although he remained partially aware of his surroundings.

The warlock's thoughts thundered in his head, much deeper and more fearsome than his spoken voice.

"Good, so what have you discovered?" he asked.

Nexus struggled a little with this new form of communication and the warlock became frustrated.

"Oh come on you moron! Just think your words in your head as if you were saying them. It's not difficult. All you've thought so far is grhmphly humpble do!" he snapped.

Nexus listened and soon had mastered the technique.

"It is pretty much as we suspected. Gorlan leads a band of riders and is accompanied by the earthlings. They have enlisted the aid of a flow rider, Jack Fishnose, commander of The Red Serpent. Our first destination is Seahome where they plan to ask for the assistance of the sea-elves."

"Hmmm. As you say, much as we thought. None of this concerns me other than the fact that the earthlings bring an unknown quantity. The sea-elves may recognise the dragon spirit in the boy Michael and may respond to his request for help. The power that Rhys possess still worries me. If he learns to control the portal flow then he will become a great threat. The girl is less of a problem. She is merely an inexperienced fire eagle rider and I can have the Shii take care of her at any point."

The warlock fell silent for a moment pondering the information.

"Nexus, I think it would be safer if the two boys were eliminated. Both bring uncertainty to any plan and I believe it would serve my purpose if you killed them both. Use the poison vials to achieve this. They will not be detectable and the others will think they have succumbed to an illness."

Nexus hesitated, the scruples of Liam Sagot leaping to the fore. He quickly suppressed these thoughts, concerned that the warlock may be able to detect them during this mind link.

"You are very quiet Nexus! Do you understand what needs to be done?"

He shook himself and replied, "Yes master. Consider it done. The boys will not live to see the sun rise tomorrow."

Nexus felt his head begin to clear and the mind link with the warlock was broken.

He flopped in a chair. Despite years of being tainted by the dark powers the thought that he may be required to assassinate his very own kin turned his stomach. The hard-nosed, tyrannical character, Nexus, was finding it difficult to cage the human emotions of Liam Sagot.

Nexus chastised himself. *C'mon you fool. Ultimate power will soon be in your reach. This is no time for sentimentality!*

Shaking himself free of his doubts Nexus examined the two vials of poison and formulated his plan for delivering the concoction to Michael and Rhys.

***

Farspell fell flat on his back with a solid thump. Stunned by the impact of the blast and his heavy landing, he laid still to give himself time to recover. As his senses returned he became aware of others close to him and felt a cold steel blade against his neck, the sharp point of the weapon pushing against his throat.

He opened his eyes and found his vision blurred. He sensed that there were five creatures surrounding him and from the shapes that he could make out through his distorted vision, two of them were holding weapons to his throat.

On the positive side they had not yet killed him which would suggest that the creatures possessed intelligence and were, hopefully, merely just being cautious.

He heard a voice, "Who are you? From where did you come? How is it that you can fly through the sky?"

The wizard tried to respond but found that all he could do was croak an unintelligible reply, his mouth and throat dehydrated from the energy forces to which he had been exposed.

"Patience Lowrunner. I believe he is injured. Let him drink from our waters." This was from a female voice, soft and compassionate.

Farspell blinked a number of times in an effort to clear his vision but no tears were secreted to clean his eyes.

He watched the shapes moving and became aware of the intense heat of the sun on his skin. One of the creatures approached him and Farspell recoiled as it brought its face to his own. He felt dry lips touch his and a warm sweet tasting liquid, water like in consistency, ran down his throat.

Understanding the intent of the creature he drank down the fluid greedily, literally embraced in a kiss of life as he felt the liquid revive his body and mind.

When the creature withdrew the wizard cleared his throat and spoke again. His vision began to clear but he had to squint against the intensity of the desert sun.

"Thank you. My name is Farspell. I am a wizard from the old world. To whom do I speak?"

There was a pause before the female responded.

"My name is Sandmover and these are my colleagues, Lowrunner, Dunebuilder and Senseteacher. We are of the Dry Dune clan. To which clan do you belong and what manner of creature are you?"

Farspell, still squinting to shut out the intense sun, continued. "I am not of a clan. I believe that I am from a different world to your own as I have not heard of Dry Dune and my surroundings feel unfamiliar."

He blinked hard again and finally tears welled up and his vision began to clear.

"I assure you I mean you no harm and, as you can see, I am unarmed. I am from Portalia and I believe I was thrown into your world while trying to repair damage that threatened both of our worlds. Something had caused a tear in the fabric of our realities which, if left unchecked, would have consumed us all."

His vision now clear he stared at the desert striders that stood above him, magnificent in their height and clearly well adapted for the dry, cruel desert world that stretched around them.

He frowned as he observed the group. He had obviously been mistaken; there were only four of the creatures not five as he had first thought. Even now his senses seemed to indicate five but there were no others in sight and he could see for some distance in all directions. To the north, west and south a great sandy desert stretched out into the distance while, to the east, a lake shimmered in the sun. There were dark clouds overhead which were swiftly dissipating and the heat of the sun was already forming a mist above the lake as the heat evaporated the waters below.

"Sheath your weapons!" the order came from one of the male creatures, clearly a little older than the others and obviously the voice of authority in the group. He addressed the wizard as Farspell stood up rather slowly and groggily.

"I am Senseteacher. I apologise for our defensive attitude but there have been a number of strange events occurring. First we lose our gatherer and then we find an enormous rain storm raging above the Wildrock Oasis. It has been many generations since rain fell on these lands."

Farspell raised his hand in acknowledgement. "There is no need for an apology. Tell me, did the rain clouds subside when I appeared?"

Senseteacher nodded, "They did indeed. Were the events linked?"

It was the wizard's turn to nod, "I believe so. I suspect that the rain storm was caused by the same powers that I witnessed. Thankfully I seem to have closed the rift but I am afraid it may mean that the rains will not return."

Senseteacher looked sad, "That is a shame. Water brings life. However, if the cause of the rain fall was not of the natural order then I am glad that you have repaired the damage. Already the rains bring relief. The plants of the oasis will have the chance to thrive once more."

Farspell glanced at the newly formed lake. "You say you lost your gatherer? What is a gatherer?"

"Not what, who." replied the female who had introduced herself as Sandmover.

"Gatherer is my mate. We call him by the name gatherer as he gathers food for our tribe. He was out on a gathering when he disappeared. We have found many of his items here at the oasis but no sign of him or any struggle."

A hopeful look crossed her face.

"We thought that he had been slain and dragged away but could it be that he too has been spirited away by this anomaly? Could he have been transported elsewhere as you have been transported here?"

Farspell looked into her eyes and knew immediately that she spoke from love.

He nodded, "Yes, it could be. When opened the rift may have pulled him from this world to another. Although, I must be honest and say that I do not know if this has happened and whether he could have survived such a journey. I think there is hope but…"

He stopped in mid flow as he espied the mountain runestone pendant hanging around Sandmover's neck. Pointing to it he asked, "Where did you get that?"

She immediately put her hand to the pendant protectively.

"It was a gift from Gatherer. He found it on his last gathering. Do you recognise it?"

"I do indeed!" replied the wizard, "It is a runestone pendant of our world. It carries great power and allows the wearer to travel great distances via a web of portal energy."

Sandmover lifted the pendant and looked at it thoughtfully.

"Gatherer discovered other items when he found this. He retrieved them from the body of a being similar in form to you but much shorter."

Farspell nodded, "I believe that the creature was a dwarf, an evil little character named Zarn. What else did Gatherer find on him?"

"A ring engraved with the symbol of a knot and a small crystallised stone," she replied.

"The runestone ring of Eumor! Where is it now?"

"Gatherer wears it. He gave me the pendant but I insisted he keep the ring."

The old wizard looked thoughtful, "These events must be linked. I am not sure how but I suspect that the forces of the runestone artefacts were somehow activated and caused the dimensional tear."

He looked into Sandmover's eyes. "My dear, if I am right then there is a good possibility that Gatherer is still alive and has indeed been transported to my world."

Sandmover beamed, "You really think so?" she asked.

Farspell shrugged but smiled to reassure her, "I cannot be positive but yes, I believe that it is highly likely."

Sandmover continued to smile as she replied, clearly her spirits had risen with this news, "I understand. There is an element of the unknown. However I feel *sure* that he is alive. I think I would know if he had passed on."

She took the pendant from around her neck and offered it to Farspell.

"Can you use this in some way to return him to me?"

The wizard shook his head.

"The runestone to which that pendant is linked has been destroyed. I'm afraid that it is of no use to us. Keep it for now as I see that it is dear to your heart."

Sandmover nodded and placed the pendant back over head.

"You also mentioned a crystal of some kind? What does this look like and where is it now?" he asked.

"It is about this size," Sandmover indicated an oblong using her finger and thumb, "and of a whitish colour."

It was now Farspell's turn to smile broadly.

"Excellent! I believe that what you have in your possession is one of the Cormion Crystals. These can be used to communicate with other wearers of the crystals. There are a set of four in total. Where is the crystal now?"

Sandmover pointed to the horizon. "It is with Tribemaker at our home at Dry Dune."

At her side Senseteacher spoke once more, "Dry Dune is less than a day's journey from here. I would suggest that we return to Tribemaker to discuss matters and decide on a course of action."

Farspell nodded agreement, "Most definitely. The Cormion Crystal could well be the key to a solution. I fear that you will need to assist me though, my legs are still a little shaky."

Senseteacher smiled, "Your frame will offer no challenge to a young desert strider like Dunebuilder." As he spoke the younger strider stepped forward and lifted Farspell into his arms.

"Light as a baby!" he said, "Lead on Lowrunner."

The wizard flinched as he was lifted but soon relaxed into the giant creature's arms as they headed back across the desert to Dry Dune.

\*\*\*

Nexus in his guise as Grant Landman watched as Rhys and Michael put their food and drinks on the table and sat down. It had been almost too easy to slip poisoned drinks to them, both tending to order sweetgrass tea with every meal.

He watched as the teenagers chatted and laughed as they ate but as he watched a tinge of remorse began to sweep over him.

*This is my kin. I should not be doing this!*

He started to feel panic rising in his gut. What could he do, it was too late to stop this. He had already administered the poison.

Watching closely in horror he noted that Rhys and Michael reached for their sweetgrass tea almost simultaneously.

Tears welled in his eyes but suddenly an idea came to him.

Pushing over the large pan of hot water he screamed out loud, "Arggghhh! Rat in the water! Rat in the water!"

The boys immediately put down their drinks and eyed it suspiciously before investigating the cause of the commotion.

Moving swiftly, his back turned obscuring their view, Grant mimed picking something off the floor and pretended to throw it into one of his covered bins.

"What was that?" asked Rhys

"Euch! A rat must have fallen in the water when it was boiling. For god sake don't drink that tea. Portalia knows what germs it may be carrying," replied the cook, sweat running down his brow.

"Here, let me take those cups from you and I'll get you fresh drinks."

Grant Landman rushed to the table and swept up their drinks. He threw the contents into the galley bilge hole and the offending fluid disappeared from site draining into the ocean.

"I am so sorry," continued Grant, "I have no idea how that rat got there. You know that I keep a clean kitchen. Please don't tell anyone, I'll never live it down."

Rhys smiled, "I reckon someone was winding you up! How could a rat get into that pot itself, you always keep it covered?"

Grant feigned surprise, "That is a very good point Rhys. I think I know who it was too. I bet it was one of those northmen! They are always messing me around. They've gone a little too far this time though. That rat could have been laden with disease!"

Rhys nodded, "Well at least you found it in time. There's no real harm done. I'd keep an eye on them if I were you though Grant."

The boys returned to their table. Michael leaned to Rhys and whispered softly, "I think he's losing it. Did you see any rat? I didn't!"

Rhys frowned, "Me neither. He had his back to us though so it may have been a small one."

"I guess so." Michael scowled at his plate as he turned over the dark meat of the stew with his spoon. "I don't want this now. God knows what's in it!"

Rhys was already tucking into his food. "Don't be daft. It's the same stuff that we always have."

"Which is?" asked Michael.

Rhys stopped chewing, "Well it's, uh, um, uh...."

"Yeah, go on," urged Michael.

"Well it's, uh........ meat!" announced Rhys triumphantly.

Michael shook his head and pushed his plate aside. "I think I'll leave you to it!" Unconcerned Rhys continued to spoon in the stew hungrily. Clearing his plate and wiping it clean with a chunk of bread he took Michael's bowl and helped himself to seconds.

***

Dunebuilder lowered Farspell gently to the ground and helped him to regain his feet.

"Thank you," said the wizard, "Are we resting here?"

They had arrived at a clear flat area surrounded by sand dunes.

Dunebuilder shook his head, "No. We are home." He pointed to Sandmover who stood deep in meditation with outstretched arms.

Farspell gasped when the dome of Dry Dune appeared before them. "Ingenious!" he muttered under his breath.

As Sandmover opened the entrance Dunebuilder bent to lift Farspell once more but the wizard raised his hand. "No. I feel much better now. I will walk."

Farspell was amazed at how quickly they had moved across the sands. He was thankful for the strength of Dunebuilder as the desert sun had beat down on them relentlessly and he realised that he would not have been able to make the journey on foot. The desert striders seemed almost oblivious to this heat but Farspell was forced to use a minor shielding spell to fend off the rays of the sun. Even so he could feel the sweat pouring from his brow and the desert striders took turns to provide him with their body water, sensing his need.

The wizard had felt safe in the arms of Dunebuilder as they skimmed across the sands and yet he could not shake off the uneasy feeling of the presence of another. On a number of occasions he had scoured the dunes, sure that there was someone, or something tracking them. On the fourth occasion that he had mentioned this to the desert striders, Senseteacher called for them to halt and he took a sensing and reassured them that there were no other creatures in the vicinity.

Farspell followed his companions into Dry Dune and they led him to the central stone clearing where Gatherer had earlier shared his last gathering. There was a buzz around the village as the occupants saw the wizard for the first time and Farspell felt many eyes watching him, some inquisitively but others with suspicion. He noticed the symbol of the sun below their feet and correctly surmised that the elder character stood at the very centre of this symbol was Tribemaker. The villagers gathered around the clearing eager to hear news from the search party and to learn more of this strange creature in their midst.

Senseteacher approached Tribemaker and spoke quietly so that others did not hear. When he had finished the elder whispered a reply, Senseteacher gave a nod of acknowledgement and left the clearing.

The clan wiseman now turned to the crowd that surrounded the clearing, circling to address all as he spoke.

"Striders of Dry Dune! The creature that you see before you is to be considered a friend. He is Farspell and he is a wizard and not of our world."

There was a murmur of amazement but Farspell felt the atmosphere relax as the tribe accepted his presence. He realised that the desert striders possessed links with their life energies as, once they had accepted his presence, they emanated a strong aura of friendship and trust which he was able to sense using skills he had developed over the years.

"Farspell possess knowledge that is beyond our own. He has offered help to return Gatherer to us," continued the elder.

A question came from one of the crowd, "Then Gatherer lives?"

Tribemaker shook his head, "That we do not know but we hope so. With Farspell's assistance we will try to find out."

Behind Tribemaker the crowd parted as Senseteacher returned.

Farspell saw that his new friend was carrying one of the Cormion Crystals and he smiled broadly as Tribemaker instructed him to hand it to Farspell.

As he placed the crystal around his neck he let out a sigh of relief as he felt the familiar glow of the magical essence still locked within. Now all he had to do was unlock that magic. He frowned. He knew that this may still not answer the mystery of Gatherer's disappearance or indeed, provide a solution as to how to return both of them to their home worlds. The weight of responsibility hung heavy on him. He now had the hopes of two worlds relying on his knowledge. He turned to Tribemaker.

"Thank you. I will now invoke the magic of the crystal. Do not be alarmed by what you see; the images are merely an illusion similar to that which you use to hide your village."

Farspell held his runestone pendant in one hand and brought the crystal into contact with it.

There was a blinding flash as a bolt of energy leapt from the sixteen pyramids that powered the dome. They struck the Cormion Crystal and the wizard was thrown into the air. The force caused him to drop the crystal and once contact with the pendant was broken the energy dissipated.

Farspell shook himself as he recovered his feet. He looked at Tribemaker.

"Ah!" he said. "I think we have a problem."

# CHAPTER THIRTEEN
## Crystals and Sea-elves

The mesh sails of the flowrider slackened as Jack Fishnose lessened the energy flow. Obediently, The Red Serpent reduced its momentum to a slow crawl and finally to a stop. Howler sat up, ears pricked. He stretched and lifted his huge front paws up onto the ship's rail. Looking ahead he let out a loud howl as he espied land.

"Hush Howler!" ordered JF. The dog looked at him forlornly, but fell silent.

Ahead of the ship, still a few miles away, loomed a large cliff face. The sea between was filled with the outline of jagged rocks. Flurries of snow white foam leaped into the air as the waves pounded against them.

Gorlan climbed up onto the bridge and followed JF's line of sight towards the distant island.

"Is that Seahome?" he asked.

JF nodded. "We will need to set anchor here until the sea-elves come to us. There is only a very small and ever changing channel through to the island. We will need the knowledge of the elves to lead us through."

Gorlan stared across the choppy waters, "How do we contact them?"

JF gave a belly laugh, "Hah! We don't. We have to sit here until their curiosity gets the better of them and they send someone to investigate."

"And if they don't send anyone..." countered the warlord.

JF shrugged, "Then we either have a long wait or we will have to push on without them."

A look of frustration crossed Gorlan's face.

"There must be a way of signalling to them," he said as his eyes searched the ship.

JF leaned nonchalantly against the thick trunk of the main mast.

"Well 'tis true that we have a number of signalling methods aboard but the elves will pay no heed." He nodded towards the island, "If they come they will come when they are ready."

Gorlan was agitated, "We do not have time to sit and wait!" He turned to the lower deck.

"Kraven!"

The Pinn rider turned to his warlord, "Yes sir!"

Gorlan gave his command, "Take your eagle and fly to the island. Give my regards to the sea-elves and ask that they grant us passage for an audience with King Treon."

Kraven acknowledged his orders as his eagle flew from the mast head. He mounted. Man and bird set off swiftly towards the cliff face.

Hours passed.

Gorlan paced the deck impatiently. Ashley tried to calm him, but after he had almost bitten her head off, she decided to make herself scarce and so searched out Rhys and Michael. She found them towards the stern of the boat. They were playing a form of deck quoits with some of the crew. This involved pitching small circles of rope towards a round target of concentric circles. Each circle, except the one in the middle, had four spikes projecting upwards from each quartile. The circle in the middle, the bull's eye, had only one spike located at the very centre. The idea was to pitch the rope rings into a sector, preferably over the spikes which doubled the points for that ring. The closer to the middle, the higher the score.

Rhys and Michael were very good at this game and made a formidable team. She watched as they narrowly beat a couple of deck hands.

"Ok if I join you guys?" asked Ashley.

"OK with us," replied Rhys, "But you'll need a partner as we're playing doubles."

A gruff deep voice boomed from behind Rhys, "I'll partner with Ashley". The boys turned to see the dwarf Trall, the ship's second mate.

A murmur went around from the crew. It was highly unusual to see Trall without his head buried in maps and charts or tinkering with the ship's equipment.

"What's up Trall? You had enough of that cabin of yours?" quipped one of the sailors.

A nervous laugh rang out amongst the crew members present.

Trall turned to the joker. His one good eye glared. The other, lost in a fight with pirates years before, was now stitched over and gave him an ominous look.

"I came to check out what that god awful smell was!" replied the dwarf, "If I had known you were out here then I would not have bothered. I thought something had died."

The joker stopped smiling as, the tables now turned, the crew now laughed heartily at him. With a mumble he stormed off.

Trall looked at Ashley and bowed. "Lady Ashley, Eagle-Rider, would you do me the honour of being my partner for a game of deck quoits?"

Ashley smiled back, "It would be a pleasure Second Mate," she said as Rhys handed her three rope quoits.

Trall stepped forward to join her. Ashley had never been this close to him before. She noted that he was of diminished height, even for a dwarf, and the top of his head only reached her chest. He sported a thick tuft of orange-red hair that was thrust out of his head like the bristles on a paint brush. Huge eyebrows wrapped themselves half way around his head and his long bushy beard, also a shocking orange-red, hung down his chest like a thick mat.

"Too formal for me girl," he responded, "Call me Trall. I apologise for not making your acquaintance before but I do tend to get a little wrapped up in running the ship and plotting our course."

Ashley laughed, "Thanks Trall, we had noticed!"

Trall turned to the boys. "So lads, what's it to be. Best of three or five? It's been a while since I dabbled with the rings but I used to be quite a demon with them."

They agreed a best of three and it became fairly obvious that Trall was not as rusty as he had suggested. After warming up during the first game, when he and Ashley had lost heavily, they struck back and narrowly took the second game.

The third and deciding game was close. Each had one quoit remaining and the scores were level.

Rhys was the first to throw his last quoit and it landed in the centre circle but not over the spike. Five points.

Ashley stepped up with her last ring. She tossed it with the flick of a wrist. It caught the edge of the spike of the second circle from the centre and, after teetering on the edge for a second, slowly slipped over it. Four points, doubled to eight.

Mike knew he needed a good throw to go ahead. The crew shouted encouragement and whistled as he prepared. Then, holding his breath he tossed the ring. A cheer went up as it not only found the very centre of the target but also landed over the spike. Maximum points for Michael, five doubled to ten.

"So," said Trall as he held his final quoit, "A four spike or five spike needed to win the game. Four spike was always one of my favourite shots. Let's see if I still have it in me!" He winked at Ashley as he prepared to throw.

He gripped the quoit lightly and with a gentle back hand toss he launched the ring towards the four spike.

The watching men held their breath as the rope ring seemed to float towards the target. It homed in on the four spike and the eight points needed for victory.

Suddenly, with a loud twang an arrow screamed through the air. Just as the rope ring fell to loop the four spike, the arrow hooked it up and carried it beyond the target. It impaled itself on the wooden deck with a loud thud.

"Looks to me like you missed dwarf!"

Trall, sword drawn had turned to the interloper. On the deck stood a sea-elf, bow in hand and dripping sea water onto the planking.

"Why you scum," exclaimed Thrall. "I should…"

Rhys and Michael were forced to jump aside as Trall leapt towards the archer who, for his part, stood fast and made no attempt to protect himself. Just when they expected blood was to be spilled, Trall threw down his sword and threw his arms around the elf in a strong embrace.

His face broke into a huge smile and he joyfully greeted the intruder.

"Trelane! It is good to see you. How are things in Seahome?" The dwarf held the elf at arms length as if to inspect for damage.

The sea elf laughed and slapped the dwarf on the shoulders. "All is well with me my old friend and with my family too. But how are you, we have heard some dark stories of times beyond Seahome?"

Trall shrugged, "I'm faring fine lad, but we shall talk more of the problems facing Portalia later. Come on, I'll take you to the captain."

***

The Pinns had searched for clues for two days but still had no more idea about what had happened to their wizard.

OverLord Toran could not hide his concern from his wife.

"Do not fret my love," she said in an effort to ease his fears. "Farspell has been regaining his old powers each day and I am sure that he is more than capable of taking care of himself. No matter what has happened."

Toran reached for her, "Melis my love, what would I be without you?"

She smiled as he hugged her tight to his chest and she nestled her head against his broad shoulder.

A knock on their chamber door broke their intimacy.

"Enter!" commanded Toran.

Tosh entered the room, Gatherer followed behind loping along and ducking his head as he passed through the doorway.

"You sent for us sire!"

"I did indeed Tosh." The OverLord turned to Gatherer.

"Our efforts to find Farspell have been in vain. We will continue to search for him but, in the meantime I must ask for your help."

Gatherer frowned at the news but responded quickly, "But of course. What do you need from me?"

The OverLord pointed to the giant's hand the runestone ring. "I am aware of what occurred in Eumor but I must ask that you use your ring to open a link to Gorlan once again. I know that this will bring you pain but we will keep the communication short and hopefully avoid any reaction."

Gatherer nodded, "I will gladly assist. It may be that Tribemaker now wears the crystal. If so I will be able to speak with my people."

"Thank you Gatherer," said the OverLord as he handed his Cormion crystal to the giant.

Without hesitation the desert strider brought the crystal in contact with the runestone ring.

Three images burst into life before his eyes.

One of them through the eyes of Ashley showed an expanse of ocean and an approaching island. Sea-elves broke the surface of the water ahead.

The second displayed an empty council chamber in Eumor as Cambor sat at a table deep in thought

The third caused Gatherer to cry out in delight as he recognised Dry Dune. The wearer of the crystal was examining one of the pyramid shaped rocks that formed the dome of the village. As the communication link was made by the invocation of the crystal, the Dry Dune image flicked violently and the wearer threw his arms over his face as he swiftly jumped away from the stone pyramid.

Toran recognised the arms immediately, "Farspell! By thunder what a relief. Where are you and how do you come to be in possession of a Cormion Crystal?"

Farspell recovered his composure as he realised that this time the pyramids offered no threat. He looked into the face of the Pinn OverLord. With a deep sigh of relief he replied, "Toran, am I glad to see you. I presume by the fact that you have opened a link that you have Gatherer there with you?"

Toran looked stunned at the mention of the desert strider but comprehension swept over him when Gatherer announced that Farspell was on his own world.

"We do indeed Farspell. However, before we speak further..." The OverLord turned his attention to the sea image. "...Ashley, could I ask that you join your crystal with your pendant. The forces involved seem to cause Gatherer discomfort."

Ashley did as she was asked and Gatherer was able to relax as he moved the crystal away from his ring finger. Ashley was now the controller of the link.

"Thank you Ashley," said the OverLord. "Cambor, please accept my apologies for disturbing you."

The image in Eumor shifted a little as the centaur walked to a mirror so that the others could now see him too. "There is no need for an apology OverLord; I was taking a break from some of my bureaucratic duties so you are not disturbing me in the slightest. Would you like me to remove my crystal to give you privacy?"

Toran shook his head, "No, not at all. Our communications will be open to you at all times but thank you for the offer." Toran shifted his line of vision back to Sandmover. "Farspell, please explain to all how you come to be on Gatherer's world."

It took a few minutes for the wizard to brief them on what had occurred with the rift. He explained how he suspected that the magics of both worlds were out of sync in some way, colliding in their energy patterns in a potentially catastrophic way.

"So is the rift now repaired?" asked Toran.

Farspell nodded, "I believe so. The storm has ceased and I presume that it was the force of the closure that blasted me here."

"So how do we get you two back to your own worlds?" asked the OverLord. The expression of frustration on the old wizard's face answered the question even before he replied.

"I am not sure. When Rhys and Ashley return we could combine the Eumor ring and pendant to recall all runestone artefacts, and their wearers, to the runestone. Although I am worried that with my presence here another such event may open an even greater tear in the dimensional flow. That said it may be that the damage is only caused when invoking Portalia forces here on the desert world. I was unable to create a Cormion link earlier but it seems that by invoking the link in Portalia there are no adverse effects. I will ponder the dilemma. I'm sure I will find a solution but, for now, both Gatherer and I are stuck where we are."

A movement was seen at the periphery of Farspell's vision and Sandmover walked into view, seemingly transfixed by the image of Toran.

Farspell once again felt the presence of another as Sandmover walked towards the projection. She reached her hand out to try to touch the OverLord and shivered as her fingers passed through the image. Farspell turned to see if anyone had accompanied her but, apart from the villagers milling around, they appeared to be alone. This time, his senses now sharper than before, he suddenly understood what they were telling him.

"Sandmover, come stand next to me." He said as he gestured for her to approach. "Toran, this is the mate of Gatherer."

Toran did not need to be told as he saw the tears in the eyes of the giant standing before him.

As they watched, Overlady Melis gestured to Gatherer, prompting him to hand the crystal to her. Gatherer looked thoughtful for a moment and then he passed it over. The images quivered and jumped as the crystal changed hands but then, as Melis held it securely it steadied and regained clarity.

"Gatherer! My love! You are alive and well!" exclaimed Sandmover. As they looked at each other there were tears in the eyes of both.

"Sandmover, I am sorry. I should have listened to you when you warned of the danger ahead. I have left you alone and I do not know how to get back to you."

Sandmover, shocked by the tears in the eyes of her usually resolute mate, quickly regained her composure, eager not to upset him any further.

"Do not worry my love. Farspell is very knowledgeable. He will find a way to bring you back."

Gatherer forced a smile. He blinked his multiple eyelids to clear his vision of tears. "Yes, you are right. We will be together again soon. Take care. Tell the tribe that I miss them and I hope to make this gathering one never to forget. I will bring back a hoard beyond their dreams."

She laughed, "I think just having you back will suffice."

They both touched their own noses with their index fingers in a sign of affection as Toran prompted the desert strider to take back the ring and crystal.

"Farspell, we have built our defences around the portal gateway but I truly need your council here in Pinnhome. Do what you must, but find a way back. I would rather not chance a runestone recall but I will do so if it is the only way for you to return."

"I will do my best Toran. I cannot invoke the Cormion crystal from here but I will carry it at all times."

Ashley and Rhys watched this exchange in fascination. Ashley had turned to face away from the island and the others could see that they were in a small boat accompanied by Gorlan. The boat was being rowed towards the island by Jack Fishnose. Overhead Ashley's eagle hovered protectively.

Toran turned his attention to his Warlord. "Gorlan, I see that you have arrived at Seahome. Once you have discussed the mission with King Treon and Queen Elena please ask Ashley to re-open a Cormion link."

"I will sire," replied Gorlan obediently.

Toran raise his hand in salute. "Goodbye all and good luck!"

He gestured for Ashley to break the connection and all three images dissipated.

Toran looked at Gatherer who was wincing and rubbing his head.

"Are you alright?" he asked.

The giant strider nodded, "Yes, just a slight head ache, nothing more."

Tosh poured his friend a glass of water and handed it to him. The desert strider looked at it and smiled. "The water of life," he said. "In my world a glass like this would be invaluable. Here you have it in abundance." He winced again in pain.

Melis placed her arm around the waist of the giant and spoke to her husband. "Toran, I think our guest may need to rest a while."

"Wait!" interrupted the giant. "Please take this." He handed the crystal and the runestone ring to Toran. "It is far more important that you hold the abilities that the ring and crystal offer and I now know you will use them to help me find my way home. I give this to you willingly."

Toran bowed his head in respect and thanked the desert strider.

Tosh took his tall friend by the arm, "C'mon big man, let's go and get that head fixed," and he led him out of the royal chambers towards the kitchens.

Immediately after the breaking of the Cormion link Farspell stared at Sandmover.

"You did not tell him!" he said accusingly.

Sandmover feigned ignorance, "Tell him what?" she asked.

Farspell looked at her and smiled. He did not reply.

Sandmover felt awkward with the silence and eventually broke it, "I do not want him to know," she added. "If he cannot find a way to return his heart would be broken."

Farspell nodded his understanding.

"Please keep my secret for now. When the time is right I will tell him." she pleaded.

Farspell agreed. As they walked back to her Dry Dune home he watched her and wondered what the gestation period was for a desert strider. How long would it be before the rest of the tribe realised that Sandmover was carrying Gatherer's child?

# CHAPTER FOURTEEN
## Seahome

J F brought their boat to a halt in a small rock hewn harbour sheltered from the thrashing seas beyond.

As he moored the boat, Ashley stared at the sheer rock face that blocked their path to Seahome.

Above this rock face the upper levels of buildings could be seen towering over them. High within she could see narrow windows and movement but, from this seaward side, there appeared to be no visible entrance to the city beyond.

As they climbed out of their boat onto the smooth rock that served as a mooring, two sea-elves leapt out of the water towards them. Ashley watched in amazement as, in mid air, the elves transformed their powerful tails into a pair of green tinged legs. As they landed nimbly on the rock she saw that each carried a handful of globe-like objects the size of tennis balls and made from what looked to be some form of silver scaled fish skin.

One of the elves addressed the new arrivals.

"Welcome to Seahome. I have been instructed to take you to King Treon." He did not smile and to the earth teenagers the abrupt attitude did not suggest a warm welcome, despite his words. Gorlan and JF did not seem offended however. They were clearly used to the gruff nature of the sea-elves.

The elves handed each of their visitors one of the skins and Rhys and Ashley watched as their colleagues stretched it over their heads to form a tight helmet. They looked like two bank robbers wearing head stockings about to carry out a heist. Rhys could not suppress a grunt of amusement.

"Place the skins over your heads," instructed Gorlan. "They will stop you swallowing sea water and also provide oxygen for you to breathe. Just as importantly they will equalise the pressure of the air in your body so that you do not get the diving sickness from ascending from deep waters too quickly." Ashley realised that he was referring to the bends that can also afflict divers on Earth.

They frowned at Gorlan and looked puzzled, "Why? Are we going swimming?"

Gorlan nodded. "It is the only way into the city. The entrance lies under the surface of the water."

The earthlings looked at each other and shrugged. They pulled the skins over their heads; they felt tight and uncomfortable and painfully crushed their noses against their faces.

As they donned the skins a second boat moored and they were soon joined by Michael, accompanied by Trall and Kraven. They too were handed skins and when all were suitably protected the elves indicated for them to follow and leapt back into the sea.

As she submerged Ashley felt the diving skin on her face soften, no longer tight and constricted but supple. She watched the elves as their bodies, now with tails once more, pushed through the water with ease. As she admired them she realised that through natural reaction she was holding her breath. Remembering the words of Gorlan she tentatively took a breath in, half expecting a mouthful of water. As she inhaled she felt the movement of water against her new artificial skin and her lungs filled with pure air as the skin filtered the water to allow her to breathe oxygen.

To her left she saw Rhys break away from the others and kick to the surface. Sensing he was in trouble she kicked her legs to follow him. One of the elves was way ahead of her and even as she changed direction the elf had reached Rhys and was supporting him on the surface of the water.

Ashley arrived to find Rhys struggling a little and arguing with the elf.

"It's no good!" he shouted. "I can't breathe!"

The elf was trying ease his fear but Rhys was in a stressed state. Ashley intervened. The familiarity of her voice calmed him.

"C'mon Rhys. Chill! It really isn't that hard. Just breathe normally." She encouraged.

Rhys settled and assisted by Ashley and the sea elf he once more dived beneath the surface. The others were treading water, waiting for them. Ashley swam next to Rhys to offer her support. Once he had taken a few breaths his confidence grew and they were soon swimming deeper following the shimmering water trail of the elves.

With Rhys now sorted, Ashley was able to take more notice of her surroundings.

The water in the natural harbour was probably some ten metres deep, so the sunlight streamed through and painted the sea bed below in a splendour of colours. Oranges, greens, blues, yellows and reds of all shades stretched out below and the waters, warmed here by the sun, teemed with life. Tropical like fish displayed their colours and patterns as the earth teenagers swam on, transfixed by their surroundings.

Still following with the others Ashley had to fight the desire to explore this new world. She noticed that Rhys and Michael had also slowed their progress, also admiring the scene that unfolded before them.

The feeling of tranquillity suddenly deserted Ashley, as a sudden injection of adrenalin shot through her body. Something had hold of her foot. For a moment she panicked but then realised that it was Gorlan. The Warlord was pointing ahead.

She looked in the direction he was indicating and saw a large ring of rock on the cliff face. The ring was around two metres thick and had a diameter of over twelve. It had been intricately carved to depict scenes and creatures from all over Portalia. Amongst the carvings, colours gleamed where pieces of coral and gem stones had been used to bring the fresco to life.

She noticed that the two sea-elves were treading water in front of the ring but the way through was barred by two large polished wooden doors. As they caught up to them, one of the elves swam to the underwater cliff face and placed his hand against a spherical projection that was mounted in the carved ring. The object was a huge pearl that glowed in the sunlit waters.

As soon as the elf touched it, the wooden doors that barred their way began to slide to either side, allowing access. Gesturing for them to follow, the elves entered and when all were through, they closed the doors by using a similar pearl mounted on the inside. Once the huge doors had closed, the elves kicked upwards.

As the group broke the surface, they found themselves in a long, wide inner harbour. The cliff face was now behind them and looked very similar to that which had faced them from the seaward side. Ashley saw that it provided a large wall that protected the real gem of the city that lay a few hundred metres behind it.

Yet again, for the umpteenth time in the last few minutes, she found herself awestruck.

The city was stunningly beautiful. The greyness of the cliffs belied the grace and complexity of the buildings that lay beyond. Buildings of differing shapes and sizes were scattered in a maze and large towers broke the skyline above. All had been built from a substance that looked very much like mother of pearl. The bright cream of the buildings shimmered with the colours of the rainbow as light refracted off their surfaces to give them a magical quality.

Beyond the buildings Ashley saw that the countryside levelled into green rolling hills. She followed the line of the cliff wall as it disappeared into the distance on either side but she could not see where it ended. She wondered if it stretched all around the island or just faced the sea on the city side, bringing protection more from the crashing and erosive waves than any invading enemy.

The elves led them to the water's edge and exited in front of a large ornate palace that seemed alive as its walls danced in the sunlight. In front of the palace a long stretch of coarse grass, bordered by beds of bright blue flowers, was cut in half by a path of shells that led to the main entrance.

Now bipedal once more, the elves walked up to the path where they were met by Trelane, the elf they had met earlier on board The Red Serpent. Trelane led them inside and they entered into a large high domed reception hall.

Comfortable chairs and soft furnishings graced this incredible room, and towards the centre, reclining in two remarkably ornate armchairs, sat a male and female sea elf. Both shone like the palace around them, their silver white hair striking against the tinged green of their skin. Ashley knew immediately that this was King Treon and Queen Elena.

As Trelane approached the Queen stood and hugged him.

"How are you today mother?" asked Trelane.

"Very well thank you Trel. I walked along the cliff tops this morning and the sea breezes seemed to have blown away my worries." She smiled at her son as she spoke. "I hope that tonight I shall sleep more peacefully."

The queen then turned to her guests and greeted them warmly. They bowed to the thrones acknowledging the status of their royalty. At Elena's side King Treon sat, stern faced. His dark, piercing eyes watched the newcomers intently. After a few moments of awkward silence he spoke.

"Why are you here Gorlan? What do you want of us?" The king directed his question at the Pinn warlord.

Gorlan had been expecting a cool reception but he was still a little shaken by the aggressive tone in the Treon's question. He took a moment to settle himself before replying.

"King Treon. I have been sent here by my OverLord to request your assistance in hunting down Weldrock and his Graav. I am sure you have heard of the events that occurred at Fortown. It is only a matter of time before Weldrock recovers and strikes once more. Our mission is to rid Portalia of his threat once and for all. In this quest we would ask for the assistance of Seahome."

The king merely stared back silently, a slight scowl crossing his face as he finally spoke, "The affairs of those beyond our walls are not our own. Weldrock offers no threat to Seahome. He visited us many moons ago and assured us that he has no plans to include Seahome in his conquests."

Gorlan raised his eyebrows in surprise. He had not expected this. Weldrock had been bold indeed to approach the sea-elves.

"That may be so King Treon but I am sure you know that Weldrock is not to be trusted. He will turn on Seahome in due course and if he is allowed to get a foothold on the mainland you will be hard pushed to resist any attack."

The king raised his hands as if to command silence, "I have considered this Warlord. Weldrock would be foolish indeed to take on the might of Seahome. It would also seem I have more faith in the strength of the combined races of Portalia than you do. I am confident that you will defeat Weldrock without the need for my sea-elves to be put at risk."

Queen Elena interjected, "But what of my dreams Treon? They become stronger each night. In them I see death and decay for all races of Portalia, sea-elves included."

Treon's expression softened as he looked at his queen. "My dearest, I have no doubt that these are one of the futures that could await us, but which path will lead us there? Are you seeing the future based on our kingdom joining forces with the alliance or otherwise? We cannot tell."

Queen Elena looked saddened, "I understand my beloved and I am powerless to help you. I do not know which path will lead to this slaughter either."

Gorlan sighed unsure of how to respond. It seemed to him that Queen Elena could be persuaded to support their cause but how to do this without alienating both the king and queen? While he pondered he noticed the king stand and approach Michael.

"And what say you dragon blood?"

Michael gave a small start as he realised the king was speaking to him.

"I'm sorry your majesty," he stammered, "Are you asking my opinion?"

Treon look directly into Michael's eyes. "Yes, I am asking you dragon blood. You do not remember do you?"

Michael frowned, unsure to what the king referred.

"Here dragon blood, take my hand."

Michael cautiously reached out to join hands with the king. As they interlocked a flood of memories swept through his mind.

*He was Fangtor the red dragon once more, flying high in the sky above the ocean. Below him a battle raged. Sea-elves protected their fortress home from a terrifying creature. A giant squid-like monster, two hundred meters in length, dark blue in colour and armed with ten long tentacles that secreted a dark oily acid, clambered up the cliff top battlements of Seahome.*

*Sea-elves attacked from all directions but their efforts were in vain. Not even their seametal arrows could harm this monster. Flaming barrages of spear and arrow were also quenched as the shafts hit a slimy protective layer which coated the creature's skin.*

*Every few minutes the creature would pause to scoop up the bodies of the fallen sea-elves from the waters below, waters now awash with dark red blood mixed with its own inky secretions. Taking the bodies in its tentacles it used its immense strength to crush them into a growing elven meatball. The creature was hungry and would eat well today. It could sense the life forces of thousands more elves in the city beyond the cliff face.*

*The dragon watched the carnage below. He knew of the sea-elves and remembered them as honourable, he had no quarrel with them, but neither did he have any reason to make an enemy of the sea monster.*

*In the city below he saw some of the elves pointing up to him. Normally he would have expected the elves to hide in fear, the usual reaction to seeing a dragon flying over their home, these however appeared to be waving to him for help. Those pleas persuaded him, he would indeed assist them.*

*It took just two passes. On the first pass Fangtor blew a warning bolt of fire over the heads of the sea monster and the defending sea-elves. The sea-elves immediately fell back, some realising the dragon's intent and others in terror of the mistaken belief they were now to fight two huge attackers.*

*The sea monster itself was clearly not so intelligent. Its large white gelatinous eyes saw the dragon and momentarily watched it fly overhead before it resumed its hunt for food, driven by the desire to eat.*

*Fangtor turned sharply and made his second pass. This time he ejected a blinding sheet of white hot flame at the creature.*

*The intensity of this flame was far too severe for the glutinous layer that protected the creature. It swiftly dried and cracked and the scorching heat reached beyond. There was a deafening noise of a high pitched scream as flesh seared.*

*The giant squid fell from the cliff face back into the ocean. As Fangtor made another pass it saw the creature dive below the surface. The waters closed over its body and a single tentacle reached out to grab the meatball that it had created then it too disappeared below the surface.*

*Fangtor was glad that the creature had decided to run rather than fight. He had no desire to slay the beast. All around he heard the cheers of the sea-elves although he noticed that many still watched him in fear, uncertain of the dragon's intentions. They need not have feared, Fangtor was not in the habit of killing other creatures without reason.*

*That day he was welcomed to the city and a great feast was given in his honour. He remembered eating until he felt ill and whiling away the night in friendly banter with King Treon and his new bride-to-be, Lady Elena.*

It took just seconds for this memory to reappear and immediately Michael understood the bond of friendship that existed between King Treon and Fangtor. Momentarily he wondered whether the king would resent the fact that Fangtor had died to save him but instinctively he realised that this was not the case as he saw the king smiling for the first time since they had arrived.

"Well," asked the King Treon. "What are your thoughts on this?"

Michael knew that the king addressed the dragon in him rather than the inexperienced earthling. As such he resisted the temptation to mimic Gorlan's plea. He paused and allowed the dragon memories to come to the fore.

*Michael saw visions of death and decay. He experienced memories of the Warlock Wars where evil did not stop its advance regardless of borders, pacts or beliefs. He remembered the aura that surrounded Weldrock in the battle of Fortown. Not as intense but so similar to that of the powerful warlock ruler Shangorth. He knew immediately what he should advise.*

"Your Majesty," he said. "The evil that drove Shangorth is reawakened in Weldrock. If the warlock is victorious on the mainland he will not stop at your borders."

King Treon nodded and a stern expression returned to his face.

"I understand but yet I am still hesitant to send my sea-elves to confront the warlock."

Behind him Prince Trelane whispered to his mother before offering a solution.

"Father, perhaps there is a way of helping the alliance and yet remaining largely anonymous at this point. Let me lead a small group of our soldiers to help locate the island in the Mists. I know the waters as well as any sea elf."

King Treon was horrified at the suggestion of sending his own son but a look from his queen made him realise that this was inevitable. She smiled supportively as her husband agreed to the request.

"Very well, but go carefully my son. I will not forgive myself if you do not return."

Gorlan sighed in relief and bowed.

"I thank you King Treon," he turned to the Prince and his mother. "And you also your majesties. We will be honoured by your presence on the quest. Prince Trelane, when will you be ready? We would prefer to leave as soon as possible."

"Very well," replied Trelane. "I will prepare immediately. I will have you escorted back to ship and will join you there."

As Gorlan and his colleagues were led away Prince Trelane hugged his mother tightly.

"Take care my son," she said as tears rolled down her cheeks.

# CHAPTER FIFTEEN
## A Fight in the Ocean

A heavy moist fog hung in the air, as Stack inspected his new legion of Graav, five hundred strong. The light, dimmed by the density of the fog, darkened the rock skin of the Graav and Stack could not suppress a shiver as he looked into their emotionless eyes of fire.

His orders were simple. He would go ahead of the main force to sweep clean the Pinnacle Mountains and foothills to the north of Pinnhome. Similarly, Tiborous commanded a force and was ordered to purge the Red Hills to the south. They were given three days to complete this task, more than enough as neither location offered any serious opposition. The vast majority of those living in the hills and mountains were smallholding farmers and huntsmen. No match for an army of Graav.

Once they had secured the higher ground, the conquest of the Pinn valley and capital would be led by the three Warlocks of the Staff of Light, at the head of one hundred legions of Graav and accompanied by three of the Shii.

With the mountains and hills to the north and south of Pinnhome controlled, the main force would then be free to focus their effort on the city itself. Weldrock was confident that the city would fall in less than a day and then he would enjoy control of northeast Portalia. From there conquest of the remaining lands would be simplicity itself.

Helender and the remaining three Shii were to remain with Weldrock's two defensive legions on the island with their master. Helender was not happy with having her Shii divided, part of their strength was in their togetherness, but she was in no position to disobey.

Stack heard footsteps approaching through the fog and the unmistakable figure of Weldrock slowly emerged from the gloom.

"Are you ready Stack?" he asked.

Stack nodded confirmation.

"I have sent Tiborous through the portal to the Halfman Forest. From there he will make his way northeast into the Red Hills to carry out his mission," Weldrock smiled as he spoke. "I think our old friend Stycich will have a shock when Tiborous appears with his army. He'll be terrified!"

Weldrock had had no contact with the halfmen creatures since his defeat at Fortown. He knew that by now the halfmen would know that they had been betrayed. Stycich headed a dying race of halfmen; with very little opportunity to reproduce, he had been promised human women as breeding companions. Weldrock knew that the women would have killed themselves before giving their bodies to the ugly halfmen creatures and so he had used the Soul Orb to control their minds. However, he also knew that there was no way that the halfmen could successfully breed with the human women but that it would take the halfmen some time to realise this, enough time to allow him to use them for his own devices.

When Farspell had destroyed the Soul Orb at Fortown, the souls of the captured women rushed back to their bodies. Appalled by what they had done, and repulsed by the halfmen, the women had turned on their captors and the creatures had been forced to slay them all. Weldrock knew that he would no longer be able to rely on the services of the halfmen clan. One day soon he would have to deal with them but, for now, they offered no threat so he would leave them be.

Stack and his army of Graav followed Weldrock to the runestone chamber.

Weldrock inserted the key and adjusted the settings. A portal shimmered into life, a doorway to the Pinnacle Mountains in the north.

As the Graav marched through, Weldrock gave one last command to his apprentice; "Remember, purge all life. The main force will attack in three days."

Stack acknowledged his understanding and followed the Graav through the portal.

\*\*\*

The Red Serpent cut its way through the waves, a long white wake trailing out behind like some intricate bridal gown. Overhead blue skies, interspersed with fluffy white clouds, would normally have cheered all aboard, but ahead the crew could see the large bank of mist fast approaching. Within a few minutes they would be engulfed by them and would have to slow their pace as they would be sailing blind. In the waters ahead swam Prince Trelane with six of the king's guard. Curiosity piqued by the sea-elves, a pod of dolphins swam amongst them weaving patterns on the ocean surface as they cut back and forth across the path of the ship.

JF slowed the Red Serpent to a crawl as its bows approached the fringe of the mists. Even the sea-elves had stopped, treading water at the edge of the foggy barrier.

JF brought the ship to a halt next to the stationary elves. Trelane swam to the vessel and a rope was thrown to him. He grabbed onto it and three of the crew pulled him aboard.

"Are you ready JF?" asked the Prince.

"As I'll ever be," replied the captain. "I will stay close behind you as you scout our path. The Red Serpent has a deceptively small draft so we can sail in shallow waters of less than two metres."

"Very good. We will be heading in a north westerly direction. My people do not venture into the mists often but there have been times when we have explored this far. There is an island chain less than half a day journey from the perimeter of the mists. We should be able to find it fairly quickly and this will give you a sheltered harbour to anchor for the night."

JF nodded and Trelane turned and dived from the deck back into the ocean below. Trelane watched the Pinn riders as they called their eagles to the ship. The eagles would not be able to see through the mists so it was safer for the eagles to remain aboard even though they could probably find their way back to their bonding partners via instinct alone.

The sea-elves formed an arrow shape in front of the boat with their Prince at the centre. This would allow him to easily communicate with each elf as they scouted ahead and to the sides.

JF shaped a small amount of energy flow into the mesh sails and The Red Serpent slowly advanced into the mists. Almost immediately the world seemed to go incredibly quiet. The thick, damp, dense mist dulled all sound. Even the splashing of the waves below was heavily muffled.

The dolphins did not follow and, as if by way of warning, they barked to the elves as they disappeared from sight.

True to their word, a few hours later the sea-elves led The Red Serpent to safe harbour. It had been tough to track the path of the sea-elves. The last two in the formation were only just visible through the mists. On a number of occasions JF had lost sight of them and was forced to stop the ship until the elves returned. Fortunately Prince Trelane had an idea to help with this. Sending two of the sea-elves to search the sea bed they returned with a string of luminescent sea weed that he called globpod. With this strung about the necks of the sea-elves they were much easier to see in the waters below and JF was then able to track them with ease.

Watching from the poop deck of the ship Ashley could not suppress a giggle when she first saw the sea-elves garbed in the glowing seaweed. She was reminded of a summer trip to Hawaii, the seaweed resembling the Pacific leis. These, however, were decorated with insipid grey almost colourless flowers and with ugly seed pods that were filled with a putrid looking liquid that that gave off the bright green glow. Unlike the leis, these globpods did not seem to offer a welcome but they were a suitable tool for the task in hand.

However, after hours of squinting and straining to keep track of his guides, JF was relieved when he docked the vessel in the natural harbour. The mists here had thinned and stars peeped through. This was the first time that the sky had been visible since they had entered this cursed region. The morale of the crew lifted noticeably, fuelled by the lessening of the claustrophobic fog that carried with it a feeling of despair. It was easy to understand why ships rarely returned from voyages into the mists. The very air itself seemed to breed discontent and despondency.

Keen to take advantage that this safe harbour offered, JF ordered nearly everybody to the shore, leaving just himself and a couple of shipmates onboard to tend the vessel. Tents were broken out and a camp set up for the night. Within a few minutes the crew had lit a campfire and joints of meat were brought from the ship's cold store and were now spitting as they roasted above the flames.

Ashley was sitting on the beach with Meld, Rhys and Michael. The sand felt good under their feet as they wiggled their toes in the grains. They noticed how cold it felt compared to the beaches back home. Clearly these beaches did not see much in the way of sunlight to warm them.

Ashley lay with her head in Meld's lap and he combed her hair with his fingers as they spoke quietly.

Rhys and Michael had watched the two grow closer as, while onboard and away from the prying eyes of the towns, the two had both shaken away the shyness that they had exhibited and finally recognised that there was an undeniable attraction between them. Over the past few days the two had taken every chance they could to be together.

"Look at those two!" said Rhys as he looked on.

"Yeah. About flipping time innit? Hopefully this will mean fewer moods from her holiness. She always seemed to get a right strop on when Meld was around," replied Michael.

Rhys laughed. He sat there a while but when Meld leaned to kiss Ashley he stood and excused himself. He suddenly realised that he did not really like the attention that the young lovers were giving each other. He didn't really understand why. After all, Ashley was just a good mate. He didn't have the hots for her or anything. Did he?

Rhys shivered; it wasn't like him to think this way. Stripping off to his shorts he called to Michael to join him and soon both were swimming and splashing around in the sea. There was nothing like the brisk ocean water to wash away the blues. After a few minutes they were joined by Grant and a game of swim tag commenced. By the time they got to bed they were exhausted but greatly refreshed by the freedom away from the confines of the ship.

On the beach Ashley and Meld were lost in their own thoughts.

"I will find you a way to get home Ash." said Meld as he stroked her hair.

She looked up at him and smiled. "I'm not sure I want to go anymore." She replied and lifting herself up she kissed him slowly and lovingly.

After a while they broke contact and Meld hugged her close.

"You must go home." He said. "You long for it I know you too well."

Tears welled in Ashley's eyes as she thought of her friends and parents back on Earth.

"I guess so." She replied glumly.

Meld nudged her and winked but she did not feel like smiling.

He nudged her again and stuck out his tongue. This time she could not help herself and she laughed.

"I suppose..." Meld said thoughtfully but stopped.

Ashley frowned, "You suppose what?"

He looked uncertain before replying.

"Well if we did find a way home for you. I suppose I could come with you." He said.

Ashley's mouth dropped open and it was a few seconds before she could respond.

"Well?" he asked.

She looked deep into his eyes and gave him a quick peck on the lips.

"I suppose so. Let's just wait and see huh?" she replied and laid herself back down on his lap.

Contented she fell asleep.

They were woken early next morning and following a hearty breakfast, everyone returned to the ship. Soon The Red Serpent was crawling its way through the dense mists once more. The fire eagles were restless as they perched on the masts but their riders dare not take to the skies for fearing of losing the ship in the foggy blanket that shrouded everything.

Boredom was one of their greatest enemies as the ship progressed slowly and the waters remained calm. There was nothing to see and very little to do as they crawled their way along. Once again moods darkened; tainted by the grey mists the crew were quiet and morose. Even Ashley felt negative despite the close proximity of Meld.

As evening drew in Prince Trelane signalled for them to stop and he clambered aboard once again. The water dripped from him as he stood before JF and Gorlan. "Two of my swimmers at the head of our line have detected a warm flow in the waters. They believe that it may be some form of volcanic activity. I have sent them ahead to investigate. As we are seeking the island of the Graav, and those creatures are hewn direct from pools of lava, it may lead us to their island."

Gorlan beamed. "What an excellent idea. I have a good feeling about this Prince Trelane."

JF was not so excited. "It is a good plan," he offered, "but bear in mind that there are a number of areas on these waters where the ocean is warmed by volcanic activity deep below. To the south there is a small set of around twenty islands that all display such features. Even if the flow does lead to an island it is highly unlikely that it will be that of the Graav."

"That is true," continued the Prince, "but at least it will give us a trail to follow instead of the directionless search that we are currently undertaking."

JF and Gorlan agreed. This was a positive lead and the sea-elves should continue to follow this plan.

The Red Serpent rocked on the gentle swell as they awaited the return of the sea-elves. It did not take long for the Prince's scouts to return and they were quickly pulled up to the deck, transforming their tails to legs as they ascended.

The first elf saluted his Prince. "Prince Trelane, we followed the flow and found that it was caused by hot air venting from a crevasse on the sea floor. This runs for a short distance before the sea bed rises sharply and lifts out of the ocean to form land, a volcanic island."

"Excellent," responded the Prince, "and how large is this island?"

"We are not sure sire. The mists were very dense. We followed the shoreline for a short distance but dare not go further for fear of losing our way back. We saw no sign of any life. The land also seemed quite stable. There was no visible evidence of volcanic activity at the surface. No telltale signs of smoke or steam, and no lava ponds."

Gorlan who had been listening carefully to the report interjected. "I still have a curious feeling about this discovery. Can you lead us there? If nothing else it would seem like another suitable resting point and another chance for the crew to step foot ashore."

The sea-elf glanced at his Prince before responding. Prince Trelane nodded his assent.

"I would be happy to," he replied. Both of the scouts walked to the ship's rail and dived back into the depths below. Prince Trelane watched his elves disappear into the mist before he spoke. "I will swim ahead with them. As usual stay close to the trailing sea-elves and they will lead you to the island."

JF did as instructed and carefully directed the flow to propel The Red Serpent forward, following the path trailblazed by the sea-elves.

They had been travelling for a little over thirty minutes and seemed to be making good progress. Even the mist, while still dense, had lifted a little and offered a few hundred metres of visibility.

They had clearly reached the area of the vents as patches of bubbling, lava heated sea water broke on the surface.

Rhys and Michael looked on from the ship's deck. Rhys pointed to a particularly large patch of bubbling water that was tinged yellow with sulphur. It covered an area the size of a tennis court.

"Look at that Mike. It must be pretty hot down on the sea bed."

Michael did not reply. Rhys turned to his friend and saw a concerned expression on his face.

"Wassup butty?" he asked, his Welsh accent and colloquialism rising to the fore.

Michael looked at him with a deep frown on his brow. He shrugged.

"I dunno." he replied. "I just have a strange feeling about this place. I think Fangtor may have been here before. I tried to focus on the memory but couldn't remember anything."

As the boys looked on a second large patch of boiling yellowed water bubbled up, similar in size to the first.

"Yeuch!" exclaimed Michael. "That yellow stuff makes the water look like puke!"

Then as the first patch started to fade a third broke out a few meters closer to the ship and Michael's eyes suddenly opened wide.

"CAPTAIN! JF! CAPTAIN!" Rhys jumped out of his skin as Michael let out a shout of alarm

"Turn the ship quickly. There is danger in the water!" he screamed.

At Jack Fishnose's side, Howler sniffed the air and let out a cry worthy of his name.

Michael was now sprinting to the bridge.

Behind him the surface of the ocean exploded as a creature of huge proportions broke the surface. Its reptilian dragon-like head sported small slit nostrils and a gaping mouth in which the savaged body of one of the sea-elves could be seen mangled amongst its sharp yellowed teeth.

A strong smell of stale fish hung in the air as the creature once more dived beneath the surface still feeding on its prey. Rhys grabbed onto the rail tightly and saw the creature's blue scaled form slide snakelike underneath the ship. Two large wing-like flippers pushed it along and a fork tail terminated its torso some twenty metres from its head.

Michael had now reached the poopdeck, but JF had already begun to redirect the energies to the sails as he put the ship into a forceful retreat.

"I remember now," said Michael gasping for breath. "This is the home of this thing. I don't know what it is but I do know it is very very dangerous and even Fangtor avoided it."

JF listened but did not comment as he was deep in concentration, maximising the strength of the energy flow to the sails.

Behind the captain Ves stood transfixed, he was literally shaking and he had gone a deathly white.

"It's the Lllllleviathan!" he stuttered through chattering teeth. "No-one llllives who sees the Lllleviathan!"

JF turned to his first mate and struck him across the face. "Snap out of it Ves. I need you now."

Ves mumbled an apology and JF returned his focus to the sails.

Suddenly, the ship was subjected to a violent shuddering as the Leviathan struck the hull. The crew were thrown around the deck, each trying to grab a handhold to prevent plunging into the waters below.

Michael was thrown from the bridge to the deck below. Rhys watched his friend fall as he too slid across the deck but with relief saw Michael recover to his feet, obviously bruised but otherwise unharmed.

He rushed to join Michael and the boys climbed the steps to the bridge.

Below them the crew had armed themselves with spears and harpoons and any time the creature showed its hide they launched the missiles at the scaly skin. It was to no avail, the weapons merely bounced off the thick hide leaving the creatures unharmed.

Once more the Leviathan attacked the vessel. This time it approached from directly below and the impact lifted The Red Serpent completely out of the water.

The crew were thrown about the deck once again and Rhys looked on helplessly as Ves was catapulted over the ship's rail. He screamed!

An expression of fear and dread crossed his face as he fell but his body did not reach the water. The Leviathan arched from the depths and with incredible speed snatched the first mate in mid air. With one powerful slam of its jaws the man was snapped in two. One second a living human the next no more than a food source for this beast. Rhys recoiled in horror at the sight and felt bile rising in his throat.

The Leviathan dived once again, but as its body disappeared below the surface it thrashed out with its forked tail and struck the mast head. Another crew member, one who had played deck quoits with Rhys only hours before, was slashed from the rigging and thrown into the sea.

As the ship steadied, Gorlan and the other Pinn riders burst through the ship's hatchway. They had been trying to reach the deck since the first attack but each strike had thrown them back below. Finally they were able to advance and, as they exited, their eagles flew down to meet them Before the two could join forces the Leviathan raised its head from the waters once again.

The creature exhibited intelligence as it observed the eagles and the approaching men. With a deep exhalation a stream of fire erupted from its mouth and sulphurous smoke poured from its nostrils.

The jet of flame intercepted their path and Gorlan was forced to push his men back into the ship's hatch to prevent them being burned to a cinder.

The Leviathan homed in on the eagles and their riders. It raised itself to an attack position but just as it seemed about to strike it let out a scream of pain. A seametal arrow had pierced its soft flesh above the right eye. More arrows flew and the Leviathan was forced to dive once more as the strength of the seametal shafts forced the projectiles deep into its body.

Ashley had not been below deck with the other riders and so she was the only rider that had been able to take to the skies. Terrified she realised that she was alone but she knew that she could not sit and wait for the others. Calling on all her training she willed her mount to attack the beast below.

The Leviathan was not even aware of the presence of the eagle plummeting swiftly towards it. With talons outstretched Ashley willed the eagle to strike at the base of the creature's neck. Claws dug in deep and the beast let out a scream of a pain as its flesh was seared with fire eagle magic.

Faced with the pain of the arrows and Ashley's attack the creature broke off its assault on the ship and retreated a little distance into the mists. Ashley and her eagle released their grip as the Leviathan slipped away. The elves continued to fire arrows in the general direction of the creature but were soon forced to stop when they lost sight of it in the fog.

The pause in the attack allowed the Pinn riders to reach their eagles and take to the air and they flew straight towards where the beast had disappeared. Finding it almost immediately snaking a circular path as it pondered its next action.

As the eagles approached the Leviathan emitted another jet of flame but the agile eagles were able to avoid this with consummate ease now that they were airborne.

Carl was the first to reach the beast, closely followed by his brother. The monster snapped at them viciously but was unable to make contact. The brothers enjoyed an almost telepathic ability when in combat and both directed their mounts to the head. As their eagles made contact with the scaly flesh their talons bit in deep and their fire magic was invoked.

The Leviathan let out another horrible scream as the magic burned deep. A searing stench erupted from the wound, but other than causing the creature intense pain and crisping the surface skin, it seemed to do it little permanent harm.

However, faced with these dangerous birds and the annoyance of the stinging arrows and experiencing the unusual sensation of pain, the great beast dived deep forcing the eagles to release their hold.

The eagles and sea-elves continued to scout the vicinity but it appeared that the creature had fled. After a few minutes searching they returned to the ship, picking up the direction from the sound of the crew carrying out emergency repairs to the vessel.

Prince Trelane climbed aboard and immediately held counsel with Gorlan and JF.

"So how bad is it captain?" he asked.

"Not good," replied the sailor. "We have lost the foremast completely and the second is badly damaged. Ves is missing and at least four other crew members. Trall is taking a roll call." JF looked at the Prince sympathetically. "And what of your elves? How many were taken?"

Prince Trelane's expression did not change as he replied. "Two. Both of the rearguard of my group. That is why we did not return to assist immediately. It took us a little while to realise that they were absent."

Trelane surveyed the intense damage that had been wreaked on the vessel.

"Are you able to limp to the island that my elves found earlier?" he asked.

JF nodded. "Yes, there is sufficient mesh left in the single sail to propel the ship. If you lead the way then we will..."

The sentence was left incomplete as suddenly an enormous explosion of water burst from the ocean to the starboard as the Leviathan thrust its body almost fully out of the water. Fire eagles attacked immediately ripping their talons into the body of the beast which let out an eardrum splitting roar of agony.

Infuriated by the pain inflicted on it, the creature was now intent on revenge, not just food. As the huge bulk started to fall towards the ship JF realised that the beast had merely been toying with them earlier. The eagles continued to cling to the gargantuan as it made contact with the ships deck, falling laterally across the vessel from starboard to port.

From her mount, Ashley watched in horror as the great weight of the Leviathan literally snapped the ship in two. She could not suppress a scream as she saw two of the riders, Herd and Green, crushed to death as the huge masses impacted.

The broken halves of The Red Serpent tilted violently and those on board started to slide towards the sea. The Leviathan snapped at falling bodies as it once again submerged, forcing the eagles to release their fiery grip.

Tor and his eagle were not so easily removed. Determined to defeat the creature and save his friends the warrior willed his eagle to stay attached. As they hit the surface of the water Tor and his eagle were knocked free and thrown over the head of the Leviathan so they now bobbed in the water in front of it. The Leviathan opened its jaws to remove the annoyance of this man and bird but in grim determination the warrior turned his eagle in the water and struck out into the air once more. As the great sea dragon lunged towards them the talons of Tor's fire eagle sank deeply into the creature's right eye. The eyeball immediately began to bubble and burn, blinding the monster as it dived deep once again to escape, this time in terror. It carried Tor with it, his eagle still clinging on firmly to the eyeball with one clawed foot as it tried to ease its way across the head to the other eye.

Behind them confusion and panic ensued as those in the water fought for their lives, reaching out for anything that could keep them afloat.

Rhys was still on board. He was holding on to a thick rope that was tied firmly to the remaining ship's mast which was now almost horizontal, parallel to the water's surface.

Further up the wrecked deck he saw JF holding onto the ship's wheel firmly. The captain was waving and shouting at Rhys but he could not hear him in all the noise and confusion. It looked to Rhys like JF was tying himself to the ship's wheel.

As the hull of the ship began to sink Rhys realised his error. Caught in the suction of the descent the rope began to pull him down with the ship. He released it but it was too late.

The force of the water and the down-pull caused by the sinking vessel was sucking him after it. As the vessel slid past him into the depths he saw JF glance at him, he was tied tightly to the ship's wheel. In true mariner style the captain was going down with his ship. With his lungs bursting Rhys struck out for the surface, trying to break the pull of the sinking wreck. It was no good, the pull was too great.

His lungs were now screaming and in panic he thrashed out madly. He was going to drown. After all this adventure he was going to die in this wet, cold, misty and miserable sea. Pain burned in his chest and he could feel his eyes bulging as he made one last fruitless effort to swim to safety, but to no avail. As he opened his mouth and the water rushed in, he mercifully blacked out as his lifeless body descended into the depths.

# CHAPTER SIXTEEN
## Survivors?

Tribemaker took a deep breath and sucked in the perfumed essence from the long, orange tinged pipe which he held in his hand. Farspell was sitting opposite him smoking a similar pipe, unsure if he was enjoying the experience. The pipes were filled with dried leaves harvested from the pulp fruit plant and the smoke had a fruity taste to it, similar to the sweetness of the fruit itself.

The tribal elder was in his 'tutor' mode, knowledgeably explaining to the wizard how the desert striders interacted with their environment and how they utilised the energies of the desert to aid them.

Farspell listened intently, exploring the information for any clues as to how it may be of benefit.

"From the description that you have provided it would appear to me that you invoke energies in a very similar manner to the way magic users utilise the portal energies on my own world," observed the wizard. "If I could learn how to touch the forces of your world I may be able to use the knowledge gained to create a little magic of my own."

Farspell sat upright in his chair and leaned toward the elder before continuing. Looking into the eyes of the old man he asked, "Will you teach me more? Perhaps there is a solution to this dilemma after all."

Tribemaker sucked thoughtfully on his pipe before answering. Then, slowly he got to his feet and smiled.

"Come Farspell. Let me show you something."

The old strider led the wizard into his sleeping chamber. A small alcove had been chiselled into the wall next to Tribemaker's bed and inside this he had arranged a number of odds and ends, mostly different types of rock that he had collected over the years.

"Each generation a new Tribemaker is chosen. Part of the responsibility of that individual is to take on the leadership and, as the name implies, to make the tribe. This involves allocation of tasks and the development of both teachers and students as required for the survival of the tribe.

"For the task of gathering the training is intense and some fail but, in this task, the student and tutor are assisted through the use of this."

Reaching into the alcove Tribemaker removed something and held it close to his chest.

At first Farspell thought it would be a stone of some kind, something that held latent power, but as Tribemaker passed the item to him, he was able to see that it was an old book. It was leather bound and a deep dark brown, aged with time and small enough to slip into a pocket.

There was writing on the cover but Farspell did not recognise the symbols and hence was unable to read it. Similarly when he opened the book the same undecipherable text stared up at him from the page.

He looked at the desert leader and offered the book back to him. "I am sorry but I am unable to read it."

Tribemaker smiled. "Place the book to your chest. Use your heart not your eyes."

Farspell hesitated but did as instructed.

At first he felt nothing but then a slight tingle touched his mind.

Words came to him. A soft female voice with a curious lilting accent spoke to him of the powers of this world. It talked of times when the planet was rich and healthy, not desert-like as it now stood.

Pictures flashed into the wizards mind, not projected from the book but built subconsciously from the words that he could hear spoken. The book had been written many years ago by the predecessors of the desert striders. They had been a noble race at the head of a great civilisation, but when the sun's rays began to scorch their world, they were powerless to prevent the changes that occurred.

Through their knowledge of the core energies of their world they developed the protective domes that still housed the tribes today. It continued with a detailed description of the energies and the uses to which they could be put. Finally a lesson was given, a brief introduction for the 'reader' to the skills of sensing.

Farspell observed all this in fascination. As the pictures played out in his mind, he began to better understand the world around him. As he brought the book away from his chest he grinned at Tribemaker. Farspell had taken the first steps towards understanding the magics of this world. Perhaps there was hope for Gatherer and himself after all.

*** 

Michael was sitting on the black sands of the volcanic beach tossing small pebbles into the water while his other hand tickled the ear of Howler. The mist had lifted and the evening brought sight of a half moon that lightly painted the beach in its soft glow. Further along the shoreline a large plank washed ashore and Michael leapt to his feet, momentarily mistaking it for a body. Realising his mistake he sank to his knees and held his head in his hands.

"I can't believe that they're gone Howler," he said solemnly. As if in understanding the Urthound stuck out its tongue and gave his face a huge lick.

A shout came from behind them. "Hey Mike! Come and eat something!"

Michael recognised the voice of Grant another one of those lucky enough to have been plucked from the water by the fire eagles. He turned towards the makeshift camp that they had swiftly constructed and saw the cook, pan in hand, beckoning to him.

Without responding Michael stood, turned his back on him and walked away along the shoreline. Howler followed close behind.

"He is finding it hard to accept the loss of his friends." commented Trall. "He clings to the hope that they will still be found but I saw Rhys go under with the ship. He didn't stand a chance."

Grant sighed. Since the loss of his nephew his persona of Liam Sagot had come to the fore, leaving the murderous Nexus behind. No matter how hard he tried he could not dismiss the feeling of loss that gnawed at him. Swallowing hard he responded. "It is a great loss for him. Rhys was his best friend and they loved each other as though they were brothers. Maybe there is still hope for Ashley though. She is missing but no-one saw what happened. Perhaps she is just lost in the mists?"

Trall nodded. "Perhaps. Many saw her flying above the ship but one minute she was there and the next gone. I hope that you are right Landman. At least we have hope for her."

A noise disturbed their conversation as Pinnel swooped down on his eagle.

He removed a leather bag from his shoulder and unpacked the contents onto a makeshift table that had been crafted from wrecked decking.

Gorlan examined the collection which was mostly made up of cloth and foodstuffs softened by the salt water.

"I take it you saw no sign of life?" asked the Warlord.

Pinnel shook his head. "No, nothing. Kraven rightly insisted that we continue looking even in the dark but it was a fruitless exercise, especially when the mists thickened. We had to keep calling to each other just to ensure that none of us went missing and to guide us back together. Even when Kraven ordered us back to camp Carl and Stern were very reluctant to give up the search."

Gorlan sighed deeply. "Time is running away from us Pinnel. We will make one last search when the sun rises in a few hours. If that is unsuccessful..."

The Warlord paused and composed himself before continuing with his statement. "...then we will have to leave any survivor to their fate."

"And then?" asked Pinnel.

"And then we push on with our mission," He almost snarled. "We must continue, otherwise those that have perished will have died for naught. There are a number of other islands nearby. Who knows? Perhaps one of these is the one that we seek. I will not give up on our search for the warlock. Not yet."

*\*\**

Stack was finding the purging of the Pinnacle Mountains almost too easy. The terrain was tough, and while the few citizens that dwelt in these parts were hardy, they were not battle trained and his Graav were relatively unchallenged as they plundered the mountain villages and slaughtered the inhabitants.

"The Pinns missed a trick here," he said out loud to the Graav. "If these mountain men had been recruited, organised and trained they would have made tough soldiers."

The faces of the stone men remained impassive. He might as well have been talking to himself.

He shook his head, tutting as he looked at the nearest Graav.

"You really are a stupid moronic beast aren't you?" he said insultingly.

Stack continued to watch for any sign of awareness to his words. "No! Nothing! Not even a glint of annoyance you rock infested devil monkey!"

Still the Graav remained passive.

Stack laughed at it. "Ah well. You serve a purpose I suppose." He waved his arm in the air like some US cavalry captain. "Let's go. There is more killing to be done."

This time the Graav did respond and, driven by his will rather than the words, they marched on.

*** 

When Michael returned to camp and heard the news that they were to stop the search for survivors he rushed to Gorlan's shelter.

"Gorlan!" he screamed. "You cannot do this! We must keep searching for them!"

The warlord had been expecting this and was prepared.

"Michael," he spoke softly. "I understand your concern and pain, but we cannot stay here indefinitely. We have a mission to complete and besides, it is highly unlikely that anyone would survive this length of time in these waters."

"No!" shouted Michael, "You are giving up too easily." In frustration and anger he struck out at Gorlan.

The warlord avoided the blow easily and stepping towards the teenager. He pulled him in close and held him tight, pinning his arms. Michael started to struggle and push away but Gorlan held on firmly refusing to let him go. Finally, Michael's struggles gave way to grief and as he went loose he broke into sobs. Gorlan relaxed his grip but held his friend close to him to offer comfort. He did not release him until his crying had subsided. The warlord whispered softly. "There is a time to grieve, but that time is not now."

In silence Michael returned to his own shelter and, for the first time since they had been marooned, he fell asleep.

Mercifully the survivors awoke to a relatively clear morning. The skies overhead were grey, masked by a high veil of mist and a thick fog bank could be seen offshore, some distance away, but for now the air was clear on the island and the neighbouring outcrops of land that dotted the area were visible in the distance.

Grant Landman prepared a light breakfast aware of the importance of protecting their rations, while Gorlan spoke in earnest to the surviving Pinn riders.

He ordered all to carry out one last search. Kraven, Carl, Stern, Pinnel, Lloyd and Flare should work in pairs as usual.

With riders dispatched Gorlan turned his attention to the island.

The eagles had not only saved Gorlan and Michael from the waters but they had also plucked two other crew members to safety, Doogie Fen and Corwin Reels, both sea-hands that had been hired from the harbour at The Gates.

Prince Trelane and his two remaining sea-elves had also survived and had been able to assist Trall and Meld to the safety of land.

All the others who had been on board were missing, assumed lost at sea. Although all hoped for a successful outcome from this last search, no-one held any realistic hope that any more survivors would be rescued. Even Michael had lost his optimism.

As the others searched the seas, Gorlan and Prince Trelane surveyed the surrounding islands.

"What are you thinking Warlord?" asked the Prince.

"One of these land masses could be the lair for which we search." replied Gorlan. "There must be twenty different islands here and our supplies are scarce."

"Do not concern yourself with regards food supplies. This grey foreboding ocean that you see before you is also a huge provider, an uncultivated farm. I will send my elves to gather food supplies while your eagles are looking for our friends. Do you have thoughts as to which island we should search next?"

Gorlan shrugged. "There is no way of saying but my gut feeling draws me to the four islands to the north. There seems to be some volcanic activity in that group." He pointed to them. "If you look carefully you can see an occasional burst of orange. It was much clearer last night but even in daylight it is visible."

"I saw that last night too. If the island of the Graav still possesses molten lava pools, which it must surely do, then I agree that logically we should follow any evidence of volcanic activity. I will get my elves to restock our supplies. When the eagles return, hopefully with good news, we can make for the first island."

Gorlan nodded. "Then it is decided. We will take each one in order working south to north. I'll speak to Trall. He is not keen on flying and has been trying to put together a boat from the wreckage but we don't have the time for that. It will take days to make a seaworthy craft. Kraven is bonded with the largest warbird of all. Michael and Trall can double up and Kraven will have to carry three. It will slow us down but it will still be much swifter than trying to sail any makeshift vessel to the islands."

Prince Trelane smiled, knowing his dwarf friend of old. "Good luck Gorlan. He is not going to take kindly to your request."

The Prince was correct but it had not been as bad as Gorlan expected. Trall mumbled and cursed but did not argue. He understood the need. He just dared anyone to tease him if he kept his eyes closed.

\*\*\*

In the Red Hills to the south of Pinnhome and the Pinn valley, Tiborous moved his forces as stealthily as possible. He had marched them northeast from the Halfman Forest to the Red Hills. If the halfmen that occupied that forest were aware of his presence then they did not show themselves. His objectives were a little more difficult than those of Stack in the mountains to the north. The Red Hills were more populated, although there were very few villages; the majority of residents living in isolated wooden shacks nestled amongst the trees in the wooded areas of the region. The hilltops themselves, painted red by the layers of rock that had been exposed by the weather, were largely barren and only a few chose to make home on these upper levels.

A seasoned fighter, Tiborous had taken a different approach to Stack. Whilst the latter marched relentlessly through the mountains slaughtering anything that crossed their path, Tiborous had hidden his main force for a day while he took a small band of Graav and surveyed the immediate area. He then set about slowly clearing this area of any inhabitants to form a base camp.

Having completed this task he had ordered a slow sweep through the hills. He knew that eventually word would be taken to Pinn of their presence but he hoped that through this tactic he could maximise the period of minimum resistance and clear the majority of the hill area before the Pinns could send reinforcements.

This tactic would have been sound but was fundamentally flawed as the Graav showed that they were totally useless in their attempts at stealthy movement. When it came to grace and gentle step, the lava-hewn creatures were about as graceful as an orc at a fairy's wedding.

Nevertheless Tiborous had used his weather controlling spells to create a thick mist bank that helped hide his forces as they moved and also deadened the sound of their progress. As such he was able to keep his band undetected and eventually they came across their first village.

This consisted of the usual hillside shack-like housing, but a community had built up in a clearing within a wooded copse. A small stream ran through the village and the residents had dug out an area to form a pond where a few of the women were busy washing clothes. Tiborous scanned the surroundings and observed that there were only a handful of men within the village; the others were out hunting and going about other daily tasks to support their families. His Graav had already dispatched some of these men when they had come across them in the woods.

In the streets of the village, young children played tag and mock swordplay, as they scampered between the dwellings. To the west noises could be heard from within a large single storey wooden structure as the older children attended school.

Tiborous had been given his orders. All in their path should be put to the sword. He did not like attacking women and children, not because he harboured any regrets about slaughtering the innocent, but more due to the fact that they offered little challenge in a battle. He was a soldier and a good one. As such he relished the thrill of a fight to the death. This would be more of a cull than a battle.

He was right. As the Graav stepped from the cover and began their relentless sweep through the village, women, children and even the men began to flee. It was to no avail though as Tiborous had arranged his Graav to totally surround the clearing and it was all over in a matter of minutes.

Leaving the slaughtered villagers to the carrion and scavengers Tiborous reformed his force and marched west.

***

Farspell clapped his hands in delight.

"Yes! It may work!" he exclaimed.

Tribemaker looked in his direction and saw that he was holding a sample of sand crystal. "You have thought of something?" he asked.

Farspell nodded. "Yes. It is just the germ of an idea but it is plausible. What are these?" he asked.

"These are sand crystals. They are formed when compacted sand granules are forced by wind and heat into a solid glass-like ball. They can grow as large as a few inches in diameter." replied Tribemaker. Farspell nodded and continued.

"Not only formed by wind and heat but also the energies of your world. These crystals almost pulse with latent energy."

"Yes," replied the old desert strider, "crystals like this are at the heart of the pyramid emitters that form our dome. It has long been known that they are powerful objects."

"Excellent!" mused Farspell. He played with the sand crystal thoughtfully, turning it between his fingers. "We know that the conflict between the artefacts of the runestones and the energies of your world are severe and the likeliest source of the opening of the rift. However, we were able to use the power of the Cormion Crystals to open a link with Portalia so this tells us that there are certain similarities that do not result in a negative reaction.

"If we take the power of the Cormion Crystal and mould it with the power that is locked within one of the sand crystals, perhaps we can forge a new artefact, a key that can be used to open a gateway between our worlds."

Tribemaker's eyes widened in excitement, "And you know how to do this?"

Farspell looked at him and grinned. "Ah, well. Not exactly but I have a theory. The problem is if that theory is incorrect I may damage the Cormion Crystal and any runestone pendant used to forge the new object which could leave us even more isolated."

Tribemaker sighed, "Not a decision to be taken lightly then my friend."

"Indeed! We will need to discuss this with Toran when he next makes contact. In the meantime I will continue my research into the differences between the energies and hopefully improve the chances of success. At least there is now a light at the end of the tunnel."

So saying, Farspell placed a small sand crystal into a mortar and began to crush it into smaller dust like particles with the pestle.

# CHAPTER SEVENTEEN
## A Captive Audience

Ashley opened her eyes and stared up at a plain grey ceiling the colour of a stormy sky.

Turning her head she saw that she was lying on a basic single bed in a small cell like room, the walls painted in the same dour shade as the ceiling. Apart from the bed the only other furniture was a wooden writing desk with two lower drawers and a matching stool.

She tried to stand but, as she raised her body to a sitting position, her vision became unfocussed and the room seemed to swim before her eyes. Propping her back against the headboard she allowed herself time to regain composure and finally was able to swing her legs around and sit upright on the bed.

A decanter of water and some plain cake had been left on the desktop and she suddenly realised how hungry she was. Standing gingerly, she moved slowly to the desk. She bit into the sweetened cake and washed it down with a sip of water. As she ate she felt her body recovering and memories came flooding back.

"Rhys!" she cried out loud. She got to her feet far too quickly for her condition and the room began to spin once more. Placing her hand on the wall to steady herself she looked to the open door and stumbled through it. As she exited she bumped straight into something. She looked to see what it was and let out a terrified scream. It was one of the Graav.

Ashley began to struggle as the stone creature had wrapped its arms around her, but she was unable to break away. Recognising her predicament, the fruitlessness of her efforts to break free, coupled with the fact that the creature did not seem intent on harm, she relaxed a little.

"Aha! Welcome my dear!"

Still secured by the Graav, Ashley turned her head. Weldrock stood with arms open and with a sadistic grin on his face.

"You!" she shouted in consternation. "What am I doing here? Where is Rhys? Is he here too?"

Weldrock waved his arms in a calming motion.

"Relax my dear," he said. "You have been through a great deal. You almost drowned. If it had not been for the Graav finding you and your eagle washed ashore then you would be dead. Instead they brought you to me and Helender revived you. You should thank me, and her, for saving your life."

Ashley felt a moment of shame as, in her confused state and concern for Rhys, she had not thought about her eagle bond partner. Reaching out she felt its presence and a feeling of relief swept over her when she realised that the great bird was nearby, although her smile faded quickly as she sensed that something was amiss with her partner.

"Where is my eagle? Have you harmed it?" she asked.

Weldrock laughed. It was not a pleasant sound.

"What. So quick to forget about your human friend! Do not fret earthling, your bird is well. Detained and sedated but well cared for."

Ashley once again tried to break free of the vice like grip of the lava man.

"Now don't be so foolish Ashley," said the warlock. "Oh, sorry, you don't mind me calling you Ashley do you? I feel we know each other so well!"

Weldrock stepped closer to her until they were almost nose to nose.

"If I instruct the Graav to release you do I have your word that you will behave? It would be so easy for me to continue to restrain you…" he paused, "…or even worse if I so chose. But I would prefer to enjoy your company. At least for the time being anyway."

Ashley swiftly considered her options and realised that she did not really have any. Reluctantly she nodded her agreement.

"Oh good!" said Weldrock. "That makes things so much easier."

The Graav released its grip and Ashley stepped from its embrace. Without conscious thought the hairs on her neck suddenly raised and she became aware of another presence, turning she came face to face with Helender.

Instinctive fear turned Ashley cold within. The creature that stood before her was daemon-like in its appearance.

"Let me introduce you," offered Weldrock. "Ashley, this is Helender, leader of the Shii. Now don't forget to thank her for saving you."

Ashley looked into the red eyes of Helender and somehow managed to stutter a thank you. The Shii nodded acknowledgement. "No thank you isss necsssesssary. I have no conflict with you and besssidesss the ssservicssse wasss ordered by the warlock."

The response confused Ashley it was not what she had been expecting. It was almost polite.

"Follow me," ordered Weldrock and led them down a corridor. Ashley noticed that there were numerous rooms leading off on either side. Most had the door closed but two were open and she noticed the same basic decoration and content as the room in which she had awoken. Weldrock came to a T-junction. The same grey corridors stretched left and right but ahead two large arched wooden doors blocked their path.

The warlock waved his hand in a circular motion and mumbled something quietly under his breath and the doors slowly opened.

Stepping inside Ashley was immediately struck by the opulence of this room, a stark contrast with the area from which they had stepped.

Crimson velvet curtains draped from large arched windows along one side of the room. Exotic and comfortable furniture was spread in a relatively tasteful manner. Half a dozen Graav stood sentry at various points. Clearly Weldrock did not feel safe even in his own living quarters.

Opposite the windowed wall a series of dark wooden shelves lined with books of varying shapes, colours and sizes formed an impressive library.

"Ah yes," sighed Weldrock. "My library, vast and full of the knowledge of many worlds. Magic and science from different lands and across many generations. A wealth of information and yet still far from complete."

Sensing the pride that the warlock held in his collection Ashley turned away and chose to ignore it. Weldrock's expression turned to anger and frustration.

"Ah, I see. Another ignorant peasant." He snapped through gritted teeth.

Ashley scanned the rest of the vast room. The warlock certainly liked his treasures. Gold, silver and bronze were spread around the room in an extravagant display. If a shelf was not inlaid with valuable trinkets then curious items sat about which she correctly assumed were part of the warlock's magical studies.

At the far end an alcove to the left served as laboratory, clearly an area where Weldrock carried out his experiments. To the right a similar alcove housed a large four poster bed. She turned and saw other alcoves at the opposite end of the room, close to where they had entered.

One contained a bathroom and toilet and the other, to her surprise, a kitchen area. She smiled, for some reason she had not thought of this evil magician as living in a condominium!

"I am sorry, I forget my manners. Please sit down. We have much to discuss." Weldrock indicated that Ashley should take a seat. He did not offer the same comfort to Helender so the Shii loomed above them as they sat.

"Now tell me. How is it that you come to be here and where are your comrades?"

Ashley folded her arms defensively.

"Why should I tell you anything," she responded. "You are our enemy and you'll use any information that I give to harm my friends."

Weldrock smiled. "Yes, that is true but I suspect that you will tell me things anyway. I sense that you are a stubborn creature so rather than waste time torturing you I will focus my efforts on your fire eagle and on your young friend Rhys. I'm sure that will loosen your tongue."

Ashley's eyes snapped wide open. "So Rhys is alive. Where is he?"

Her thoughts turned back to the attack by the Leviathan. She had watched from above as Rhys was dragged down by the sinking ship. Realising the danger, girl and bird wasted little time and plunged into the sea. The shock of the cold water was intense and she had to force herself to remain conscious. She hardly needed to will her eagle on, it already knew what she wanted and was using its great wings as flippers, pushing against he water to dive down to Rhys who was being pulled away from them.

Down and down they plunged until Ashley felt she could breathe no longer. She remembered the great bird stretching out its leg and clutching at Rhys' foot but then blackness until she awoke in her room at Weldrock's lair. It would appear that they had been successful, to a certain degree, although it seemed the rescue had been too much for her and her eagle and so they now found themselves in the clutches of the warlock. *But at least we are alive she thought.*

"Yes, he is alive but again you have to thank Helender for this." Ashley glanced to the Shii and nodded. Helender did not respond. She stood there staring at the warlock. *Was that hate in those eyes?* She filed this away in her mind for future reference. It may be that this creature was not as faithful to her master as it first appeared.

Ashley raised her hands to her face and sighed deeply into them. "Thank God," she said.

It was at this point that she noticed that her pendant was missing. She put her hand to her chest, almost involuntarily. Weldrock noticed the movement. "Ah yes. My thanks for the pendant. It looks good in my collection."

"Give it back!" Ashley screamed at him. "It's mine!"

Weldrock roared with laughter. "Such spirit. You amuse me but alas you are mistaken. I could give it *back* if I so chose but it is not *yours*, it is now *mine*, so why would I?"

Ashley glared at him. The pendant may offer the only hope of getting back home again and this miserable old man had stolen it from her.

"In fact," continued the warlock. "I was lucky enough to get a matching pendant from your friend. So kind and, as if you hadn't been generous enough, you also gave me a Cormion

Crystal to help me…" he paused for dramatic effect. "…keep on top of things."

At this point their conversation was interrupted by a hammering on the chamber doors. Weldrock opened them and allowed entry to two Graav. They dragged a barely conscious Rhys into the room and pulled him to the centre where they dropped him into a chair, a few meters from where Ashley was sitting.

She jumped to her feet but Helender placed her hand on Ashley's shoulder and pushed her back to a sitting position.

Rhys flopped in the chair and barely acknowledged his surroundings.

"What have you done to him?" She demanded an answer from the warlock, who merely waved a hand in response.

"Do not concern yourself he is merely drugged. His ability to create portal openings intrigues me and I would know more of this but I cannot afford for the young man to create a portal here and escape my grasp." He pointed to Rhys. "In this state even if he creates a portal subconsciously he is unlikely to be able to use it. I had ordered for him to be killed but fate has been kind enough to deliver him to me so I can experiment with his mind a little."

Ashley scowled at Weldrock. "You're a psycho! Why don't you just curl up and die you jerk!"

Weldrock feigned thoughtful consideration of this request by tilting his head and replied. "Hmm, let me consider that request. Ummm, no, I don't think I will. Thanks for asking though!" He tilted his head back and let out a loud laugh at his own jest.

Rhys let out a groan and opened his eyes a little further. "Uhhh." He looked towards Ashley and a spark of recognition ignited. "Ashley," he said groggily, "What is going on?"

Weldrock signalled to Helender and the Shii grabbed the boy by the hair. She pulled his head back roughly and poured the contents of a vial down his throat. Within seconds Rhys returned to an almost trance-like state.

"You'd better not harm him!" exclaimed Ashley.

"And if I did?" snapped Weldrock. "What would you do then? Be silent girl. The boy's abilities may offer me riches but you I merely tolerate as a bargaining piece. I could easily be rid of your whining and insults once and for all if I so chose."

Ashley fell silent, she realised that the warlock was dangerously insane and that she should not push him too far.

"That is so much better," declared Weldrock. "Now tell me. What happened? How did you come to be here and where are your colleagues?"

Ashley thought quickly and decided on a partial truth.

"Dead." She replied using the memories of those that she had actually watched die to bring tears to her eyes.

She then told of him of the attack of the Leviathan and how she had dived on her eagle to save Rhys. She added that she had pulled his body from the depths and that she had seen no other survivors. Finally she recounted how, exhausted and water sodden, the eagle had probably dropped them both as she remembered no more until she had found herself in Weldrock's 'care'.

The warlock considered her story.

"How ironic. To travel all this way to find me only to fall to the Leviathan so close to your goal. Perhaps you are correct and that your colleagues all died too, drowned or eaten, but if you two survived then others may have done so."

Weldrock turned to the Shii.

"Helender, take your sisters and search the nearby islands. If there are any other survivors bring them to me. Try not to harm them unless you must. If Gorlan and any of his men survive they will not be taken easily."

Helender left to obey and immediately two Graav took her place behind Ashley.

"So tell me about this one," demanded the warlock waving his fingers at Rhys. "How does he control the portals?"

Ashley lied again.

"He can't do it anymore. He's lost the ability."

Weldrock flicked his head and one of the Graav struck her roughly across the face, knocking her out of her chair.

"Do not lie to me!" screamed the warlock.

He asked her again but met with the same stubborn response.

"Enough!" he snapped.

Turning to the Graav he voiced an order, more for Ashley's benefit than anything else.

"Take them back to their cells and this time lock them both in. Feed the young man but not the girl. When she is screaming for food and water perhaps she will be more willing to speak to me civilly and honestly."

The Graav responded even before the warlock had finished the speech and within minutes Ashley found herself back in the grey room where she had awoken earlier. This time though the door was shut and when she tried the handle she confirmed that it was indeed firmly locked.

\*\*\*

Rhys was floating. At least that was how it felt.

He remembered being wet and seeing Ashley, her face all contorted, moving towards him slowly but now she wasn't there anymore.

Where am I? He thought.

Am I in a portal gateway?

He tried to take in his surroundings but they seemed to be constantly changing as things do in a dream.

One minute the blue ooze of a portal, next the blackness of space, then floating in a pool and then sinking in water.

Sinking in water! Why was that so important?

He tried to grasp onto that thought, but his concentration wavered and he found himself on the back of a giant pink ant scuttling through a field of tree sized grass stalks.

"Ash, where are you?" he called from a great distance. But there was no reply.

A wave of black overcame him once again and Rhys returned to the relative tranquillity of unconsciousness.

\*\*\*

The fire eagles had picked their way slowly across the sky to the nearest island. Finding nothing of interest they had then island hopped to the next one in the chain and it was while searching here that Gorlan and Meld, working close together on the northern tip, spotted the approaching Shii.

Too late to alert the others Gorlan let out a loud shout of warning for anyone in earshot and drew his sword.

The Shii homed in and Meld took up a battle stance alongside the warlord.

With swords raised they prepared themselves for a fight to the death as they faced the demons that approached.

Helender broke off from her sisters and guided her flight path towards the men, to their great surprise, rather than strike, she came to a standing halt just a few meters from them, making no move to attack.

"My name isss Helender, leader of the Shii. Who of you leadsss?"

Gorlan lowered the tip of his sword but retained his battle stance.

"I have that honour. My name is Gorlan. Warlord of the Pinns."

"Ah yesss. I have heard the warlock ssspeak of you. I have no love for your kind Pinn but I sssuggessst we call a trucssse. We can be of help to each other."

Gorlan raised his eyebrows, this was certainly an expected turn of events.

"Speak then Helender," replied Gorlan.

At his side Meld found the hoarse and whisper-like tone of the Shii unsettling and he muttered a warning to the warlord. "Surely we cannot trust this abomination?"

Helender snapped her head around to look at him. "Sssilencssse. Normally I would not choossse an alliancssse with sssuch asss yoursslevesss but our needsss are sssimilar. Both of usss want to sssee an end to thisss warlock."

Meld bowed an apology, although Helender noticed that he kept his sword raised and retained a battle position.

Gorlan stepped towards her.

"Go ahead Helender. Tell me what you propose."

"Asss I sssaid, a trucssse. Weldrock hasss the girl Ashley and the boy Rhysss held captive. Likewissse he holdsss the Shii in hisss ssservice through the ussse of a sssmall black orb. Help me recover the orb and free my Shii and I will help you defeat the warlock."

Helender waited for a response.

"Go on," encouraged Gorlan.

"Weldrock hasss ordered me to capture any sssurvivorsss in your ranksss. I sssensssse that besssides you there are othersss here. Order your men to ssstay on thisss island and allow me to take sssome of your number back to Weldrock. He keepsss the orb on him at all timesss but I cannot touch it asss it hasss a powerful hold over me.

If one of your men could sssteal it and return it to me then we would be free to act independently."

Gorlan looked at the Shii. He must admit there was nothing about them that would suggest he could trust these creatures. He had no doubt that they needed his help but likewise his instincts told him that once free these demons would not care for past alliances and may well fall upon those that had helped release them.

Helender continued. "Thossse that come with usss will be temporarily imprisssoned but my Shii will releassse you at the firssst opportunity ssso that you can sssteal into the warlock'sss chambersss and recover the orb."

Gorlan pondered the suggestion. He did not like the thought of being imprisoned but this presented an opportunity to get right to the heart of the warlock's stronghold.

"Very well," he replied. "I will gather my men to discuss your proposal. I will return within the hour."

It took thirty minutes for Gorlan and Meld to gather together the survivors of the shipwreck and Gorlan briefed them on the request from the Shii for assistance. Despite the seriousness of their situation, the group were lifted by the news that Ashley and Rhys had survived and Michael simply beamed with delight. Yes they were at the mercy of the warlock but at least they were alive and where there was life there was hope.

"I don't like this Gorlan," said Prince Trelane.

"Me neither," said the Warlord. "I don't trust these creatures they are of demon spawn and care little about anything other than their own kind. However, this could be a way to get deep into the heart of Weldrock's domain."

"But anyone taken will be held securely and who knows what methods the warlock has at his disposal for gleaning information from captives," continued Trelane.

Gorlan nodded. "I know that the risk is great Prince, but I am willing to take it. I will not ask anyone else to be taken captive, but if there are three or four of us then it may serve our cause better from within and will also help to persuade the warlock that all are captured."

Michael stepped forward, "I'll come. If he has Rhys and Ashley then I want to be with them."

Gorlan nodded, "Very well." He did not question Michael's request.

Meld also volunteered. "If I can get on the inside then I will find Ashley. A thousand Graav and an army of warlocks will not stop me." And he too stepped forward to stand at the Warlord's side.

Grant Landman, also known as Nexus, shrugged and raised a hand. "Ah well, you only live once." He said as he joined them. In truth he had jumped at the chance of a return to the stronghold as during the sinking of the ship he had not only lost the leaves that allowed him to communicate with the warlock but also his precious cloak of invisibility.

His band of four now in agreement, Gorlan continued.

"I am not sure if this is the correct thing to do but I just feel that having us on the inside may benefit our quest greatly." He turned to Prince Trelane.

"When we have gone I want you to wait an hour or so and then make your own way to the island. If we are able to free ourselves and determine the best route into the citadel we will find a way of signalling to you. If you do not hear or see anything that suggests our freedom, you will need to find a way into the fortress yourselves. It may be that we are unable to assist."

Prince Trelane frowned , "I still don't like this. Why don't we slay these Shii and stay together."

Gorlan shook his head. "I have a feeling that these Shii would not be as easy to slay as you think. I'd rather have them at least partially on our side as totally against us."

He looked around at the assembled faces.

"No. It may be that we offer ourselves cheaply but I feel instinctively that more is to be gained this way. I trust you to arrive and free us, even if we are secured and unable to free ourselves. I have decided. This will be our path."

No more was said, the decision had been made.

***

Weldrock felt the familiar tingle of the Cormion Crystal energising. Acting swiftly he closed his eyes tight shut. It would appear to the other crystal wearers that Ashley, who they thought still held the crystal, was sleeping and would not arouse their suspicions. In the meantime he would be able to listen in on their conversation.

"Toran!" the voice belonged to Cambor leader of the centaur council in Eumor. "Is all well in Pinnhome? We have heard rumour of attacks in the mountains to the north and hills to the south."

Toran reassured them that Pinnhome was not yet under siege.

"We have contemplated sending out troops to protect the villages but reluctantly we have decided against this. The tactics being used seem to be trying to draw us out, to weaken our stronghold here at Pinnhome. We have sent troops into the Red Hills to help protect our citizens but only in small numbers."

"Regrettable but understandable," offered Cambor, "Sometimes we have to make some tough decisions, sacrifice of the few to protect the many."

There was a sad silence for a few seconds before Farspell lifted the gloom.

"Toran, I have an idea that may offer a solution for Gatherer and myself."

The expression of the OverLord changed from concern to one of hope. He listened intently as Farspell detailed his ideas of combining the energy devices of both worlds.

"So how would you join the crystals?" he asked.

"Not just the crystals but also the runestone pendant," replied the wizard. "I believe that this will be the critical component to enable the device to provide a safe opening between our worlds."

Toran pondered the idea aware of the risk that it presented to the runestone artefact and crystal.

"Tribemaker," he directed his next question at the old desert strider, "What are your thoughts on this. You are familiar with the energies of your world. Could this work?"

"OverLord, my skills and knowledge fade into insignificance in comparison to Farspell, even in his reduced state of recall. I believe he should advise us on this."

Toran nodded, "Well Farspell? What do you advise?"

Farspell frowned. "I am sure that the key can be forged but I need to work on the method of that forging. Some of the ancient spells would be needed to combine the elements, powers similar to those that Weldrock used to destroy the mountain runestone in Dargoth.

"I am sure I can master these spells but I will need some time to practice and perfect the method."

Toran could not hide a look of concern as he responded, "So many unknowns but I see no other option. Very well! Focus on this. I need your skills back here as much as Gatherer's tribe want to see his return home."

"ASHLEY!" Toran raised his voice to rouse her. Weldrock flinched but did not open his eyes.

"ASHLEY! WAKE UP!" he shouted again.

There was an ominous pause before Cambor broke the silence. "Something is wrong Toran. The link is open so she wears the pendant but she will not wake. I believe she may be unconscious."

Toran swore and tried again. "ASHLEY! WAKE UP! WHAT IS WRONG?"

Weldrock suddenly found the situation extremely funny and could not prevent a quiet laugh as he pictured the panic that ensued. Unfortunately the warlock forgot that this almost inaudible laugh would be amplified and communicated to the others. Farspell shouted a warning. "Close the link! Do not speak further! This is not Ashley!"

"Damn it! And just as it was getting interesting. I really do need to control my sense of humour but your floundering really was too much!" Farspell recognised Weldrock's voice almost immediately.

"Weldrock!" The hate was clear in his voice. "What have you done with Ashley? If you have harmed her or any of those earthlings you will answer to me." Farspell blurted out in frustration.

"My dear comrade, calm yourself. The children are fine. They are my...*guests*." Turning his attention to Toran Weldrock continued, "I am afraid that I do not have such good news for you OverLord. Your forces have somewhat, how shall I put it...dwindled."

Toran did not react; he did not want the warlock to see his sadness at losing his men. Recovering his composure he challenged. "Stop this now Weldrock before it is too late. You cannot win this battle. Even in the unlikely event that..."

"Unlikely!?" interrupted Weldrock, What do you mean 'unlikely'? We both know that you will not be able to resist my forces. That said, with Farspell isolated on his little desert world your chances will have improved greatly." He roared with laughter at his own quip. No one else commented.

"As I was saying," Toran continued. "If you surrender to us now I will offer you clemency."

Weldrock stopped laughing and his eyes narrowed. "Now you bore me fool! Enough of this," and without hesitation he removed his pendant breaking the link.

"Toran you must prepare, the warlock knows we are weakened and he may choose this time to attack. I think it is more likely than ever that Pinnhome will be his next target," said Cambor.

"I agree," replied Toran. "Can you spare any more centaur troops to bolster our forces?"

Cambor shook his head. "I'm sorry my old friend. I have barely enough to protect Eumor should he choose to strike here first. I have already provided all that I can."

Toran accepted this and understood. "Farspell, we need you back. Start work immediately on trying to build the key. It may be that time is running short. I need your counsel especially as we can no longer use the crystals without being spied upon."

With a brief acknowledgement Farspell accepted the request and the link was closed.

\*\*\*

A few hours passed before Helender returned to the warlock bearing her 'gifts' of four survivors from the wreckage of The Red Serpent. She delivered their catch to him in the runestone chamber and Weldrock almost screeched in delight when he saw the prize presented.

He examined the four captives. "Are there no other survivors?" he asked.

Helender shook her head. "None that we sssaw."

"No sea-elves lurking in the waters?" prompted the warlock displaying uncertainty.

Helender shook her head once more. "We did not sssenssse any other life on the islandsss or in the ocean."

Weldrock reached into his robe and withdrew the orb. As he squeezed it the Shii convulsed in agony.

"You are sure aren't you Helender?" he asked squeezing the orb once more.

Gorlan held his breath. He could see why Helender needed their help but wondered if under this pain she would give away the alliance. He need not have been concerned.

"We are sssure warlock. If the sssea-elvesss sssurvived then they mussst have returned home," she stammered through the pain.

"Good," said Weldrock as he placed the orb back inside his robes.

With a flick of his hand he ordered the Graav to secure the prisoners.

"Take these away and lock them up. Put Michael and this one," he pointed to Grant Landman, "in one of the apprentice rooms next to the earthlings. The other two can be thrown into the cages. I'll deal with them later."

Helender looked at Gorlan in consternation and she quickly hissed a suggestion, "Weldrock! Would it not be better to quessstion thessse sssooner rather than later? Why not lock them in the apprenticssse roomsss with the othersss. It would be much fassster to get them for quessstioning than from down below in the cagesss."

The warlock eyed the Shii leader suspiciously. "My, this is unexpected. A sudden interest in what would be best for me. I don't suppose you are planning anything are you Helender?"

Weldrock removed the orb once more and Helender and her sisters shuddered.

Laughing he put it away without using it and repeated, "To the cages with them. I will have plenty of time to deal with them later." Looking at Gorlan he continued, "I have a score to settle with this one. Torturing him will be a pleasure and a gift to myself but it can wait until we have taken Pinnhome.

"Warlocks of the Light! Step forward! Farspell is absent from Pinnhome, Gorlan now captured, the earthlings are in my control and many of the Pinn flyers and eagles are lost. Fate is smiling on me. The time has come to lay siege to Pinnhome. Gather your Graav and prepare. The glory shall be yours to share."

Gorlan and Meld exchanged anxious glances as three warlocks stepped from the shadows brandishing their staffs of power. Suddenly their alliance with the Shii did not seem such a good idea.

# CHAPTER EIGHTEEN
## The Staffs of Light

Despite the knowledge that the portal could be a threat, the Pinn guard were slow to react as the first Graav poured through the gateway. Months of tedious sentry duties had led to boredom and, despite the efforts of their commanders and the impending threat, a level of lethargy had set in.

As a result it was almost a full minute before the alarm was raised and, by this time, the Graav had already begun to scale the walls of the pit.

Shocked into alertness human, dwarven, elven and a handful of centaur reinforcements surged towards the pit where their comrades were already in action.

Time had allowed for comprehensive preparation and the Allies had built a significant source of weapons for defence of Pinnhome. Many of these had been given a boost of magic by Farspell to make them far more effective against the protective collars of the Graav.

Orders were screamed out and the soldiers on the battlements above the pit loaded huge boulders into large slingshot catapults. The catapults were angled downwards and aimed across the pit enabling the Graav to be picked off as they scrambled up the steep walls. As in previous encounters with the Graav, these met with limited success. Although they were effective in knocking the attackers back to the pit floor, very few were harmed, other than a few lucky shots that decapitated the lava-hewn creatures. Even some well placed head shots merely bounced off the protective collars that each Graav wore.

The defenders were aware that this would be the case and merely used the catapults to stall the enemy advance. As more creatures fell from pit walls elven archers arrived at the battlements, armed to the teeth with thousands of magically imbued arrows from the trees of Lorewood.

Taking up their positions the elves set to work on the wholesale slaughter of the Graav. The Lorewood shafts screeched through the air, piercing the collars and often completely severing the heads of the creatures. Smoke and ash started to fly as the dying Graav exploded into piles of hot lava-rock rubble.

Great cheers went up from around the battlements as the Graav began to fall in droves. Soon the pit floor was covered in the ash and rubble of the creatures but still more poured from the gateway. The constant wave of Graav meant that the catapults could not handle their drive for the surface and, as such, an increasing number of the marauders were scrambling out of the pit and had begun to smash their way through the wooden battlement defences.

The Graav possessed incredible strength and their concentration on conquest was not to be deterred. Even as their comrades fell around them, the creatures smashed and clawed at the wood until they had breached the defences in a number of places. The Graav were now able to advance beyond the battlements and small pockets of hand to hand fighting had broken out.

Protected by their collars, the creatures were extremely difficult to defeat in one on one combat, but the Pinns were well briefed. Their training had shown the men how to work their bodies into a position where they could pierce the necks of the stone creatures, by sliding their blades underneath the protective collar to remove the heads of their fierce opponents. In addition, those equipped with enchanted blades were clearly marked with a blue sash and the Allies worked hard to steer the individual tussles to those so armed. Even so the ratio of Graav slain in hand to hand combat was intimidating. Three Allied soldiers would fall for each Graav beheaded. Fighting the creatures at close quarters was not a strategy for success.

Fortunately for the Allies, the number of Graav that breached their line was relatively small and they continued to hold the creatures at the pit.

A great cheer went up as OverLord Toran arrived at the battlements, armed and ready for combat.

As more of the Graav fell, the pit became littered with their rubble and Toran frowned as he observed the floor level slowly rising, the portal gateway rising with it. Even though the pit was very deep, Toran prayed to himself that the enemy lacked sufficient forces to lift the floor back to ground level.

Suddenly there was a lull in the Graav flowing from the portal.

Three figures appeared in the gateway. There was a slight pause in the actions of the defenders too as they looked at the newcomers but it was very brief and within seconds the Allies had started to resume their fire.

Some shot at the new figures as they appeared but, as boulders and arrows alike flew to their intended targets; three devil-like winged creatures flew from the portal to block them.

The Shii had been given their instructions. Defend the Warlocks of Light at all costs.

The Allied forces watched in amazement and consternation as the boulders and arrows that struck the Shii merely passed into their dark bodies. They simply disappeared from existence, their matter and energy absorbed.

Toran turned to Kul who had joined him. "By all the gods what are these creatures?"

Kul shrugged, "I have never seen their like sire. I wish Farspell were with us. If anyone would know then it would be him."

At the pit floor, in unison Zephyr, Fenwaer and Ryne stood back to back and invoked the power of the Staffs of Light. Each emitted a ray in a large arc of around one hundred and thirty degrees. With all three warlocks thus employed the entire pit area was illuminated by the energy that beamed from their staffs.

The ruby on Zephyr's staff pulsated as it emitted a red arc of light which shone out of the pit to illuminate the battlements above. Everything in its path, Graav and Allied defenders alike, were affected by the red beam and immediately time for them slowed almost to a halt. For those watching it seemed that those tinged in red had become frozen. Closer inspection showed that they continued to fight, but at a rate that was incredibly slow and hardly perceivable.

The blue arc of light that spilled from the sapphire of Ryne's staff also kissed all that fell within its beam. As each creature came under its spell, each became despondent and Toran watched in disbelief as hardened warriors broke down in tears and threw their weapons to the floor, falling to their knees in abject misery. Not even the stone faced Graav were immune to the power. Where they were bathed in the blue glow they stopped and looked around in confusion, unable to understand as they tasted emotion for the first time. Soldiers rushed in to help their colleagues but were immediately overcome with despair as they also became victims.

But it was the emerald green glow that offered the greatest threat to the Allies. Fenwaer stood and projected his force. As the soldier were touched by its light, their faced turned a jaundiced yellow. Human, dwarf and elf alike began to vomit and their strength was sapped from them as their weapons fell helplessly to their sides. Toran, shaded from all the beams by his vantage point high in one of the towers, watched in horror as those in the path of the green beam were struck defenceless. The Graav, although their reactions were slowed by the touch of the staff, did not suffer in a similar way, and so were able to continue their progress forward, slicing and killing prostrate opponents as they advanced.

Toran screamed orders to his commanders and the word was passed to the green bathed zone for the defenders to fall back, away from the power of the staff. Fortunately, with the warlocks still deep in the pit, only a small area of the rim was affected and the defenders were able to successfully rebuild their defensive line a short distance away from the edge.

For the first time Toran turned his attention to the skies above and saw that his eagle riders had also been forced to retreat from the pit's edge. The beams from the staffs' continued their projections high into the sky. As eagle and rider were touched by the light they too fell under its influence. In two sectors the response was dramatic as those bathed in red and green literally dropped out of the sky.

As luck would have it, when each fell, they moved beyond the direct line of the beams, allowing them sufficient time to recover their senses and to avoid smashing into the ground. However, with the eagles now pushed back, the power of the staffs had, at least for the moment, rendered ineffective their aerial threat.

Even in the blue sector the birds were neutralised, seemingly frozen in a moment in time as, for them, time slowed.

Realising that their position at the bottom of the pit still left them vulnerable and largely ineffective the warlocks changed their tactics.

Turning as one they brought the light of their staffs together. As the three arcs converged, the individual beams of red, green and blue flared to a brilliant white. The warlocks lowered the trajectory of the beam and focussed its power onto the pit wall.

Graav that were caught within the beam exploded violently, white hot rock splashing into the air. The earth barrier offered poor resistance to the intense glare of the combined staffs and began to bubble and disintegrate. Slowly the warlocks were burning a wide upward slope.

With the power of the staffs now redeployed, fighting had once again broken out all around. Increasing numbers of Graav fell but were just as quickly replaced as reinforcements poured through the open portal. Despite their cold, lifeless demeanour, the creatures were quick to learn that they should remain outside the arc of white.

The Allies continued to hold their lines but Toran looked on with a worried expression aware that the tide of the battle would turn if the warlocks were able to burn a pathway to the surface.

He shouted orders for increased efforts on attacking the staff wielders and within seconds the projectiles aimed at the magic users increased ten fold. Toran nodded in satisfaction as a wave of boulders and arrows screeched through the skies towards the three protagonists. Positive that this barrage would finish them he even allowed himself a smile.

That smile did not last long.

In an incredible display of speed and unbelievable accuracy, the Shii leapt from projectile to projectile, their bodies a blur as they absorbed boulder and elven arrows alike. Not one arrow penetrated the defence of the Shii; the creatures provided a living force field around the magicians.

Ignoring the battle overhead, the warlocks increased their efforts on the destruction of the pit wall and the growth of the pathway accelerated at an alarming rate. Toran realised that they would be at the surface within minutes.

Adjusting his strategy he signalled for the fire eagles to return to the pit and sent Kul to give them orders to eliminate the warlocks.

Ten riders mounted and, swords raised, riders and eagles swooped into the depths as the catapult bombardment stopped to allow them safe passage. However, the elves, confident in the accuracy of their archery, continued to fire shafts at the enemy below.

As the eagles dived towards their intended targets one of the Shii looked up towards them.

"Sssissstersss! A challenge at lassst. Come!"

Two of the Shii broke off, leaving the last to protect the warlocks. They flew to meet the eagles, emitting an unholy screech as they closed in on the huge birds.

The eagle riders soon found that their swords were useless. Their blades struck the Shii, their metal sliced easily through the flesh but immediately started to sizzle and disintegrate. As the swords literally fell apart, the incision that they had made quickly sealed leaving the Shii completely unharmed. In consternation the riders realised that they would have to rely on the fire magic of their eagles to defeat this foe.

The Shii were fast. Too fast.

The plan had been for half of the eagles to occupy the Shii as the others attacked the warlocks. The speed of their foe prevented this and the two female demons moved from rider to rider, slicing deeply into human and warbird with their long claws. Time and time again the eagles flailed their legs hopelessly, each time finding only clear air as they failed to grasp the Shii in their own talons, hence unable to invoke their fire magic.

In their efforts to trap the Shii, the eagles were forced to weave in and out and confusion began to take hold. Some of the birds collided with each other and one rider was knocked from his mount. He fell to the pit below and the Graav were quick to finish him off. Immediately his eagle flew skywards, heading westwards into oblivion.

The Allies watched in horror as some of their finest riders were torn to shreds by the claws of the Shii. Rider and eagle continued to battle, but now all were bleeding heavily from numerous deep wounds.

Time seemed to stand still for a while but, in reality, in a matter of less than a minute the remaining nine eagles and riders fell into the pit, victims of the ferocity of the devil like creatures. These fire eagles would have to travel to oblivion in spirit alone; they would not be taking their bodies with them.

With the reduction in the aerial barrage the Graav started to pour over the rim. In some ways it was fortunate, heavily involved in holding back the attack of the stone men, it left little time to fully realise the defeat of the fire eagles. The Graav continued their slow advance as human, elven and dwarven defenders fought courageously and fiercely to repel the assault.

The Staffs of Light continued their destruction of the pit wall and Zephyr, Fenwaer and Ryne now began to advance along their light hewn pathway. The dirt at their feet still smoked as they strode upwards continuing to build the path ahead of them. Boulders and arrows rained down, still protected by the Shii, the warlocks remain untouched.

As the pathway continued to grow, Toran changed tactics.

Kul, now mounted, led a full blooded high speed cavalry charge in the hope that the strength and speed of the horses would give them access beyond the Shii allowing them to confront the warlocks. The large war horses, now clothed in battle armour, were breathtaking as they roared forward, the polished metal reflecting the light of the staffs. Urged on by their riders they galloped towards their targets. When they reached the edge, and with the pathway still some four metres below, the first horses leapt into the air and down onto the marauders below.

It was another slaughter! Touched by the brilliant aura of the combined staffs, the cavalrymen and horses suffered a similar fate to that of the Graav. Within a fraction of a second the intense ray had turned them into cinders as they erupted into balls of white hot flame. At the head of the column, leading by example, Kul was the first to die. Toran, watching from his vantage point, felt cold pains stabbing his stomach as he saw his friend slain.

The speed of the attack was so great that a large number of the cavalrymen had no time to turn their mounts. Twenty more horses and riders perished with the last few falling in their effort to stop the advance, the horses losing their footing as they slipped off the edge of the pit, down to the pathway, now only two metres below.

Observing the death of their comrades and the fruitless impact of the advance, the remaining cavalrymen turned their mounts to the side. Galloping to the left and right, they were able to sprint away from the warlocks avoiding the focus of the beam that brought instant death.

As the warlocks neared the surface they were able to lower the elevation of the projection and defenders had to run for cover as the white beam levelled across the open field. It burned everything in its path, yielding to neither Allies nor attackers in its quest for death.

The pit rim now breached, the three warlocks returned to their previous strategy and split the emanations from their staffs into three once more. Now level with their enemy the impact was even greater as the beams were able to travel a significant distance.

The colours of the staff painted the countryside a curious mix of hues. Green faced forward, allowing a steady progress as the Graav piled into this sector, slaying the vomiting defenders as they slowly advanced. To the left the battlefield had gone deathly quiet as the red beam froze time while to the right, Graav wandered in confusion around humans, elves and dwarves, who, in turn, were sat on the ground in utter despair. For some the level of misery was so intense that they took their own lives. Occasionally a Graav would seem to remember why they were there and would strike.

Where the arcs of light overlapped the land and creatures were stained a new colour, cyan where the power of the emerald and sapphire touched and yellow, where that of the ruby crossed with the emerald.

Behind the warlocks more Graav ambled out of the portal and up the newly forged pathway. The warlocks separated to allow the reinforcements to pass through the centre of them and into the green zone. All three warlocks roared as they displayed their powers and enjoyed utter mastery of the battle.

\*\*\*

While the battle for Pinnhome raged on, in the Sea of Mist, Prince Trelane led the small band of Pinns and sea-elves to the southern tip of Weldrock's stronghold. Graav roamed freely around the island so they were careful to move under cover and as silently as the terrain allowed. Fortunately, the buildings, isolated out here on this mist shrouded island, were not built to withstand attack and they soon found unguarded access to the main structure through a drainage system.

"I'm glad we left the eagles behind," whispered Carl to his brother. "They would not have been able to get down these drains."

The Prince agreed, "Very true, but Howler seemed less than happy being left behind. I think he sensed what we intended and wanted to come too."

Wading through the shallow waters the Prince led them into the domain of the warlock.

When they came to a crossway, Prince Trelane paused. "Trall, any thoughts on which tunnel we should take? Winding our way in the dark like this has removed my sense of direction."

The dwarf, now clutching a short battle axe that the elves had recovered from the wreck, shrugged.

"Aye, it can do that to you when you are not used to it. We're more or less facing in the same direction as when we entered. Straight ahead would lead us deeper into the building. My guess would be that the warlock would sit at the centre of his domain so I'd say we take that tunnel."

Prince Trelane accepted the advice and led them on. A few minutes later they reached a circular area that was lit from above and looking up they could see a large drain cover. A hard wood ladder was conveniently secured to the tunnel wall leading up to the surface.

"This must be for maintenance access." Prince Trelane smiled at Stern and Carl. "After you gentlemen."

The brothers bowed and began to climb. When they reached the drain cover they paused and listened. All was quiet.

Lifting the cover they climbed out of the tunnels and found themselves in a small courtyard at the centre of a rectangular building. Doors led into the courtyard from all four sides and a grey stone-clad two storey building seemed to cage them in. Checking that all was clear the brothers signalled for the others to join them.

The group slipped over to the wall and flattened themselves against it. No windows looked out onto the courtyard, so no-one could observe them from inside, but neither could they see anyone who may exit from one of the doors.

Stern ran to the first door and listened. Hearing noises within he shook his head and signalled for Carl to try another.

Straining his ears at the wooden entrance, Carl waited to be doubly sure that no-one was within before trying the handle. The door popped open and he eased inside. The others waited for his signal to proceed. Seconds went by and they became uneasy. A minute passed and as Stern looked questionably at the Prince his brother suddenly appeared and waved them forward.

As they entered, Stern saw the telltale sign of steaming rubble, testament to the fact that Carl had had to dispatch one of the Graav. The Prince indicated to his elves that the rubble should be hidden and then they were creeping forward once more. Ahead the corridor turned sharply to the right. Pausing at the junction the Prince cautiously glanced around the wall.

Ahead was a long grey corridor that led down to a set of arched wooden doors.

Twelve rooms were offset to this corridor, six on both sides and midway down Graav stood sentry at four of the doors.

"The Graav must be taken swiftly and quietly to prevent the alarm being raised." Prince Trelane turned to the Pinns. "Pinnel, I want you to draw their attention. You are the fastest runner of us all and your speed can be used to our advantage. The Graav are single minded but cumbersome. Sprint past them and take a stance at the far end of the corridor but do not step beyond the junction in case other guards stand sentry. The Graav should be drawn to you and we can then attack from behind."

Pinnel nodded and Prince Trelane turned his attention to the Kraven, the bard warrior.

"Kraven, you are the only one of us to possess a blade that has been blessed by Farspell. You will need to move fast. The guards must be taken down quickly and efficiently." Addressing the rest he continued. "My elves have no seametal arrows but they do possess arrows honed from Lorewood and these will pierce the protective collars of the Graav."

He looked into the eyes of the men and elves and saw grim determination in all.

"On my count...one...two...three...sprint!"

Pinnel burst around the corner of the corridor and pumped his legs faster than he had ever done before. He sped past the four Graav, taking a cursory swipe at two of them with his sword.

As he reached the end of the corridor he stopped and, with sword raised, turned to face the guards.

"Damn!" he cursed out loud. The Graav may be cumbersome but they were not stupid. As two advanced on him the remaining two took up a battle stance and remained at their post. As a result they were able to respond immediately as Kraven turned the corner backed by the two sea-elves.

The bard warrior leapt towards the first Graav and with one mighty swing his weapon bit deeply into the collar. Even given the strength of that strike the blow did not cut deep enough to severe the head and the Graav was able to strike back, forcing Kraven to block and take a defensive stance.

Almost simultaneously two Lorewood arrows flew from the bows of the sea-elves. The first completed the decapitation that Kraven had started and bit its way through the remaining lava rock, completely severing the head of the creature. As the lava man burst into molten ash, Kraven received painful splashes on his bare skin forcing him to take a step backwards to avoid being severely burned.

His movement intercepted the path of the second arrow which luckily skimmed off the edge of his armour. Unfortunately the deflection of the arrow was sufficient to take it off its intended path and it continued its flight harmlessly over the head of the second Graav.

As much through instinct as through sight, Kraven realised his predicament and his years of battle experience told him to continue his backward motion. As he pushed with his legs he leapt into the air and carried out a neat back flip. During his brief flight he heard two telltale sounds. The first that of the stone sword of the Graav whistling past his head, as his foe missed, and the second the sickening impact of a Graav sword slicing through flesh. Although he registered the significance of that sound, Kraven did not take time to contemplate it. As he landed on his feet he realised that he was off balance and defenceless. The Graav struck again but this time the sword slash was met with a loud clang as stone sword met battle axe.

"I don't think so laddie!" snarled Trall as he blocked the death strike.

With time bought for him by the dwarf, Kraven adopted a forward striking stance and dwarf and Pinn simultaneously struck at the neck of the second Graav. The combined strength of the magic tinged sword, together with the dwarven axe allowed the blows to bite deep, travelling straight through the collar and stone to remove the head of the creature. The force of the blow smashed through Kraven's arms and his sword was torn from his grasp. It slid noisily along the floor out of his reach.

Even as it fell, Kraven, now weapon less, was running down the corridor towards Pinnel. Turning he heard the swish of another arrow and a third Graav erupted into a smoking pile.

He noticed that the fourth Graav was chest to chest with Pinnel and suddenly, in horror and despair, he realised that the sword of the lava man protruded through the body of his comrade. Pinnel was skewered but still alive.

Realising that their success depended on his preventing the Graav from escape, Pinnel summoned up all of his life force and began to sprint. His body screamed with pain but with his last breaths he somehow managed to call forth immense strength and began to push the stone creature backwards, forcing it towards Kraven and the elves.

"Shoot the damned thing!" said Kraven as loud as he dared.

The sea-elves were already firing but to no avail. They had exhausted their supply of Lorewood and seametal arrows.

Continuing his run towards the creature Kraven closed in. Stooping as they made contact, Kraven scooped up the spent Lorewood arrow that he had earlier deflected off target and slammed the shaft under the neck band of the Graav. The energy from the arrow spread swiftly around the creature's head and it too fell into a pile of ash with a satisfying popping sound.

Kraven stood with hands on his thighs, bent almost double and gasping for breath. As the others caught up to him they looked down at Pinnel's body, now lifeless.

Prince Trelane slapped Kraven across the shoulders. "Well fought bard but I am sorry for your lost rider."

On the island to the south, a faithful fire eagle took to the skies and flew west into oblivion.

# CHAPTER NINETEEN
## Two Fronts

High on the protective wall of Pinnhome, Tosh stood with Gatherer watching the carnage taking place below. He paced up and down, frustration and worry mixed on his face.

Finally he stopped and turned to the giant.

"I am sorry my friend. I know my orders were to remain here with you but I cannot watch on idly as my men die. I must ride with them."

Gatherer understood and nodded. "I will come with you." It was a statement, not a question.

Tosh shook his head. "No, this is not your battle. You should remain here where it is safe."

The desert strider snorted. "It may be safe at the moment but not for long and then the battle will be as much mine as your own. Come, let's fight side by side!"

Tosh recognised the truth in the giant's words. Sensing his need his eagle had already landed, ready to carry his soul partner to battle.

"We will have to land to the rear of the warlocks to avoid the power of their staffs," suggested Gatherer.

Tosh shook his head. "No, I don't think so."

He pointed to the battlefield below. "Look at where the arcs collide. It would seem that the powers of each staff are negated when two overlap."

Gatherer looked in the direction that the Pinn indicated. Where the ground was shaded yellow and cyan the Graav and Allies were fighting normally, unaffected by the sorcery of the staffs.

A wide grin stretched over the hairless face of the giant as he followed the lead of Tosh and swiftly climbed up onto the back of the war bird. With both firmly seated the bird stepped off the town walls and glided towards the havoc below.

The rider hugged the giant bird. Tosh always felt a deep sadness when he rode the eagle into conflict. So far they had both been fortunate and always returned from battle unscathed, but the thought of what could happen made him feel cold and sick inside.

As the eagle descended Tosh held his right hand aloft, fist clenched. Surveying the skies around him he screamed at the top of his voice, "Eagle-riders! To me!"

***

Prince Trelane opened the first cell. Michael and Grant Landman beamed widely when they saw him.

"We thought you'd never get here," they joked.

Moving swiftly, Michael helped free the others and as Ashley left her cell he swiftly gathered her up and squeezed her body so tight she ached. She didn't mind though and she hugged him in return equally affectionately.

Rhys was still drugged and while able to walk he needed to be half propped, half pulled along by Stern and Carl.

"The room ahead is Weldrock's condo." offered Ashley. "It is quite heavily guarded and the door is secured by some form of magic. I think the runestone chamber is that way," Ashley continued, pointing down one side of the T-junction, "but I don't know where that corridor leads." she added as she turned and indicated the other branch.

Michael offered his advice, "I think the Graav headed down that way when they took Gorlan and Meld away. I only got a quick glance as they exited but I'm sure that is where they went. Perhaps it leads to the 'cages'."

Prince Trelane looked along the corridors. "Then we shall take that route. Our first priority should be to free Gorlan."

"...and Meld!" exclaimed Ashley.

Led by Prince Trelane they made their way along the empty corridor. At the end he opened the door and saw a dimly lit stairway that descended straight for a few metres and then turned ninety degrees to the right. There was no sign of any guard.

Moving as silently as they could they followed the stairway, peeping around the corners when they came to a change in direction. It seemed that the route zigzagged downwards, a change to the right shortly followed by a turn to the left but always following a steep descent.

Eventually, they came to an arch that opened into a large chamber. They crept through the arch and saw that they were on a stone ledge that overlooked a great chamber.

At the centre of the chamber a huge fire roared brightly, so severe that the heat filled the entire cave-like room.

From the roof a series of strong chains led down to twenty or so cages that hung suspended high above the fire. Six chambers appeared occupied, two by Gorlan and Meld. A set of narrow winding stairs led down to the main chamber and the floor was teeming with Graav.

Prince Trelane frowned at the scene. "Does anyone have any ideas on how we get those two free?" he asked.

He looked at each of his comrades searching for some inspiration. The others noticed a sudden change in his demeanour. "Where is Landman?" he asked.

The others looked around and scanned the area but there was no sign of him.

Suddenly they heard heavy footfall approaching from above them on the stairwell.

"Seize them!" Weldrock commanded and within seconds they found themselves surrounded by the Graav. Sharp lava hewn sword points pricking at their throats.

At Weldrock's right stood Nexus, known to them as Grant Landman, and he was grinning from ear to ear.

The warlock laughed, "You have done well Nexus, your loyalty shall be rewarded."

Waving a hand towards the cages he continued. "Free those two and bring them all to my chamber. It is time to rid myself of this troublesome band."

***

Above Pinnhome eagle riders rallied to their captain.

Tosh hovered with his eagle and soon the remaining thirty war birds were formed up behind him in a triangular formation. Looking down at the growing carnage below his men awaited orders.

Tosh indicated the overlapping arcs where the power of the staff was nullified and signalled for his forces to divide into two. He commanded both lines to attack and, as his riders swept past, he increased his own altitude to await his chance, hovering as his men met the Graav with full force.

The ferocity of the eagle attack was awesome.

In the battle for Fortown the fire eagles had found that their fire attack would merely replenish the energies of the lava hewn Graav and their efforts to remove the heads of the creatures with their claws had only met with a limited success. However, since then the riders had had time to prepare and during their drills they had practised for this moment. As the birds made contact with the Graav they locked their talons around the necks of the creatures, just above the protective collar. Once in their firm grip the eagles struck out violently with their huge wings to swivel the head as they pulled.

The effect was dramatic. The rock heads of the Graav were torn off and the creatures exploded with an audible pop and hiss of releasing gases. One rider, caught in the act of removing a head did not see the approach of a second Graav. As the eagle twisted it also dipped and the back of the rider was suddenly exposed to the advancing lava man. With one swift plunge of its sharp stone sword the rider was slain, falling from the back of his bird. Tosh winced as he watched the eagle climb and fly away to the west.

Returning his gaze to the fighting, he saw that his men had been successful in clearing a path to the warlocks and their protective Shii. With a huge roar he instructed his eagle to dive. The battle cry of the warrior was joined by the high pitched scream of the eagle and a roar from Gatherer as he held his scimitar aloft.

Talons outstretched Tosh's eagle screeched toward the warlocks. One of the Shii leapt to defend the intended targets. Eagle and Shii struck each other with an almighty slap that was heard all over the battlefield. Gatherer was thrown from the back of the warbird and flew through the air to land inside the emerald green zone. All around him the Graav were murdering the Allied forces as the defenders lay vomiting and writhing.

As the two creatures met, more through luck than skill, Tosh turned his eagle onto its back. The movement took the Shii by surprise and as she threw out her own claws to strike at the war bird she badly mistimed her strike. The momentum of her swing forced her arm onto the talons of the fire eagle. The sharp claws pierced the dark flesh and the eagle immediately reacted, invoking its own magical forces to call on its phoenix like powers of flame.

The cries of the Shii reached an unbearable level as she burst into flame. For a moment her two sisters paused to cry out in agony as they watched their kin die. One remained to protect the warlocks and the other advanced on Tosh.

The captain of the riders was quick to recover and with a huge flap of its wings his eagle soared upwards to safety, momentarily out of reach of the attacker. The Shii, infuriated by Tosh and the eagle, contemplated chasing after them, but her attention was drawn to the green zone where Gatherer now stood, his scimitar a blur as he waved it from side to side decapitating Graav with a ruthless display of deft skill.

The desert strider had removed his tunic and stood battling bare-chested. His chameleon-like skin had changed to match the green aura of the staff. This made it difficult for the Graav to follow his movement as he battled ferociously.

Tosh watched the scene unfold. A shiver went down his spine as he looked at the desert strider. The calm, gentle creature that he had come to know had been transformed. In its place stood a pure hunting and fighting machine, its face as impassive as that of the Graav.

The Shii did not pause. She leapt towards Gatherer as the Graav retreated to allow the female a clear run at him.

The giant desert strider stood poised as the Shii made her attack. Gatherer had not seen anything move that quickly and his first defensive strike was in vain as the creature knocked him to the ground, drawing blood across his chest as it raked him with her talons. Large red welts formed on his green tainted flesh.

Gatherer regained his feet and once more stood with sword poised. The warlocks looked on somewhat confused, not only by the sight of this strange giant of a creature but also by the fact that he appeared to be immune to the power of the emerald staff.

The Shii looked down on him and grinned with pure malice as Gatherer struck out with his sword. She made no effort to block the blow. The blade sliced deep into her flesh and she laughed as it was engulfed by her body. Unlike the weapons of the Pinn riders though, Gatherer's sword did not disintegrate and, as it left the body of the Shii, a large black bubble of blood welled up on her skin. She immediately stopped laughing and stared at the wound in disbelief. Hope arose from those that looked on, but just as swiftly, it was quenched as within seconds the wound healed itself, leaving the Shii unharmed. All that the blow had achieved was to make her even angrier.

This time more cautious in her approach, the Shii used her speed and strength to strike at the desert strider from the left. Once again a line of claw marks raked across his chest and, as he fell, she swung her other arm around swiftly to strike him across the side of the head.

Gatherer was immediately stunned and everything went black. He lay there defenceless, shaking his head to clear his vision. The Shii stood over him and prepared to drive her talons deep into his body.

\*\*\*

The island runestone rocked beneath the feet of the Graav as the line of warriors continued to pass through the portal to bolster the ranks of their kind at Pinnhome.

Weldrock stood leaning against the runestone pedestal watching his forces advance and surveying his prisoners that he now had grouped together.

"Well! Well! So it seems there were a few more survivors than my 'faithful' Helender reported." He turned to face the senior Shii. "How is this Helender? How could it be that you missed so many?"

Helender remained silent.

"Shall I show you what happens to those that betray me!" snapped the warlock viciously.

Still Helender remained impassive.

Whipping out the orb, Weldrock began to pull and stretch it with as much violence as he could muster.

The Shii began to screech in agony as their bodies contorted, their forms moving in horrific deformity as the orb was squeezed and twisted.

The tormented cries of the creatures assaulted the ears of the captives. Men and elves covered their ears to silence the sound as the Graav continued their relentless advance through the portal.

Only one of the humans remained unmoved. Still standing in a trance-like state, Rhys was suddenly awakened; some semblance of the anguished cries had reached his mind and slowly freed him from the effects of the drugs.

As his sense returned the first scene that registered was that of Weldrock torturing the Shii. Behind them the Graav continued to pour through the portal. Rhys knew instinctively that the Graav were heading for battle and his deep distrust of the warlock fired his impulses as he immediately reacted in defence of Helender.

Forming the picture of a portal in his mind he focused on the warlock and began to create a gateway, one targeted directly on the physical form of his enemy, not merely in empty air. Static sizzled around Weldrock and his grey hair began to stand on end as the portal began to form. Recognising the feel of the portal as it grew around him the warlock turned angrily to Rhys. Furious, he raised his hand and a bolt of blue energy scorched the air. It flew towards the young man striking him centrally in the chest. Rhys was thrown across the chamber.

While manipulating the orb in his right hand, Weldrock continued to pour energy into the beam of power and Rhys began to convulse and shudder as his body began to burn. Ashley and the others made to protect him, but were easily forced back by the Graav that surrounded them. She screamed when she saw Rhys' hair begin to smoke and a scorching smell filled their noses. He was being burned alive.

# CHAPTER TWENTY
## End Game

On the battlefield at Pinnhome, Gatherer saw the figure of the Shii looming over him, still dazed he was powerless. Talons outstretched, the creature focused on the desert giant's chest, intent on tearing out his heart. As she made her forward thrust to finish her foe, she suddenly dropped to her knees and began to convulse and writhe in pain.

A few metres away, her sister was suffering in a similar manner. From his eagle, Tosh looked on in amazement as both creatures fell to the ground, their bodies contorting and convulsing. Their flesh appeared to be twisting and bubbling, as the creatures rolled around in agony. He allowed himself a sigh of relief, his new comrade in arms had been so close to death.

Gatherer regained his feet and recovered his composure, a savage grin crossed his face and stepping towards the Shii he struck out at her, cutting into her flesh with a single sweep of his sword. As before the weapon sliced through but the wound sealed itself over. The Shii, still thrashing around seemed oblivious to his attempts. Gatherer grunted in frustration. Taking careful aim he brought his blade down in a sweeping arc to slice through her neck.

Almost as quickly as the flesh was cut, it reformed behind the blade. Although defenceless before him it would appear that his weapon could not permanently damage the creature. Gatherer, realising this turned his attention to the warlocks.

With no Shii defending them, the warlocks had swiftly appraised the situation and, as one, they moved their staffs back together to re-form the blinding white ray of death. Gatherer and the Shii were engulfed in the beam.

Tosh screamed a warning, but too late. Momentarily, before the light blazed full on, he saw the first Shii start to bubble and melt as the rays touched her skin. Thankfully the intensity of the light prevented him witnessing the same fate for his desert strider friend.

In the path of the beam Gatherer stood staring death in the face for the second time in a matter of seconds.

He closed his eyes and thought of Sandmover as the rays bathed his whole body and he felt the searing heat.

Seconds passed and realisation dawned. He recognised this power.

It was not identical, but it had the feel of the core energies of his desert world. The familiarity of powers used during his sensings.

He opened his eyes once again and, using his additional eyelids as filters, he ran straight along the path of the beam.

The Warlocks of the Staff of Light, blind to the approaching giant, did not have time to react as Gatherer burst upon them. With a rolling dive and three sweeps of his scimitar the desert strider impaled two warlocks through the chest and removed the head of the third.

Immediately the staffs fell to the floor, their power quelled.

Taking the opportunity that this presented, Toran and his eagles fell on the second Shii who was still writhing on the floor. Weakened by the damage that had been inadvertently dealt to her as Weldrock punished Helender, she was only able to offer a token effort and the eagles swiftly invoked their fire magic to incinerate her flesh.

A major victory had been won by the Allied defenders though the battle was far from over. The Graav continued to pour out of the pit and had succeeded in overrunning the battlements along the pit rim.

Toran screamed orders to his commanders and the Allied troops started to fall back to the city walls, their second line of defence. Gatherer, now facing the Graav alone was suddenly pulled off his feet as Tosh's eagle lifted him to safety. He made a fruitless grab for the staffs that lay on the ground but missed and the wooden shafts were soon trampled into the soil by the advancing lava men.

Humans, dwarves and elves streamed towards the city, their retreat helped by the slow advance of the Graav who continued their steady march forward. The fire eagles continued to attack, striking at the Graav to allow their comrades time to regroup within Pinnhome.

It was a dangerous task for the eagles. In the action of twisting to remove the heads of their opponents, the rider was left exposed at times and five more eagles lost their soul mates during the sprint for the city.

Their deaths were not fruitless though and had bought the time needed for the forces to flood through the gates repositioning themselves on the ramparts.

Tosh dropped Gatherer onto the battlements alongside Toran before turning to rejoin his men. The fire eagle captain counted twenty-nine eagles still picking off Graav.

The stone men continued their resolute advance, finally reaching the city. Here they started to work on the wall itself, driving their swords and fists into the stonework in an effort to batter their way through, or to manufacture handholds to allow them to clamber up to the walkways above.

The Pinns had been prepared for this eventuality too and along the ramparts they had built multiple defensive engines. These wooden devices had been designed by Toran himself. Driven by water, which was housed in large purpose built tanks, buckets mounted on a large wheel were filled. This turned a device that resembled a windmill, the blades of which were shaped like large wooden spoons. As the arms revolved, they were loaded with boulders, fed to the spoons by another water driven ramp.

With the weight of the stone now loaded, the device turned slowly. As it reached the apex of its rotation, the large wheel met supporting rails that prevented the rocks falling from the scoop. The water continued to power the wheel, sliding the ammunition along the rails until it passed over the city wall. Here the rails finished and the boulder was released onto the Graav that clambered up from below.

Although the trajectory was ineffective for decapitating the Graav, the engine was very effective in striking multiple attackers from the city walls. The timing of the rotation was sufficient to prevent the attackers from reaching the top of the walls before another barrage of boulders fell on them. Time and time again the stone men approached their goal only to be struck back to the ground by a well placed bombardment. Although accurate, the engines had only a few degrees of lateral movement and so in many places, more traditional and manual methods were needed to repel the onslaught. Some threw rocks at the Graav while others used their weapons and bare hands to push the creatures back as the Graav breached the protective wall.

The Pinns, in an effort to quell the fires of the lava born Graav, even tried large barrels of water and ice but they soon gave up on this as this proved less effective than the boulders.

Occasionally, those fighting hand to hand would find themselves in an unbreakable grip and would themselves be dragged to their deaths by the falling Graav.

Despite the defeat of the warlocks and Shii, the size of the Graav force was beginning to turn the tide of battle back to the aggressors and enemy reinforcements continued to pour from the portal. Fire eagles and even some lorewood arrows dented the numbers but still they continued to come.

***

Grant Landman, now in his role of Nexus, right hand man to Weldrock, stared in disbelief. He was fighting against the rising turmoil that welled within. Liam Sagot, a loner and completely self-centred had never been faced with the prospect of having kin of his own and he did not want to see Rhys die in this way.

With a sudden move, the real character of Sagot came to the fore and as his persona as Nexus died he made his move. Exploding into action he leapt at Weldrock.

While in midair he drew his knife and, as he made contact with the warlock, he thrust the blade deep within, puncturing Weldrock's dark heart from the rear.

Caught in mid spell and suffering the shock of blinding pain the warlock lost control of the forces and the energies reversed, now focusing on his own body. As the warlock became consumed with his own force, the runestone artefacts in his possession appeared to amplify the reversal of the spell. The Cormion Crystal pulsed as it fed the energy fire and even Weldrock's own island ring and pendant fuelled the inferno, helping to destroy their creator.

Locked together, Weldrock and Sagot burned brightly as the forces enveloped them. The momentum of Sagot's strike pushed them forward and they fell onto the runestone pedestal. The forces locked within the pedestal clashed with those of the energy spell and now it too burned brightly incinerating the bodies that hung over it. As the heat intensified and burned to an almost white tone, the pedestal and artefacts began to melt. The portal to Pinnhome closed.

The warlock and Sagot writhed in the aura as they were seared by its power. The black control sphere of the Shii fell and rolled across the floor to come to rest against Helender, still on the ground herself after her torture at the hands of the warlock.

With a roar of triumph Helender snatched the orb. She wasted no time. Turning to stare at Gorlan and the others, who were still held by the Graav, she let out a loud and aggressive hiss before she and her sisters evaporated. They had returned back to the dark dimensions from where they had been summoned. Gorlan sighed with relief but had a strong feeling that their paths may cross again some day.

The bodies of Weldrock and Nexus were now cooling as the energy dissipated. Next to them lay the remains of the Island runestone pedestal and key. The runestone pendants that they had been wearing could be seen as small patches of white ash against their bodies.

The warlock was still unmoving. As they looked on a sudden change came over both charred bodies.

Weldrock's began to flake and crack as his lifeless shell fell to dust.

Grant Landman appeared to flare momentarily and his form was reshaped.

A few metres away Rhys recovered his feet and with singed hair, he looked at the transformed Nexus. While the body was still extremely charred there was something familiar about the face.

Rhys jumped as a croaking sound was heard. It came from the throat of Nexus.

"Rhys," it cackled weakly. "Forgive me. I have been so stupid!"

Rhys bent to the dying man.

"I was never a good man Rhys but I lost my way when I came to Portalia. Tell your Aunt I have always loved her, even when I was unkind and cruel."

Rhys gasped. A vision of old photographs flashed through his mind. This was his Uncle Liam!

"Rhys, listen to me. There is a gateway, the Shimmering Gate. It lies in the mountains to the north. Deep within the Pinnacles where few travel. It..." Sagot coughed and a dribble of blood ran down his blackened chin.

"...it leads to Peru. You can get home."

"Quiet Uncle, you need to rest," replied Rhys, but he knew it was too late. With one last request from Sagot for forgiveness Rhys watched as the last wisps of life left his Uncle's body.

There was no time to mourn. Standing Rhys turned to face the Graav that guarded him and his friends, unsure of his next course of action, or indeed how the creatures would react. Should they remain passive or attack before the lava men had time to strike?

The Graav solved the dilemma for him as they retreated from the chamber, leaving them all free and unmolested. The line of Graav warriors that had been advancing through the portal also turned and retreated.

Prince Trelane and Gorlan frowned and looked at each questioningly. "What's happening?" asked the Prince.

Gorlan shrugged. "I don't know but I think it may be a good time to get out of here before the Graav change their minds and decide they don't like our presence here. My guess is that they are in a confused state due to the death of Weldrock."

The others did not need a second invitation to flee.

Rhys gave one last look as he was helped from the chamber by Carl and Stern. The runestone stood undamaged but was now useless without the pedestal.

As he turned to leave Ashley pushed her way back into the chamber and shouted.

"Wait, the pendants! We need to get the pendants!"

She ran to the body of the warlock. It was no good. Anything that he had been wearing was destroyed along with his body. In desperation she looked around the chamber but had no idea where to look.

Rhys joined her. "I can't see them!" she shouted.

He looked around the chamber. As he scanned the room he focused his mind. He could now sense the portal energy, not only from the area of the runestone but from a large set of drawers to one side. "There!" he shouted. "I can feel them. They are in there!"

Ashley rushed to the area where he pointed and pulled open the top drawer. Inside was the warlock's collection of runestone artefacts.

She grabbed them out of their slots. Throwing one of the Eumor pendants to Rhys she put the other over her head. The rest of the artefacts she bundled up and placed in her pocket.

"C'mon, let's go!" she shouted and they sprinted from the chamber.

The group rushed through the corridors passing numerous Graav that paid them no heed. As they turned a final bend to face the exit, Ashley broke away once more.

"Ash! What are you doing?" shouted Michael.

"Go on!" she replied, "I will be fine. I have to get my eagle."

Michael and Rhys made to follow her but a strong hand pulled them back.

"No! Stay with us. She will be fine." It was Gorlan forbidding them from following their friend.

Meld was not so easily persuaded though and he ran after her, seemingly oblivious to the shouts of Gorlan for him to stay with the group.

The Warlord led the escapees through the exit and they streamed into the sunlight. All around them they saw the Graav streaming towards the hills to enter the lava ponds, submerging themselves in the molten rock as if purging themselves of the touch of the warlock.

They did not pause to determine why this was occurring. In the sky the Pinn eagles had already struck out towards their riders.

As the eagles swooped down and the Pinns mounted, Michael and Rhys hesitated.

"We have to wait for Ashley! We can't leave without her."

Gorlan turned back frowning. He knew they should make haste but he too did not want to leave without Ashley and Meld.

As they paused he considered whether he had been wrong to allow Ashley to carry on alone but then, as doubts grew, Ashley's warbird swooped through the exit and they saw both Ashley and Meld clutching tight to the back of the great creature.

Gorlan beamed, "OK, let's go!"

The escaping group returned swiftly to their island base. As the fire eagles landed Howler ran around, jumping up on each of them and licking their faces with his huge tongue.

Soon they were rejoined by the sea-elves who had swum from the island of the Graav.

Gorlan hugged Prince Trelane in relief as he stepped from the ocean.

"Well met Prince!" he said.

The Prince momentarily returned his embrace before turning to more serious matters.

"What now Gorlan?" he asked.

"Now?" replied the Warlord. "Now, we return to our homes and the sooner the better."

Prince Trelane indicated the Urthound. "What do we do with Howler?" he asked.

Gorlan looked at the huge dog.

"Oh I think he can look after himself. We'll leave him food and later, when things are settled, you could travel back here to collect him and take him back to Seahome."

The Prince nodded. "Yes, I will do that."

"Good, thank you," said Gorlan, "especially for your aid in this quest. We could not have succeeded without the help of yourself and your elves." Prince Trelane did not reply he just smiled to acknowledge the compliment. Thirty minutes later, with their camp now re-packed they were embracing again. This time in farewell.

# CHAPTER TWENTY-ONE
## Combination

Farspell grabbed a second handful of sand crystals. He placed them into a stoneware pot and started to grind them into a fine powder. He looked towards Sandmover and held his hand towards her. "It is time".

She frowned and toyed with her runestone pendant before reluctantly removing it.

As she handed it to the wizard she asked, "Are you sure this will work?"

"No. I'm not sure at all." Now it was his turn to frown.

He placed the pendant into the pile of crushed sand crystal. The wizard pulled open his cloak with his right hand and with a slight wave of his left a pocket appeared.

Sandmover raised her eyebrows in surprise. "Nice trick!"

Farspell smiled. "I was taught that one many years ago. A handy little energy pocket that can slip in and out of the gap between worlds. I think that opening it causes minor disruption though so I do not use it very often. I'm led to believe that each time it is opened something is transported into the void. My theory is that this is where you will find all those lost socks and hosiery together with a myriad of missing writing quills and implements."

Reaching into the pocket he drew out a small bag.

Opening the bag he removed a pinch of dark powder and added it to the bowl before re-securing it and placing it back into his inter-dimensional pocket.

"What is it?" asked Sandmover.

"This, my dear, is the catalyst for the spell. It is the crushed claw of Fangtor, last of the red dragons. The use of the claw will allow me to focus my will on the alchemic reaction that will occur when we heat the pot. It is this that should permit me to forge a new key, a key of relocation."

Carefully lifting the pot Farspell placed it above a roaring fire.

"What now?" asked Sandmover.

Farspell raised his hand to request silence. "We wait. But please, I need quiet, I must focus."

The old wizard stared into the bowl and Sandmover saw a slight shimmer in the air between the bowl and his eyes. Waiting patiently she stood and watched in silence.

At first nothing happened but, as the ingredients began to melt in the heat, they started to bubble and congeal. A high pitched squeak came from the pot and it began to glow.

Brighter and brighter it became, until she had to turn her face away from the glare. Farspell continued to stare into the pot, trancelike.

There was a bright flash and weak *fwishh* sound, not unlike the opening of a bottle of fizzy drink that has lost most of its pressure.

As the light from the pot faded Farspell and Sandmover looked at each other.

"That didn't sound right." she said, gloomily.

The wizard could not hide his concern. He removed the pot from the flames and reached inside where he found a flat disk, a few millimetres thick and the size of his palm. It was jet black.

Handling it gingerly he was surprised to find that it had already cooled. He removed it from the pot and showed it to Sandmover.

She looked at the disk. "Will it work? Is this the key that you had hoped for?" she asked.

Farspell shrugged. "There is only one way to find out."

Pulling his Celtic knot pendant from within his robes he lifted the disk and brought it into contact with the newly formed key.

Sandmover instinctively shielded her vision closing her multiple eyelids as a bright flash erupted from the wizard. When she opened them again Farspell was gone.

***

Those defending Pinnhome saw it closing and this raised their spirits. Despite the intensity of the fighting the casualties on both sides were extremely low. The Graav were armed with swords which only helped them in hand to hand combat and similarly, the defenders were unable to strike at the heads of the attacking horde. The siege defence machines were effective in keeping the Graav off the walls but they made little impact on their numbers. Even the elves were now powerless having spent their supply of Lorewood arrows.

At least the fire eagles were making some inroads into slaying the creatures as they continued to tear the occasional head from the shoulders of an attacker.

However, it seemed as if the stalemate would soon be broken as the Graav changed their tactics. Instead of trying to scale the perpendicular walls of the city they began to pound at the stonework with their fists and swords.

Toran looked on, he knew that the stone was very thick but it would not be able to withstand indefinitely the battering that the Graav were inflicting upon it. Stone and masonry were flying everywhere as the creatures drove their bodies further into the walls.

The Pinns tried acid as a deterrent in an attempt to burn the creatures below but the acid merely reinforced the efforts of the Graav and it had no effect other than to paint a few dark stains on their hard exteriors.

On the ramparts above the battle Melis, OverLady of Pinnhome, had joined her husband.

Toran spoke to her and she noticed the edge of fear in his voice. "If they break through we will need to retreat once more. Take command and order our forces to divert men to reinforce the outer city buildings. They can use sand and dirt bags to raise a second barrier. We may need more time to develop a strategy."

"Of course my love. What are you going to do?" she asked.

"I am going to try to contact Farspell. There must be a way of fighting these creatures more effectively."

He rushed to one of the guard towers and dismissed the men who were taking refuge there.

Lifting his hand he touched the ring to the Cormion Crystal...

The images formed slowly and the quality was poor. Rather than the sharp although ghostlike three-dimensional images that were normally displayed, these were speckled and blurred. Toran squinted at them but it was difficult to make out any clear detail. However, as he waited, the images slowly came into focus as if the signal needed to tune in to the imagery.

Two clear images solidified. Curiously, when they had become focussed the quality of the image was even sharper than it had been in the past. Toran noticed that only two images were evident. Curiously both images showed the same Eumor city street scene but from slightly different angles.

"Cambor?" said Toran uncertainty in his voice.

"Yes. Hello Toran. I was just about to make contact with you. I have a surprise."

The aged centaur turned his head to look at his companion. Almost in synchronisation the second Cormion image turned in the opposite direction until one showed the centaur and the other...

"Farspell! You are back." exclaimed the OverLord.

The wizard smiled. "I am indeed but only just. I thought my little experiment had gone awfully wrong at one point."

"But how do you come to be in Eumor?" asked Toran.

Farspell held up his newly created artefact. "With this! I call it the Key of Relocation. It is formed from matter and energies of both our world and that of Gatherer's planet. If my supposition is correct it will allow safe transfer between both worlds. But there will be time for this later."

Farspell paused and double checked that there was no third Cormion image being transmitted. "It appears that Weldrock has removed his crystal. Good! We can speak openly. Tell us, what is happening at Pinnhome. I see you are in one of the wall towers."

Toran gave them a brief summary of recent events. When he had finished Farspell looked thoughtful.

"I don't understand why Weldrock has closed the portal. Victory was in his grasp. Even now our forces are struggling to hold back the Graav. If more had been sent then the city would have been over-run."

"Perhaps he has no more Graav to send," offered Cambor.

"Perhaps," the wizard replied, "But I would have expected him to have a far greater force than that which currently threatens Pinnhome."

"Do you think he plans to attack another location?" asked the centaur. His eyes opened wide as a sudden fear gripped him. "Could it be that he is going to focus some of his forces here at Eumor?"

Farspell nodded. "I think it would be foolish for him to split his forces but we know that he does not always do things logically." The wizard looked around the city. "Cambor, I think we should prepare your people for battle. I will assist you."

Toran was not pleased, "But Farspell, I need your council here."

Farspell looked downcast. "There is not enough time my friend. You will have to fight the Graav alone. By the time I reach you the battle may well be done. It is better that I stay here in Eumor and assist Cambor with his preparations."

Toran looked angry, but realised that there was sense in the words of the wizard.

"Very well, but I fear for what the coming hours will bring. I must return to my soldiers. I will make contact again later."

The images closed as Toran broke the link.


The OverLord raised his hands to his head and rubbed his temples. A headache was thumping and his skull felt fit to burst.

"There must be a way of defeating these accursed creatures!" he said out loud.

There were no seats in the guard tower so the OverLord sat on the floor. He lost himself deep in concentration searching for an idea that would swing the battle. He stayed that way for almost an hour before suddenly jumping to his feet. Rushing from the tower he called for his OverLady.

"Melis!! To me!"

His wife was at his side quickly.

"Melis. Where is Ophra?" he asked?

"She is below tending the wounded. Why?"

"Go and get her quickly. Tell her to get together the women and children of the castle and to gather as many snow blooms as they can find."

"But why?" she asked again.

"Not now!" he snapped, "I will explain later. Just go and get her and tell her to be swift."

Melis did as she was bid and ran to find her daughter. She did not understand the request but she recognised the urgency in the voice of her husband.

*** 

Cambor's brow was furrowed with worry as he gave orders for his people to prepare for battle. In the weapon store Farspell too was working feverishly, adding enchantments to as many bows and swords as he could, but with each weapon requiring individual attention he made slow progress.

The wizard was putting the finishing touches to a bow when Cambor approached. After checking that they were alone the centaur elder spoke.

"Farspell, I will continue preparations but you should ride to Pinnhome. Should we be attacked your presence here would be a boon but we both know that Eumor is not built to withstand assault as it once was."

The wizard shook his head, "No. I cannot desert you. It will take me days to ride to Pinnhome and by then the battle may be over...resolved one way or another."

"You do Toran an injustice. He will find a way to hold the Graav at bay. Leave now. Common sense would decree that you will be of more use there than here and I have a way for you to get there faster."

The elder whistled in a low tone and the sound of hooves was heard. Farspell turned expecting to see a centaur but, instead, he looked on the form of DiamondCrest, his cloud horse.

The old wizard welled up when he saw his old friend and he threw his arms around him in welcome.

"Ah my old friend. It is so good to see you again." He spoke quietly as he stroked the horse's neck.

Cambor rubbed the neck of the cloud horse. "I believe that he has come to carry you back to Pinnhome. He too senses the need."

Farspell looked at the old centaur and nodded.

"Very well." He saluted the centaur as he climbed onto DiamondCrest's back. "Good luck Cambor. We will meet again soon."

Farspell turned his mount and they walked from the building. Once outside the city DiamondCrest sped along as if carried by the wind, demonstrating why his breed were called Cloud Horses.

***

Toran, turned his back on the battle that raged below, no advance had been made by either side. He looked from the battlements towards his city.

The Graav had begun to focus their efforts on one particular section of wall, combining their force to make a greater impact on the tough stone that obstinately stood before them.

Toran thanked the heavens that Pinnhome had been built from granite hewn from the Pinnacle Mountains. The metamorphosed rock made it hard work for the Graav but they were making slow progress as small chips began to fly from the continuous pounding of the lava men.

Although this synchronised effort was resulting in faster destruction of the city wall, the tactic of focusing their effort actually fitted Toran's new plan.

Behind the wall where the Graav toiled, the OverLord had instructed his forces to construct a large corridor. Rock, stone, sand and dirt bags had been used to build a passageway that offered almost sheer sides and which would channel anyone entering through a breach in the wall at this point, down the makeshift corridor towards the very heart of Pinnhome.

The end of the corridor had been left totally open to the town beyond. Toran realised that this was a desperate tactic and if his plan failed, the Graav would be free to stream into Pinnhome leaving all his people open to slaughter.

The OverLord directed his gaze to the tops of the walls where Melis was issuing instructions as more workers, mainly the women, children and the elderly, transported masses of snowbloom flowers from the fields to the North, piling them into large mounds at regular intervals down the length of this rocky channel.

Once more the Graav assault had played into his hands. The focus of their attack flowed directly from the south where the portal had opened, so the north of the city remained open, not only allowing a route for retreat but also allowing access to the snowbloom fields located there.

A large cracking sound caused him to turn his attention back to the attacking Graav and he winced as he saw a large section of granite crumble under the bombardment.

"Hold on Pinnhome! Hold on!" he said out loud. He needed just a little more time.

***

In the snowbloom fields Ophra worked tirelessly as she harvested the blooms. At first oblivious to why her father had given her such an order, rumour and word of mouth had persuaded all that this was an integral part of the OverLord's plan. Wild suppositions were raised as to what was to be done with the blooms but all were united in their mission, to gather as many of the white flowers as quickly and as efficiently as possible.

*** 

High above Pinnhome, the fire eagles were tiring, an unusual occurrence and alien to most of the riders. Again and again they had picked off the Graav, but they were making only a small inroads on the numbers. Tosh was climbing back to a hovering position when he heard the wall finally give way.

With a large hole now gaping in the defences of the city, the very structure of the defensive boundary was weakened and, as the Graav continued to smash their way through, the hole became larger very swiftly. The enemy began to pour through, filling the newly constructed makeshift corridor beyond.

Faced with sheer walls on either side but a clear path ahead the Graav continued to advance as thousands flooded into the passageway, driving for the heart of the city.

As the first of this attacking horde of Graav approached the city end of the passageway, Toran waved a command. Soldiers snapped to readiness and as the first dozen or so Graav left the passage began to pour tons of small rocks into it at either end, blocking the exits to the north and south.

Repositioned catapults fired heavy projectiles into the growing pile of stone and rubble and teams of horses were used to pull large boulders across both exits, adding weight to the blockage.

Almost ninety percent of the Graav were now temporarily trapped, but they had already begun to climb up the rubble blockade.

Another signal from the OverLord instigated the second part of his plan.

Additional catapults, now loaded with snowbloom, fired the blossom into the passage. At the same time well placed 'sweepers' began to pile more of the flowers down onto the Graav below.

It was an uncanny sight. The usually impassive Graav began to show signs of panic as the snowbloom touched their exteriors as the ice magic of the blooms sapped the heat-energy of the creatures. As the lava men began to thrash about wildly the scene took on a strangely wintry appearance as the falling blossom seemed to float down like snow. A freezing snow of death slowly engulfed the fire formed creatures.

More and more of the snowbloom were piled into the passageway until the Graav disappeared from sight, buried under the wispy white soft petals of the plant.

For a few minutes blossom could be seen flying into the air as Graav thrashed and struggled within its hold. Slowly all went still as the struggles ceased.

The sound of battle diminished significantly as the Graav were silenced. In support of their town folk fire eagles now focussed their efforts on picking off the few Graav that had managed to clamber out of the flowery death-trap. The silence awed and unsettled the defenders as they stared into the snowbloom filled channel. Slowly they began to realise that the OverLord's plan had worked. In one swoop they had utilised the power of nature to defeat their enemy. Shouts of joy and victory began to break out spontaneously.

Even Toran stared in disbelief. He had hoped that the ice magic of the snowbloom would succeed in slowing the advance of the lava creatures, but the effects were far more dramatic than he had expected. Looking across the town and breathing a sigh of relief, he allowed his people a few moments of celebration before shouting out new orders. Many surviving Graav still remained outside the city wall and they were continuing their assault.

The tide of battle had turned but there was still a victory to be won. The remaining Graav offered a threat and were continuing their relentless assault.

The OverLord summed up the odds and decided that the superior numbers of the defending forces called for a change of tactics. Under the instruction of their leader, commanders rallied their troops and led by warriors carrying enchanted weapons, they flooded through the city gates to rush headlong into the remaining enemy forces.

Blood began to flow and rubble exploded as the Allied soldiers fought at close quarters with their foe. Toran felt pained with each death, as more fell to the stone swords, his heart began to beat fast and his anxiety rose as doubts began to surface about this desperate tactic. He had underestimated the strength of the remaining force, but it was too late to retreat. Final victory depended on his field commanders and the skills of the fire eagle riders.

# CHAPTER TWENTY-TWO
## Return to Pinnhome

Farspell had reached the peaks of the Red Hills. Galloping to a suitable viewpoint he brought DiamondCrest to a halt and looked across the valley towards Pinnhome. To his surprise there was no sign of the massive Graav army that he expected would be stretched out on the plain. Squinting hard he tried to focus on the land surrounding the town but it was still too distant to make out what was happening.

Turning his head slowly he scanned the horizon, following the contour of the mountains to the north. Out of the corner of his eye he saw more movement to the west, this time in the sky, and as he focussed he observed half a dozen specks dotted against the wispy clouds. Although the objects were far away he recognised the fire eagles. Six in total.

"What do you think DiamondCrest? That doesn't look like a scouting flight. Whoever they are they seem to be headed for the city. Come, we must intercept them, it may be that they are flying straight into the hands of the enemy."

The wizard urged on his mount and once again DiamondCrest responded. They sped in a northerly direction and he guided his mount towards the centre of the Pinn valley where he waited for the oncoming flight to reach him.

Kraven was the first to notice the lone figure on the plains below and he swiftly alerted the others.

Even at their high altitude they recognised the figures of Farspell and DiamondCrest. Ashley was the first to fly down to the wizard. Meld rode with her and held on tightly to her waist. Carl and Stern, carrying Michael and Rhys were next, followed swiftly by the others.

As soon as her eagle touched the ground Ashley jumped from her mount and running to Farspell threw her arms around his neck in a huge hug.

"Oh Farspell! It's so good to see you!" she said in delight despite her weariness.

She was soon joined by Rhys and Michael. The others kept a respectful distance for a few seconds to allow the boys to greet their mentor too.

The sharing of their adventures took far less time than one would have expected. When Gorlan and Trall had explained how Weldrock had been defeated the old wizard frowned. He looked relieved but sad.

"What's up Farspell?" asked Rhys. "You look fed up. Aren't you glad that Weldrock's dead?"

Farspell shrugged, "I guess I was hoping that he would come round and return to his old self. He was a great wizard once, long ago. I called him friend then."

A silence followed. All present had forgotten that the two wizards once fought side by side.

It was Farspell himself who broke the awkwardness.

"At least now we know we can use the Cormion Crystal openly. We should make contact with Toran to find out what is happening in the city."

They all gathered around the wizard as he invoked the power of the crystal. The aura of the energy shone in the eyes of those assembled. Six eagles remained from those that had set out on the quest, those belonging to Ashley, Flare, Lloyd, Kraven, Stern and Carl. These eagles and their riders had carried survivors back to Pinn; Gorlan, Rhys, Michael, Trall, Meld, and the two crew members from The Red Serpent, Corwin Reels and Doogie Fen. Gorlan looked at each of them and remembered those that had fallen on the mission. He shook off the feeling of misery that threatened to engulf him, there was still much to do and there may yet be more deaths to witness before this day was done. No time yet for grief or pity.

Two different Cormion images came into focus; they were markedly opposite in what they portrayed.

The first, from the eyes of Cambor showed the centaur standing on a hill overlooking the sweeping grassy plains around Eumor. All looked peaceful. The second showed Toran in bloody hand to hand battle with the Graav.

No discussion was needed. Immediately breaking contact Farspell shouted instructions.

"Come, we must help our comrades," he said as he leapt onto the back of his cloud horse.

As the others returned to their eagles Gorlan raised his hand to stop the passengers.

"No. The eagles will fly faster without a second body to carry. I will ride with Farspell. The riders will fly alone." He addressed Meld and the boys. "I am sorry but you will have to continue on foot."

Meld nodded in agreement. "We will move swiftly Warlord. Fight well and we'll drink a toast together to celebrate our victory later today."

Gorlan smiled, "Aye, that we will." He looked towards Ashley and spoke to her, "Ashley, you should stay with Meld and the others. Help protect them."

Ashley was about to object but Stern did so on her behalf. "Warlord, Ashley has proven herself in battle. She should fly with us." Gorlan hesitated but could see in Ashley's eyes that she agreed.

"Very well. Fly quickly," said Farspell as he offered his hand to help the Warlord to mount DiamondCrest. Gorlan held on tightly to the wizard as the cloud horse once again accelerated towards Pinnhome.

\*\*\*

Supported by the fire eagles the Allies fought fearlessly, many laying down their lives to ensure that those with enchanted weapons were protected and given a chance to strike at the heads of the lavamen. Graav numbers continued to fall but not as fast as those of the defenders.

Toran was now fighting side by side with the giant figure of Gatherer, his skin now the colour of golden sand but streaked with Graav ash and his own blood. Few had seen the skills of the OverLord in battle and many marvelled that day at his hidden talent with a sword. Brandishing an enchanted blade, kissed by a spell from the dark-elves of Rusinor many generations before, and flanked by the savagery and power of the desert strider, Toran had driven a wedge into the Graav and now found himself at the very front of the defensive battle line.

As if sensing the threat that the pair posed, the Graav closest to them suddenly changed their strategy. Ignoring any other Allied forces they turned to focus their attack directly on Toran and Gatherer. Rather than the handful of Graav that had faced them in one on one combat up to this point, they were suddenly faced with over forty Graav warriors bearing down on them. Both realised that as a result they had been cut off from the others. They were completely surrounded by their enemy.

Now back to back the pair mixed defensive blocks with strong attacking blows. Despite their skills, the numbers that they faced were overwhelming and, as Toran tired, Gatherer was forced to block attacks aimed at the OverLord as well as himself.

The desert giant was also beginning to tire and as realisation dawned that he could not continue much longer he whispered a farewell to Sandmover. His body screaming and muscles beginning to cramp, his scimitar point began to fall and all seemed lost.

Suddenly, as one, the Graav stopped their assault. A strange silence fell over the battlefield as the lavamen lowered their weapons and stood immobile. Not one soldier struck out at the Graav, themselves confused by their enemies' sudden cessation of battle.

Together, the stone creatures turned their backs on the city and looked south and walked slowly away from the fighting. The Allies watched, completely dumbfounded by the sudden change.

Toran and Gatherer looked at each other.

"What in Portalia is happening?" said the OverLord.

\*\*\*

Farspell remained seated on DiamondCrest with the Warlord still perched behind him.

They had reached the edge of the portal pit and were about to enter the battle when the wizard brought his mount to a halt. Ahead of them the Graav had turned and now stood before them. All faced the wizard and the Warlord.

"I think they've seen us!" commented the Warlord with irony, as he jumped down to the ground and drew his sword.

"Hold your weapon Gorlan," said Farspell.

The Warlord looked at the wizard quizzically. "What?" he asked.

"Hold you weapon. I can feel them," replied Farspell.

"What do you mean?" responded Gorlan uncertainty etched on his features as he looked from the Graav to the wizard and back, unsure how to react.

"They sense me. They know I am a wizard. They are looking to me for direction."

Farspell raised himself on DiamondCrest as high as he could and checked around the battlefield.

All around the city the fighting had stopped and Graav were streaming to join those that stood before him.

"Stay your sword Gorlan. I am going to order them back to the pit," continued the wizard.

Almost immediately the Graav lowered their weapons and began to stream back into the pit where they stood motionless.

Gorlan did not lower his weapon as the lines of Graav marched towards him, but the lavamen obeyed the will of Farspell and paid no attention to him as they returned to the pit. As the withdrawal continued a path to the OverLord opened and Farspell urged DiamondCrest forward.

"Farspell, it is good to see you," the OverLord gestured towards the retreating Graav with his hand. "Nice trick. How did you do it?" he asked.

Farspell smiled, "I didn't. The Graav were already programmed to obey me, or I suspect, obey the next wizard or warlock who may have come along. Weldrock has been slain. It seems the Graav need direction from magic users. With Weldrock slain, I can now command them although I have no knowledge as to how or why they were created and why they need guidance from such as me. You need not fear them. They obey my will and will probably do so until I am replaced."

"Let's kill them now," said Gatherer, "While they are defenceless."

Farspell raised his hand in objection.

"No! They are merely pawns. They will not attack you now that they are aligned to me. In fact they will fight for us if I so chose. However, they do still possess their own survival instincts. They will not just surrender themselves to you. If you attack them they will defend themselves, whether I will it or not," said Farspell.

Toran added his command. "We will leave them. If Farspell says he has them in control then that will suffice." The OverLord looked to the wizard, "However, I believe my people would feel more comfortable if they were out of sight, away from the city."

Farspell acknowledged this request. "I will send them home."

Those that had defended Pinnhome watched in amazement as the Graav began to move once more.

Some thought that attack was being renewed and raised their weapons but soon relaxed when they saw their enemy marching westwards, the Graav were heading back to their island.

Farspell made a request of the OverLord. "I know that your men are tired but please send some riders ahead of the Graav. Others should be told that they will not cause harm if they are left alone to continue on their way. They will return to the shores and then travel through the waters to their island. They will not stop until they reach their destination."

Toran responded and gave orders for cavalry riders and two fire eagle riders to clear the way ahead. Additionally messengers were sent out to inform commanders of the change in status of their former enemy.

As the last of the Graav left the area the Allied defenders began to shout in celebration.

Soldiers overjoyed that they had lived to see another sunrise, rushed towards Toran and Farspell and bore them through the streets, the citizens shouting the OverLord's name in adoration and homage.

When Ashley arrived with the other five riders it was to a city that was celebrating. They had flown over the retreating Graav and had feared the worst, but were soon comforted when they saw the city intact.

After checking in with Gorlan, Ashley took back to the air. She directed her eagle westwards once more, directly towards where Meld and her friends Rhys and Michael would be approaching on foot. She wanted to get there swiftly before they met the Graav.

"Boy have I got a surprise for you guys!" she said smiling from ear to ear.

# CHAPTER TWENTY-THREE
## Aftermath

The clean up of Pinnhome would take months to complete.

Soldiers and civilians alike toiled tirelessly to return normality to the city. The initial priority was to bury the dead. There were no mass graves here as there had been after the initial assault at Fortown. All were honoured.

Next they turned their attention to clearing away the piles of rubble that littered the outskirts. Filling large wagons full of the lava rock, all that remained of many of the Graav, the citizens used it to fill much of the pit that they had built to protect their city. Mound after mound was poured into the manmade hole and slowly the ground was cleared.

Behind the city wall the snowbloom filled passage still remained as it was left at the end of the battle.

The petals had now started to brown and fade and the once fragrant scent was now stale. As wagons were released from their task of carting rubble, they were redirected to clear the passage and snowbloom was transported to the pit and laid in vast piles which would provide for a fertile soil.

Gradually the citizens of Pinnhome reached the Graav, buried deep within. As the stone men were uncovered people came from all around the city to look on. The lava men that had received the kiss of the snowbloom had been perfectly preserved. Thousands of their stone bodies remained solidified in the position in which they had met their deaths, the fires within their hulks extinguished by the cold touch of the ice magic of the blossom.

Rhys looked across the inert forms of the Graav, "They look a bit like those warrior statues that they found in China. Y'know the ones that were supposed to guard someone or other when they died."

"The terracotta guardians," said Ashley. "I saw some of them at a museum in San Diego and there was a video showing that told you all about them. You're right Rhys. Even the way the Graav fill the passageway, it is just like how the terracotta figures were arranged."

Toran was also impressed by the sight of the frozen Graav. Following a brief discussion with Gorlan and Farspell it was decided that the lifeless forms would remain as they stood and that the large area would be segregated and turned into a memorial for all those that had died while protecting Pinnhome.

With all the activity of clearing the residue left by the battle, three days passed before Ashley, Rhys and Michael were able to spend time with Farspell. Although they had told him much of their adventures they had not shared everything. Finally, as the city returned to its old ways, there was time for lessons with the old wizard once more.

Ashley was the first to surprise him. Under her arm she carried a rolled up cloth. Laying this on the desk top she smiled at Farspell. "I have a present for you!" she said as she unravelled the bundle.

Farspell could hardly believe his eyes as Ashley revealed a number of runestone artefacts. The first set bore the symbol of the mountain. Ashley grouped the items together and Farspell saw that of the mountain set she had recovered the keystone, the ring and three pendants.

However it was the final item that caused the wizard to exclaim in surprise.

"By all that is holy! The keystone of the Forest of Old." He picked up the keystone which was emblazoned with the image of a tree in full leaf. "This was thought destroyed years ago. How did you come by these?"

Ashley explained that she had taken them from the warlock's store when she recovered her own pendant.

Farspell shook his head in disbelief before speaking, "Eumor is the only working runestone left in existence. The runestones of the tree and mountain are both destroyed and Weldrock's latest island runestone now lacks a control pedestal. However, with these items and the knowledge I gained when I created the Key of Relocation, I may be able to utilise the energies locked within these items. Who knows I may even find a way to return you three to your world!" He turned to Ashley and the boys, "Thank you. You truly are remarkable."

They blushed a little and there was a brief awkward silence before Rhys spoke.

"Farspell, there is something else. We may have found another way to get home without the need to use the runestones."

The wizard raised his eyebrows in surprise, "Go on," he encouraged.

Rhys continued and explained the comments made by his dying Uncle and his reference to the Shimmering Gate. When he had finished he looked hopefully at the wizard. "We had hoped that you may have some idea of where we could find these ruins. If the Shimmering Gate is still working then we could use it to go home."

Farspell sighed, "I am sorry. I don't remember any mention of this place. If it exists then it must be hidden deep in the mountains. Are you sure that your Uncle was telling the truth?"

Rhys nodded, "I think so. I know he did some really bad things, but he seemed truly sorry in the end. I'm sure he wasn't lying."

"Then we must discuss this with Toran. You have been away from your families for too long. If this place exists we will find it. Even if we have to search every single peak in the Pinnacles."

The earth-teens smiled and felt encouraged by his words. They knew how tough a task it would be trying to find what amounted to looking for a needle in a haystack, but things were turning their way at last. With Weldrock defeated and peace reigning across Portalia, Farspell could focus his efforts on helping the teenagers find this Shimmering Gate. It may take a while but they knew that they would find it."

Farspell, his enthusiasm now overflowing, pulled a large map from one of the shelves. He unrolled it to reveal a topographic chart of the Pinnacle Mountains.

Pointing to the grid that was overlaid on the map, Farspell spoke excitedly. "We can use this grid to do a search." He ran his fingers across the first horizontal section formed.

"We can take it a row at a time, sweeping northwards until we find the ruin. There are more peaks beyond the range of this map but once we have completed the search in this area we can start to map anew and strike out further northwards."

Farspell looked at the teenagers, "What do you think?"

"Sounds good to me!" said Rhys.

"Way to go!" replied Ashley.

They looked at Michael who had remained silent. He was staring at the map with far away look in his eyes...

*He was flying high in the clouds. Other red dragons chased each other and weaved intricate patterns in the air. Charcir, his closest companion, swept past Fangtor nudging him with her rear legs as she went by.*

*"Come on slow coach. Race you to the valley," she said as she beat her wings feverishly and accelerated away from him.*

*"Oh no you don't!" he chuckled as he gave chase.*

*Charcir knew she could not win the race while up here in the open sky so she nose dived to the mountains below where her smaller frame and nimbleness would give her the advantage over his more powerful frame.*

*For his part Fangtor humoured her and followed. "OK, we'll play it your way but you still won't win." He said as he roared with pleasure.*

*The pair entered a ravine that twisted from left to right. Fangtor began to fall further behind but when it opened into a clearing he was quickly back on her trail again, the open air allowing him to use his might. As he bore down on her he playfully grabbed her tail in his teeth and gave her a twist.*

*Charcir rolled to the side, tumbling through the air. "Hey that's cheating!" she shouted. She turned to Fangtor to object just as he passed her and flashed into another crevasse to the right.*

*She smiled as she gave chase, aware that he was giving her a chance to make up the lost ground.*

*The walls of this ravine were steep and close together making it extremely hard for Fangtor to turn and she was soon on him again. She descended as she approached to pass him from below but he blocked her way preventing her progress.*

*She moved quickly to counter and as the pair swept around a left turn she climbed again and passed over his head as the tight passage turned almost ninety degrees to the right. As her body moved a whole length ahead she took her revenge and whipped the top of his head with her tail. It gave a satisfying slap and she roared with laughter so deep that with a little embarrassment she inadvertently emitted flames, a bodily function which was deemed impolite in the dragon world.*

"*You human!*" *shouted Fangtor by way of mock insult.* "*Where are your manners?*"

The walls forming the crevasse had become increasingly shallow and as Fangtor closed in once again the pair of dragons burst out above the Pinn valley, two red streaks cutting a line against the blue sky.

"*I beat you!*" *she shouted and turned around but Fangtor was gone.*

"*Up here!*" *She turned to see him climbing high in the sky and she ascended to join him.*

"*Let's go and buzz the Kar-ar-cal children!*" *said Fangtor.*

"*Oh can we?*" *she replied,* "*I love playing with the little humans. They are so much fun.*"

In answer Fangtor turned his flight to the north east and together they beat a path to the settlement.

As the mountain dwelling of the humans came into view they gave a roar. The humans looked up and waved, unafraid of the sight of the enormous red dragons approaching. Children ran from the town carrying small baskets of light brown nuts. Sprinting to take up a position in a small grassy clearing on the outskirts they spread themselves out and held a handful of nuts in the air above their heads.

Fangtor and Charcir went into a dive and fell towards the clearing, levelling out as they approached the ground. As each dragon approached, each child watched their flight path and when they were close they threw the nuts high into the air, straight into the path of the oncoming dragons. As each dragon passed overhead the children would stretch up and stroke the huge creatures as they flew past. At the same time the dragons breathed out a sheet of flame that instantly roasted the nuts in mid air. As the treats fell back to the ground nearby children raced eagerly to gather them and munched happily on the tasty, hot kernels as they dipped their hands into their bucket to grab another handful ready for the next fly past.

"MIKE!" Rhys shouted at the top of his voice and Michael finally regained his senses.

Eyes wide he looked at Farspell and then down at the map. Lifting his right hand he extended a finger and brought it down on a point directly to the northeast of Pinnhome.

"This is where it is," he said. "I've just been there."

# CHAPTER TWENTY-FOUR
## The Shimmering Gate

There's nothing here!" screamed Ashley, as she turned her head to shout at Michael who was perched behind her on her eagle.

"But there must be. We've been following Fangtor's flight path exactly as I remember it." Tears welled up in Michael's eyes as he responded defensively and bitter disappointment began to replace his feelings of excitement.

"There's nothing here Mike. Goddamn nothing." repeated Ashley, her anger rising.

The other fire eagles swept over to them and Rhys shouted from the back of Carl's bird.

"What now Mike? Where do we go next?"

Michael, uncertain how to respond, merely shrugged. "I, I, errrr, I, errr, don't know," he stammered.

Rhys was confused. "Whadja mean you don't know? You said you knew the way." He replied accusingly.

"I thought I did," Michael snapped back beginning to get annoyed too. "But something is different. It should be here. It's not my fault."

Farspell, riding with Tosh, called to them.

"Steady young ones. You are losing your tempers but it is through frustration," he addressed Michael, "Mike, are you certain that we are where we should be. Remember, your memories are ancient and things will not be as they once were."

Michael calmed himself and looked around drawing forward the dragon memories that were still fresh in his mind.

He looked at the mountain ahead and pictured the scenes that Fangtor had seen aeons before.

There. Looming above the settlement. The same mountain, now much smaller but with the same characteristic shape.

Michael nodded, "Yes, I am certain." He pointed to a flat rocky area below. "It should be there, but it's gone."

The authoritative voice of Tosh rang out, "Then that is where we land. Follow me." And so saying the rider captain directed his eagle down to the plateau.

The eagles landed smoothly on the hard surface.

They dismounted and in silence they looked around the lifeless and featureless area of bare stone.

Ashley felt here frustration rising once more.

"There's nothing here Mike. Not a goddamn thing!"

Meld stepped to her and placed his arm around her shoulder in an effort to calm her.

"Steady Ash. We know what this means to you but it's not Mike's fault." He said.

Ashley took a deep breath to calm herself and mumbled an apology to Michael.

Farspell ambled to the edge of the plateau and looked over and down. Below and beyond were thick trees and vegetation. The trees had grown so tall that you could almost step from the ledge onto the top branches.

"Mike, could the village be amongst the trees?"

Michael stepped to the edge and looked.

He shrugged. "I guess so. It could be that Fangtor's memories are slightly out. It should be right here, where we are standing."

A shout from behind them caused them all to turn. Stern had not gone to the edge with them and they could see his head and torso sticking out above the rock, he had found a pit of some kind.

"Over here!" he said.

They rushed to where he stood and saw that the rock had fallen away at this point to leave a gaping hole in the plateau.

Rhys whistled. "Blooming heck the things hollow!" he said.

Michael gazed down through the hole.

He pointed excitedly to the edge of where their vision was obscured by the rock.

"I told you!" he shouted. "Look, there! A statue."

The others followed the direction indicated and sure enough, they saw the lone shape of a human statue partly hidden by the vines that grew around it.

Ashley grabbed Michael and hugged him. "Mike you are an angel." She planted a kiss on his cheek and he blushed. "Sorry I doubted you."

The hole was not large enough to allow an eagle to pass through and it was a sheer drop below so they mounted the birds once more and circled above the tree canopy looking for the best way to enter the forest.

It was not easy but Tosh finally chose a point and they carefully made their way downwards, slowly picking their way through the thick foliage. On a number of occasions the eagles were forced to break off smaller branches as they progressed but, eventually, they made terra firma and were soon walking into the ancient settlement.

They looked in wonder at the ornate buildings that stood in ruins, intricate carvings and what had once been delicately decorated structures were evident below overhanging vegetation.

"Who built this place?" asked Rhys directing his question at Farspell, but it was Michael who answered.

"Humans. A race known as the Kar-ar-cal." He said.

"What happened to them Mike?" continued Rhys.

Michael shrugged. "Dunno, but something bad must have driven them away. From what I remembered they were a happy and peaceful people."

Many of the buildings had crumbled into disuse but there were still numerous structures with sufficient cover to hide what lay within.

Farspell called for them to halt as he inspected each building, trying to evaluate its purpose. Finally he pointed to a small domed structure that was nestled towards the forest side of the city.

By comparison to the other buildings this one was fairly basic in appearance. Its walls were a pale cream and once would probably have gleamed in the sunlight, but now long vines hid most of the structure from view. Long strings from the same vines snaked across the open entrance which once would have housed two large doors.

As they passed through the entranceway Ashley pulled the lighter vines aside and rubbed her hand across the wall. She noticed that there was a faint pattern engraved on the surface and tore away more of the overhanging plants.

"Look guys," she said, "there are images here showing humans and centaurs and what look like small suns. They look similar to the things that the Incas used to do on Earth. We studied them in High School and I remember being amazed by them."

Rhys and Michael examined the walls and saw what she meant although neither knew much about the Incas so could not confirm Ashley's observation.

The group continued inside and entered a long narrow hall. The way became darker, the only illumination provided by small holes high above them in the wall. They proceeded cautiously until they entered a square room, also dimly illuminated by window slits above.

At the centre of this room there stood a large, rectangular slab of rock, that stretched upwards from the floor for some five metres, towering above them all. On one face a symbol of a sun like object had been carved. It had a circular centre and beams of energy were depicted flowing from the core like long wavy tentacles.

Farspell looked at the earthlings. "I think this may be what we are searching for."

The wizard walked to the carved face and ran his hands over it.

"It's warm!" he exclaimed, "And it is vibrating slightly." Farspell's tone suggested caution.

Michael placed his hand on the slab. "Yeah, feels like a washing machine on spin cycle."

Rhys laughed and placed his palm on the stone to feel it for himself.

As soon as his hand touched the rock, the vibration became intense and a loud hum could be heard. Rhys quickly removed his hand but it was too late. His touch had triggered the device.

A gust of warm air blew from the stone into their faces, strong enough to ruffle their hair. A smell of old books tinged the air as if something had been opened that had lain dormant for some time.

The etched circle began to glow and a sphere bubbled from it seemingly leaking from the stone slab to fully form and float in mid air. It was a deep blue, almost dark purple in colour. As they watched in fascination, the orb began to revolve and long tentacles, identical to those in the stone depiction, speared out from its core to touch both floor and ceiling.

The hum pulsated in their ears and in unison the light shimmered and danced.

"The Shimmering Gate!" said Farspell. "You have opened the gate Rhys. You have found your way home."

Rhys, Michael and Ashley stared at each other, dumbstruck in disbelief.

"Go on! Why are you hesitating? Use the gate before it fades," said Farspell earnestly.

The three teenagers looked around at the faces of their friends. Since being thrust into the world of Portalia they had worked towards this end, to find a route back to their own world. Now, faced with the solution to their quest they paused, unsure.

"Come on then. Just think about all those things that we've missed," said Rhys as he stepped towards the portal.

"Yeah," added Michael, "Fish 'n' chips, pesky sisters, rugby, decent music..."

"Real football, Playstations, TV, films, cuddles from yer Mum..." continued Rhys.

The boys were now up close to the portal and to those watching their forms seemed to be shimmering in rhythmn with the gateway.

They turned to look for Ashley and saw that she was hugging Meld.

"I don't want to leave you." she said as she pulled him close, tears streaming down her face.

"You must," he replied. "You do not belong here and we both know I could not survive in your world. From what we have discussed your ways are too alien to me. I would be lost."

Tears continued to pour as she squeezed him harder than she had ever done before, daring him to push her away.

Farspell placed his hand on her shoulder.

"You know Meld is right Ashley. You must return to your world. You would regret it if you did not."

Meld began to gently prise her arms from around him and she finally succumbed to the words of her friends and the desire to see her family once more.

She gave him a long kiss goodbye and finally pulled herself away from him. Turning she shouted loudly.

"Come on then you guys! What are you waiting for?" Without looking back she sprinted towards the Shimmering Gate and launched herself into the air as she leapt through.

Rhys and Michael waved to the others and they followed her in. Both had butterflies as they entered the portal. Fear of the unknown knotted in their gut.


There was no sensation of floating as there was during a runestone portal transition. One second they were in Portalia and a few steps later they exited into a dark chamber which was only illuminated by the light of the Shimmering Gate.

Rhys and Michael exited together and almost walked into Ashley as she stood there in front of the portal, still crying.

"Come on Ash," said Rhys as he put his arm around her. "We need to get out of here before the gate closes." "Yeah, c'mon Ash," added Michael. "Don't worry. We'll go back one day."

She glared at him, "I'm never going back!" she snapped and shaking off Rhys' arm she made towards the steps.

Rhys looked at Michael and shrugged.

"Women," he said, "I just don't get them."

Michael nodded and the boys followed Ashley out into the bright sun of the Peruvian hills.

Behind them, the Shimmering Gate fizzled and died as it closed and threw the chamber back into total darkness, hiding its secret once again.

# EPILOGUE

Where are the Earthlings?" Tiborous asked Stack as they watched the events unfold in the ancient city.

"They did not leave the temple," replied Stack. "They entered but never came out again. They must still be inside."

The pair watched as the rest of the group recovered their fire eagles and left the city. One eagle, Ashley's, looked crestfallen as it flew with the others, empty and with head bowed in dejection.

Stack frowned and contemplated these strange events.

"Tiborous, I think this calls for some investigation," he said.

They watched until the fire eagles were out of sight before breaking their cover.

Walking to the temple they entered together. They followed the long hallway and entered the chamber of The Shimmering Gate just in time to see the glow subside as the gateway closed.

Stack turned to face Tiborous. "Now that is what I call curious."

\*\*\*

Gatherer hugged Sandmover and placed his hand gently on her torso. He could feel their offspring moving.

She looked over her mate's shoulder towards Farspell. "Thank you for returning him to me!" she said.

"Oh, think nothing of it," replied the wizard. "Now that we have created the Key of Relocation we can use it to travel freely between our worlds. I expect to watch your young grow to be as great as their parents."

The desert striders smiled at his words.

"What of Rhys, Michael and Ashley? Do you think you will see them again?" asked Gatherer.

Farspell laughed, "Oh, I think we will meet again one day. The Shimmering Gate is hidden but still operational and Rhys and Ashley still possess the Eumor pendants. I think that when they become bored with their world they may pay us a visit. Who knows, if they do not come here I may go and visit them on their world. It sounded so different to our own."

Farspell had a far off look in his eye and Gatherer knew that the wizard was keen to make the journey to Earth. He probably would have left already, but Toran had forbidden it and had even dispatched Pinn infantry to guard The Shimmering Gate to prevent its use.

"Anyway, enough talk. I'm eager to try one of your famous Razorback patties," prompted Farspell.

Sandmover laughed again. "They are not that good!"

"Ah my dear, you do yourself no justice. They are wonderful."

She smiled and made for the kitchen area. Behind her Farspell took a seat and lounged back into the large and comfortable chair. At last, for the first time in many months, he could enjoy some peace and tranquillity.

He closed his eyes and fell asleep in seconds.

## THE END

# GLOSSARY

| | |
|---|---|
| Ashley Rees-Jenkins | USA Girl of 14 when the adventure starts. Becomes a fire eagle rider. |
| Auntie Glenys Sagot | Rhys' Auntie lives in Pembrokeshire, Wales |
| Ben | Fortown—Brianna's brother |
| Black Eagle | Portalia—Giant Eagles corrupted by magic |
| Borst | Dwarf scout |
| Brianna | Fortown female—Molt's friend and partner |
| Calem Ford | Landlord of the Traveller's Tavern in Ralle |
| Cambor | Centaur—Eumor Council Leader |
| Carl | Pinnhome Warrior—blue eyes. Twin to Stern |
| Centaur Armour | Decorative and functional wrought ore armour |
| Centaur Pipe Music | Centaur magic that can enchant humans |
| Ceremony of Choosing | Pinn ceremony where an eagle chooses its bond partner |
| Charcir | Red dragon—Fangtor's mate |
| Chisel | Dwarf—Son of Swiftaxe (eldest) |
| Chot | Fortown Town Guardsman & clayball player |
| Clave | Pinn owner of the Unfurled Sail inn in Norgate. |

| | |
|---|---|
| Clayball | Portalia—Human sport played with a clay ball and wooden bats + three bases |
| Coastal Range | Portalia—A range of low mountains running parallel to the coast |
| Cooburrows | Portalia—Small rabbit like creatures—like grassy hills |
| Cormion | Ancient Wizard—created the Cormion Crystal |
| Cormion Crystals | Four white crystals linked with the artefacts of the Celtic Knot. Allow communication over great distances. |
| Cornbread | Portalia—Cornbread! Bread made with corn! |
| Cortina | Fortown—One of the women who escaped the Graav |
| Creel | Pinnhome Warrior |
| Cyretha | Last red dragon breeding pair (male) |
| Dargoth | Portalia—Mountain region in west—dark region |
| Desert Striders | Desert World—race of intelligent creatures that are adapted for the hot sandy environment |
| DiamondCrest | Cloud Horse Lan's mount |
| Dragon Heart | The gift of life from Dragon to other creatures |
| Drenda | Portalia—Home of the Dwarves in the White Peaks |
| Drengtor | Last red dragon breeding pair (female) |
| Dry Dune Tribe | Desert Strider tribe—homed at Dry Dune |
| Dry Lake Creeper | Desert World—Lake weed. Hot and spicy seed pods good for cooking. |

| | |
|---|---|
| Dunebuilder | Desert Strider—member of the Dry Dune tribe |
| Eumor City | Portalia—Home of the Centaurs on the Plains of Eumor |
| Fangtor | Last of the red dragons |
| Fangtor Claw Ball | Created after Fortown battle by Farspell |
| Farseeker | Horse—Rhys' mount |
| Farspell— | Powerful wizard—old friend of Weldrock now his nemesis |
| Fenwaer | Warlock of the Staff of Light—Green Emerald staff |
| Feyberry | Portalia—Healing and pain killing properties—found throughout Portalia |
| Fire daemon | Portalia—Ferocious daemon—enemy of dragons |
| Fire Eagle | Pinn eagles born of a phoenix and an eagle. Possess fire magic and are bonded to their riders. |
| Firmstar | Horse Chestnut—Mike's mount |
| Flare | Pinnhome Warrior |
| Fleck | Fortown—Brianna's Uncle—town counsellor |
| Flowriders | Ships skippered by captains with the ability to channel portal energy into their sails to power the vessels |
| Foile | Pinnhome Warrior—cousin to Stern and Carl |
| Folken | Pinnhome Warrior |
| Fortown | Portalia—outpost town on Dargoth border |

| | |
|---|---|
| Fyros | Centaur—Kyrie's father—9 feet tall |
| Gabriel | Lorewood Elf—Archer leader |
| Gareth Stillwaters | Farming family—formerly of the Gates but moved to Fortown |
| Gatherer | Desert Strider—Gatherer of the Dry Dune tribe |
| Globpods | Portalia sea—luminescent sea weed |
| Gorlan | Warlord of Pinnhome |
| Graav Legion | 500 Graav warriors |
| Green | Pinnhome Warrior |
| Griff | Captain of the Centaur Soldiery |
| Halfman Forest | Portalia—Forest to south of Yew and Snake |
| Halfmen | Small half human carnivores that live in the Half Man Forest—a vicious but dwindling race |
| Helender | Leader of the demon spawn female Shii |
| Herd | Pinnhome Warrior |
| Hesh | Centaur—Eumor Council—over ambitious council member |
| Horn of Summoning | Summons a red dragon to fight for the Warlord |
| Horos | Centaur Eumor Council—knowledge of magic |
| Howler | Jack Fishnose's Urthound pet |
| Hyrax | Portalia—A large wild boar like creature—size small horse found on Eumor Plain |
| Hyrax Patties | Portalia—Hyrax burgers served with blood sauce! |
| Jack Fishnose (JF) | Captain of the Red Serpent |

| | |
|---|---|
| Jade & Amber | Fortown—Sisters to Molt and Meld |
| Kar-ar-cal | Ancient human race that built The Shimmering Gate |
| Karia | Centaur—Kyrie's mother |
| Kelp Wine | Low alcohol fruity wine made from fermented kelp in The Gates |
| Key of Relocation | Forged by Farspell when on the Desert World. Can be used to travel between worlds. |
| King Treon | King of the sea-elves |
| Korgan | Pinnhome Warrior |
| Kraan | Low skill warlock—part of Weldrock's coven |
| Kraven | Pinnhome warrior sergeant and bard |
| Kul | Pinnhome Warrior |
| Kurl | Centaur—Assistant to Cambor young male |
| Kyrie | Centaur—Young female—plays banned magic pipe music in secret |
| Lady Kiss | Pinn flower—Bright crimson red spring bulb (tulip-like)—strong bouquet. Shaped like a pair of lips and used for courting couples |
| Lan | Mad old man of unknown origin |
| Lava Cavern | Portalia—Where Graav are created from the lava rock |
| Leviathan | Fearsome sea monster in Portalia ocean |
| Lloyd | Pinnhome Warrior |
| Lorewood | Portalia—Home of the Wood Elves of the Forest of Lorewood |
| LowRunner | Desert Strider—member of the Dry Dune tribe |

| | |
|---|---|
| Meld | Fortown—Molt's brother—age 18 at start of the Chronicles |
| Melis | OverLady of Pinnhome |
| Mike Evans | Welsh boy of 13 when the adventure starts. Resurrected with the memories of a dragon. |
| Molt | Fortown—Meld's brother—age 17 at start of the Chronicles |
| Mountain Hamlets | Portalia—Four hamlets in the Pinnacle Mountains |
| Nexus/Dark Assassin | Originally from Earth. Once advisor to Toran but became a minion of Weldrock. Possesses a cloak of invisibility |
| Niles | Fortown Messenger sent to the Gates |
| NorGate / Sougate | Portalia—Home of the River Folk on the mouth of the Snake River |
| Ohrhim | Unique Shapechanging creature from another dimension, not of Earth or Portalia |
| Ophra | Pinn daughter of Toran and Melis |
| Pinn Roses | Pinn Flower—Climbing flower mid Spring to mid Autumn, Reds, Yellows and Purples. When the rose leaves are covered in runestone dust and dried in the sun can create a mind link between two consumers of the rose leaf. |
| Pinnacle Mountains | Portalia—Northern Mountains |
| Pinnel | Pinnhome warrior GRAAV on Weldrock's Island |
| Pinnhome | Portalia—Home of the Pinns (Human), located in the Valley of Heroes |

328

| | |
|---|---|
| Portal Lady | Mysterious lady who appears to Rhys in his dreams and who resembles his mother |
| Portalia | The world where the teenagers find themselves |
| Portalia Meadows | Portalia—Meadows of farmland of central Portalia |
| Pulp Fruit | Desert World—Edible fruit of the desert cactus—yellow and bulbous |
| Queen Elena | Queen of the sea-elves |
| Quickhoof | Horse Ashley's mount |
| Ralle | Portalia—River Town on Snake River—multi race |
| Ramsey | Fortown—Shepherd |
| Razorback | Desert World—vicious carnivore kangaroo-like with tough leathery skin. Down it's long back it has a large ridged spine |
| Red Dragons | Portalia—Rare beasts of the far north (ancient) |
| Red Hills | Portalia—Southern border of Valley of Heroes |
| Rhys Morgens | Welsh boy of 13 when the adventure starts. Develops the ability to create portals. |
| River of Yew | Portalia—Tributary of the Snake from Red Hills, and through Elfdom |
| Rose-petal Wine | Portalia—Very low alcoholic wine made from roses |
| Rusinor | Portalia—Home of the dark-elves in the Forest of Old |
| Ryne | Warlock of the Staff of Light—Blue Sapphire staff |

| | |
|---|---|
| Salmonfish | Portalia name for salmon |
| Sam | Ashley's pet Labrador |
| Sandmover | Desert Strider female—Gatherer's mate in the Dry Dune tribe |
| Sarah Evans | Michael's sister—aged 5 when he disappears |
| Sea-elves | Ancient elves that have become merfolk and live in the sea locked home of Seahome |
| SeaHome | Portalia—Home of the Sea-elves on the Island of Llan |
| Seametal | found beneath the water level off the southern coast of Llan. Immune to any enchantment, possessing their own magical ability. |
| Senseteacher | Desert Strider—member of the Dry Dune tribe |
| Sensing | Desert Strider ability that allows them to relate to the energies of their world |
| Shangorth | Ancient warlock—slain during the Warlock Wars |
| Shangorth Towers | Portalia—Domain of Shangorth the Warlock |
| Snake River | Portalia—River runs from Pinnacles to the sea at Norgate & Sougate |
| Snowbloom | Pinn flower—with fist sized white blooms of forty or so petals. Possesses a freezing ability |
| Soul Orb | Weldrock's weapon—Amber in colour small and round—captures essence of life |
| Stack | Man—Weldrock's lead apprentice |

| | |
|---|---|
| Staffs of Light | Three powerful staffs—red, green and blue each unique but together form a blinding ray of power |
| Stern | Pinnhome Warrior brown eyes—twin to Carl |
| Story-songs | Stories told in song by the bards of Portalia |
| Stycich | Leader of the half men |
| Sweetgrass tea | Portalia—brewed from the red sweetgrasses of the Meadows. |
| Swiftaxe | Dwarven king—Drenda—lost in portal web |
| Tea Rain | Portalia—Storm rain heated by the southerly winds |
| The Dramkaan | A magical creature that guards the Cormion Crystals and is tasked with maintaining the integrity of the portal energy network |
| The Flame | Dragon journey of death |
| The Graav | Lava rock made creatures with hearts of fire. Impassive. |
| The Lifebreath | Red Dragon life force |
| The Peak | Dragon essence of power—now waning |
| The Red Serpent | Jack Fishnose's Flow Rider ship |
| The Shii | Seven sister demons led by Helender |
| The Spider Gem | Mounted on a wooden staff—controls arachnids |
| Thorn Cactus | Desert World—Dark green with vicious thorns. Poisonous but not deadly |
| Tiborous | human Northman—large frame powerful 0ver 6ft—good at weather manipulation |

| | |
|---|---|
| Tor | Pinnhome Warrior |
| Toran | OverLord of Pinnhome |
| Tosh | Pinnhome warrior captain / sergeant |
| TownMaster | |
| Cortrain | Fortown Leader of Fortown (Deceased) |
| Trall | Dwarf 2nd mate of The Red Serpent and navigator. Friend of the sea-elves |
| Trelane | Prince—son of above |
| Tribemaker | Desert Strider—Leader of the Dry Dune tribe |
| Urtwatch | Portalia—human Desert town |
| Valley of Heroes | Portalia—Pinn Valley |
| Ves | Human First mate of The Red Serpent |
| Weldrock | Warlock—formerly a wizard friend of Farspell |
| Wildrock Oasis: | Dried up oasis on Desert World. |
| Wrought Ore | light weight armour from the White peaks the density is such that it resists blows from other metal weapons |
| Yam | Dwarf scout |
| Yanto Flow | Gatesman messenger |
| Zarn | The White Dwarf—albino— messenger of Shangorth—minion of Weldrock |
| Zephyr | Warlock of the Staff of Light—Red Ruby staff |

# AUTHOR BIOGRAPHY

Taff Lovesey was born in 1959 in the valleys of Gwent in South Wales, United Kingdom.
He enjoyed a successful career in the electronics and IT industries from the mid 70s which eventually led him to four years living and working in Oregon, USA. Lovesey returned to the UK in 2002 where he now resides in Lincolnshire with his wife and two children.

These days Lovesey makes a living from his writing supplemented with some IT support for home and small business users and some other freelance activities.

A fan of all things fantasy and inspired by writers such as Garth Nix, Stephen Donaldson, Tolkien, Phillip Pullman and Edgar Rice Burroughs, Lovesey enjoyed success with his first novel of the Portal Chronicles, The Spider Gem, during 2006.

Over the coming years, Lovesey has plans for further episodes of Portal Chronicles. Additionally he will produce fantasy novels and short stores.

If you would like to discuss writing, publishing or just general life experiences, Lovesey is available via his web site and more than happy to attend events and talks around UK (or even further afield).

To keep current with his work, or to request attendance at an event or book signing, or merely just to natter via email, please visit Lovesey's self managed web site and blog at http://www.lovesey.net

846996

Made in the USA